How the

How the Dice Fell

John Roberts

Matador
9 Priory Business Park,
Wistow Road, Kibworth Beauchamp,
Leicestershire. LE8 0RX
Tel: (+44) 116 279 2299
Fax: (+44) 116 279 2277
Email: books@troubador.co.uk
Web: www.troubador.co.uk/matador

ISBN 978 1780880 914

British Library Cataloguing in Publication Data.
A catalogue record for this book is available from the British Library.

Typeset in 11pt Minion Pro by Troubador Publishing Ltd, Leicester, UK
Printed and bound in the UK by TJ International, Padstow, Cornwall

Matador is an imprint of Troubador Publishing Ltd

For my children,
Alex and Joe and Kate

Contents

Part 1:

Three Journeys

7th July 2005

1.

Departures and arrivals

7 July 2005

4.30 am.

Amjad is startled by the rapping of knuckles on his door.

"Your turn for the shower. May Allah bless you."

He hears the footsteps shuffle away. Then there is silence. His head is aching, his eyes stinging from lack of sleep. He feels light-headed from fasting, his shoulders are stiff. This is not how he wants to be. He wants to be whole, alive, vital, sensitive, his mind clear, his body ready.

In the shower he lets the soap-free water run down his body, feeling it bring him alive again, fresh. With his fingers he scrubs to the roots of his hair. Then he begins to wash himself following the ritual he had learned, because this washing will cleanse him of his sins. He knows too that it is a way of avoiding the first tensions of a physical fear that flutters in his stomach. From a plain metal bowl he pours water over his hands three times because then the sin of everything he has stretched out his hands to will come away with the water, coming out even from under his nails. Three times he fills his cupped palm with cold water and washes his mouth and nose. Then he washes the rest of his face so that the sin of everything that he has

3

looked at with his eye comes away with the water. He puts his two forefingers into his ears and wipes the back of his ears with his thumbs, as is proper. He washes his right arm from the fingertips to the elbow three times, then the same with his left. Finally he washes his right foot to the ankle three times, and then the left foot and uses his little finger to wipe between his toes so that every sin that his feet have walked towards comes away with the last drop of water.

Now he is cleansed. He feels renewed, smiling as he thinks of meeting the Prophet 'the blazes shining from the wudhu', his sins washed away. He takes the clean clothes he had neatly folded and puts them on: the white ironed shirt, the new jeans and new shoes he had bought especially. But he has to look normal. He puts on his zip-up tracksuit top to hide the newness.

'We love death as much as the infidels love life': the words of Osama bin Laden. Amjad isn't afraid of dying in a few hours. All through his training they had talked about death. There is a high and impenetrable wall that separates humans from paradise or hell. Pressing the detonator on the train will open a door in the wall. It is the shortest path to paradise.

He is a chosen one, with his four fellow martyrs. But he is so alone, a tiny figure under a spotlight in a dark arena with the world waiting and the Prophet witnessing. Soon, very soon, his actions will propel him into meeting the Prophet Muhammed. He cannot believe it. No, that is not right. He can believe it, does utterly believe it. What he cannot do is imagine it. He feels overwhelmed, awestruck. He is such a frail creature. His training has cast a shell around him, hard and polished. But inside is his warm soft flesh and his beating pulse. That too is a gift of Allah.

He stands up and moves to the window, pushes aside the dirty net curtain and looks down at the street three storeys below. He remembers looking down on his own street at home eighteen months ago. He has not been allowed to contact his mother for three months. If she thinks of him, she will be sad and angry with him, disappointed. He is her only son and she must think he has abandoned her, forgotten her. She will imagine him going to his studies with his briefcase and his books.

4

Amjad turns abruptly from the window, rests his forehead against the cool grimy wall and clenches his fists.

Jalla jalaluh – May his glory be hallowed, he chants to himself as he rocks his head against the wall. She will not be proud of him when she discovers what he will do today. She will not be proud, ever, that he is shaheed, a martyr in battle. Tears come into his eyes. He does not care that his father will be angry and will disown him, be ashamed of the praise that others will pour upon his martyrdom. But his mother – he will break her heart, she who had carried him in her body and fed him, brought him up to be a decent hard-working boy.

Later today the TV will be on in the living room and she will hear the sudden announcement about breaking news. She will hear reports of an explosion, an attack, several attacks, and come in from the kitchen to watch with a concerned interest and then with horror. She will see pictures of chaos, bodies, fires. When will she realise her son is responsible? She would never think of it as a possibility. He had not wanted to record a video: it would have been too cruel for his mother to see it broadcast on TV, to see his face and hear his voice when he is dead after what he has done.

5.25 am.

Mike settles into his seat on the first London train of the day from Leeds, due in at Kings Cross at 0805. He stows his sports bag in the luggage compartment in the middle of the carriage where he can keep an eye on it. The train is filling up: most people carry briefcases or laptops. It will be a working journey. He looks at the glossy file he's placed on his fold-down tray. He hasn't read any of it yet except for the venue and start time. There might be a preliminary exercise to do, some self-analysis no doubt – but he now has two hours on the train in which to do it.

Exactly on time the train pulls out. Newspapers and laptops are opened, the first mobile phone calls are being made. A man hunched in an overcoat reads Terry Pratchett, a woman works her way through a puzzle book. The Elland Road grandstands are passed.

5

Why is he coming on this leadership course? Sue had thought it was an experience he should not pass up – if only to help him decide what he didn't want to do with his career. She is right. Sue is organised, has plans – not a timetable of career advancement and a date set aside for giving birth, but she knows clearly where she wants to go. She relishes extra responsibility and is confident she can carry it out. He prefers to believe things will happen, situations develop when the time is right. *Serendipity*, is it called?

He opens his mobile phone to look at the photograph of Sue. She looks so open and uncomplicated and positive. All of those qualities were expressed in her smile. Her smile had started it all, the most captivating smile he had ever seen. Was he drawn to her because her qualities were what he lacked? Because she complemented him? If so, could she be drawn to him in the same way? How did his comparative solitariness attract her? His doubts beneath his idealism? Was it her nurturing instinct that drew her to him? Maybe it is all of those. He looks at her picture again and snaps the phone shut.

The refreshment trolley arrives and he buys a coffee. He can't put off any longer opening the file on the course *Leadership Skills for New Managers*. A quick flip through shows there is no exercise to complete – good news. He isn't a New Manager, of course, but some people, including Sue, think he has the potential. That's why he's here.

So you have just been promoted to lead a team in your organisation. You are now thinking beyond your function and are starting to deal with strategic issues. What does your team expect of you as a leader? Someone who's working long after they've gone home? Someone who reads Sun Tzu's 'Art of War' in between barking out orders? What kind of leader do you aspire to be?

What sort of a leader would he be? He reads on...*increase your level of managerial maturity... be engaged in functional strategy....mind sets of high-performing first level leaders... balance personal mission, needs and accountability... work through collaboration and conflict within teams...manage the Amygdala Hijack.*

The what? He's already glazed over when he comes to that phrase.

Is it a route across Icelandic glaciers? A terrorist attack? His curiosity is aroused.

It's all about becoming a subjective objectivist.

He laughs to himself. Jesus, is this the kind of crap I've got up early for?

He sighs and looks out of the window. The passing landscape is not inspiring: beyond rusting railings are fields full of thistles and tussocks of dead grass; some sheep feed on diced turnips spread across a ploughed field. There are cooling towers in the distance, a collection of scrap metal in a yard with a pile of concrete sleepers, yellow-necked cranes and dumper trucks.

His mind drifts to his favourite memory: his first meeting with Sue had been at that presentation he had given. At the end she had held out her hand to thank him, and smiled at him. As he shook her hand, blood had surged into his face. This was a physical connection he had never experienced before. He knew, at the same instant, that she felt it too. He could not speak, felt gauche. He saw a blush rise to her cheeks. He felt the lovely surprise of it, the mutuality of it. As he held her hand he felt the briefest of tremors in her fingers, and thought he saw in her soft grey eyes a bright, startled, happy acknowledgement. He had watched her walk away, her neat body attractive in her understated clothes, moving confidently. *She looks at ease with herself,* Mike had thought. He had wondered at the time if he had imagined that connection. How right he had been to believe she had felt something too.

6.15 am

His hands cupped behind his head, Lee lies on his bunk staring up at the barred window with its thick glass. Many nights he has watched the constellations cross that small square of sky his cell allows him. Soon he will feel the warmth of the sun. Every day for a year he has followed the progress of the sun hidden behind the high stone prison building, watching the shadows of the bars brighten and fade, the bright patches of sunlight on the wall disappear leaving just the dull even greyness of the dirty wall. This will be the last time.

7

The key rattles in the lock at 6.35 am. and the heavy door grinds open. The warder has brought an Aldi plastic shopping bag and Lee carefully puts his photos and his books into it. The door clicks closed behind him and Lee and the warder walk along the corridor, the cool blue paint scuffed and scratched. The prison echoes with their steps on the metal gangway and down the stairs, the clang of steel doors and the rattle of keys. Lee looks up at the bright sun shining through the roof windows high above. Never will he come back to a place like this. This stage of his life is over. He has paid the price demanded.

They come to the exit office. Lee is given his own clothes back and the small pile of the rest of his property. He signs the forms to confirm he has received them and goes to a booth to change out of his prison uniform for the last time. In the office the Release Officer gives him a travel warrant that will take him on a single journey to Bradfield. He is given a discharge grant of £46.75 and written instructions about the Probation Service in Bradfield to whom he has to report.

"All the best, Lee," says the officer and shakes his hand.

"Thanks," says Lee, as if he is leaving a Bed and Breakfast.

The prison officer opens a small gate beside the big gates where the vans drive in and Lee steps outside. The door clunks shut behind him and he stands for a moment on the pavement of the street already busy with buses and cars and with the steady roar of traffic on the nearby Westway. He breathes in deeply, wishing for the smell of cut grass that had occasionally wafted into the cell, but all he can smell is petrol fumes. He feels the warmth of the early sun and a soft slight breeze on his face that makes him realise how the air, even outside in the exercise yard, has been stale as if imprisoned itself. He looks the length of the street, along the row of shops to an office block and the spire of a church. It is the longest view he's had for twelve months. There are no walls hemming him in. He looks up and sees a whole sky, not just a patch through the cell window or an octagon above the exercise yard. He is free to go in whatever direction he wants. But he is going home. He had deliberately preferred a prison far from Bradfield, wanting to isolate his time in prison from the rest of his life. How right that decision had been.

It is a ten minute walk to East Acton underground station on the Central Line: the first part of his journey to Kings Cross and the north. It is warm and Lee turns right and strolls along. His time is his own – not just that he doesn't know the times of trains departing north, but that no routines apply, no instructions to be followed. He can make his own decisions. The pavements are already busy with people hurrying to work, all with their own purpose and destination in mind. The sunlight flashes on taxi windscreens. The legs and arms of women are bare in their summer dresses: how lovely and free they are, how normal. The women pass him, their skirts swaying. They do not register him, his happiness in seeing them, his pleasure and the kick of desire. Release, he thinks, is almost as traumatic as first imprisonment – an equal assault on the senses.

6.45 am.

There is a second knock on the door.

"Come in," says Amjad.

The door opens. A man he doesn't recognise says: "The commander is ready for you now. Please follow me."

They go down a flight of stairs. The man knocks quietly at a door, opens it and they enter. Four men sit cross-legged on the floor, their backs to him, facing a man in shalwar kameez with a full black beard. He motions to the four men to get up. They stand.

"Meet the final member of the team," says the bearded man. "We are now complete."

They each step forward and clasp his hand.

"Allahu akbar," each of then intones quietly. "Allah is great, all praise to him."

"Sit down," instructs the bearded man. Amjad sees a glittering hardness in his dark eyes. The room is lit only by a low power, bare electric bulb, curtains closed with just a fringe of daylight round the sides and along the top. They are sitting on a shabby rug, the room empty except for a small wooden table in a corner. Amjad had imagined something grander. This is a poor, gloomy, stale-smelling place. He looks at his fellow shaheed. They look as ordinary as he

9

does in their casual western clothes, two wearing spectacles. Are they disappointed, too, he wonders? They are looking up at the face of the bearded man who stands above them. Amjad thinks they are about the same age as himself.

"You do not know each other's names," says the bearded man. "And you must not. Your names are immaterial now to you but tomorrow they will be in every newspaper and television programme across the world. Tomorrow your Muslim brothers will praise you as shaheed, sacred martyrs. Although death will come to you, you are not seeking death. You are seeking to glorify Allah and be his instrument."

He pauses and smiles down at them. Amjad lowers his head, sees the man's sandals below his pale frayed trousers, the toenails yellow and thick like horn, the skin paler underneath the big toe. The leather of the sandal is scuffed and worn. He breathes deeply and closes his eyes, smells the faint sweetness of the man's sweat. He almost retches, has to swallow quickly three or four times, hopes the commander has not noticed in the poor light.

"Today you will face many challenges. When you begin to feel weak – and you will feel weak, suddenly, unexpectedly – you must be strong and steadfast. Allah will stand with those who stand fast. Ask Allah for guidance and help. The hours left for you in this life are very few. But then you will be entering an infinite paradise, the happiest and ever-lasting life."

He waits a moment and then walks over to the table. He sits on the corner of it and Amjad looks at where the trouser has risen up and exposed his leg, thick with dark hair, the calf tight with muscle, his sandaled foot dangling.

"You know your routes; it is essential to keep to your times. You will leave the house at intervals. Do not look behind you. You will not be followed. Nobody knows about you. Your missions must be completed as we have instructed you. Finally, remember your prayers as you step into the trains."

He motions to them to stand and goes over to them. He shakes hands with each of them. Amjad looks into the commander's black eyes. Similar eyes had looked into his own in the heat of the training camp when he had been given his first rifle, felt the cool steel in the heat and dust. The commander's two hands clasp his own, they are firm and warm and dry.

"Allahu akbar," he says quietly in his rich voice and smiles. "Today you will do great works. Remember you are the chosen ones. You are ready. Today you will be in paradise. There is no God but Allah, we are of God and to Allah we return."

They file out, their eyes not meeting, Amjad the third to go. He climbs the narrow stairs back to his room and closes the door behind him. He has said nothing to his companions.

Now there are only his final prayers. He must do them with perfect correctness, his clean body and clean mind concentrated on Allah, his thoughts far above this scruffy room. He prostrates himself with feet, knees, hands and forehead touching the floor.

"Glory to my Lord, the highest.
Glory to my Lord, the highest.
Glory to my Lord, the highest.
Allahu akbar."

He sits upright, his hands on his knees, his left foot tucked underneath his body and, careful this final time that he do it properly as the prophet had described, his right foot erect with only his toes touching the ground. He bows again and repeats the prayers, then stands up. He takes a deep breath and relaxes his shoulders. It is time for the warrior's prayer. He speaks aloud in a measured resonant voice.

"Oh Allah, raise the banner of Islam and its helper.
Help those who fight Jihad for your sake
And who in obedience to you have sacrificed themselves."

He bows his head. His hands are trembling.

7.00 am.

It promises to be a bleak day. His worst fears will be confirmed. Mike skims through the rest of the folder. Certain phrases trigger an immediate Amygdala Hijack as he snorts with cynicism: *the four circle model... the six leadership styles... the six factors of*

11

organisational climate..., developing meaningful coaching conversations... leading towards transformation towards higher performance...leadership is a journey and you will need a roadmap.

Bollocks! What had Sue said to him? *"Leadership is when you value the people who work for you more than the people you work for."* That was more like it: simple, common sense, no jargon or management speak. He takes a swig of water from his bottle, peels a banana and looks at his travelling companions. What journeys are they on? Are they necessary? Is his necessary? *"At least you may find out the direction in which you don't want to go,"* Sue had said, *"or even surprise yourself and see where you do want to go."*

He looks at the pylons with their power lines transmitting electricity across the land, at the concrete pillars which support the motorway over the railway line, the motorway already full of constantly speeding cars and lorries, racks of containers from China Shipping, P&O, Hamburg Sud waiting in yards for further distribution. Everything is a swirl of movement and transition, of change. It is supposed to be exciting. The train slows and he sees collections of homes, estates, settlements – tilled allotments, a garden with a bright plastic climbing frame, territories bounded by strong lap-fencing. A place to return to is more vital than the journey. He loved running across the wild open spaces but he loved it more because he came back to a home, and that home was Sue. She was the core of it.

Now they are past the suburbs and into north London: the long terraces of three story brick houses with rusting fire escapes and unkempt gardens. They overtake suburban trains in their different gaudy garbs, an inter-city roars past them on its way out of London. They slow through brief dark episodes of tunnel. Passengers reach up to luggage racks, laptops are folded away. Mike puts his folder back in his kitbag. They are twenty minutes late. Then the huge curving roof covers them and the railway lines fan out to platforms. For Sue's sake he will try to take the leadership course seriously, try to keep an open mind. But already he is looking forward to his run in the park this evening.

7.10 am.

Lee is hungry. He will go into the first café he comes to – he has his discharge grant and the £35 he had on him when he'd gone into prison. He opens the door of Big Man's and the smell of frying bacon envelops him, the roar of the coffee machine frothing up the milk. It is already busy with a queue of people wanting carry-out coffee and most tables are occupied. He takes a place by the wall, dumps his bag on a chair where he can see it and joins the queue. There are choices he can make – different sizes and kinds of coffee. All these customers are here of their own free will. So is he. Some are in a hurry but he isn't. He is not impatient, he relishes the waiting, not being in the shuffling disgruntled queue at the prison canteen with just thirty minutes to eat.

"A large Americano, with hot milk, please."

"Anything to eat with it, sir?"

He feels a slight panic, hastily chooses what is just in front of him in the glass cabinet.

"One of these apple Danish, please."

He takes a fiver from his wallet and pays, pockets the change and takes his small tray over to his seat. It seems odd, dealing with normal politeness, making a simple exchange. He sits and takes his first sip of the hot coffee: how strong and substantial the taste, a real taste not the pallid prison stuff. Already he senses his body awakening from an enforced hibernation, realising how it had shut down in some kind of natural defence mechanism to reduce disappointment. The breeze in his hair, the natural stride of his walking, the noise of car engines, the wide sky, women's bare legs and now the coffee – all are sensations brilliant and vibrant. It is a fog clearing and the sun emerging. Best of all, he is picking his son Ben up from school this afternoon. They will go to the park for a kick-about and then the Pizza Parlour for tea. He knows they will both be shy but soon they'll be natural again with each other. Real life is beginning again for him.

He looks around: some people are reading newspapers, some just sitting and staring. A young woman putting make-up on entrances him. With painted fingernails she is carefully putting lipstick on, using a small compact mirror. She has full lips and long blonde hair. Christ! He needs a woman! Does he smell of prison, he suddenly wonders? Is the pallor of his light-deprived face a give-away? Or does he look as ordinary as them? It seems so, nobody is taking any interest in him. He realises there is no threat here, no sense of frustration or anger that could easily ignite at a wrong word or wrong look. He is ordinary too; he has a family.

Through the wide café windows he watches buses pass. It will be good on the upper deck, riding through London, perhaps seeing some of the tourist sites he has never yet seen, looking down on pedestrians, looking into windows of houses or flats above shops, seeing people's real lives again, waiting in traffic, taking his time. But he doesn't know the routes or how long it will take. No, he had better take the underground, as planned. He finishes his coffee and his Danish pastry. *I can stay a bit longer,* he thinks, *or I can leave now. I decide.*

His other important meeting in a couple of days is with his mate Barry, down at the Bobbinmakers'. They had a lot to talk about. His first cell mate had been Jason – a member of the British National Party. He wanted to see what Barry thought about Jason's ideas.

7.45 am.

There is a third knock on Amjad's door, as if the man outside has been listening and waiting for this moment. Amjad does not hesitate, cannot hesitate. He strides to the door and opens it. The same old man is there as before.

"Follow me," he says and begins to descend the stairway.

Amjad follows him into a first floor room, completely empty apart from two rucksacks in a corner. So three have gone already. He recognises his own. The man gestures towards it and Amjad goes over to it. It is exactly as he had left it, neatly buckled and strapped, bulky but evenly packed. He looks at it, bends and hoists it onto his shoulders. It is heavier than he remembers it from yesterday. He adjusts it so that it is evenly balanced on both shoulders. He checks his watch: exactly on time. The man is staring at him then he walks forward and clasps his hands in his own. Amjad thinks he sees a moistness in the old man's eyes.

"You are a true shaheed," the man says, still holding his hand. Then from a pocket in his loose jacket he gives Amjad a pocket-sized Qu'ran.

"Carry this next to your heart," he continues. "May Allah bless and protect you."

Amjad tries to thank the man but no sound comes, his throat is dry. He nods his head, turns and leaves the room. Down the stairs he goes and along the hall to the front door of the house which, like his home, opens directly onto the street. As he opens it he is startled by the bright sunshine and the gentle warmth of the air. He is suddenly dizzy and has to lean against the door frame to balance himself. The moment passes. The street is busy with ordinary life as he eases himself into the flow of people. He is intensely aware of the weight of his rucksack, the bulk of it making him manoeuvre carefully on the crowded pavement so as not to knock into people. To calm himself he rehearses his route: a ten minute walk to the bus stop, the number 81 to Liverpool Street underground where he will pick up the Circle Line to Kings Cross.

He feels surrounded by the press and purpose of people, hurrying to their jobs, carrying bags or briefcases or small rucksacks towards offices and desks, to shops and stores. Most are silent but he hears laughter and chatting, sees the bare arms of women in bright summer dresses, smells the coffee in takeaway polystyrene mugs. A news vendor shouts at his stand on the corner of a street. Amjad buys a *Daily Mirror*. He must look ordinary, blend in. A young man bumps into him and mutters an apology before hurrying on into the crowd. He holds their lives on his back, the power of life or death. The sense thrills him – that he could in a moment transform the expressions on their faces into horror and bewilderment. He seems to float above them all.

He had felt the same when he came out of the leader's tent at the training camp in Waziristan. He had been summoned at night, wrapped in a blanket against the desert cold, his keffiyeh flung round his neck as a scarf. Three men sat behind the trestle table, only half-illuminated in the light of burning oil lamps. The rest of the tent was in deep shadow but he felt carpet under his feet. This was the moment he had trained so hard for. He would be made or broken by the decision. His life would pivot on the next words he heard. He stood to attention.

"You have done well, Amjad Khan. Stand easy," said the man who sat on the right of the three, his full beard ebony in the gloom, black eyes bright, his teeth gleaming white in the lamplight as he smiled.

Amjad dared to hope.

"You have been chosen."

The man did not stir from his chair, did not hold out his hand in congratulation. There was just his voice, the words Amjad had prayed for.

"From now on you are *al-shaheed al-hayy,* the living martyr. You will go to London where you will join your martyrdom cell. You will be allocated your task. There is a great plan to be accomplished. Your name will be honoured forever, you will be spoken about in sermons in mosques."

He had sworn an oath on the Qu'ran, a pledge not to waver – the pledge called *bayt al-ridwan,* after the garden in paradise that is reserved for prophets and martyrs. His would be the sweetest jihad. If done for Allah, all martyrdom operations hurt less than a gnat's bite.

Outside the tent he had stood and looked up at the shining constellations in the sky, imagined them sliding across space as they always had done, indifferent to the doings of men, the moon partly shadowed as if it had been broken. At that moment he had felt humble and yet glorified: just a man but also an instrument of Allah. Around him were the dark shapes of tents, a few fires burning low, the mutter of men's voices, a wolf howl up in the mountains. Those millions of glittering stars. How small he was, how large the purpose, how all-encompassing.

Back in the tent, while others snored and muttered in their sleep, and the mountain wind keened around the canvas, he could not sleep. How cleverly had Allah guided him to this point. Where had his journey begun?

8.40 am.

Clattering down the escalators at Kings Cross, his heavy sports bag held awkwardly in front of him and bumping into standing passengers, Mike curses GNER's late train arrival. He hates hurrying, hates when people turn to look at him if he's late, hates the press of people. Down into the depths and then across a yellow-tiled concourse – people criss-crossing, dodging and weaving but somehow oblivious of each other, a weird almost-silence of voices among so many – to another escalator, his arms aching now with the sports bag that contains his laptop, running kit and folders for the management course where he will arrive hot and flustered. Thank God he's had the foresight to book a through ticket which includes the underground to the conference centre in Bayswater. At least he's missed having to queue for separate underground tickets, the queues to the machines snaking into the passing crowds and adding to the pressures.

At last he emerges onto the platform, at the back of a solid mass of people. Adverts for Chanel perfume and Audi curve up the wall on the opposite side of the tunnel. More people push in behind him. There is the oncoming rush of air, the screech of wheels and a train pulls in, the doors open, the taped message drones out. He sees people forcing their way through the crowd off the train and surging forwards but there is still a line of people between him and the doors. He can't force his way through and in any case he can see the bent backs of those already in the carriage crouching inwards from the doors.

"Mind the doors."

They close with a squeal of rubber. He notices the lit destination board. This is a Metropolitan train going to Amersham; he would have had to change at Baker Street. The next one due in four minutes, is a Circle Line which will take him direct to Bayswater. That's lucky: he should just get there for the introductory coffee. He begins to relax a little. He keeps hold of his bag, careful to keep the shoulder strap looped over his wrist. London, the anonymity, the news stories of mugging, make him nervous. The platform seems to pack even tighter with waiting commuters. People do this every day. *Incredible*, thinks Mike.

8.45 am.

Lee gives himself a couple of minutes and then leaves. It is only a short walk now to the station. He examines the large scale tube map on the wall. There are several ways to get to Kings Cross. He realises he wants to walk into Kings Cross from the open air, from a street, not along underground passageways and up escalators straight into the concourse, hurrying with others at their pace along a set route in artificial light. He will take the Central Line to Notting Hill Gate, then change to Circle Line and get off at Euston Square. He will walk along the crowded Euston Road. He wants to be among travellers, going to or from Kings Cross or St Pancras – travellers on their own individual journeys to work or home or holidays, but going to different destinations in their lives, to meet people: their decisions, their choices.

At the turnstile he shows his travel warrant, a sudden reminder of where he has been as he looks at the face of the checker for any sign of understanding. But the face is expressionless, the gate opened with a slight nod. He rides the escalator, his kit-bag impatiently pushed into him as a young man hurries down on the left hand side. At the bottom he needs the East route. The platform is crowded with rush hour travellers. There is a rush of wind and the train pulls in, the doors slide open and a few people get out of the crowded carriage. Somehow he forces his way in, half dragged and pushed by the momentum of others.

"Mind the doors."

Somewhere behind him as he stands pressed into the crowd of bodies, the doors close and he lurches, almost overbalances, grabs for a hanging strap as the train pulls out. He can just see the underground plan on the curve of the carriage roof, between the hands and arms of the straphangers. White City is the next stop – dog racing and athletics? Then Shepherd's Bush – BBC? Next will be Holland Park – is there a park? And the Notting Hill Gate with its carnival – his stop. How little he knows of his own capital city, just a series of headlines. At each stop more passengers get on, though it seems impossible to cram more in. No one complains, leaning on each other, swaying together as the train rounds curves with a screech of steel on rail. He lurches forward as the train stops, people push past him.

8.50 am.

Amjad waits with a serene patience in the queue at the bus stop. His secret is precious, delicate yet all-powerful. Traffic passes in roaring spasms, then stops, engines idling, revving as traffic lights change. Petrol and diesel fumes hang in the air. His throat is dry again and he tries to swallow saliva. So much noise and rush all around him, while in his head there is calm and his own holy purpose.

"Excuse me, is this bus going to Euston?"

A young black woman is asking him. He realises it is the second time she has asked him. He can't bring his mind to bear on the question, can't even take in her face as he turns to her. He sees just a blur of black skin and a smile of white teeth.

"Er, sorry, I don't know, sorry," he manages to splutter out. She speaks to someone else. He is alarmed by his panic, inability to reason. He must remain clear-headed.

When the 81 comes he goes carefully upstairs, manoeuvres off his rucksack and sits towards the back with it on his knee. He visualises its contents that he packed so meticulously yesterday. A trained engineer had mixed the TATP explosive from drain cleaner, bleach and acetone. He has forgotten what TATP means. His task was only to pack the plastic containers in the required sequence: 1 kilogram tubs of vanilla icecream and lemon sorbet, some of which contained explosive and some shrapnel: screws, tacks, nails, nuts and washers. On top of these, just beneath the rucksack cover on which his left hand is now resting, is the detonating device. All he has to do is complete a circuit by snapping two connectors together. He must not unstrap the cover before he gets on the tube. He must remember that. He must keep focused.

The bus halts in a line of traffic. But he can't keep his concentration.

He is fascinated by other people, as if seeing them for the first time. On the opposite side of the aisle sits a young white woman, her legs bare, her feet in sandals. He dare not look directly at her face. Her bag rests on her lap, on the thin material of a brightly coloured dress, smoothed tightly over her thigh. Her arms are bare. There is a glint of gold at her ears under blonde hair. He wrenches his mind away and turns to look out of the window. He has never been inside a woman. Will the virgins in paradise have real warm bodies? Would he have been a good lover, a good husband, a good father?

An image – his father and himself at a Test Match at Headingly, watching Pakistan beat England, the white-clad cricketers, the green oval, the tiers of spectators, the scoreboard, the constant movement of people going for drinks and food, the smell of vinegar on chips, his father and he sharing earphones as they listen to Test Match Special, cheering and clapping, the crack of bat on ball, his father holding his hand as they leave the ground among the crowds.

Amjad has disobeyed only one instruction. In his wallet is a photograph, creased now and with a tear at one corner. He knows it so well. He should not have it with him but he had decided long ago that he would die with it. It will be destroyed in his death, no one will find it. It is a simple snap: his father and mother sitting in the centre of the sofa, he and his three sisters beside them. His father looks serious but all the rest are laughing. Will they ever understand? He feels such love for his mother, wants so much for her to accept him, to accept with joy the high standing she will have in the community as mother of a shaheed, a martyr, and confident of her place in heaven. But he knows she will not. He has to put that sadness away from him, as he had to put the childish laughter and quarrels of his young sisters. They are too much of this world. He looks at his father.

Amjad had hated his father but because of that owes everything to him. He forgives him his errors; his father never wore qameez, even to the mosque, always western dress, even a tie. His father told his mother she should wear her face uncovered when she went outside because the burqa made white people suspicious and this would stop them being accepted by the community. His father allowed his eldest daughter to wear western make-up and skirts, even at home not insisting on the traditional shalwar qameez, encouraged her to go to college and promised that he would never arrange a marriage for her.

The bus lurches forward. He must put his family out of his mind. He will go crazy, he will panic, he will fail. Control, he must regain control. He needs other memories: how Allah had changed this hatred of his father into a positive force. In turning away from his father, he had been enabled to meet Waheed and learn that he had a part to play. He remembers watching through the shop windows in Leeds as the planes flew into the Twin Towers, the plumes of smoke, the collapse of the buildings. He concentrates fiercely on quotations from the books he was given when he was inducted into his cell of Hizb ut-Tahrir. *'Religion and politics are one and the same in Islam. Islam is a way of life and must be enshrined in the state. We have to conquer and convert, attack the crusaders. We must spare neither life nor property. That is jihad.'* He recalls the newsreels the Young Muslims had shown, of war in Iraq and Pakistan and Afghanistan. Especially he remembers the video of the war in Bosnia and the imam who said: *'They did not protect us, the UN troops did nothing. 7500 Muslims were slaughtered. If the British would not protect Muslims in Bosnia, is it not obvious they will not protect us here in Britain? We have to grow strong to protect ourselves, my brothers. And our main weapon is the spreading of fear.'*

Amjad remembers the swelling of his heart, his understanding of his mission. He remembers their drive in the bouncing back of the lorry, across the desert on a rough track through the night after the flight to Islamabad; his fever of fatigue, excitement and apprehension as he and his companions crouched on the dry cool gravel of the cave in Waziristan, the deafening reverberations of the American helicopter blades overhead.

And he knows where it all began: at school. He was nearly fourteen years old and trying to do Ramadan properly, wanting to follow the rules for a proper adult. He has never forgotten the name-calling: *Pa-ki, Pa-ki, Pa-ki, poppadum boy,* their mocking mimicry of the muezzin's call from the mosque as he, the only one devout and brave enough, ascended the stairs to the prayer room past the chanting boys. His uncle Hussein had requested the school to provide this during Ramadan, much to his father's disapproval. He remembered entering the small prayer room, closing the door to shut out the row and the crude ignorance below. He had ten minutes to make his prayers. As he took off his school bag and put it down in the corner, it seemed like all the mundane details of the rest of the world and of the day were loosened from his shoulders. He took off his shoes, washed his hands and feet in the bowls of water provided – noticing they had not been refreshed from yesterday. There was a dull film of dust on the surface. He stepped out from behind the curtain that partitioned off the small washing place, knelt on the bright red and gold carpet, closed his eyes, knelt and bowed with his arms stretched out in front of him. The ritual repetitions of what he chanted to himself in a low, low voice acted as a screen that slowly drew to shut out everything except himself and his God – his supplication, his humility, his obedience, his head bowed. The bare emulsioned room with a few desks cleared away and stacked in the corner, with a copy of the Qu'ran on a shelf, was filled with the enfolding and absorbing spirit of Allah to whom Amjad devoted himself: his disciple, his example of peace and acceptance.

He had prayed, his forehead on the rough weave of the carpet, conscious of the rough scratch of the wool on his temple but not shifting to ease the irritation. At the same time he felt uplifted into some vague bright but insubstantial light, absorbed into a wider compassion and love. He gave thanks for the self-control and willpower Allah bestowed upon him. He celebrated the purity of his body and soul. And so he had stayed until the crude hammering metallic bell sounded out in the corridor and summoned Amjad back to this day and place and his next lesson.

Now he understands how that experience primed him, prepared him. Now today he is fully ready. He feels strong again. He opens the *Mirror* and forces himself to read about Tony Blair's jig of joy that the Olympic bid has been successful. *That joy will be short-lived*, he thinks grimly. He looks out of the window to get his bearings, checks his watch. Then at last the bus slows for his stop.

On the pavement Amjad slings his rucksack over his right

shoulder. It is now only twenty minutes to the detonation. Wherever he is on the tube at 9.35 am he must explode the bomb. Twenty minutes to live. He knows his final prayers off by heart but he must check, leave nothing to chance. He finds an empty shop doorway and takes the folded typed piece of paper from the Qu'ran in which he had placed it. He repeats the prayer to himself, his heart beating hard, then checks the paper. He has it correct, his last supplication to Allah. He folds the sheet of paper back into the Qu'ran, hesitates, then takes out his photograph. He sees the smiling faces of his sisters, the restrained smile of his mother, the serious face of his father. He feels a surge of sadness coming up from his stomach and his heart. But all that is past, is irrelevant. He puts the photograph back in his pocket.

He looks across the road to the Liverpool Street Underground sign, hitches up the rucksack on his shoulder, then remembers, slings it off and unfastens the straps of the top, but keeps the draw-strap tight and loops the rucksack back onto his shoulder. He is ready now. He straightens his back, pushes his shoulders back. He is the warrior now, the sacred shaheed with his mission for the love and glory of Allah.

Devoid now of feeling, as if programmed, he crosses the road when the green man permits him, not hurrying. He descends the concrete steps, stands in the queue, slips his coin into the ticket machine and takes out the ticket, slides the ticket into the turnstile machine and stands on the descending escalator. He is not thinking of anything, his hand on the warm black rubber of the moving hand rest, staring at the neck and shirt collar of the man on the step below him, feeling the strap of his rucksack biting into his shoulder.

The platform is packed with commuters. The person behind him squashes the rucksack into his back. Amjad feels the shape of the tubs packed with explosives pressing into his spine. Then the rush of wind and the train roars in from the curving tunnel. The doors open and passengers alight into a crushing melee of people. He is carried along by the surge of bodies. But there is no room for him, the last bodies curve their backs to avoid the closing doors. Amjad steps back.

"Mind the doors."

Then the train pulls out. The sign says two minutes until the next train, a Circle Line.

9.17 am.

The Circle line train curves in, red and ramshackle compared with the aluminium of the Metropolitan. A few passengers get out and a few get in, the rest waiting for another line. Mike gratefully sits down in the one empty seat, hoisting his heavy sports bag onto his lap. On the diagram above the doors he counts the stations, just six to Bayswater. As the train draws away he looks around the carriage, immediately conscious he is the only one doing so. The others are reading or staring straight ahead or have eyes closed, some with earpieces isolating them inside their music. A few are talking, not English but he cannot recognise the language, perhaps some eastern European. Two white women are conversing, their dark hair pulled tightly back from their foreheads, carrying empty shopping bags. He recognises Italian and Spanish headlines in newspapers, all with the same pictures of London celebrating winning the 2012 Olympic Games. He notices skin colours too dark to be English, and a couple of African students studying files of notes.

He wonders if he is the only Englishman there, how many are visitors, how many in temporary residence, in what small poky homes they live in the poorer areas of London, the service jobs they do, why they stay here, why it is better than home. Do they like London more than he does, this collection of foreigners? Next to him an elderly man with glasses is licking his finger and sorting through a handful of papers resting on a laptop case. A day and a half of management speak, some boxes ticked, jargon learned, papers collected, slogans memorised, and then tomorrow the late afternoon train home. This evening he'd manage a run in Kensington Gardens before dinner and tomorrow early before breakfast.

He looks at his watch. Paddington will be the next stop. He'd be at the course on time after all. Thank God Sue didn't love him because he was a future leader. She was strong but sometimes she needed his support. She didn't win every time in the classroom.

When she came home angry and frustrated, he was glad to be able to calm her down. They were a good team. They would endure, he was sure of it.

9.22 am

At Notting Hill Gate Lee pushes his way out and follows the yellow signs and arrows to the Circle Line. He is part of a moving crowd – up steps, down steps, escalators and tiled tunnels. And then out on to another platform. Above him the electronic sign states *Edgware Road,* a District Line train. That is no use to him, he would be only half way there. But underneath that the sign also states *Circle Line 4 minutes.* That was lucky – perfect! He's getting used to this already. This platform is less crowded. He can see adverts for *March of the Penguins* and *Star Wars Episode 3* on the curved tunnel wall above the rails. He peers at the diagram of the journey: Bayswater Road, Paddington, Edgware Road and then just Baker Street and Great Portland Road before Euston Square.

The train roars in and this time there is a seat for him. The train accelerates out of the lighted station and into the dark tunnel. He looks around his fellow passengers: some are reading paperbacks, others newspapers, turning the pages with difficulty in the confined space, some have eyes closed, some just stare ahead. Some are chatting but in languages he can't understand. There are small rucksacks on laps, briefcases, laptops, plastic bags, handbags. Everyone has a destination and a purpose. He feels caught up in the excitement of the city, the movement, the freedom. His carriage empties and re-fills, a constant re-shuffling of bodies, each separate but each part of an intricate network of pathways, crossing but disconnected from each other.

He looks more carefully at their faces; the range of colours in which white is a definite minority. He counts the white faces: less than 20%, he calculates. There are faces black, brown, sallow, yellow, Asian, African, Middle Eastern, East European. It seems the whole world is represented in this carriage – tourists, workers, immigrants, going to homes, to jobs. How many are ex-cons like himself? What secrets do they hide? Are those two young Pakistani men connected with the things Jason had told him? London is now the centre for Islamic radical fundamentalists, he'd said. Islam is now the second biggest religion in Britain and far more active than Christianity.

Looking round the carriage again, he feels a sudden sense of isolation, of being an alien in his own land, outside the networks. At Edgware Road a couple struggle in with large suitcases with airline luggage labels. Are they returning from a trip or setting out? He is doing both, he thinks. He has Ben this afternoon, he will have a job in a couple of days, he will be living again in his mother's house – his house now, but it will always be his mother's. But beyond all that, what will he do? What seemed to be clear in prison seems cloudier now, his direction more uncertain. Where does he fit in this multi-racial carriage? Barry will help him. He needs help. In the last few weeks back in prison, thinking about what Jason had said, and reading, he had felt a renewed purpose. Now he is not so sure.

He senses the train slowing. It will be Paddington next. People begin to get up and press their way to the doors. He sees the first pale electric light of the station on the dark tunnel walls. And then the platform opens out and they stop. People crowd out and in.

9.31 am.

Amjad stands behind the yellow line on the platform and watches the red rear lights disappear into the tunnel. He will be first into the next train, a Circle Line. The electronic board above his head states two minutes to arrival. He stares ahead at the adverts on the curved wall but registers nothing. The train roars in out of the tunnel, doors open, the same surge of commuters.

"Oh, Allah," he intones silently to himself. "Open all doors for me. Oh Allah who answers prayers, I am asking you for your help. I am asking you for forgiveness. I am asking you to lighten my way. I am asking you to lift the burden I feel. Allah, I trust in you. Allah, I lay myself in your hands. I ask with the light of your faith that has lit the whole world and lightened all darkness on this earth, to guide me until you approve of me. And once you do, I have achieved my aim."

26

He pushes his way in first, slings his rucksack off his shoulder and takes the only seat, placing his rucksack on his knees.

"Mind the doors."

And the train pulls out. He looks at the underground plan. He knows the stops: Moorgate, Barbican, Farringdon, Kings Cross. It is there, at the busiest place, that he must detonate the bomb. He checks his watch, he is on schedule. Tense now, his eyes stray to the other passengers but he takes in only the standing shapes, the sitting forms, the sway and rocking of the train. His head seems full of a haze of blood but his throat is dry. He licks his lips. They are drawing into Kings Cross. The carriage half empties and then fills up again with another crush of passengers.

"Mind the doors."

They clunk shut. Now is the allotted time. But there is a child standing in front of him, her dark eyes looking intently at him, staring at him. He sees her pale hand holding her mother's. He looks around. Suddenly he can focus, see the newspapers and spectacles and bags, the colours of coats and trousers and dresses, feel the warmth of close bodies, hear someone laughing among chatter. The top of the unbuckled rucksack is inches from his face, the drawstring tight. But he is paralysed. He cannot move his hands to loosen the cord. His mind is numb, barely conscious of the waves of commuters leaving and joining the train at Euston Square, Great Portland Street, Baker Street and Edgware Road.

Mike looks across at the Asian man sitting opposite him, dark-skinned, black eyes staring forwards, with a bulging rucksack on his knee. Next to him the old man is tidying his papers away. Three young women are standing in front of them. He can smell their perfume as they talk and laugh.

The Asian man's eyes look straight into his, their blackness seems to shine with an unnatural intensity as if he is communicating a message to him, sharing a triumph. His lips move slightly as if reciting a prayer, like the Catholics Mike has occasionally seen fingering their rosary beads.

The train slows. An old lady wearing a red scarf jostles and prods her way along the carriage towards the door. They are slowing up at the station, pulling in next to a stationary train on the other platform.

Lee's train begins to move out of the yellow-tiled brightness into the tunnel.

Mike watches the Asian man staring at the girls' bare arms as they stretch up to the hanging straps, thin black straps on their shoulders, dresses taut across their breasts. The train lurches and the girls' bodies sway.

Mike watches the man quickly put both hands inside his rucksack, fumble with the drawstring and loosen it.

The man closes his eyes and rocks slightly back and forwards, rhythmically, his lips moving.

Lee stares across at the lights of the carriage passing him, slowing down as his own train accelerates.

Mike is still watching the Asian man who seems to be struggling to get something out of his rucksack. Suddenly the man screams:

"No!"

There is a sudden blinding, all-encompassing white flash. Mike has a heavy smothering pressure on his chest as if someone has pumped the carriage full of air. There is a searing heat and massive deafening explosion.

Lee feels the air sucked out of the train, hears the smash of glass, is back in the bombs of Basra, and is hurled out of the air by the surge of pressure.

Mike falls to the floor instinctively as a shower of glass hits him and then he is blown out of the doors, his back hitting the tunnel wall. Immediately a crushing metal weight lands on his legs. An excruciating pain shoots up and explodes in his head.

Part 2:

Two Tunnels

July 2005

2.

Explosion

7th July

9.35 am. London

Mike plummeted into blackness, flung like rag doll, limbs flailing as he was turned and twisted by the force. He was the man leaping from the Twin Towers and falling. He was in an endless lift shaft, nose-diving down the narrow dark metal tube, tumbling over and over in slow motion through air that was thick and hot as tar. Flakes of images – of sunlight caught in a curl of water, of a smile – flickered fast as a subliminal film across his brain and disappeared. He plunged past screams, muffled and torn away from him. The blackness throttled him and filled him. *This is death*, he thought. And then the timeless fall ended in an instant. He crashed down into a hard floor, his back slammed into a steel pole. A weight crushed his legs.

*

Alongside, in the other underground train Lee, too, was thrown onto the floor. His back, curled instinctively to protect his head, was forced up hard against the seats. There was a sharp pain in his elbow, jammed into the hard floor by the weight of people thrown and squirming on top of him. His face was muffled by someone's coat which he scrabbled in a panic to clear so he could breathe. He felt the train judder as it ground to a halt, the metal of the wheels screeching on the rails. Lights had gone out and the darkness was filled with a choking black smoke. He heard screaming but it sounded distant and echoing as if he was partly deafened. There was a sharp chemical acrid smell.

He felt the body directly on top of him lift its weight off.

"I'm so sorry," a female voice said, bizarrely courteous in the chaos.

His head still on the floor, Lee felt the scraping of shoes vibrating in his jaw bone. He felt other bodies moving around him, shoes nudging him as their owners stood up. Some part of him recognised how – even in this extreme – they were diffident and careful not to hurt him. He pushed himself up into a sitting position which meant, he thought, that his arms were still working. He bent his legs, flexed his feet: all working. Lee stood up, holding on to unseen neighbours to balance himself. He seemed unhurt.

The tannoy crackled above shouting and moans: "This is your driver. We have a problem. Don't panic. If there is anyone with first aid knowledge please make your way to the back of the train. Otherwise stay where you are. The emergency lights will be on shortly and we will then evacuate the train."

People around him were beginning to talk, the screaming seemed more distant, a woman was sobbing softly somewhere to Lee's right. A man was groaning. The air was warm, choked with dust and the smell of burning rubber. In the darkness he saw tiny panels of light flicker on as people used their mobile phone LED screens as torches. Through the broken windows he heard the screaming more sharply, saw the mangled shape of the other train next to him on the other track. As his eyes adjusted to the gloom, he saw a man a few yards down his own carriage breaking the door windows with a fire extinguisher, the thick safety glass eventually shattering like a windscreen, falling to the floor, some of the pieces glittering momentarily from some unseen light source.

Lee moved forward and followed the man through the window space, clambering across into the adjacent train. Lee climbed over the twisted metal door frame, using his hands to find his way, his feet treading on debris, on shattered glass, on the softness of a body. Then the emergency lights came on – pale greeny yellow bulbs of light at intervals in the tunnel and he could see smoke billowing out of the buckled frames of windows. He stood still to get his bearings, covering his nose from the acrid smell, coughing to clear his choking throat. The situation was much worse in this train. He saw a woman still sitting on her seat: she was completely naked except for a pair of knickers, her body naked and grey from the blast, her head streaked with blood. She was dead but her eyes stared open. There were moans and cries all around him, the carriage shattered and twisted. Bending down, he cradled the back of the woman's head in his left hand and closed her eyelids with the fingers of his right hand.

*

Further down this train Mike felt movements around him, voices calling but as if from a great distance. His ears and teeth still rang with the explosion. He tasted blood and his mouth seemed full of sharp sand. His tongue felt swollen, dry as ash. He licked his lips, dry and scabbed with dust, felt fragments of glass on his tongue and spat them out, a sudden panic at the sense of glass in his throat and lungs. He felt a covering of something on his eyelids, fought the panic. He flexed his fingers, revolved his wrists, carefully lifted his arms. He had to brush his eyes clear of glass. He had to get them absolutely clean. With the back of his forefinger he brushed across his eyebrows and the side of his nose, first the left and then the right. With infinite softness, he brushed his eyelids and eyelashes to the outside corner of the eyes and then flicked away the debris. With fresh saliva he moistened his finger and stroked it across his eyes, cleansing any last remnant of dust and powdered glass. He was isolated in his concentration. He was alive and he had to do this first task right. He had to protect his eyes.

He opened them carefully, blinked. They were fine, but instantly stinging with the smoke. He smelt burning. He was slumped half on the floor, half up against the cushioned fabric of a seat. He heard shouts, calling out, screams – but faintly from far away. His ears must have been damaged by the blast. He tried to shift his body, to ease the pressure on his shoulders. It was then he realised he could not feel his legs, the bottom half of his body was numb. A massive weight lay on them. Terror and panic surged up from his stomach.

"Sue!" He didn't know whether he cried it or whispered it or said it inside his head. "Sue!"

He saw her face so clearly, her soft grey eyes. He groaned with despair, he wanted her holding him. If he could concentrate on Sue he would survive. Something terrible had happened. But he would not let himself die. He had to stay in control. Sue's final image of him must not be of his suffering and dying down here in the dark and devastation. Some help would come. This was London, they would know what had happened. They would not be allowed to die, trapped in a wrecked train. He had to stay awake until someone came, until he could see an approaching torchlight. Yet it was so tempting to drift into sleep.

Now he could see shades of grey within the darkness, shapes moving. There was an echoing in his ears but the sounds were a little sharper. He had to breathe steadily, calmly, wait. He turned his arm, looked at his watch, the luminous figures on his training watch. He watched the green digits, the seconds flick past. He read the date, THU 7, watched the digits climb to 59 and 00, the minute tick over to 31, the seconds start again at 1. It was 9.37. He would live a minute at a time. He would stay alive for Sue. But he had to make sure whoever came would know he was alive.

"Help me," he called but his voice echoed in his head and he did not know if he had spoken aloud.

*

Lee, now in Mike's carriage, shuffled forward past bodies. This was like a war zone. He stopped when he saw a man whose upper body was protruding from a crater in the carriage floor. His eyes were staring open in shock, his arms making involuntary jerking movements. Gently Lee placed his hands in the man's armpits and tried to lift him free but he couldn't move him, the man silent and unable to co-operate. Lee peered down through the hole. But he saw the man's legs were lying on the track in a mass of gleaming black blood. Lee turned to the man. He was still lodged there but his head had lolled forward, his arms were still. He was dead.

"Thank God for that!" muttered Lee to himself.

One or two other people were moving about now, groans and cries were getting louder. Then he heard a male voice just to his left and low down in the gloom. It was quiet, restrained, almost polite.

"Someone help me, please."

Carefully, Lee moved towards the voice. He crouched down over the man.

"My legs," said the man. "My legs are gone."

"OK," said Lee. "I'll see what I can do. Don't try to move."

Lee gently ran his hand down over the man's stomach and slowly towards the man's right thigh. He paused his hand and inched it down. The thin trouser was already soaked in blood. Then his fingers touched a mushy sludge of flesh like papier mache, and a metal pole embedded in it. The man flinched and cried out. In the dim light, Lee saw the man's smashed leg was mangled round the pole. A twisted curved carriage door, its glass smashed, lay at an angle alongside the man and resting on, or actually in, his left leg. Lee knew immediately from his army training that he had to elevate the man's legs above the level of his heart and try to stem the bleeding from the artery. He had a sudden memory of Mac tumbled into the seat beside him in the jeep, his hand to his shoulder, the blood streaming around his fist.

"The weight on my leg," said the man, and groaned.

Lee looked at the angle of the door, saw in the gloom where it was balanced against an empty seat, worked out how he could lift it free and manoeuvre it into a space. It had to be one movement, one shift of position so that it did not fall out of control back onto the man or on to someone else. He had one chance, that was all, or he could make things even worse. With both hands he grasped the rubber seals of the door side, slippery with blood, tried to gauge its weight,

35

then lifted and jerked it up as fast as he could. The man screamed and Lee angled the door away so that it flipped partly over and rested on the wrecked edge of a seat. Lee tested its stability: it would not move. Then he saw that the man's other leg was also crushed.

Lee was pouring with sweat, his heart thumping like mad. The man was groaning quietly. He knew he had to keep him awake, try to make him talk, keep his brain operating.

"What is your name?" His mouth was close to the man's ear, almost touching it. He smelled burned hair.

"Mike, Mike Cooper."

"I'm Lee, Lee Norton. I'm going to try and stop your legs bleeding."

Lee started to take off his shirt, then looked up and saw a woman slumped across a seat. She had a silk scarf around her neck. Not knowing whether she was dead or unconscious he carefully took it off and ripped it in two.

"I must move your legs," he said. "Be ready, it will hurt for a moment."

Mike made no reply.

I am going to keep you alive, Lee said to himself, *this one is not going to die on me.*

Rapidly Lee used the scarf strips as tourniquets, pulling them tight. He wedged some chunks of metal debris to try and elevate the remains of Mike's legs. Mike howled with the sudden spasm of pain. Lee knew the risk: cutting off the blood supply could lead to the necessity of amputation. But the alternative was rapid loss of blood and Mike's death. It all depended now on how quickly the emergency medics took to arrive.

"You'll live now," said Lee. "How old are you?"

Mike knew too that he must not go to sleep. He felt a draining that was more than blood, a seeping away of some kind of life force, spirit. Drowsiness was seeping into him. He forced himself to answer Lee's question.

"Twenty eight," he said.

"What's your date of birth?" asked Lee.

Mike closed his eyes, focused on figures as on an application form.

"24th July 1977," he said.

"I can't hear you," said Lee. "You'll have to speak louder."

Mike dragged up some energy and concentrated it into his throat and mouth.

"July 24th 1977. Stay with me, please. Don't leave me, I must not die."

Lee held Mike's hand firmly.

"I won't leave you."

Mike focused on Lee's grip, feeling it warm and strong.

"Tell Sue I love her," said Mike.

"You will tell her yourself," said Lee. "The medics will soon be here."

Where are those fucking medics? This was worse than Basra, worse than a battlefield. These were civilians, ordinary people not trained soldiers. He couldn't work out what had happened. He couldn't remember his train crashing. It had come to a controlled halt yet there had been an explosion. It sounded like a bomb. There was less screaming now. He knew the soft groans were those of the badly wounded, too weak to scream.

"What's Sue's full name?"

Mike forced himself to remember, dragged up the name from beyond the darkness and chaos that surrounded him.

"Sue Whitehall."

"Can you spell that for me, please? I want to write it down."

He had to keep him focused, had to force Mike's mind to work. Lee ripped a piece off a newspaper lying on the floor and found the pen in his pocket.

Mike spelled it out to him and Lee wrote the names in block letters.

"Where do you live?"

"Bradfield," Mike managed to say, his throat was so dry, his tongue so thick.

Lee added the name of the city, folded the paper and crammed it firmly into Mike's shirt pocket.

"I have a son, Ben," said Lee, shocked that this was the first time he had thought of him.

At last Lee saw torchlight bobbing along the tunnel, huge shadows curving on the tunnel walls, yellow fluorescent jackets climbing into the carriage. Slowly they made their way towards them along the carriage, bending, talking. They seemed to be working in pairs. A torch shone into his face.

"Not me, him." Lee nodded to Mike. "It's his legs. They're very bad. I've tried to tourniquet them."

The torch beam swung over to Mike. Mike shut his eyes against the sudden brightness. Lee watched the torchlight quarter down Mike's body and stop at his thighs, the shirt strips already soaked red with blood.

"Priority One," said a voice.

Another man, his jacket sleeves livid lemon in the beam of light, looped a tag around Mike's neck

"You've done well," said the voice to Lee.

The two moved on. Lee squeezed Mike's hand.

"You'll soon be out of here."

Mike understood that Priority One meant he would be the first to be treated, but this also meant he was one of the most badly injured. His legs. He dare not picture them. His running. It was strange he felt no pain in them, the pain was in his head and in his shoulders. And he was so tired, weary with aching and the difficulty of breathing, the heat, his parched throat. He had to keep Sue's smile in his head for a little longer, keep it there, her face blocking out all the rest. He couldn't give in now.

"Priority Ones," announced another male voice at the far end of the carriage.

"Over here," shouted Lee.

Mike opened his eyes, felt Lee let go of his hand. His fingers scrabbled to keep hold, to keep Lee there. In the half light he saw men, maybe four, bending over him, felt them lift him, groaned out of the very centre of him as pain at last shot up like red-hot fire around his legs, felt himself placed in what seemed like a hammock, soft as blankets. He heard muffled male voices, calm, measured, knowledgeable, loving. He felt tears in his eyes.

"Stay with me, Lee" he whispered.

And he heard Lee reply, "I'll stay with you, Mike. I'll just be alongside with you. The medics are taking you out now, out of the tunnel."

Mike tried to smile. He could let go now, relax. He had done all he could to keep himself alive. He had stayed awake. Lee and he had survived. He was safe, he could trust these men, give himself up to them. They knew how to help him.

Lee followed the four stretcher bearers as they moved awkwardly through the carriage. They were trying to hurry, he heard the anxiety in their voices as they manoeuvred the makeshift stretcher through the wrecked carriage and out through the door onto the track. They had to pause as one man changed his grip. In the wider space of the tunnel Lee could walk alongside the stretcher. He found Mike's hand again. Mike just felt the warmth and strength of the grip, the connection, just heard Lee's voice:

"Stay with us, Mike. Come on, Mike, you must stay with us, stay with us for Sue."

Sue, Sue. But Mike could not keep her, her smile was fading, the joy in her eyes dulling over, her face receding. The warmth of sleep was brimming over him.

They were shuffling forward single file.

"Priority One! Priority One!" shouted a man at the front of the stretcher.

The line of other rescuers moved to one side to let them through as they stumbled and jogged in the gloomy greenish light of the smoky tunnel, crunching broken glass under their feet. Lee heard people talking, even laughter: jokes that controlled their fear, minimized the horrors – *it was the same after a patrol*, he thought.

Then the lights became brighter and Lee saw a line of men in fluorescent jackets waving them forward towards the platform. He had to let go of Mike's hand as the stretcher was tilted up onto the sloping end of the platform. Lee grabbed a bottle of water from a woman who was handing them out. He saw people lying on the platform, leaning against the walls, staggering. Some were covered in blood, all were blackened as if with soot. Mike's blanket stretcher was laid on top of a proper one. Now they ran along the platform, Lee jogging along behind.

Across the packed station foyer they ran and out onto the street. At the very end of his consciousness Mike smelled the fresh air, opened his eyes to sunlight. Lee stood by the stretcher as a medic efficiently fixed a saline drip into Mike. His stretcher was thrust into the ambulance.

"Can I go with him?" asked Lee. "I'm his friend."

"Sorry, no room, mate. Thanks for your help."

The ambulance doors closed. The medic ran round to the passenger door. The ambulance accelerated away, the siren blaring. Mike felt the ambulance move off and heard the siren. He could give in now. He lost consciousness.

Lee watched the ambulance turn a corner. He hadn't asked which hospital it was going to. He stood, feeling suddenly bereft, exhausted. *Ben*, he thought. *Ben*. He should be seeing Ben this afternoon. And suddenly the fact of his own survival overcame him, that he was still alive for Ben, that Ben still had a father. It had been a thought that came to him after every patrol in Iraq. He slumped down onto the pavement, his back resting against a wall. He rested his head in his hands.

Lee felt bewildered. Why did he feel so shocked? He'd seen death and terrible injuries many times before. Was it the thought of Ben without a dad? Was it because he was alone, not with his mates, not with his patrol? Was it because Mike was just a civilian, an ordinary man on his way to work on an ordinary week day, not in a war zone? Was it because he had got to know a little about him?

Was it because he was not a soldier any more?

And what had happened? Had the trains crashed? But he remembered an explosion and, in Mike's carriage he now realised, the unmistakeable smell of explosive. A bomb?

He was too tired to think. For the first time he realised he did not have his kitbag with him. He patted his back trouser pocket. He still had his wallet, and in it was his travel pass that would get him home. He looked around. Other people like him were slumped against walls, some had their arms around each other in small groups, there was blood on faces. He looked at his own hands and sleeves and trousers: there was blood everywhere, Mike's blood and blood from the man who had died. He noticed a man in shorts and white socks slowly panning round the scene with his video camera. There were fire engines and ambulances and police cars, flashing lights and sirens. Two young girls arm in arm staggered past, their bare legs bandaged. Lee felt for his mobile phone. It had gone. Somehow he had to get home, let Ben and Ben's mum, Nikki, know he was OK. They'd see stuff on the TV, know he was somewhere in London, out of prison. He had no money but was desperate for something hot to drink. He'd emptied the bottle of water. He saw a café across the road and stood up. He hoped they'd give him a mug of tea.

*

Mike became aware of distant voices speaking calmly, he sensed light on his eyelids. He flickered them open. The bright metallic light blinded him. He shut his eyes. He heard a female voice close to his ear.

"Can you hear me? You are in St Paul's Hospital, Paddington. Don't worry, we'll look after you."

Mike was aware of lying absolutely still and calm. He couldn't move, had no desire to move. He felt no pain, felt at peace, safe, the voices around him reassuring. He opened his eyes again, looked round, saw tubes and drip containers, people in green moving.

"We need to know who you are," said the voice in his ear. "You've been involved in a major accident."

Though Mike could feel the warm breath of the woman on his ear, the voice sounded as if he was underwater. But he could not move his mouth or tongue or make a grunt. After a first feeble effort, he did not even want to try. There was something obstructing his throat. There was a mask over his mouth and nose.

"You're OK. But we want to know your name. Can you blink for me? Blink once if you understand me."

Mike concentrated for a moment then blinked, screwing his eyes tight then opening them again into the glare.

"That's fine. You will be able to tell us your name. I'm going to go

41

through the alphabet one letter at a time. When I come to the first letter of your first name, blink once."

The woman's voice soothed and comforted him so much that Mike felt himself drifting back off to sleep. But he wanted them to know who he was. Was Sue here? Where was Lee?

"A, B, C, D, E. Let me know when we get to the first letter of your name. A real blink to let us know."

Mike focused all his concentration on her voice.

"H, I, J, K, L, M."

Mike blinked.

"M. Is it M? M is the first letter of your name?"

Mike blinked again.

"Brilliant! Now we'll start again to get to the second letter. Blink again when we come to it."

Mike heard the letters enunciated clearly in his ear but progressing so slowly. He had to resist the temptation to doze off, float away. It was like a child's guessing game. The woman's voice started again at the beginning of the alphabet. Mike concentrated and waited.

"E, F, G, H, I ..."

He blinked with all his might.

"That's excellent, your first name begins with MI. Is that right? If that's right blink once, please."

Mike blinked. He was getting tired.

"I'm going to have a guess now. Blink once for me if I get it right."

She paused.

"Is it Michael?"

Mike forced himself to keep his eyes open, staring into the light. He wanted to shout his name, just tell them, and tell them about Sue, but there was this thing down his throat. He felt frustration tightening him, wanted to drift off to escape it.

"Is it Michael?"

Mike felt a great sense of relief wash through him. He blinked, held the blink and then opened his eyes again.

He saw a woman's face close to his, smiling, eyes bright, caring for him.

"You are Mike?" she asked him softly.

He blinked again, wanting to cry this time, as if he had been lost and had now been found again. There are other faces now, on either side, smiling down at him.

"Now, Mike, we need to know your last name, your surname. We will go through the alphabet again. I know you are tired but you want us to know who you are, don't you?"

Mike blinked. How much force and meaning he wanted to express in that blink as if it might burst through a mighty barrier between them and all would become clear. Then he heard a change in the pitch and tone of the voices around him, people were moving about. The woman's face appeared above him again. She showed him a torn piece of newspaper.

"We found this in your shirt pocket. Are you called Mike Cooper, my love?"

Mike felt tears fill his eyes. He looked at her. He blinked. He saw her face break into a smile. He blinked again, wanting to make certain, now at the every end of his energy.

"And is Sue Whitehall your girlfriend?" said the voice with so much tenderness.

The sound of her name came from this voice and void outside him and instantly melded with the silent syllables floating in his head, lighting them up, giving them form. They knew about Sue. They would tell her. She would come.

He realised his eyes had closed as he visualised her.

"Is Sue Whitehall your girlfriend, Mike?"

Oh Yes. Oh Yes. He wanted to shout and sing it out.

He blinked, and again he blinked, salt tears stinging his eyes, the only part of him he could feel, all his being centred in the stinging living part of him.

"And you live with her in Bradfield?"

Yes, yes.

He blinked again. How did they know that?

"You've done wonderfully well, Mike," she said. "You can sleep now. We are looking after you. You'll be alright. We'll bring Sue for you."

Already Mike was letting himself slip away. He would sleep and when he awoke Sue would be there. It was alright. It would be OK.

The surgeon saw his eyes close.

"Right. Let's get to work. It will be a close run thing," he said. "He's lost so much blood. He arrested twice in the ambulance."

3.

News

7th July

9.00 am. Bradfield

Sue was drawing down the blinds on the windows opposite the white board as her sixth formers sauntered in to their first lesson of the day. The classroom was already warm with early morning sunshine. The dimmed light made it even more drowsy.

"Oh good, miss, we can have a bit more sleep."

"No, it's work today, Jenny."

Gradually the class assembled, spread around the room, slinging rucksacks onto table tops, chatting.

"What's with the blinds, miss?"

"You'll see."

Last in, as always, was Grum. He closed the door this morning, without being asked.

"Mornin'," Grum said and grinned at her in his open friendly way. He was invariably polite, a real charmer.

She watched him as he strolled to sit, as usual, on his own. His green-dyed hair was tied in a top-knot. This way, as he had explained to her, it could be hidden beneath his MacDonald's cap when he went to work. His black silver-buckled biker boots, steel-tipped, thick

45

rubber-soled, were oddly silent on the composite floor. His leathers creaked loudly as he sat down. How absurd it was to try and wrench his mind from his 500cc gleaming red Kawasaki to a 16th century Flanders painting – all their minds from boyfriends and girlfriends and all the insecurities of teenage years. *Teaching is a crazy business,* she thought, as she walked to the front of the room and stood next to the whiteboard.

"OK," she said. "Let's get your minds into gear."

The desultory chatting continued as if she wasn't there. They weren't being deliberately rude, their lives were just elsewhere.

"Come on, Chris. Katie. Let's get going. I've got a picture for you."

Sue waited a moment, saw she had enough of their attention. She tapped her pen on the arrow icon and the whiteboard was filled with her picture.

"Pieter Bruegel the Elder, 1558," she said. "Now, tell me what you see."

Silence, bemusement.

"Have any of you seen it before?"

A few grunts, barely perceptible shakes of the head.

"Grum, start us off."

She could usually rely on him to start a discussion.

"There's that farmer, that guy in the red shirt ploughing the field. Great plough."

"He's wearing a pleated skirt," added Katie.

"Cool," someone muttered.

Silence.

"Come on, what else?"

"Sheep – and that shepherd leaning on his stick, staring up at the sky," said Chris.

"Yes, good."

"Some old ships."

"It's windy, look at the sails."

Someone noticed the city with its harbour, the rocky islands.

"What's that guy doing in the corner? Is he fishing?"

"Look at those legs," said Jenny. "Someone's fallen in."

"Well spotted," said Sue. "And that's the point of the painting."

"What do you mean? What's the point?" asked Grum.

"Well, has anyone in the painting noticed him falling in?"

"Some bloke on the ship might have."

"But no one Bruegel painted has noticed," said Sue. "A guy is drowning."

"You mean they don't care?" asked Jenny.

"No, I don't think it's that," said Grum. "They're just too busy, getting on with their own lives."

"Absolutely, and that's the point. Someone's dying, it's a tragedy. And people don't notice."

Sue clicked on the pen tool and drew a red circle round the flailing legs.

"And see where Bruegel's put Icarus in the painting – not in the centre but pushed away to the side. You have to look for him. He's not obvious."

"Who's Icarus?"

There seemed to be a bit of interest. Some were looking at the picture more closely.

"There's an interesting legend behind the picture," said Sue. "It's called Landscape with the Fall of Icarus."

She told them the story of Daedalus, the great craftsman, and his son Icarus: how Daedalus had built the Labyrinth for King Minos so that the half-man, half-bull Minotaur could be kept imprisoned in it; how King Minos had then imprisoned Daedalus and Icarus in a tower so they could not tell people the pathway through the Labyrinth; how Daedalus, desperate to escape, had made wings out of birds' feathers for him and his son, sticking the feathers together with wax. Before they leapt from the top of the tower, wearing their pairs of wings, Daedalus warned his son not to fly too near the sea because the foam would wet the wings and make them too heavy, but nor must he fly too near the sun because its heat would melt the wax. But the youthful Icarus was too full of the joy of flight and escape, and of course he flew too near the sun.

"So the wax melted as his father had warned him and there he is, falling into the sea. A good story, eh?"

"Yes, but what's the message?" said Grum. "It seems to mean that we shouldn't try too hard, don't aim too high or you'll get your fingers burned. But teachers are always telling us to be ambitious."

"Yes," said Katie. "My dad's always on about trying to reach further than you can grasp or something."

The discussion was going in a different direction from the one Sue wanted. A pity! They were a good group once they got going.

"We'll talk about that another day. It's a good subject. But now I want you to read this poem."

A groan. Sue tapped the board again and the picture disappeared. The room dimmed a little. She briskly handed out the photocopied sheets.

"It's called *Musee des Beaux Arts*" and it's by W H Auden. I'll read it to you."

And so she read it.

About suffering they were never wrong,
The old masters: how well they understood
Its human position; how it takes place
While someone else is eating or opening a window
Or just walking dully along;
How, when the aged are reverently, passionately waiting
For the miraculous birth, there always must be
Children who did not specially want it to happen, skating
On a pond at the edge of the wood:
They never forgot
That even the dreadful martyrdom must run its course
Anyhow in a corner, some untidy spot
Where the dogs go on with their doggy life and the torturer's horse
Scratches its innocent behind on a tree.
In Bruegel's Icarus, for instance: how everything turns away
Quite leisurely from the disaster; the ploughman may
Have heard the splash, the forsaken cry,
But for him it was not an important failure; the sun shone
As it had to on the white legs disappearing into the green
Water; and the expensive delicate ship that must have seen
Something amazing, a boy falling out of the sky,
Had somewhere to get to and sailed calmly on.

"Ha, so I was right," said Grum.

"Do you think it's true?" asked Sue.

"Well, it has to be," said Jenny. "Life has to go on. Everything can't stop just because someone dies."

"It's sort of cruel, though," said Katie.

The class was suddenly quiet as if everyone had drawn in their breath. They all knew that not long ago Katie's Mum had died of cancer. Sue had to break the silence.

"I remember," she said, "when my father died. I was sitting with my Mum in the lead mourners' car. The windows had that darkened glass so people couldn't stare in at us. My Dad's coffin was in the hearse in front with white flowers on it. We were driving slowly through the town to the crematorium. I was looking out and I saw a young boy in the barber's, getting his hair cut; his mother was sitting at the back flipping through a magazine. And then there was a postman in shorts, turning into a gateway, holding a white envelope in his hand. I remember thinking, how could they just carry on when my Dad had died."

The class were intent. They always listened when she talked about her own life. It was real, like theirs, not part of literature. That was the trick – to get them to see that literature was about life.

"I remember the cortege stopped at a traffic light and I saw a woman standing with a bulging shopping bag outside the co-op checking the till receipt. She was oblivious of us."

Her voice faltered. She knew they were watching her.

"Right!" she said. "Work! When you get home tonight, I want you to write some notes about something very ordinary, possibly something you do every day. Think about it but be vivid and brief. For me it might be making a mug of proper coffee with a percolator. Then look through the newspaper or watch the news for some story about suffering, or even better choose something that's happened to you or your family. Again, be brief, try to note down just the essence of the experience. In class tomorrow we'll put the two together."

"Very jolly," muttered Grum.

Then the bell rang and they were immediately putting their books and folders away, the poem and her anecdotes forgotten.

49

Tidying away her photocopies of the poem, she thought of Mike down in London. She smiled to herself: he'd be hating that leadership stuff, sitting at the back of the group, sceptical, silently mocking it, hating that who-are-you-and-what-are-you-hoping-to-get-out-of-the-course? exercise, already looking forward to his run in the park in the early evening. He'd be running, she'd be marking, both pushing themselves, both in their own worlds, in their own heads. She liked the symmetry of it. Then a moment of doubt: was she pushing him too much with this leadership thing? Was she aspiring for him rather than just letting him be?

At break in the English department staff room, there was already the smell of coffee and the chink of coffee mugs being washed at the sink from yesterday. The microwave was humming, doubtless with Peter's morning Pot Noodle. The place was always a bit of a tip: pigeonholes stuffed with papers and envelopes and small packages. Piles of exercise books, files and folders lay on tables. The photocopier in the corner was ticking out A4 sheets. Rick was slumped in a chair in the corner, looking desperate for the fag he was no longer allowed to smoke here and not wanting to trail across to the staff smokers' room. Sue went over to the cold water fountain. Then Lisa rushed in, the noise from the corridor wafting in with her through the open door.

"Have you heard? On the radio, there's been some huge explosions in London."

Nobody took much notice, milk was stirred into coffee. The copier continued.

"No, it's really serious."

Sue's heart thumped.

"I'd just driven Gavin Wilson home, he'd been sick after PE and his bloody mother wouldn't come in and collect him. On the way back I turned on the car radio. They think it's bombs."

"Bombs!" said Sue. "Where?"

"It's on the underground," said Lisa. "First they thought there were power surges and trains were stuck in tunnels. Then a London bus was blown up and now they think the underground has been hit by bombs. There's injured people everywhere."

"So it's our turn now," said Rick. "This is our 9/11. It was bound to happen."

Lisa was making a hurried coffee, hoping to get a few gulps down before the end of break. A conversation had started and Sue heard Iraq mentioned and the march against the war which Rick had been on. No one in the room knew that Mike was in London. *Just his luck,* thought Sue, *the only time he's in London and this happens.*

"Do you know what time it happened, Lisa?"

Lisa turned from the electric kettle.

"I think it was rush hour."

Sue realised she didn't know where Mike was going in London. He was going to phone her this evening. He'd talked about running in Hyde Park so it must be near there. How was he getting from Kings Cross to Hyde Park? Presumably by underground. She didn't know the routes or the lines, had only a vague memory of that underground map. The chances of Mike being involved were minimal – all those underground trains, Mike there for just two days. She took out her mobile and tapped in his numbers. It rang steadily and then: *This phone is not available. Please leave a message.* She rang off. He'd be in a meeting by now, hunkered down somewhere at the back, sullen, watching his companions. She was about to text a message when the bell rang. People levered themselves out of chairs, broke off conversations, picked up books and bags. From the corridor a blast of noise came in as the door opened. She'd leave it until lunchtime. It would be OK. Coincidences like that didn't happen.

She found herself going out of the staffroom doorway at the same time as Lisa.

"Mike's in London today on a leadership course," Sue told her.

"Oh no!"

Then each went in different directions along the corridor. *He'll be alright,* thought Sue. *With all those trains and all those commuters the chances must be a million to one. Mike will ring me at lunchtime to re-assure me he is safe.* With that thought, she switched into work mode but deliberately left her mobile on.

When the next lesson ended and the classroom was empty she

heaved a sigh of relief. She was grateful the lesson had demanded all her concentration. Now, as the corridor slowly quietened, voices moving outside to the canteen and playing field, her mind switched straight back to Mike. She took out her phone and tapped in Mike's number. She looked at her watch as it rang. 12.30. Surely it would be lunchtime on the course now. She decided to send a text. *Heard about bombs. R u safe? Xxx*

And now, in spite of herself, she felt herself tightening up. It wasn't possible, the chances were infinitesimal. But there was a chance, she had to admit. Why hadn't he phoned or texted? Surely there would have been an announcement at the course about what had happened so that people could phone home. Her heart began to thump at the realisation of this. Suddenly she was panicking. Her stomach felt hollow. The door opened. It was Lisa.

"Are you OK, Sue?"

"Why hasn't he phoned me?" Sue blurted out. "He could have phoned me from the course he's on to tell me he was safe."

She was almost crying. *Hold on,* she thought, *this is ridiculous.*

"I don't know what's happening. I need to know what's happening. I've phoned him, texted him, and there's no answer."

Lisa came over and put her arm round Sue.

"I'm sure he'll be OK, Sue. He's probably busy, doing some stupid role play or having to make conversation with the others."

But Sue wasn't reassured.

"I need to know what's happening," she said. "I'm going to sit in the car and listen to the radio."

"I've got a better idea," said Lisa. "There's a TV in the caretaker's office. He watches it when he's on duty on parents' evenings. Let's see if we can get in."

Sue agreed and the two hurried down through the noise of a school lunchtime – young boys chasing each other round, yelling in their high-pitched voices, queues for the canteen, the smell of chips. Lisa knocked on the caretaker's office door.

"Come in."

They went in. Dave the assistant caretaker was there, his box of sandwiches open, his mouth full, the TV on.

"If it's something you want, you'll have to find Terry. It's my lunch-hour. Have you seen this?" he said. "It's terrible."

"Can we watch it for a bit? Sue's feller's in London and she's worried. We don't know where there's another TV in the school. They're all just monitors."

"Christ!" said Dave. "Of course you can. Bloody hell!"

He shifted up a bit. Sue manoeuvred the only other chair so she could see the screen. Lisa shifted some papers and sat on the corner of the table.

"Oh God!" exclaimed Sue.

They were looking at a picture of the red double-decker London bus, its top blown off, wreckage all around. Then the scene shifted to outside an underground station. A woman with her face completely bandaged was being led away. Sobbing distraught people were being comforted, their faces blackened, clothes torn. The reporters were talking of three attacks on the underground, of the possibility of suicide bombers. They were interviewing people who described the explosion and their long walk up the tunnels.

Sue was transfixed, terrified. All her optimism had vanished with the sight of the tunnel survivors. It was just Mike's luck. He was bound to be in the wrong place. He was always so fatalistic. All central London roads were blocked, the underground system closed, mobile phone networks down. Sue had a brief surge of hope: that was why she hadn't been able to get through, why Mike hadn't contacted her. Then as quickly the hope faded away. She began to cry quietly, eyes closed. Dave didn't know what to do. He stood up, muttered he had to check something and went out.

"I'll be back in a minute, Sue, stay here," said Lisa. She hugged her and left, closing the door carefully behind her.

Sue couldn't believe that this was happening, that she was involved in the far away capital city. He was somewhere in London, somewhere doing that stupid course she'd pushed him into going on. *God! It's my fault he's down there,* she thought.

She had to look away from the TV screen and watched the monitor for the school's security cameras, slowly evenly swinging back and forth across the all-weather pitch where several games of football were in progress. Unfolding on the screen was a tragedy, Mike's whereabouts unknown, and she was sitting here in this small room with a faint smell of disinfectant, racks of keys on the wall, a plan of the school marked with fire alarm locations. Dirty mugs were piled in the sink. On the whiteboard was written: *Thursday – Lights out on science stairwell, Fire doors opposite drama studio.*

Five minutes later Lisa was back.

"I've seen the Head," she said. "I've told him the situation and he's said you should go home."

"Home?"

"Yes, and I'm coming with you. I'll sort your lessons out. You get your stuff and we'll meet at your car."

Sue felt stunned. Things were happening so quickly. She suddenly did want to be away, with her mobile and her home landline waiting for a call from Mike. But going home like this also seemed to imply that the worst might have happened.

"Thanks so much, Lisa. But I'm OK and I think I'd rather be on my own."

She drove home with extra care and deliberation. How ridiculous if something happened to her, some minor collision which would entail the tedious time-consuming process of police taking statements and exchanging insurance details. Once at home Sue immediately turned on the TV. The scenes were the same, the people different. There were stretchers and paramedics, police and firemen, interviews with survivors, station staff. Then a Hotline telephone number appeared on the screen and a list of the hospitals to which casualties were being taken: Royal London, St Paul's, University College Hospital…

She snatched up her mobile to ring it, starting tapping in the number. Then stopped. She should use the land line. That would leave the mobile free in case the network was up again and Mike was trying to get through. He would expect her to be at school not at home. She dialled from the landline. But it was engaged, she couldn't get through. She went to redial and held the receiver to her ear, hearing the tone repeating and repeating. Mesmerised, she watched the TV screen, saw the blackened faces, the shock and bewilderment, people taking charge, managing things, organising, saw the concern and frantic energy, the desire to save and comfort. Where was Mike? What was he doing? She wanted to pray but forced herself not to: she didn't believe in God. To pray would be hypocritical and in some irrational way she thought it might count against Mike.

Finally a voice startled her. She was through. She panicked but the voice was calm and business-like asking for her name, her relationship with the missing person, his name, her address and contact numbers.

"I need to ask you this," said the voice. "I need some details about him."

She asked for Mike's height and weight, his skin colour, eye colour, hair colour, any distinguishing marks or features. Sue had to close her eyes to answer: forcing herself to see Mike in front of her to answer the questions. She forced herself to keep her voice steady. When she put the phone down she was trembling. She hadn't been able to think of a distinguishing feature but the colour of his hazel eyes had been so clear to her.

Now all she could do was wait. She couldn't stand those images on the screen any more. The authorities were pretty certain now that the explosions were the work of suicide bombers, all the hallmarks of an Al-Qaeda operation. With the remote she turned the TV off. The room was suddenly hushed. Remote in hand, she sat staring at the blank screen. She noticed Mike's dark blue sweater that he'd thrown onto the chair last night. Now she did need to be alone. It was as if by concentrating on Mike, keeping her mind focused on him, she could somehow protect him and ensure his survival.

He was in the darkness, in a tunnel somewhere, injured, in pain, alone. In the silent, comfortable living room Sue sat and cried: a sudden gush of sobs and wails and a long plaintive angry *No, no.* Gradually she recovered herself, wiped her eyes, stood up and looked out of the window. She had to do something. Ironing. She'd do some ironing, lose herself in that. She went into the kitchen, put the mobile on the surface next to the microwave, took the ironing board out of the tall cupboard and set it up in its usual place, where she could look through the kitchen window into the garden. There were three white

55

shirts flapping on next door's washing line, bright in the sunshine. She plugged in the iron and went to get the plastic basket of fresh washing. On the creel above her head were two of Mike's shirts. There was a moment's indecision and then she took one down, his favourite blue one. He would need it in the office, she told herself, on Monday.

She spread out his shirt, draped it over the board, carefully manoeuvred the point of the iron around the collar, smoothing it down. She did the first half of the body, shifted the shirt across the board, then the second half. Thinking of nothing, her mind was absorbed in her movements, the strokes of the iron, the warmth, the familiar rhythm of movements. She completed the first shirt, put it on a hanger and hung it on the hook behind the door to cool down, ready to take upstairs and put in the wardrobe. She took down his second shirt and then the door bell rang.

She propped the iron up carefully. The bell rang again, insistent. Then it came to her: the police. Her heart raced, she leant on the ironing board. The police, they'd found him. She clenched her fists and moved to the hallway. She stopped and returned, unplugged the iron with an icy calm, forcing herself to move normally.

Through the frosted glass of the front door Sue could see two figures. Her heart was thumping hard. She felt her stomach lurch, the blood drain from her face. She turned the yale latch and opened the door. Looking past the two figures she saw the yellow and blue police car parked at the gateway just behind her own. She just stood there. Mike was dead. She knew.

"Are you Sue Whitehall?" asked the woman.

Sue heard immediately the professional concern in the woman's voice, noted that it was the woman and not her male companion who had spoken. Sue nodded. She heard them say their names, saw them take out their identity cards, but nothing registered.

"Can we come in?" the man asked.

She knew.

"He's dead, isn't he?" said Sue, not moving, not looking at them. She felt flat and beaten and helpless in a way she had never done in her whole life.

"Are you asking about Mike Cooper?" asked the woman. "Does he live here?"

Sue raised her eyes and looked into the policewoman's eyes.

"He lives here," she said slowly. "Mike is my fiancé." She emphasised the 'is', defiant now of fate, refusing to accept it.

"We need to come in and talk to you," said the woman.

Sue had heard only the sounds. Something had stopped them being decoded into meaning. She turned, the core of her numb as another part of her fell and soared and fell. She leaned against the wall and the policewoman held her arm while the man closed the door behind him. The door to the living room was open and Sue let the woman lead her in and sit her down in the armchair. The police sat on the edge of the couch, leaning forward. Sue noticed they were not in uniform.

Sue said nothing. She waited. Her swirling head was steadying. What had the man said? She dared not remember. She too sat forward, her elbows on her knees, her hands in the form of praying cupping her jaw.

"We need to tell you about Mike," said the police woman. "He was involved in this morning's bombings in London."

Sue stared at her, perfectly still, poised, balanced as if the slightest movement would send her toppling into a terrifying darkness. A syllable could push her over. Every part of her was tensed, ready to collapse and fall or to stand and hope. She closed her eyes and bent her head into her hands. She steadied herself, prepared to accept the worst, the inevitable.

"Tell me," she said. "Please."

The police woman spoke towards Sue's bowed head. Her voice was calm and measured.

"Mike is alive but he's badly injured. He's in St Paul's Hospital in London, near Paddington station. He's in a critical condition."

Sue opened her eyes.

"Mike's alive?" she asked.

"He's alive," repeated the police woman.

Sue breathed deeply, her breaths snagging in the tension of her chest. Straightaway she knew he would survive, she would will him to survive. He was strong, fit, he would fight. Together they would bring him through. Elation flamed up in her, renewal. She stood up and walked towards the light of the window.

"How is he injured? What's wrong with him?" she asked and turned.

"We don't know, I'm afraid. He's probably being operated on right now. He survived the explosion but we don't know, no one knows, if he will pull through the operation."

Sue looked at her then turned again to the window. She was calm now, determined, knew what she had to do.

"I'm going to him," she said.

"We can help you," said the police man. "There's a Kings Cross train leaving in forty minutes. It's the quickest way to get to London, you'll be there in a couple of hours if there's no hold up. We can take you to the station in the car. We'll fix up a police car to meet you at the other end. Transport's still in chaos down there. The car will take you straight to the hospital."

The way opened out in front of her, things were happening. Time once again was ticking. Sue looked at her watch. 17.05.

"Right! Brilliant! Thank you so much. Five minutes to throw some things in a bag and then I'm ready."

She knew that this was what she did well – organising, being strong for someone, being busy.

"Will you be OK on your own? Don't you want a friend or a relative to go with you?"

"No, I'll be fine, I'll be better on my own."

She didn't want anyone else to be concerned about. She wanted to sit on her own to beam out her will to Mike, to send it along the rails and streets, over buildings to focus in on his operating table.

*

The train pulled out on time. She saw the guard on the platform, looking up and down the train, saw him wave his white paddle-shaped signal, put the whistle to his lips. He was the ploughman.

It was almost exactly twelve hours since Mike had left on the same journey, twelve hours in which their lives had changed, maybe for ever. She felt the train swing over points, pass gleaming new office and apartment blocks and Elland Road stadium. Somehow she had to put herself into a trance to get through the next two hours which she knew would pass with agonising slowness. He had to know she was with him, that he was not fighting this alone. It was the two of them together. He had to believe they would win, whatever the odds, whatever the damage to his lovely body. He had to believe in himself and in them, together.

Somehow she had to recall for him, confirm for him the love they shared, strengthen his purpose, his reason for living. Mike – gentle Mike, only she knew how gentle he was, that gift he had given her of his vulnerability. Others knew of his will, his self-discipline in his running – qualities that would serve him well in this ultimate challenge. They recognised the idealism that lay behind his work but they didn't know his fears about compromising his principles. Nor did they know how romantic he could be. She remembered her birthday when he had lit candles up the garden path to welcome her home, the Christmas when he had laid out a treasure hunt that led her through the frosted garden and round their rooms, following clues to a large box wrapped in his usual clumsy cellotaped fashion but which contained under all the bubble-wrap a small box with a ring in it.

There was a long delay before the train eventually pulled into Kings Cross. In front of her an old lady with a big case took ages to negotiate the step down to the platform. Down at last, Sue hurried with the other passengers. But their conversation was subdued, checked as they passed policemen in bulky flack jackets, guns nestled in their arms, their eyes interrogating the arrivals. Incomprehensible announcements blared and echoed. Was she the only one on this mission? Were other footsteps urgently hurrying to meet or find loved ones? How much did all these people know about what had happened? Was this the last train allowed to arrive? The noise of waiting trains, their huge engines idling, was deafening.

Ahead of her at the barrier there were crowds of waiting people, peering over shoulders, searching anxiously. Several were holding up cards. She scanned across them. There! A woman was holding up a card with her name scrawled on it in capital letters. Next to her stood a man she somehow recognised as being a policeman. They were in plain clothes. The queue of people slowly moved forward to the barriers. Sue waved and caught the eye of the woman. Then she was through and into another melee.

"Sue Whitehall?" checked the woman without any preliminaries.

"Yes," said Sue. "That's me."

They shook hands.

"We'll get you to the hospital as soon as we can, but it's chaos out there."

They escorted her through the crowded concourse, a babble of noise and tightly packed bodies. They told her many trains had been cancelled and these crowds were waiting in the hope they could get home that night. Among them she saw several with torn blackened clothes, some with bandaged heads, faces weary and dirty. She sensed tension and stoicism in equal measure. She couldn't know that she passed a man called Lee, sitting on the tiled floor with his back leaning against the window of WH Smith's, half hidden behind those standing.

4.

Hospital

7th July

8.30 pm., London

At the hospital, Sue was hurried out of the crowded noisy reception area by a hospital liaison officer who introduced herself as Janet Williamson. They turned into a long corridor that stretched into the distance, their footsteps tapping on the floor. Nurses hurried along in both directions, a trolley was wheeled past at a jog, a man beside the trolley holding a drip in place. A porter hurried past, wheeling a wire cage full of oxygen bottles. Doors opened off on both sides of the corridor. Sue noticed a sign *Chapel*. She strode on quickly, impatient. This wasn't right. They had told her nothing, she knew nothing. Then the liaison officer slowed, opened a door and gestured for Sue to enter. The door clicked closed behind her. The room was quiet, still, empty.

"For God's sake, will you please tell me how Mike is?" Sue wanted to shake the woman out of her professional calm, so bloody collected. And yet she knew she must not antagonise her, knew the woman was doing her very difficult job. She knew she would need her help.

"Please sit down," said the woman.

This meant bad news, the worst. Half challenging, half pleading, she looked at the woman's face searching for some sign of what she knew.

"I don't want to sit down! I want to see him, I've come all this way. Where is he?"

"Mike's just come out of the operating theatre. The doctors are waiting for him to come out of the anaesthetic. It's been a complex operation and it's too soon to say if it has been successful. He was in a very bad way when he arrived here."

The woman spoke in such a measured way, sitting there, so composed in her smart suit and identity badge. Sue bent her head, clenched her fists to stop herself from shouting or crying. She walked a couple of paces towards the window, stopped and turned.

"But what was wrong? How badly was he injured? What have they done to him?"

"Please sit down, it's easier to talk with you sitting down."

Sue ignored her. Fiercely, enunciating each word slowly and clearly, she said: "What has happened to Mike?"

"I'm sorry, Sue, but it's bad."

"Just tell me! Tell me!" Sue shouted at the liaison officer. There was a pause and then the woman spoke.

"They had to amputate both of Mike's legs, one above the knee, one below."

"Oh God!"

Sue stood there, her hands covering her face.

"No, no," she moaned.

Janet stood up and put her arms round Sue's shoulders. Gently she helped her to a chair and put her arm round her but Sue shrugged it off. *His legs,* she thought, *how will he cope?* Hope drained out of her, she felt empty, hollow, just a bleakness. She broke, crying uncontrollably, tears saturating her face. When the liaison officer put her arm around her this time Sue leaned into her, buried her face in her arm and shoulder. She heaved with sobs. Janet stroked her head, saying nothing.

Slowly Sue's crying slowed with exhaustion. There was a box of tissues on the small coffee table. Janet took her arm from Sue and handed her the box. Sue wiped her face.

"Does he know?"

"Not yet."

"He's a runner," she said. "He runs across the moors and mountains. It's what he loves most."

She paused, sobbed, wiped her face again with the soaked tissues.

"And he was only down here in London because I told him to come."

You fucking, fucking stupid woman, she screamed to herself inside her head.

"It's normal to think like that, to feel somehow it's your fault. To blame yourself," said the liaison officer. "But it wasn't your fault. Mike was just unlucky."

"Unlucky!"

"It was chance, pure chance that he was in that carriage on that train at that time. It's terrible but it was just bad luck, random chance. You can't blame yourself."

Sue sat, tissues scrunched up in her palms.

"Can I get you a cup of tea?" asked Janet. "There's a canteen just down the corridor."

"When can I see him?"

"The doctors know where we are, but I'll go and see if there's any more news. Are you OK on your own for a while?"

"Yes, I'm OK."

The door closed and Sue was on her own. She closed her eyes and sat back in the chair. It was so quiet and peaceful in here. Her body heaved again, shuddered. This wasn't happening. She stood up and paced about the room. She had to do something, couldn't just wait. Police had raced through cities for her, given her an escort – all to rush her here. And now she was still waiting, held in a limbo in this room. Mike had had his operation, why couldn't she see him? Something must have gone wrong. Was he awake yet?

Then she thought of Mike's father, his only living relative, living now near Vancouver with a Canadian wife. But she hadn't got the number. And he was seriously ill, anyway. What could he do? She'd deal with that later. Thank God his Mum wasn't alive: she would not have been able to bear it. She didn't want to tell anyone else, not even

Lisa. It was too stark, too brutal. She had a sudden shocking image of bandaged stumps, white tight bandages stained with red blood. Mike would need so much help – not just looking after and learning to walk, but coming to terms with it. He had to learn to live with his new self, to look at himself. He was so bound up with physical fitness, he averted his eyes from disfigurements and disabilities. He couldn't look at the woman in the newsagents with a purple birthmark across half her face. He had to leave the supermarket café when a group of the mentally ill were sometimes brought in, faces twitching, voices incoherent and too loud, making strange sudden noises. He was scared by all that, couldn't handle it. He was squeamish, too, not even able to push out that splinter from her finger. His future nightmare ballooned inside her. How could he endure it?

The door opened and the liaison officer came with two mugs of tea. Before she could place them on the low coffee table Sue announced: "I'm not waiting any longer, I'm going to find him."

She moved towards the door but the Janet was in the way.

"I've told them you must see him," she said. "Even if he's not yet awake. It's asking too much of you. They'll be along in a couple of minutes."

"Thank you so much."

"They're very busy. There are so many injured."

The tea was hot but she gulped it down, her throat dry

A few minutes later the door opened and a tall man entered. He was stooping, grey-haired and looked exhausted.

"Hello. It's Sue isn't it?" he said.

"Yes."

He shook her hand. His arm was bare from the elbow down in his short-sleeved green theatre scrubs.

"I'm John Hutchinson, I'm the consultant surgeon who lead the team who operated on Mike."

Just tell me, please, just tell me.

"He's certainly had a rough time and was very badly injured in the explosion. Before we take you through to him we need to talk to you about his condition."

Sue swallowed, braced herself. Something had gone wrong.

"I'm afraid we had to amputate both Mike's legs. I think you know that. He lost a lot of blood before they got him here. His heart stopped beating twice and he was starved of oxygen for extended periods of time. I have to tell you there is the possibility of damage to his brain and severe cognitive loss. His chest must have taken a tremendous blow, either something heavy landed on him or it's when he was hurled onto the floor by the explosion. He has pulmonary contusions – which is bleeding into his lungs, caused by the pressure of air in the blast of the explosion. He's on a ventilator, breathing a mixture of air and oxygen, and to ensure this works properly he's been sedated. The operation has been successful but it's obviously a very traumatic one. He's in intensive care, his body needs all its strength to recover."

Sue almost staggered, put out a hand to steady herself against the back of a chair. Damaged brain. The image came to her of the young man with dark floppy hair in the wheelchair at the supermarket: his head lolling, his face twisted to one sound, the strangled sounds he uttered as remnants of communication.

"But he's fit and strong, as you know," the surgeon continued, "and his body has already shown a strong will to survive. The next forty eight hours are vital."

Sue nodded. "Please take me to him."

The surgeon explained he had to go back to theatre for another operation. A sister and the liaison officer accompanied Sue down the corridor. It was the longest, loneliest walk she had ever done. She seemed to be walking in a vacuum, cut off from the rest of the world, in a state of suspension. Yet normal work went on – an orderly was buffing the corridor floor, a nurse pushed a white trolley loaded with coloured files. They passed through swing doors on the left into a wide corridor, past a door with a red light above it, staff hurrying by all with identity badges on blue lanyards round their necks. Sunshine streamed in through the wall of windows, the heat was close and stuffy. They came to the last door at the end: Ward 17 Intensive Care Unit.

"Are you ready, Sue?"

Sue nodded, she could not speak. She was scared, scared of what she would see through the door, the version that Mike had become.

They moved towards a pair of double doors. The sister held the door open for her. She stepped inside. There was a series of curtained bays. At the far end, the sister pulled back the curtain and they stepped through. Sue saw first a sort of white gantry across the width of the bay with tubes and wires and bags – one red as blood, two full of transparent liquid, one caramel-coloured – descending from it, rows of machines with screens, and then below them the bed. There he lay.

"Mike!" she said and lurched forward to him. Swiftly, ready, Janet strode after her, prepared to hold her, catch her if she stumbled.

"Oh, Mike!"

Sue stood by the bed, looking down at him. Two tubes were angled into his mouth and nose, taped in place. There were bandages around his head, only the area around his eyes was visible. She gasped at the livid green purple bruising on his white face. His sun-browned dark-haired arms lay on the pure white sheet, with clips and tubes attached. She wanted to touch his fingers, just touch him. But she dared not. His chest was bare but bruised, with patches of red grazes and cuts, there were sensors stuck on with white medical tape with wires leading to a monitor. Another clip was attached to his finger, wired to another unit. Fixed on the gantry and on stands around him were the monitors: pulsing graphs of yellow, green and blue, digital read outs flickering, green lights steady.

She shook her head. All this needed to keep him alive. It was at the same time frightening and reassuring. The lights and graphs proved he was alive, sentient.

"Mike! Mike!"

It was the sister who held her gently at the crook of her arm.

"Can I hold his hand?" she asked him meekly.

"Of course."

His fingers were warm. She stroked them. She saw the rise and fall of his chest as he breathed steadily. She saw his scorched eyebrows and the singed lashes on his closed eyes. Her eyes travelled down his chest to the sheets folded at his waist, tracing his shape. She paused and took a deep breath, let her eyes continue over the shape of his torso. It was so short, the abrupt L-shaped ending of his body, one leg now longer than the other, a slight rise because of the bandaging and dressing underneath, and then the flatness to the foot of the bed, the sheets neatly tucked under at the side. Two drains of plastic tubing emerged from beneath the sheets, leading to bottles half full of blood. Sue gasped and put her hand to her mouth. It was done, final, irrevocable.

A dark-skinned white-uniformed nurse came in and checked the monitors, competent, busy, checked the drip bottle, filled in squares on a huge chart already half full of figures clipped to a wooden frame.

"He's doing well so far," she said to Sue. "He's a fighter."

"Yes, he is," said Sue.

She leaned forward to kiss him on the brow.

"We should leave him now," said the sister. "He'll be monitored closely overnight."

Sue hardly heard her words. He is still Mike, my Mike, she was thinking. Beneath all that paraphernalia he was the same man. He was in front of her and alive. Her dread and fear were draining away. The urgency to add her will to his – to live – returned.

"When will we know about his brain?" Her voice was barely audible.

"We will know more when he wakes up," continued the sister. "We can only hope. We'll keep a close eye on him. We're doing everything we can."

"I know. Thank you," muttered Sue.

Sue looked at Mike's closed eyes, wanting to see the slightest tremor that showed he was conscious and yet knowing that it was better if he did not wake yet. *A help meet for me,* he had once whispered to her while he stroked her forehead, *you are my helpmate and I am yours.* She would be that for him, they would be that for each other, they would need each other. Together they would get through this. But she would need to be careful: Mike would not tolerate pity or condescension.

"Shall we go now?" said the sister. "There is nothing more you can do."

She bent and gently kissed him on the forehead again. His closed eyelids so delicate, the bruises around them so lurid, the tang of singeing.

Outside in the hospital grounds she followed the signs to a rose garden. She sat in the darkness there. She was exhausted, yet it was only five hours since the police had knocked on her door back in Leeds. Five hours which had seen her life thrown in a new direction.

That she had no one except his father to phone about him made him even more vulnerable, made her even more indispensable. He was happy in his comparative solitude – but only, he had stressed to her, in the context of being with her. His contradictions intrigued her: his desires for solitude and companionship, his strength and neediness. There were layers to him that she wanted to experience and find out about just by living with him. Her own approach to life seemed so much more straightforward – and she knew this was what he found so fascinating and energising about her.

Her mind filled with the picture of Mike in his bed wired up to instruments, she felt the weight of responsibility. She loved him, she would care for him. That was all that counted for now. The future was shadowy and uncertain – she had assumed a family for them but had never made this explicit to Mike. Was it less than twenty four hours ago that she had talked about Icarus, his bare legs thrashing the air as he plunged into the sea?

5.

Playing

10th July

Bradfield

Lee pulled the front door to behind him and stepped directly onto the pavement. The sun was already lighting up the stone walls of the terrace of houses and there was a warmth in the air. He was looking forward to the day. He put his rucksack in the boot of his car and threw in the football. He'd packed the beans and sausages. All he needed now were a couple of packets of crisps and a can of orange for Ben from the shop.

As he walked down the road an old Asian woman was slowly approaching him, wearing the usual Asian clothes, her head covered with a black scarf, and holding a Morrison's carrier bag in each hand. She passed him, her head lowered, moving at a slow shuffle, her brown feet in sandals. Lee turned the corner and paused to look down the narrow back street lined with tiny yards. Washing was already out on the lines but it wasn't the kind of washing his mother used to put out. The line was full of glittery shalwar kameez – purples, golds and greens – and the white wide floppy trousers the men wore, and those long shirts like night shirts. His Mum would have said *A good drying day* because of the sun and a slight breeze.

But it wasn't Monday, it was Friday. His Mum, and all the other older women of the terrace, only put washing out on a Monday. Lee remembered wet Mondays with washing draped over the wooden maiden in front of the fire, his Mum ironing, the scratch Monday tea of potato hash.

One of the few white residents still in the street, his Mum had never said a word against the Asians. "They're all very nice," she'd said. "They sometimes do me errands if I'm feeling a bit off. They're no trouble. The kids are a bit noisy but so were you and your mates."

He passed Diva's Boutique, full of kalwar suits, and the Kashmir Crown Bakery and Sweets. Neither was open yet. The Snooker Club on the corner had its grey metal security door pulled down and padlocked. There was still the Fish and Chip shop. A young Asian woman in a smart shalwar kameez and blue headscarf, carrying a laptop and her car keys, strode along the opposite side of the road. A white bloke was already washing his car, soapy water running along the gutter into the drain.

"Grand morning," Lee said to him.

"Aye."

Lee felt a sudden kinship with him, a solidarity. He certainly didn't feel at home here any more. Across the big Asda carpark he saw the new mosque. It was a long two story building with those pointy windows they always had, its two twin green domes topped with the gold crescent and star that shone brightly in the sun. It was imposing, paid for by its own worshippers which he had to admit was impressive. But it didn't fit in, rising above the low crammed terraces of dirty Yorkshire stone with their net curtains and satellite dishes. Neither did Asda, too, come to think of it. Three men were going up the steps into the mosque, wearing western jackets over their pyjama things. Everything was mixed up. It wasn't a community any more, like when he was a kid.

He walked past the mosque. Above the door there was Arabic writing with an English translation underneath. He read: *There is none worthy of worship but Allah. Allah is the name of the most affectionate and the most merciful.*

He snorted. Tell that in Basra where they murdered each other.

More Muslims had been killed by other Muslims than by American and British forces combined. Tell that to Mike and the others killed and maimed in London. He should contact that hospital, see if Mike had pulled through. He turned away. There was a car parked on the road. The driver's window was down. A dark-skinned bearded man was looking intently at him, arm at the open window, smoking, his front seat passenger leaning across the seat to watch him as well. Two other Asian men were in the back seat, both staring at him. They didn't say anything.

His mind flashed back. The Red Route was happening, out of bounds because it was so dangerous but now the quickest route into Basra. Clattering Blackhawk chopper blades overhead were happening, screaming engines, 50 calibre tracer arcing up through the night, savage bursts of AK47 assault rifles from balconies and roofs and wall corners, rocket-propelled grenades. Rounds were shooting past with high-pitched hissing sounds, hitting the ground and spinning off into the air, or punching through the steel bodywork of the Snatch landrover as he wrenched it round piles of rubble and down narrow streets; the smell of cordite, sweat and sewers.

They were racing through the streets, called out because there were reports that some of their soldiers had been pulled in by the local Iraqi police and were being held in a police station, with a mob of men armed with stones and sticks and rifles demonstrating outside the station. They were desperate to get to the men before the mob did or before the police allowed the mob to. There's no such thing as a prisoner of war out there. The lads knew what would happen to them if they were captured: orange jump suits and decapitated on TV.

The leap from the landrover, the charge through the howling mob in the half-light of flames from buildings, racing and slamming through the old wooden door, rifles cocked and ready to fire, not knowing who was inside: speed, action, reaction, instinct, ferocity, no time for thought.

Four soldiers inside – three men and one woman – their feet tied to chair legs, their arms tied behind the chair backs. The men had been beaten about the head, blood everywhere. The woman's uniform had been ripped down the front and her breasts were exposed. When they burst into the room there were three Iraqi policemen – or three men dressed as Iraqi policemen – sitting behind a table and one man standing next to the prisoners with a pistol in his hand, holding it by the barrel. Yelling and shouting, prodding with rifles, shirt suddenly cold with sweat, smell of cordite and petrol and smoke, the woman's face looking up at him in the half-light. Getting the Iraqis into a corner, disarming them, covering them with rifles, freeing the captured soldiers. The guards leading the way, hands on their heads, rifles prodding their backs, getting back to the landrovers, hoisting the guards into one and our soldiers in the others, getting out fast, under fire from every direction. His foot grinding the pedal to the floor, praying for acceleration, zeroing in on the road, the landrover lurching, tyres clipping the kerbs, RPGs coming in, making himself a smaller target, hunched down, elbows tucked tightly in to his body, head shrunk into his shoulders. He'd received the Queen's Gallantry medal for that. Much good it had done him.

He shook his head and looked at the car again, the men still staring at him.

Lee moved on, deliberately casual. This sense of menace, of hostility – he could feel it, here in his own country, in the streets where he had played and grown up. He wasn't welcome here. He was the foreigner, not them.

Fuck 'em.

He passed Patal's Cloth House. Next to it was the Pakistan Community Learning Centre, with more Arabic script. 'Empowering the community,' it said. *Yeah, like those bombers in Leeds. Hadn't one of them worked in a community centre? Subsidised by taxpayers like him and Barry.* He was looking forward to seeing Barry. He'd have something to say about it. And what sort of a world was Ben growing up into? He'd picked him up from school the other afternoon – he'd been in a minority of white parents. In the gabble of conversations in the playground he hadn't heard any English spoken. He'd never seen anything wrong with different sorts of people living together. He'd drunk with Poles and Russians, Ukrainians and Irish in pubs before he'd gone away. He liked the look of Sikhs in their turbans, always manly and dignified. Chinese and Balti takeaways were great. But it was all too much now.

By now he'd arrived at the Kashmir Food and General Store. They didn't bother with window displays – just the backs of cardboard boxes or untidily written notices of price discounts. Outside the door just piles of boxes of oranges or string sacks of spuds. No pride, no workmanship. But the prices were good, he had to admit. A woman came out, her face and hair tightly covered by a black scarf.

"Good morning, Mr Norton," she said and passed him.

He recognised her as the wife of the shop owner. Very occasionally she served in there.

"Morning," he replied, smiling at her.

Then two younger women came out, carrying bags of shopping. Both wore those niqab things, with black lace over the eye-slits. One was speaking into her mobile, he could hear voice. She laughed. If you couldn't see people's faces how could you know them? It was the hostility of the young men and the separateness of the women – this aggressive assertion of being different and somehow superior, this defiant refusal to fit in. That's what pissed him off. Made him somehow feel uneasy about being English. He went into the shop.

"Morning," said the shopkeeper with a smile. "Another fine day."

"Aye," said Lee. "I'm taking my lad out for the day. Need some crisps. Salt and vinegar's his favourite. And some Fanta orange."

He liked the shopkeeper, a Mr Hassan. He worked hard, putting in long hours. The shop was open till late, very useful. And a couple of times Mr Hassan had let him owe a bit when he'd not brought enough money out and needed fags on the way home. His daughter was in Ben's class.

"Enjoy your day," said Mr Hassan.

Lee walked back to his car. On Nightingale Street there was Rajpak Jewellers – *authentic elegance*. Everything was broken up now. His boyhood England had gone. He felt robbed. He unlocked the car, added the crisps and drink to the rucksack, and got in. Enough of that. Today was for Ben.

It wasn't far to the council estate where he lived on the edge of town. Social housing, they called it now. Not a bad place – and not a coloured face in it. He wondered if Ryan would be in –Nikki's new man. She'd told him about Ryan in a letter to him in prison. He hadn't felt any sexual jealousy – all that was long past. But he had felt a real anger about being usurped as a father. There was no logic to it, he knew: he had broken the marriage and had to take the consequences, one of which was being only an intermittent father. It had been OK while Nikki and Ben were on their own. But another man in the house was a different matter: another man playing football in the garden with Ben, kissing him goodnight, telling him off, shouting at him, even smacking him. That was hard to come to terms with. Another man with his own ideas, replacing him. *Life was just too fucking complicated sometimes.*

He drew up outside the grey pebble-dashed semi. And there was Ben in the front window, waving like mad and then rushing down the path to greet him as he got out of the car.

"Hi, Dad!"

The best word in the world.

Lee picked his son up and whirled him round.

"Hi, my beauty! We've got a busy day."

Lee put him down and they walked up to the front door, holding hands. Such a warm small hand. Nikki was leaning against the open door.

"Morning, Lee. Everything OK?"

"Aye. Everything's great!"

"Come in a minute while I get his stuff," invited Nikki. "I found the fishing net you asked for. Where are you going?" asked Nikki.

"Up Crimhope Dale. Remember it? Good times we had then, eh?" he said, grinning at her.

"It was a long time ago, Lee."

"Not so long."

"Long enough!"

"You haven't forgotten. Have you?"

"Course I haven't, Lee. And didn't you go there first with your granddad?"

"Aye, fishing."

There was no sign of Ryan except for a donkey jacket hanging in the hall. Perhaps he was still in bed.

"Sorry, Nikki, but can I use your bog?"

"Loo! Of course."

Lee went upstairs. Ben's bedroom door was open. He peeked in at the unmade bed, Lego and dinosaurs over the floor, a wooden garage in the corner with more model tractors than cars. Nikki's bedroom door was closed. He went into the toilet and locked the door – it wasn't his home. With Ryan living here, Lee felt like a trespasser, an intruder into his son's home. He relished having a shit here, leaving his spraint, marking his territory with that unique sweetish smell of his own shit. He flushed the toilet but left the seat up and deliberately closed the louvred window. He wanted Ryan to smell his presence here. Childish, pathetic really, but satisfying.

Going down the stairs he heard Ben excitedly talking to his Mum in the kitchen.

"Ready, Ben?"

"Yes, Dad. Bye Mum."

Ben turned to kiss her. She hugged him.

"Have a good day, you two. See you back at tea-time."

"Don't worry, I won't be late," said Lee.

They got into the car and Lee belted Ben in. The fishing net and Ben's bag were put on the back seat.

"First stop, adventure playground," said Lee.

"Brilliant!"

It wasn't far. The playground was in the park, the grounds of what used to be a millowner's grand residence with its show-off fake battlements and turrets so it looked like a castle. Ben ran straight over to the rope ladder that led up to a wooden house with walkways and sliding poles.

"Look at me, Dad, I can do this now."

Ben climbed up to the top of the swaying ladder, swung himself across, grabbed the edge of the window space and levered himself in.

"Magic, Ben, well done."

He was a strong little lad, Lee knew from play-fighting with him.

75

Ben disappeared into the inner workings of the playhouse. Lee looked around. Christ, there was hardly a white kid here. Hardly any parents, either. The little Asian kids were with what looked like their elder brothers and sisters, most of them talking excitedly into their mobiles – but he could hear no word of English.

Ben slid out of the playhouse, stood up, saw there was a vacant swing and ran across.

"Push me high, Dad," he shouted.

"No, push yourself, you know how to do it."

He sat on a bench with the football under his arm and watched Ben leaning his body forwards and backwards in an exaggerated way, trying to get up momentum.

"Fancy a kick about?"

"Yeah!"

Ben jumped down, snatched the ball and kicked it away, chasing after it towards the gate that led onto the open grass. Lee made a goal out of four empty flattened lager cans he found in the bushes. They played shots and passes. Lee was the goalie. Ben was well co-ordinated, he had a strong and accurate kick. *Better than most kids of his age,* thought Lee.

"OK, five goals past me and then we'll have a drink."

Ben was determined, getting closer and closer before he shot.

"You win!" said Lee.

They sat down on the warm grass and Lee got out the crisps and drink.

"Do they have a footie team at school?" asked Lee.

"Yes, but only for the older ones."

"Well, when you're in the team…"

"But I don't want to be in a team," interrupted Ben.

"Why on earth not?"

"I want to be like Ryan. He doesn't like teams."

Lee said nothing but it cut him to the quick. Somewhere in Lee's head had been a picture of him in a couple of years going to watch Ben play on Sunday mornings, shouting him on from the touchline with other dads. Being in a team was important.

"Do you still go to Mini-Dribblers?"

"Yeah, it's great. I go with my friend Thomas, his Dad gives us a lift."

So that Ryan and Nikki could have a 'lie in' on a Sunday morning.

"I can take you next week."

"I'll have to ask Mum. Can you take Thomas as well?"

"Of course."

"Where are we going now, Dad?"

"I know this place. It's not far away, by an old ruined mill. We'll do some fishing in the stream after we've cooked dinner. It's a place I used to go with my Grandad."

They drove out of the town along the bypass, turned off at a roundabout, steadily climbing, the moors opening up around them.

"My Grandad and me used to bike up here on a Sunday."

"It's a long way."

"There's short cuts you can't take with a car."

"Can we do that?"

"When you're older, sure. When you've got a big bike, a two wheeler."

"I'm really starving now, Dad."

"Not far!"

An hour later they came to a narrow valley. The lane ran along it, half way up its side. On the other side was a rough track that led to a solitary cottage. It had been abandoned when Lee was a kid, probably gentrified now. The road on this side ran up to the watershed at the top of the valley, cutting over the moor ridge and descending to a small hamlet on the other side. There was a For Sale sign on the only cottage they passed. A bit further on Lee spotted the footpath that led down to the small river in the valley bottom. He pulled onto the verge and checked there was room for farm vehicles to pass.

Lee led the way down, along a stone wall to a field corner, over a stone stile and down what had once been a green way where animals were taken to market. There was a trickling sedge-choked ditch bordered by twisted hawthorns, the fields were patched with clumps of reeds. The ruined walls bent right, the path descending steeply now under beech trees to a narrow pack-horse bridge over the river and up to the walls of the old ruined mill. By the bridge there was an open grassy patch.

"Right, food first," said Lee. "We need to build a fire. Can you collect some dry grass and small twigs for me, Ben?"

Ben went off foraging and Lee made a circle of old wall stones. He showed Ben how to start the fire with grass, blowing on the flame from the match, adding small twigs when the flames flared up.

"Don't put too much on too soon," said Lee. "And we need a good stock of twigs."

Soon the fire was going. Lee brought out an old frying pan and an even older milk pan that his mother had used when he was a kid, blackened inside now. He shaped tin foil into the two pans.

"The hardest thing about camp-fire cooking is the cleaning. This makes it easier."

They sat and watched the sausages frying, sizzling, the skins splitting open.

"I like sausages a bit burnt, just like my Grandad used to," said Lee.

"I do, too," said Ben.

When they were ready Lee put on the baked beans in the old milk pan. He waited until they bubbled, stirred them round and then spooned them out onto the two plastic plates he'd brought. He divided up the sausages. They sat on the grass in the sun, the river bubbling by, birds flitting across the trees, a couple of crows squawking.

Lee was content, listening to Ben chattering on. He felt a great warm love for his son, already he seemed such an individual with a mind of his own. When they'd finished they screwed up the dirty tinfoil and carefully packed it in a plastic bag. They wiped the pans with green bracken and swilled them in the stream. They played together with the fishing net but found no fish, only an old sheep bone. They made a dam with rocks and formed a little pool. They threw sticks into the stream from one side of the bridge and rushed over to see them float down the other side.

Lee looked at his watch.

"Time for home, Ben. We said we wouldn't be late for your Mum."

They gathered their stuff together and walked back up the slope to the car. As they drove back, Ben suddenly said: "Why does God give men ideas about killing people?"

"Wow! That's a good one," said Lee, flummoxed. "I don't think God does. They're men's ideas."

"But God makes men think ideas," said Ben.

Lee had no answer to this.

As he pulled up outside the house, he saw Ryan turn away from the front room window and move out of sight. Again that sudden spasm of bitterness that undermined the whole day's goodness. Ben was unbuckling his seat belt. Lee turned and gave him a huge hug, wanting to envelop him.

"I've had a great day, Ben," said Lee.

"Me, too, Dad. When are you coming again?"

"In a few days, Ben. And then we're going off on holiday. I've just got to sort it with your Mum. I'm going to hire a camper van and we'll go to the coast."

He saw the front door open and Nikki standing there.

"Now, off to your Mum. A last kiss."

Ben turned and gave him a quick kiss. Ben ran up the path, hugged his Mum and went inside. Nikki waved at him and closed the door. Lee sat there. What did the day mean? It had been so good. It had ended so quickly. Without fuss. That was good. Ben seemed happy. That was the main thing. This was how it would always be: a part time Dad, a weekend Dad. Ben deserved more. But he dared not let himself think in that direction. He put the car in gear and pulled away.

Back at home, in what he still felt was his mum's house, Lee washed up the picnic stuff and put things away. He felt exhausted but pleased with himself. He'd given Ben a good day. No doubt about it, he was a bright lad and had the makings of a good footballer. He'd already got a strong shot on him. He hated leaving him at the door, it was a kind of betrayal. Did Ben feel this way or did he just switch into the next activity? He knew he would now inevitably be only an occasional observer of Ben's growing-up – hearing second-hand about what he did, his new interests, new things learned. But if he'd stayed in the army it would have been the same. In fact he'd probably see more of Ben under these arrangements. The problem was Ryan. For Lee, Ben and Nikki living together was cosy: the bedtime stories, walking to school. But Ryan's presence changed things. Was it just rivalry over another male? He didn't think so. It was the influence Ryan might have over Ben. That team thing Ben had mentioned. Ryan would bring Ben up in a different way, with different values. But there was nothing he could do, another of those things he seemed powerless over. He just had to believe it would add to Ben's experience, give him a wider view of life. Presumably Nikki was happier with Ryan and that should make her a happier Mum. But you heard bad things about step-parents. If he found out that Ryan ever laid a hand on Ben, he'd really sort him out.

On the mantelpiece was his favourite photograph of himself, Ben and Nikki on a beach in Ibiza. He had looked so often at their faces in the photo to see traces of strain but had found none that might foretell divorce. Ben had been three. Lee had played with him in the hotel pool and in the sea, explored rock pools with him, rubbed sun cream into his shoulders, taken him on walks along the coastal cliffs while Nikki lounged and read. They'd been good times. Then had come Camp Sandbox in Iraq, court martial and prison. He hadn't wanted Ben to visit him in prison, though Nikki had volunteered to bring him down. He would explain it all to him when he was old enough to understand. He sighed. That was all in the past.

6.

Wakening

10-15th July

St Paul's Hospital, London

During his third night in the ICU, a brightness beyond Mike's eyelids registered for a moment, then dulled and he sank back again. A distant muffled clattering of metal instruments, even a voice, impinged at some deep level and faded away almost immediately. The scent of a woman flared and was snuffed out by his morphine.

A few hours later Mike's eyes flickered open then closed again. Slowly consciousness returned, seeping into him. He opened his eyes again, this time voluntarily. He was in a dim light. His eyes flicked round, seeking a focus, discerned vague tubes and the edges of flickering coloured light, red and green. He saw the outline of a figure bending over him. A face bent close to him, out of focus, and next to him another pale face with a white shape on it. His throat moved instinctively to say something but it couldn't. But even this brief awakening exhausted him and he slipped back into sleep.

Sue sat and held Mike's hand. She did not know what this awakening meant, how she could help or what she could say. Was this as far as he could emerge? Was this the limit of his brain? Or was this the beginning of his return to life? He was completely still, his face bandaged and impassive, grey and bruised. He needs me. He will need me to survive. She understood that more than medical care was needed now. She loved him, she knew that with a greater clarity than ever before. A sense of her own strength surged through her: she would rise to this challenge. She stroked his slender fingers, his hand so still on the smooth, tucked-in sheet, dirt under his nails, knuckles scraped red from his struggle in the wreckage. She saw his eyelids flicker.

Mike became aware of a slight coolness, a hardness on his mouth and nose. He did not want to open his eyes, wanted only to concentrate on the sensations on his face. In his head he tried to re-form the shape of his face. He tried to focus his attention on the slight restriction which he realised was around his nose, he felt the comforting softness on which his head lay. His throat was parched and clogged, painful. He relaxed into the softness, felt sleep seeping into him again and was thankful, letting himself drift back into that warmth of sleep, the sensations on his face disappearing. Then his mind leapt up with a sudden twist as a sharp acrid smell burned into him. His eyes jolted open, staring in terror. Sue felt his fingers jerking, scrabbling. Mike felt smothered by something strapped onto his face, constricting him. But he couldn't move his head, saw tubes hanging over him. He was shut in. He tried to lift an arm but nothing happened. The sharp acrid smell was in his nostrils, screams and hacking coughs. He remembered his legs twisted and grotesque, the blood everywhere. His legs! He tried to lift his head to look down the bed but he could not. His eyes were bright with panic, with desperation. Then he felt each of his hands grasped with warm fingers. They were firm. They knew: somehow they knew what he was desperate to ask.

Some time later he remembered a man's face leaning towards him, pale, grey-haired, lean. He felt his warm clean breath on his forehead. He remembered hearing the man's soft voice and the sounds of words, watching his lips move. He wasn't sure if he had replied or nodded. He watched the man move away. Was it a couple of hours or a day later that he returned? The man was talking again, gently. Mike heard him pause then say: "I'm sorry, Mike. We couldn't save your legs. I'm so sorry."

Mike felt the enfolding fingers tighten on his hands, comforting him. But he wanted to retract his hands away from the warm living hands, to curl up in his terror, to hide his stunted torso in a darkness, to be unseen. And then piercing through the darkness he heard Sue's voice, Sue here in all this bleak wilderness.

"Mike, I'm here. Mike, my darling, I'm here. I love you, my sweetheart. It's OK, I love you."

But he could not bear her so near to him, didn't want her joined with him in his nightmare. His eyes burned with fear and then spilled over in a rage of tears. His running legs were gone. He would not walk, could not stand. He collapsed back into himself, closed his eyes. Why him? He wanted to turn away, sleep, to give in, switch off the pain, pretend nothing had happened. He did not want to breathe through a tube, he did not want to breathe. He wanted the wires and tubes ripped out so he could die. He wanted to take his hand away from Sue. But he could not wrench it clear. He could not move. He was pinioned. He felt her warmth still holding him and was revolted by it. At last he managed to jerk his arm away. Immediately a machine began to bleep. Sue looked up in a panic. A nurse swiftly came to Mike, readjusted the tube on the arm he had shifted. The machine stopped bleeping.

"He is so distressed," she said. "He must rest again. That was nothing serious. Moving his arm put a kink in the cannula and that blocked the flow of the antibiotic fluid so it set off the alarm. He may ask again about his legs, I'm afraid. Some patients can't accept it or believe it. They are in denial."

The doctor increased the morphine infusion to ease him, Sue stroked his forehead, mopping away his moist sweat until the morphine took effect. She was terrified. All her confidence had drained away as she saw the fear and horror in his eyes. *This would be the worst time, the very worst,* thought Sue. This now was what had to be faced, the brutal unambivalence of it. Mike knew.

"I know his distress is difficult to witness," said the doctor, "but it is a good sign. It means he understands. It means that his brain may be undamaged. He may have been having a flashback, a memory of being in the train. It often happens."

Sue nodded. She understood that this might be more a curse than a blessing. Because of his fears and phobias, his squeamishness, his love of physical fitness, his absorption with physical beauty – this was the worst that could happen to him. He had told her once that hell for him would be to constantly see the workings of his interior body – the blood circulating, the pumping heart muscle, the filling and emptying of his lungs, microbes scurrying everywhere. Now this kind of hell would be visited on him: every day he would see his deformed body, imagine the chaos of serrated nerves and tissue in his stumps.

She watched him as he slept. Could he be the same Mike again? She remembered one of their first weekends away when after far too much to drink in the pub they had literally rolled their way home, wrapped round each other, giggling like kids, along the grassy lane to their tent. She remembered camping on the Gower in a field by the sea, the mist thick and low and damp in the late evening, both of them warm in their double sleeping bag. And then hearing the sound of singing: rhythmic, ululating, rising and falling, rich and foreign. They had opened the tent to see a group of Africans on the shore in bright robes, reds and yellows and greens, bodies and arms swaying, the mist drifting round them, their wonderful voices warm and strange. They found out later they were a touring Christian choral group. Sweet, sweet Mike! Somehow with him interesting things happened.

What should her love of him really mean? If she could, should she let him escape this hell, let him …die – to avoid the pain, not just the physical pain, but the mental and emotional anguish he would surely suffer? She looked at the shape of his thighs beneath the sheets. She shuddered – his…stumps. Involuntarily her hand went to her mouth. Her beautiful Mike, whose legs she loved wrapped around her in bed, warming her in winter, those legs that sped him into the wild places he loved. What right had she to decide that he should suffer? Was she being selfish, did she want him alive for her own sake rather than his?

"When he wakes," said the doctor, "you'll need to speak slowly and clearly. We think he will understand everything."

Too well, thought Sue. She looked up at the doctor with scared eyes and watched him go. She envied him: his duty was clear, to keep Mike alive, to restore him as best he could. She sat and took Mike's left hand in hers. She had learned that the tube in his mouth was a breathing tube and that in his nose was a nasogastic tube to feed him. Monitors checked his heart rate, the pressure of oxygen in his blood, his rate of breathing. The nurses on their thirteen hour shifts changed tubes and cannulas, measured urine output and the fluid input, checked his blood pressure and temperature. All was meticulously noted on the giant chart every hour. Mike was visited by the anaesthetist who ran the unit, by a vascular surgeon, a respiratory team, even by a physiotherapist who cupped her hands and clapped his chest so hard Sue wanted to intervene.

A middle-aged, dark-haired woman, slightly built and brisk, had introduced herself as Kathy. She would be the lead physio for Mike throughout his rehabilitation.

"We must clear the secretions," she had explained, "the things you and I would cough up. If we don't it could allow infection which would lead to complications like pneumonia. Patients usually call us the physio terrorists because we do hurt them. But after these bombings they might change the title."

This, thought Sue, *is what the NHS is all about: care and professionalism and technology, all there for ordinary people.* It was humbling. She felt a sudden pride in being British.

The following day she was sitting in the same position when Mike's eyes suddenly opened. It wasn't a bleary slow awakening, he was wide awake immediately. She saw his dark hazel pupils adjust to the light and then focus on her. He looked at her steadily and she tried to read some meaning into his gaze. Did he recognise her? He seemed to be examining her with a frightening detachment, weighing the alternatives in a calculated way. Or perhaps it just appeared as if he was back in this room with her but in reality was still back in his head, his brain still not functioning properly, his gaze an unseeing blank.

She squeezed his hand, wanting desperately to feel him respond. But there was nothing, just a limpness. She saw his eyes slowly close as he surrendered again to the morphine, soothing and warming him, rescuing him from the brightness, the pain and maybe from the beginnings of thought. Sue stroked his hand endlessly.

Sue moved aside and watched the nurses wash him: first one side and then the other, with flannels and warm soapy water, drying him with rich towels, rolling him first one way and then the other, deftly whipping out the old sheets and replacing them with new at the same time. The nurses bantered with each other and they always explained to him what they were doing even though he was unconscious or asleep – as if he could co-operate and hear them. They spoke loudly because the blast had caused Mike considerable hearing loss. Sue copied them.

"I love you, Mike. We shall be fine."

She repeated it, the loudness of it making it sound melodramatic, soap-operish. But there was no response.

The vital first four days were almost up but Mike's body had been exhausted. Were his organs too tired to carry on? Was knowing about his legs the final blow?

"Be strong, Mike," urged Sue. "Be strong. We can do this. I love you. Squeeze my hand and let me know that you love me too."

Sue knew that within his sleeping form a titanic struggle for life was going on: it was terrifying and awe-inspiring. The instinct to live, the temptation to die. Was it just instinctive to want him to live? Or was it her love for him? Was it her own defiance of fate? Her own positive optimism? Or was it simple selfishness? Whatever it was she found herself bending close to Mike's ear and speaking into it, her lips touching his skin.

"Mike, stay with me. Stay with me. I want to live with you, marry you, go places with you. There is so much to do, so much to enjoy. Come back to me, Mike. Don't leave me."

It was like a prayer, an incantation.

She watched the day's routine: the calm, purposeful visits of the medical staff, the cleaners who would always chat with her, enquire about Mike and move on. But still she waited for him to wake, still anxious about his brain, anxious about his mind and how he would adapt.

The next day Sue felt a relaxation among the doctors and nurses as they checked the readings and graphs. The vital signs were starting to improve, they told her. In the middle of the morning Mike's eyes opened again, more naturally this time. This time she saw a softness in them – not detachment or anger or misery, but a peace. The nurse took the breathing tube out of his mouth and placed an oxygen mask over his mouth and nose.

"We can do lots of things," said a nurse. "Maybe it's the power of love that makes the difference in these acute cases. We really thought we were going to lose him early on. We believe he has gone through the worst."

Mike still could not move his head which was in a brace. He saw Sue's face clearly for the first time, saw through his loneliness the love and concern that filled her face. She smiled at him and he felt her squeeze his hand. He tried to smile back, to help her, but his mouth seemed numbed. He wanted to speak but his throat was badly burned and very painful. His eyes filled with gratitude that she was there, the only person he wanted to be there. He felt the warm plastic tubes brush against his arm as he shifted position slightly.

Then Sue suddenly felt her fingers grasped by Mike's fingers, like a baby's, grasping and curious. It was his only way of thanking her. Did she understand? She leaned over him and kissed him again on the forehead. He felt the softness of her lips. And he needed to ask so much. To understand so much. He could not speak, his throat was dry. He felt an overwhelming thirst. His legs! Involuntarily he wanted to squirm away, to hide from her. He didn't want her to see him.

Sue saw only bewildering fast-changing expressions in his eyes. How much did he understand? Was his brain functioning properly or was it juddering in stops and starts? There seemed to be intelligence bright in his eyes as well as anger and fear. The doctor had told her he would possibly be able to speak when he was off the ventilator but he couldn't. She felt Mike's fingers again. Were they trying to stroke hers? Was there an intention there, not just a response? She felt his fingernail scratch her hard. She looked round at a nurse.

"Could he be trying to tell me something?" she asked.

"If he was, that would be wonderful." She added more softly, "We still don't know for certain if his brain has been damaged. If he is trying to communicate, that would be a very positive sign."

"His fingers seem strong," said Sue. "Let's try."

The nurse brought her a pad of paper.

"Mike, can you try and write? I'll help you."

She looked to his eyes but could not interpret what was in them. She placed a biro in Mike's fingers and felt him enclose it. But his hand did not move. In the cloying glue of his mind the beginnings of words and questions surfaced and sank again. How long had he been here? And then he had a sudden vivid picture of the man called Lee, of the darkness and the smoke. His fingers held the pen more firmly and he cocked his wrist. He knew what he wanted to ask. Sue eagerly felt his movement and guided his fingers as they moved the pen jerkily, minutely across the paper.

Mike saw the black shape of the letter he wanted to write, clear across his mind, concentrating.

Sue watched the letter form. It was spidery and faint but without doubt 'Y'.

His hand relaxed, collapsed after the effort both physical and mental. She looked at him but his eyes were closed. 'Y'. *You, yes* were the first words that came to her. What was he trying to say? Mike let the pen fall. Had he forgotten what he wanted to say, could not continue the word because it had floated out away from his mind? Despair filled her. She remembered another hospital bed she had visited as a child with her mother: the aged aunt propped up in bed, her mouth dribbling, uttering quiet plaintive moans, another woman standing and ceaselessly tapping her forehead on the ward wall, talking gibberish and laughing. Ever since that day at the hospital Sue had been terrified of mental derangement – Mike's clear vision veiled, his ideas mangled.

Perhaps he was trying to say 'You.' She wedged the pen into his fingers again but there was no response. His eyes were open again now, looking dully at her.

"What do you mean? Do you mean me?"

She pointed to herself, smiled, made herself look happy. But his eyes did not change. Mike had made his effort but he was still locked away from her, had not made himself understood.

"Y," said Sue. "What do you mean, Y?"

And as soon as she said it aloud she understood. What a fool! How slow! He knew clearly what he wanted to know. It was her stupidity that was at fault, her slow brain, not his. She grasped his writing hand with both of hers.

"You want to know why it happened."

She saw his eyes brighten. In her B&B in the evening she had read the papers avidly, poring over the appalling photographs, reading survivors' stories, watching the TV news. Some of what had happened had become clear, but not everything. She would keep it simple. What explanation, if any, would make it easier for him to come to terms with? She looked at his eyes, still questioning her. She would be honest, tell the truth as she knew it. She spoke loudly and slowly as the consultant had advised her, articulating her words as if she was speaking to a deaf man.

"It was a bomb, Mike. There was a bomb on your train. An Islamist suicide bomber. He blew himself up and you were in the same carriage. There were other bombs, too, in another two trains, and one on a bus. They were terrorists."

Sue tried to interpret his eyes. Was there fear, incomprehension, anger? Mike closed his eyes in bewilderment. He felt stunned: a suicide bomber – like in Baghdad and Palestine and Israel. It had never occurred to him. It was as if the revelation scarified his brain, wire-brushed and de-clogged it. The electricity zipped again, the synapses connected. He'd assumed it was an accident, a crash, a derailment not a crazy religious zealot. A vicious hatred surged up in him at the man's arrogance and ruthlessness, a hatred born of his own absolute irrelevance to the bomber's mission, of his sheer bad luck. There was nothing he could have done about it – the coincidences, the late train, the missed first tube. He heard again echoes of screams, cries and groans from the train and the tunnel. He raged, unable to move, unable to hurl something, to pace, to shout or scream.

All Sue heard was a low gargling growl which, because his throat was raw, turned into a cough and coughed up black fragments of stuff he had ingested and inhaled in the tunnel. The nurse wiped it away with a tissue.

"Here's some water," she said.

She dipped a piece of pink sponge into some water and wet his lips. Then she squeezed it into the side of his mouth.

"Is that better?"

Mike felt the drops gliding past the tube and into his throat – beautiful, cool, soothing. It was a moorland stream where he ran, dappled with light as it twisted and fell between rocks. He snapped the image shut, it was too painfully bright.

Supervised by the nurse, Sue dripped more water into Mike's mouth, wiped around his lips and the inside of his mouth.

During the next night, Mike awoke horrified to realise he needed a shit. He needed to tell someone, needed help. He was like a fucking child again, asking for his potty. A nurse wheeled in a contraption, all white and beige plastic and silent on rubber wheels, but still looking like an updated version of a medieval instrument of torture. Curtains were drawn round his bed. Three nurses supervised as straps were placed under his arms and thighs. A button was pushed, the machinery quietly hummed and he was slowly hoisted up into the air, swivelled round, and lowered so that his arse hovered over the commode. His muscles were paralysed by his utter humiliation, he loathed himself as he dangled there, steadied by the nurses' hands. And then the choking smell of his shit as he could resist no longer. It filled the room, gross in all this antiseptic cleanliness. Calmly the nurses went about their tasks. He was hoisted higher and his arse was wiped. These nurses were martyrs. He was swivelled back and lowered.

"Not so bad, was it?"

Mike grimaced.

"All in a day's work," the nurse replied. "Don't worry about it."

Mike rested back on his bed. Surrounded by care, by life-giving machines he nevertheless felt utterly alone as the minutes of the small hours ticked slowly by. He loathed this dependency.

7.

Barry

13th July

Bradfield

Lee switched on the TV evening news. There'd been a vigil, a two minute silence in London for the victims of the bombing. A man in a suit was speaking to the crowd. Lee presumed it was a politician and turned the sound off. It was easy to be glib, especially if you thought you had God on your side. He'd heard the army padres. Hypocrites! He watched as the camera swung around Trafalgar Square. It was beautifully sunny, the crowd in t-shirts and shirt sleeves, men and women in shorts, some wearing sunhats, one woman held a Union Jack across her body. Then they all bowed their heads and stood still – builders off sites in their yellow fluorescent jackets, holding their helmets under their arms, office workers in ties and shirts; Muslim women in headscarves, men with skull caps, Africans in their bright dresses. All races, all colours were there, it seemed. There was a huge sign *London United One City One World*. The camera settled on a couple holding a banner *We are not afraid.* There were huge piles of flowers at the foot of Nelson's column, men in tears, women wiping their eyes. A sign announced that there was a Book of Condolence that could be signed.

Lee turned off the TV. It was all so far away. And yet it was so close. Some of the bombers had come from Leeds only a few miles away. He thought of Mike and his girlfriend Sue. Was she with him? Was he alive? He could remember scenes in that wrecked train more clearly than combat zones in Iraq. He looked at his watch. He'd just make it in time. He hated being late, keeping people waiting. He liked the Bobbinmakers' Arms, the Bobbin as it was known locally. He liked the semi-circular bar and the dark wood the place was done out in. It was only a five minute stroll to the pub and when he entered the bar, Liz the barmaid was taking glasses down from above the pump handles to wipe the shelves clean.

Her arms were bare in a short sleeved blouse. Lee liked to see her muscles moving under her skin as she pulled back the gold and black handle. She had a hard man-weary face that had seen it all and not been too impressed. But she had a nice pony tail. Perhaps she was soft underneath. Music was pounding out, Sky Sports with the sound turned down on two big screens at opposite ends of the big room.

"Quiet tonight."

"Same as usual, it's early."

Over in the corner, three what looked like sixteen year old girls were concentrating on the Deal or no Deal machine, its red and yellow lights flashing up and across the screen. All three were overweight, wearing too tight jeans, short hair, one dyed bright red. There was no one at the snooker table in the back room.

Lee took his beer and sat at a table in one of the little areas separated from each other by dark wooden balustrades. An old man looked up at him from a table opposite and waved a hand.

"Evenin', Reg," said Lee.

Reg looked down again at his paper, making notes on it with the stub of a pencil. His Racing Post, Lee knew. Three pints and he'd pick up his Morrison's bags and be off home, a bus driver with a bald head, ruddy face and big belly. Barry was late. Then the door swung open and in he walked in his busy fashion, black leather jacket and jeans, trainers, his usual roll-up in the corner of his mouth.

"Hi Lee, sorry I'm late. Got a long phonecall."

"No problem. I'll get it. What you drinking?"

"Pint of Carlsberg, ta. Hi Liz."

They stood together at the bar while Liz pulled the pint.

"Did you have a good day with your lad? Was it yesterday?" asked Barry.

"Couple of days ago. Had a great time, thanks. He's going to be a good footballer, that lad. Bloody knackering though. We went to the park. Then down to the river where we used to go as kids."

"You mean Crimhope Dale?"

"Aye."

"By, we had some good times there. Remember that ruined barn we tried to sleep in?"

"We were terrified. Us hard city men out in the country!"

They sat down at the table.

"Did you see that video on the news last night?" asked Barry.

"Video? No. I saw that stuff tonight on the vigil in Trafalgar Square. Brilliant. Brought it all back. Very moving, I thought."

"It was Mike wasn't it, that guy you saved on the tube?"

"Yep. Mike. I don't even know if he survived. Last I saw of him was that ambulance racing away."

"That video, Lee. You should have seen it."

"What was it?"

"It's one of the bombers, not sure if it was the one who did you lot. It's a tape he made, deliberately to be shown after he died. A suicide video, they call it. It's vicious stuff."

"What was he saying then?"

"He was so bloody calm, that was what got me. It was spooky. He's just sat there, on the floor, like they do. He's so casual, relaxed, looking straight at the camera. He's got a pen in his hand and he keeps jabbing it at us. He's got one of those Arab scarves tied round his head. But what was really weird was he was talking in a Yorkshire accent, just like you and me."

Barry took a drink of his pint and ran his hand through his hair.

"What did he say? Was he trying to justify himself?" asked Lee.

"Yes, that was it. He said he'd given everything up, like

thousands of his brothers, to take revenge for all the innocent Muslims killed by us and the Americans. The British public elected a democratic government and that government killed Muslims in Iraq and so the public are just as responsible. He talks about us gassing and torturing and bombing his brothers and sisters."

"But that's crap, Barry. They kill each other more than we kill them."

"He doesn't care about that. There's no logic to it, Lee. It's a war. He sees himself as a soldier, like you were. That's what he says he is – a warrior."

"Some fucking warrior – killing ordinary civilians who can't defend themselves," said Lee fiercely.

He looked up as the girls at the slot machine burst into a fit of giggles. A couple came in, ordered halves and sat at a table near them, under the huge gilt-framed mirror over the empty fireplace. The man put his arm round the woman who nestled into his shoulder. He kissed her. She squirmed away.

"Sorry, it must be the garlic prawns," said the man.

"I took Ben down the park," said Lee. "He was the only white kid in the playground. Then there's that bloody great mosque they've built just round the corner from where I live. It's not England any more. It's bollocks. I was out in Iraq fighting Muslims, risking my life to protect my country, and my country's half bloody Muslim. I've seen mates killed out there. Those Arabs use women and children as human shields. Soldiers! That's a sick joke. They know we won't go into their holy mosques so they hide in there and snipe at us. And beheading those workers they kidnap. With a huge bloody sword on TV. It's disgusting."

"We're soft on them over here, you know."

There was the clack of a woman's heels on the wooden floor. Lee looked up. Really high black heels and black tights, a short skirt, blonde shoulder length hair done properly, a gold bag over her shoulder. Up for it. She joined the girls at the machine. Lee turned back to Barry.

"How do you mean?"

Barry lowered his voice.

"In this town everyone knows they run the drugs and prostitution gangs. Every so often their gangs fight each other when they think they're trespassing on each other's territory. Your part of town is the High-enders. At the other side of town, round Lawkfield, it's the Low-enders. There's even fights at school between the younger brothers of the gang members. It's anarchy, mate. There was a bloody cricket match a few weeks ago. Two Asian teams in the league. Do you know they have Asian-only teams?"

"No, I thought that was against the law."

"But it doesn't apply to them. Anyway, the cricket match is going on when three cars roar up to the pavilion. A gang of Asian blokes get out, armed with iron bars and baseball bats, run out onto the pitch and start beating up some of the players. Really beating them up. Then they drive off. Three ambulances had to come. Two guys got fractured skulls. It's like fucking Islamabad."

There was a sudden burst of laughter from the group of girls now sitting at a table. The blonde was gesturing. Some story about a bloke, no doubt. Music was still thumping out its heavy beat. Reg was peering up at the darts on Sky Sports.

"You don't know the half of it," said Barry. "We don't know the half of it. They don't want us to know."

"Who doesn't?"

"The government. The police. The bastards in charge."

"But why not?"

Barry leaned forward conspiratorially, his eyes bright with excitement, and said in a low voice, "Cos they're scared. Scared there'll be real riots if the whites knew what was going on – like there was in Brixton and Liverpool a few years back."

"What do you mean? What's going on?"

"I just talk to people, get information And there's stuff to read. Books, the internet." He paused and then added: "And there's meetings."

Lee frowned in puzzlement. "What meetings?"

"Once or twice I've been to a group called The English Patriotic League. Just ordinary blokes who are getting pissed off that no one's doing anything about anything. But I think they're just whingers and thugs. They won't get anything done, maybe wave a few flags and beat up a few blokes."

"So what are you wanting to do?"

"Dunno yet. But something that will make people sit up and take notice. If you're interested, Lee, your experience in the army would help. But we've got to keep it just between the two of us."

"You know me, Barry, I won't say anything."

Barry stubbed his fag out and immediately started rolling another. Lee would be a good bloke to have on your side. He was broad-shouldered, his pale blue shirt tight over his chest and biceps. He still had his short military – or was it prison? – haircut. A broken nose gave a rough edge to his square face. He wasn't a man to be messed with.

Barry lit the new fag.

"And they're setting up Muslim schools so they can keep separate," he continued. "They don't want to be part of us, join in. But we're supposed to accept them."

"If they don't want to be part of us, if they don't like the way we live, why don't they just fuck off home to Pakistan?"

"Good question, Lee. But for a lot of the young ones, home is here. They were born here."

"So we're fucked, then!"

A young lad had joined the girls at the table. Their laughter was louder.

"Look, I've got to go in a couple of minutes, Lee. Just a couple more things to think about, since you seem interested. These Islamist attacks are happening all over the world, not just here – Tel Aviv, the Philippines, Madrid where they killed 192 on the trains. But London is the biggest centre of Islamic activists in the world."

"That's what Jason said."

"Muslim leaders have been kicked out of their own countries for inciting violence and they've come here and been allowed to stay. I'll give you just two examples. There's a guy called Abu Hamza. He's been connected to terrorist cells all over the place. He was allowed to preach in the Finsbury Park mosque in London. While he was in charge, Richard Reid the shoe bomber stayed there, as did one of the 9/11 Twin Tower planners, and a guy who tried to bomb the Los Angeles airport. Another preacher was Omar Bakri. He was expelled from Saudi Arabia. He founded a group called Hizb ut-Tahrir in London. He aimed, he said, 'to fly the Islamic flag over Downing Street.' He claimed the Prime Minister was a legitimate target for assassination. His sect wanted to cover England 'with our blood through martyrdom, martyrdom, martyrdom.' And this guy is living on £300 a week in social benefit handouts. See what I mean?"

"I don't believe it."

"It's true. And here's something else. When the government does decide to do something, the lawyers fuck it up with their human rights. Anyway, I must go. Someone important to see."

He got up and patted Lee on the shoulder.

"Think about it. See you sometime."

Barry got up and walked briskly out. He was a white man, that was for sure. His skin so pale, his face white as a fridge door. A wiry little bugger, Lee remembered. Legs and arms like sticks but so strong, a grip of iron. You didn't want to get on the wrong side of him. When they were kids and playing Nazis he'd once asked Barry to hold a burning cigarette close to the back of his hand, wanting him to just touch it to the skin to see if he could bear it. But he'd pulled his hand away at the last second. Barry had laughed.

"Coward!" He'd said.

"I'll do it to you, then," Lee had retorted. "See if you can."

"Don't be bloody daft," Barry had answered. "I'm not a nutter like you."

But if he hadn't pulled his hand away, Lee knew Barry would have touched him with the burning cigarette. Who was the nutter?

Lee hadn't been prepared for so much. It was more of what Jason had told him. Islamic bookshops and newspapers glorified terrorists, imams trained jihadists and planned operations in which British-born Muslims had carried out a human bomb attack in Tel Aviv, kidnapped and murdered a US journalist in Pakistan and tried to blow up an airliner with a shoe bomb.

London was the base, Jason had said, for organisations linked to

Al-Qaeda – the Muslim Brotherhood, the Hizb ut-Tahrir which was banned in many countries, the Islamic Foundation. Jason mentioned names of Muslim radicals who now lived freely in London preaching and inciting hatred of the West while living on benefits paid for by the taxes Lee paid. Lee had never heard of Abu Qatad, Omar Bakri Mohammed or Abu Hamza.

Lee had been shocked. He did not recognise the country he'd been fighting for. It seemed like nobody was on his side. Maybe there was still a part for him to play. He didn't know how but he knew there was a gap in him that needed to be filled. Perhaps he could get something organised with Barry.

He'd been fighting for a country he didn't really know. He thought of Andy, a paraplegic now after Basra, his mind blown apart too, his life destroyed, existing on crap compensation. A land fit for heroes! And that preacher bastard living on benefits. Who was doing anything about it? Who had any balls? The Muslims were changing his country. They didn't live by his values: forced marriages, honour killings, halal food, burning books, those bloody veils. They were toxic. They didn't want to fit in. He looked across at Reg, his head tilted back, draining his pint. Reg put the pint glass down on the table, stood up, took a purse out of his pocket and carefully slotted some change into it. He was a decent bloke was Reg. He wouldn't know anything about all this. Everything was changing round him while he drove his bus and drank his pints in peace.

What was that group Barry belonged to? He might go along, find out more. He finished his pint, put the empty glass on the bar.

"See ye, Liz, behave yerself. See ye Reg."

Walking back he passed the hardware store with its shutters down. Next to it the lights were on in the Direct Claims office. He looked in through the window. Three young Asian men sat there at desks with computers on, one was eating some sort of fast food. They stared at him as he passed. Their cars were parked outside, on double yellow lines. *They don't give a shit*, thought Lee, *the rules don't apply to them. Somebody should do something about it.*

8.

More News

Jackdaw Road, Bradfield.

Across the city, it was 2 am. as Amjad's mother switched the light off and peered through the curtains of her front room. They were all gone – no, there was a man a few yards down the road sitting on the pavement, his back against the wall, his coat wrapped round him, his long lens camera beside him. She checked again: he was the only one left. She closed the curtain, stood for a moment then walked slowly back into the living room where the television was still on, the sound low so as not to disturb her husband upstairs. She knew he would not be asleep either. He'd gone up unable to watch any more of the constant new updates, the re-runs of shots of the bombed bus, the injured and the dead being carried out of the tube station, the scenes in hospital, the interviews. She had been horrified when it had happened a week ago but now it was like an addiction. She could not stop watching it all. Amjad did this, my son did this. Because it was incomprehensible she watched and listened for clues that might explain her son to her, knowing at the same time that she would never understand.

She was exhausted, her head thumping, her eyes dry and aching.

But she could not sit still, let alone sleep. Her mind circled endlessly, dizzily after a day in which her world had collapsed. At six this morning they had been wakened by loud knocking on the door, shouting, two police cars outside with their flashing blue lights. Her husband had opened the door and police had pushed past them into their house. They had to go immediately to the police station. But what about the girls? Arrangements quickly made for a neighbour to look after them and make sure they went to school as normal. Their bewilderment and tears, kisses and re-assurance. The girls waving fearfully to them on the doorstep as she and her husband were escorted separately into the two cars. Seeing other police dressed in white suits moving into their house.

Sitting in that bare room on a hard plastic chair at the police station, a man and a woman at the other side of the table. "You are not being arrested," they had told her. And then the shock that had paralysed her, had seemed to stop her heart. "Your son Amjad was one of the London bombers." She had needed her husband but they would not allow that. "We are searching your house for evidence." Then the endless questions about Amjad. "Where had he been living, what had he been doing, had he been a student, who were his friends, which mosque did he attend?" And all the time she was refusing to believe it was true. It could not be. She tried to give clear answers. That was easy, she was simply honest, she had nothing to conceal. He was a good boy, a hard-working boy. The only friends she knew about were his old school friends. She didn't know about after he'd gone away to study.

She heard herself speaking but her voice seemed to be coming from deep down beneath the waves of shock and grief and anger that swept over her. After five hours they had let them go. Driven back together in a police car they had held hands but sat in stunned silence, already in separate worlds. As the car turned into their road, the second shock had come. Outside their house there was a mass of people, cameras, TV cameras, vans and cables. As the police escorted them through the melee to their door the shouted questions, the microphones thrust at them, the flashes of cameras. Their heads bowed they had hurried in, terrified. And there had been Hussein,

Amjad's uncle and his wife. They closed the door behind them, the voices outside still loud. Curtains in all the rooms were drawn and the lights on.

"No interviews," Hussein had said. "Speak to no one."

Then her husband had exploded at Hussein, shouting at him, insulting him about his faith, blaming him for leading Amjad astray with his primitive beliefs. "It started with that prayer room at the school. That was your idea." It had been terrible. She had never seen her husband like that. Hussein had just nodded, head down, saying nothing. Finally her husband had stopped. "Get out of my house," he had said, in a fierce whisper. "Never come here again." At the door Hussein had told her he would collect the girls from school with his wife and bring them back later. He would tell the reporters outside that there would be no interviews. He opened the door to more shouts and baying questions, more camera flashes then he and his wife were gone.

Her husband was slumped in a chair, tears rolling down his cheeks, breathing heavily. She went to comfort him but he pushed her away. She put on the television just in time to hear the announcement of Amjad's involvement, seeing scenes outside their house, watching the police car return with them. Their mobile phones were ringing, their land phone was ringing. She had nothing to say to anyone. She switched off the mobiles and unplugged the phone. The only sounds now were the television reporters, interviews with police and – she recognised some of them – community leaders. She stared blankly at the screen, their words just blobs of sound.

For a time her husband had watched, too. Then he had gone upstairs. She heard the bedroom door closing, the creak of the bed above as he lay on it. She had turned the lights off and wandered the gloomy, eerie, silent rooms with their fringes of light round the curtains. Always she came back to the television. She made one phone call, to Hussein, asking him to take the girls round so they could stay the night with their best friends. She had to think, to absorb what had happened, to think about Amjad.

How could she have been so ignorant of her own son? So remote from her own flesh and blood? He had been so studious, such a dutiful and loving son. And yet, somehow, she must have done something wrong. Mothers create their sons. If he had begun to prefer the company of bad people as he grew up, it was because she had not given him something in his childhood. If he had got in with the wrong sort at college it was because there was a need, a gap, in him. But she could not identify this lack. She had always been confident she was a good mother: not just feeding and clothing her children, but listening to them, being loving and affectionate, giving them clear boundaries of what was right and wrong.

Her husband had played his part, too: an honest man, working hard, never hitting his children as other fathers did, attending the mosque regularly. He enjoyed his children, playing with them at the park, making time for them in his busy life. She had seen Amjad's antagonism to his father as he became a teenager. But this was normal, she had thought: it was part of the male process of growing up, of becoming independent.

She remembered her husband's own growing independence as they courted. He wore only western clothes, allowed her to choose what she wore, insisted on speaking English at home, preferred English food. In their early days together she and Amjad's father had spoken about all this. One of the reasons she had fallen in love with him was his passionate belief about the future: that they were part of a clash of cultures, Islamic and British, that as the first generation of Muslims born in Britain they had a duty to resolve this clash. He had talked so logically and quietly about this duty. If they got it wrong the future would be difficult for their own children. Their skin colour alone would always identify them as different but you had to minimize the differences, seek what was common between them, fit in, adapt, integrate.

She had been excited, inspired even, as he spoke about how he wanted her to be, as his wife: fully equal to him, able to make her decisions, free from the need for chaperones. Of course they were Muslims and they went to the mosque, but religion was a private thing. It had not been easy. She knew Amjad disapproved of some of this – but she had thought it was just a convenient peg on which to hang his adolescent defiance of his father. Hussein had criticised them for betraying their faith and his heritage. Although he lived only three doors away, they hardly spoke or acknowledged each other, bringing up their families in different ways. Hussein's wife was only allowed out of the house in her burka, and she was content with this. But tonight at least Hussein had tried to help, until her husband had dismissed him so violently.

Amjad's father had always been enraged by Hussein's interpretation of the Qu'ran and of his lifestyle: the burka, he said, was more than a garment. How could anyone be so stupid as not to understand that it was a symbol? It was a public display of disapproval of the English culture in which you lived, it shouted that you were different, separate and implied you were superior. It set people apart. It made non-Muslims apprehensive, made them wonder what it was that they had allowed into their towns and onto their streets. And it wasn't in the Qu'ran. Tonight he had blamed Hussein and people like him.

Amjad was the result. She could not put out of her mind the images of destruction, the stories of mutilation and suffering, the interviews with survivors and relatives of the dead, pictures of the wounded. Her son had done this. Her husband had locked himself away in his head, was hardly able to comfort her. She knew he was trying to erase Amjad from his mind: it was his way of coping. She knew he would now lose himself in their daughters' lives.

She heard the snap of the letter box. Wearily she got up. On the floor by the door was a white piece of folded card. She bent down, picked it up and unfolded it. Scrawled across it in black ink were the words: *Your son is a blessed martyr.Inshallah.*

She stared at it. The letters swirled as she felt dizzy and she had to steady herself against the wall. When she was steady again she went into the kitchen, opened the lid of the swing bin and tore the card into shreds. She stuffed the pieces far down the bin. Her husband must never know.

9.

Exercise

15th July

St Paul's Hospital, London

At their weekly meeting Mike's team decided he was well enough to start exercising. His throat was healing too and they took the feeding tube out of his nose. Kathy, the physiotherapist, came in with another physio. Mike had not even savoured his new freedom, not even dared to tentatively clear his throat when Kathy said:

"I'll be responsible for looking after you, Mike. We're going to work together with Louise here to get you independent again. It's our job to get you strong again, ready to walk."

"Walk!" exclaimed Mike. The word came out as a croak.

"Yes. You'll be surprised how quickly you'll learn. You're young, fit. You were a runner, I understand. How long do you think it takes?"

Mike thought. He hadn't expected to be having this conversation or even talking at all. He certainly hadn't considered walking again. It was an impossibility.

"Six months," he finally croaked out.

"That's what people usually say," said Kathy. "What if I tell you you'll be walking – with crutches, of course – in six weeks. And you could be at home."

Sue was amazed. That was fantastic. She looked at Mike.

"You're joking," he whispered.

"No, it's real. We don't set targets because that's too much pressure. But I'd be very surprised if it takes you longer than that."

It was obvious that Mike was sceptical.

"Anyway," continued Kathy, "we need to get busy. The longer you lie in bed doing nothing, the weaker your muscles will get and the harder it will be to recover. Sit up off your backrest, please."

Mike pushed with his fisted hands on the mattress and shuffled upright. Kathy held him.

"The first thing you have to learn all over again is to balance. I'm going to push you sideways. You need to resist me. It will be OK, I won't let you fall over. Louise will be behind you. Trust us."

Mike felt the sore sensitivity of his stumps as he moved. Kathy held him by the shoulders and pushed him. Mike resisted to remain upright. She did this three times from each side, forcing him to increase his resistance. Sue watched. She could see him concentrating. It must be good just to take him out of the introspection into which he could so easily fall.

"That's a great start," said Kathy. "You were really strong. I had to push hard."

"I'm like one of those self-righting punchbags," croaked Mike.

Sue laughed.

"You just can't knock me over," added Mike.

"We haven't finished yet," said Kathy.

She produced two plastic bed blocks and put them each side of Mike on the mattress.

"Grab hold of these two handles and lift yourself up off the bed."

He gripped hard and pushed down, straightening his arms. He felt the weight of his arse lift off the bed, just for a moment, and then he had to lower himself. Kathy was holding him all the time. He did it twice more. He was sweating with the effort.

"Great. I'm going to leave them here. You can practice when I'm not here. Sue can hold you instead of me. I'm also going to leave you these."

From her bag she produced two weights.

"You need to hold these in each hand and then lift them above your head. It's to strengthen your biceps. We have to work on strengthening your upper body, getting your balance and developing your core stability. Now just one more exercise to help this. I'll hold you to keep you steady. Sit up straight. Now rotate your trunk from side to side like this."

She demonstrated. Mike followed.

"Would you like to try and hold him, Sue?"

Sue and Mike's eyes met for a moment. Apart from kisses of greeting and farewell, it would be the first time their bodies had made contact. But there was no time to think about it.

"Come on, Sue," said Kathy briskly.

So Sue held him and Mike rotated his body from side to side. When he had finished, Sue squeezed his warm shoulders and quickly kissed one before she sat back down.

"Some new things tomorrow," said Kathy, "but that's enough for this session. I'll see you tomorrow. You've made a really good start."

Mike was exhausted and breathless.

"Well, you've done brilliantly," said Sue.

He nodded but said nothing. It seemed impossible to him that, exhausted by a few minutes fairly minor activity now, he would in six weeks be doing some kind of walk. What must he have to endure in between? Yes, he'd been fully involved in the activities, trying, pushing himself. But afterwards he felt himself slithering down into despair. Sue watched him fall asleep, worried that he had not been more positive.

During the night he slept fitfully. Each time his body shifted position a little, his stumps grazed the bed and the pain woke him. He lay awake in the early morning, listening to the hum of all the machines that were monitoring him or keeping him alive. So much was needed. Their traces and graphs and figures stood out green and red as the first light undimmed the room. Nurses' voices were speaking quietly around the corner at reception. They were re-assuring. Hearing her footsteps squeak across the floor, he closed his eyes when one came to his bed to check him and fill in the chart. He looked down at the sheets neat over his thighs, still not daring to envisage what was there. He remembered going into a shop when he was young and seeing the woman behind the counter. Her right arm ended just below the elbow, and there was an odd stubby finger-like projection at the end. He had looked away partly because he didn't want her to notice him looking. But it was mainly because he was repulsed by it – the deformity, the paler pink of the stub and, most startling, that the stub had a finger nail and it was painted in bright silver nail varnish. She had been a thalidomide baby rather than an amputee.

Gingerly he put his right hand, the arm which had no tubes and clips fixed to it, under the sheets and rested it carefully on his bandaged thigh. He pressed down slightly but it was so sensitive. He tried to flex his thigh muscle but felt nothing, relieved he could feel only the thick wrapped bandaging. He edged his fingers until they came to the escarpment of his stump end. He shuddered, almost retched. After a pause he forced himself to cup his palm tentatively around the bandaged stump. His eyes closed, his imagination refused to take him further. With a start he touched a tube that came out of the bandaging. *Perhaps for seeping blood,* he thought. He transferred his hand to his left leg, the longer one. By bending forward just a little he could cup his hand below his knee. The same soft but firm bandaging. Another tube. Would he still be able to bend his knee? Would it be easier to operate this leg? He extracted his arm from the sheet and relaxed back onto the raised pillows.

He was alone in the curtained room – he and his stumps and the machines. A thin band of sunshine arrowed in from the curtain edge, bright and warm, like a taunt. He couldn't bear the day when he would have to see his stumps, see them pink and scarred. How could he live, disgusted by his own body?

The next morning Sue arrived at the ICU with a sheaf of newspapers.

"They're from Yorkshire, Mike. The bombers are from Leeds, one from Bradfield. Armed police and bomb disposal teams have carried out raids in Beeston and Holbeck, in Dewsbury and even one in Bradfield."

Avidly he listened as Sue told him about the evidence of CCTV footage, of documents found in the debris at the bomb sites that had led to the raids at 6.30 in the morning. Explosives had been found at another site in Burley, also in Leeds, and 600 people evacuated from their homes. A controlled explosion had been carried out. The same day a car had been found outside Luton railway station with some suspects caught on CCTV. Another raid had been carried out at a house in Aylesbury in Buckingham.

Mike looked at the latest photographs and listened to the stories of survivors, all of them praising the emergency services staff. He learned which of the bombers had been on his train. Mike had told Sue all about Lee, that his tourniquets on his legs had probably saved his life. Sue asked the hospital staff but all she could discover was that Lee had accompanied Mike and the paramedics as they brought him to the ambulance, that Lee had left the ambulance men a torn piece of paper with the names of Mike and Sue on it. After that Lee had disappeared. In the aftermath of the explosions little could be done to find him. But Mike was determined that some time he would discover him. Sue saw that as a good sign: after his original horror at his injuries, Mike was, perhaps without acknowledging it to himself, finding reasons to live.

Then Kathy and Louise arrived, cheerful and brisk and without saying a word, Kathy threw a soft purple fluffy ball straight at Mike. Instinctively, with his free arm, he caught it.

"Nothing wrong with your hand-eye co-ordination, then."

They repeated the balance work of yesterday, Kathy pushing, Mike resisting, Louise ready to support if necessary. Then they extended this to Mike's first attempts to roll over in a controlled way.

"OK, a bit of a rest," said Kathy. "Have you noticed, Mike, how the stump with the knee is resting flat against the bed, but the other one, the shorter one that ends above the knee, is sticking up a bit, not lying flat?"

Mike looked at her suspiciously and nodded.

"I'll explain why. The muscles in the stump with the knee are still intact. They're working almost normally. But the other leg is different because the muscles were cut."

Sue flinched and tensed. She wasn't sure whether Mike wanted to hear this.

"You need to know this," continued Kathy. "It's better if you understand."

"I'm not sure about that," said Mike.

But Kathy was determined. He had to accept, could not stay in denial.

"On this leg," said Kathy and lightly rested her hand on his short thigh stump, "the quadriceps and the hamstring had to be cut."

Kathy watched Mike's face carefully. It was impassive. Sue feared he might retch but thought he'd tuned out, wasn't listening.

"And the adductors were cut, too. They're the muscles that stop your legs splaying out. And our first exercise will be to get them working again."

Mike closed his eyes and breathed in deeply, calming himself. He pushed aside images of red cut sinews and muscles. Kathy placed a pillow between his legs.

"Squeeze as tight as you can."

At first Mike could not make the muscles work. Then there was a twitch and he felt a tightening. Next, lying on his side, he began to work on hip extensions.

"This is the start of controlling your legs again. It's a matter of becoming aware, conscious of what you are doing, in a way you didn't have to be before."

It was tiring work. Kathy left with instructions about repetitions to be supervised by Sue. For once, Mike felt wide awake. The endorphins, he supposed. Sue chatted away, read more of the papers. She told him stories about her pupils at school – she made him smile as she told him of the things they said, of their antics, but behind that he understood her real affection and care for them. He was awed by Sue's love of him, her dedication to him. He saw from the brightness of her eyes that she was elated by his efforts and determination. He rediscovered her beauty, watching her mouth as she read, astounded that her smile could still make his heart lurch as she leaned to kiss him, the smell of her skin as she came close. More peaceful than he had felt for a long time he drifted off to sleep to the comforting familiar sound of her voice, lively and lilting.

Sue watched his eyelids close. There was still the pale purple-green of bruising around his eyes but his lids were clear and pale. His long dark lashes were strangely soft and rich in his thin face. He was a gentle man and she felt it a private privilege to be the only one who knew that. She looked at his strong lean arms warmed with dark hair, his shoulders brown in the shapeless white hospital gown. She knew he needed her, that he had come to life with her – and she had never been attracted to needy men before. What a paradox of strength and determination and vulnerability he was. She filled up with a sense of a possible future. The rehabilitation of him into an independent man again became something they could achieve together. She would help heal him. He would never run as had used to but she had begun to read about paraplegics and their whole alternative sports set-up. There were activities he could do that could replace running. He could successfully continue as the man he was. Slowly he would come to terms with his amputated legs. He would retrain his body and find another form of fitness.

Yesterday, infiltrating her fingers under the smooth, white tightly folded sheet, she had dared to rest her hand on his thigh, needing to re-connect physically, wanting to confirm to him her acceptance of his changed body, but with a sense of mischief, too. But at the first touch of her fingertips his eyes had blazed with anger. She had been shocked at his intensity. She should have known better, she had misjudged. Each time the nurse came to dress his stumps, Mike dismissed her from the room. He could not bear to let her see them, in fact she knew he could not bear to look himself. But it was a matter of time, she knew.

Nobody had said anything to her about the possible effects on his virility. Would he be impotent? Would he still be able to have an erection? Surely they would have warned her – or perhaps they didn't know. If together they couldn't work it out, then nobody could. But she was confident. That was a challenge she would look forward to.

Sue had even begun to plan the kind of place they would need to live. She would research the adaptations necessary to facilitate his mobility and independence. All things were possible and she believed in them as a pair. She remembered how she had told him on one of the first occasions he had woken from his coma and his medication, speaking directly into his ear, that she wanted to marry him. She had been so right about that. She wondered if Mike remembered. Tired, dulled by the heat of the room, at peace with herself, Sue fell asleep in her chair.

Mike didn't remember. He had only the haziest of memories of those first moments of consciousness. Later he woke to see Sue asleep. He had marvelled at her loyalty, sitting for hours on end by his bed. He now watched her, catalogued her integrity and her beauty. More clearly he began to recall their times together, understood how much he needed and appreciated her. He remembered their last evening at home – how many days ago was it? Sue playing his favourite piece on the piano, the total beauty of making love together, her jokes about leadership and initiative. And his last lovely run across the hills. The dull ache down there was back, an ache he did not want to locate precisely. It was a void under there, a terrifying dark unknown place, a horror beneath the pure white sheets. He still closed his eyes, refusing to look when the nurse came to dress his stumps, felt only a temporary soothing coolness as she put a fresh dressing on him. He had brusquely sent Sue out of the room to wait in the corridor even though he knew his dismissal hurt her. At those times he recognised a coldness in himself which gradually began to harden first into a realisation and then loomed into a huge question. How could he punish Sue for the rest of her life with his needs and his deformity? She deserved so much more – she was positive and active and sociable and he would hold her back, would be a brake on her high spirits.

He looked at her: the blonde highlights in her thick curly hair, her long neck as her head lay back against the chair, those full sensuous lips that smiled and laughed so readily, her slender legs in her neat conservative skirt, her hands, fingers half curled, that lay on her lap, her ever-so-slightly lilting walk, the hint of a limp in her brisk stride, the softness of her body, the deftness of her fingers on him. So generous she was. She represented life to him, she danced around his dourness and made him easy.

Not long ago he had been strapped down, staked with tubes and

111

wires and braces which supported and arranged him like a Japanese bonsai, training him into his future of restricted movement. Now he was moving again, gladdened by such small advances. Around him the hospital was busy with the continual everyday bustle which mocked him.

He was different, in a world apart. He was beginning to enjoy the physiotherapy, the feeling of working his body. But after the exercises his perception was confirmed: he was not a normal human being any more, no matter how Sue pretended it was not so. He was a member of a separate species now. A mutant, a deformity, incomplete, broken. He remembered photos he had seen at school as a boy of dark-skinned Indian children holding out their hands for alms, crouched on the dusty roadside, their limbs deliberately broken and twisted by their parents so they could earn more as beggars. Someone had deliberately deformed him and now he too was a beggar, forced to live on other people's kindness and charity. He remembered a picture of a legless man on a home-made trolley, pushing himself along with skinny arms. He shuddered.

How could he inflict himself on this woman to whom life with a whole man could give so much? What could he give her as she watched him over the next months and years, struggling to learn to walk like that first lizard-like creature that flopped up out of the sea and somehow hobbled painfully over the mud onto dry land?

Even now, as he looked at Sue he felt himself drawn to relax back into the certain comfort of his medication and the constant care of nurses, the machines and expertise around him, ready to cope with any emergency. He could live in this artificial self-contained world of support where even his lungs could be worked for him if necessary. He could enjoy this dependence without responsibility, being looked after. Without Sue. Without the obligation to her, without the need to keep her happy, to work in tandem with her.

If he stayed with her he would slowly strangle her, squeeze her spirit out of her. She would challenge him, would not give up on him and his inadequacy. And he knew his inability to rise to her challenge and her belief in him would send him into anger, silence and a deep depression.

As he struggled to this conclusion about himself and Sue, he came to another about himself alone. He would have to re-create himself, build another identity. He could never be the Mike he once had been, the Mike who had met and fallen in love with Sue and been loved by her. He could never run again. This immobile, self-obsessed person he had become had not evolved over time; it had been a sudden quantum change, been dumped on him. The only way he could deal with and develop his new self was on his own. He knew he had always been a bit of a loner and had often resented and regretted this part of himself. Now maybe it would be a necessary strength. He had run mountain marathons on his own, without support from waiting friends or previously dropped stocks of food. He had deliberately wanted to cut out support.

Running was over. He had to compel himself to remember it, accept it as it had been, acknowledge the beauty of it, confront it then put it for ever to one side. Mercilessly he called up his first run after first kissing Sue. He would spare himself no detail. It was his early morning regular long fell run, as he did three times a week. He was pleased that the rain had turned to cold. That morning he seemed to float. He didn't have a particular image of Sue in his head, her presence filled him. No woman had affected him in this way before. She seemed to inspire his mind and body; his movement was lighter, his running smoother. The air was still, a few almost motionless clouds in a blue sky, a pale crescent moon still just visible, the low sun bright on fields, trees casting long shadows. His feet padded with an even rhythm along the lane and then he turned off up a track that led onto the moors. A frost glittered on the heather and rabbits bolted away as he approached. Up he went past the grouse shooting butts, the path skirting the tumbled stone walls of a copse of pine trees. He felt easy and relaxed, his breathing controlled, his steps regular, the only sound his trainers on the gravel.

Up at the reservoir just below the skyline he slowed and stopped. Leaning into the stone wall of the dam he stretched his quads and calves. Then he looked around – at the endless expanse of moor stretching away in all directions, the narrow path winding back among the heather, the flat expanse of black water, rocks and rushes, the sky wide and blue. He felt the winter sun's warmth on his shoulders and on his face. He threw his head back and his arms in the air and shouted "Yes," with a jubilation that became part of the landscape around him. He felt so good, so fit, so happy. He watched a kestrel hovering, heard the slap of a fish jumping in the reservoir and turned to see the ripples spreading outwards. A soft breeze scuffed the surface leaving a ruffled pattern that then faded and disappeared. Life and movement flickered everywhere among this immense spread of moorland that freed him. He felt tuned to the delicate vital beauty, the quick of it, hidden beneath the louring melancholy of this wild place. He wanted to lose himself in Sue as he lost himself in these wild places. He started back and ran with the wind of his speed in his ears, the sound of his trainers in the splash of ice-skimmed puddles. His mind became his body with a great contentment – just a rhythm of steps, of easy breathing, of the swing of his arms, an almost unconscious fast sure-footed selection of where to put his next step. He leapt down the descents, became his instinctive physical body in a maze of unconscious reflex adjustments, a kind of madness in which the rational brain had to be disengaged, disregarding pain and danger. He loved the idea of trusting in man's primeval physical reflexes honed over millennia of hunting and escaping. He celebrated the jarring, the burning in ankles and knees and soles of the feet, all absorbed in a blur of adrenaline, excitement and daring and a pure joy in being able to do this, alone and unseen. And the exhilaration of knowing he would see Sue again that night.

Now all that was over; it was a different lifetime, another world. He looked across at Sue as she shifted in her chair, still asleep, re-arranging her body to ease some stiffness. It was all bleakness. Mike understood with a sudden blinding clarity that if he was to survive and create himself anew he had to cut off not just his past running but his love, too. He had to amputate love, cauterize his heart. Amputate anger, too, and longing and revenge.

He looked up. Sue was stirring again, stretching. When she opened her eyes she would see no difference in him, no change in his position. She would smile and welcome him back. He shut his eyes again. He could not face her. She would notice some change in his eyes. It would be the beginning of a long loneliness.

Sue woke and for the first time thought of her friends at school and who would be teaching her lessons. It was nearing the end of term and her absence would not be so important, no important exam work was being missed. She was supposed to be going on the week-long Highland Hobble into the wilds of Sunart and Ardnamurchan in the far west highlands of Scotland with twenty or so kids – a mixture of the very troubled and deprived and a few 'normal' ones and half a dozen adults. Mike had encouraged her to take part. She had been looking forward to it. But that was now impossible and she would have been replaced on the team. They would be leaving for Scotland any day now. Her place was here with Mike.

10.

Separate

17th July

St Paul's Hospital, London

After ten days in Intensive Care, Mike was moved into a small room off a general ward. Outside his window there was a gap of maybe three yards to a dirty red/yellow brick wall, angled across by grey plastic pipes. There was an air vent from which steam constantly rose, and three frosted glass windows with rust-stained frames. But across the right hand side of his window jutted the branch of a tree full of the maple-shaped leaves of what Sue told him was a plane tree. Mike could see the leaves turn and shake when a breeze blew. Sometimes a blackbird would perch, its glossy tail cocked up, its yellow beak bright. It didn't come every day but when it did come it was always about four in the afternoon. Mike would wait for it to appear, knew that if it had not arrived by the time the clock on the wall said 4.30 it would not be coming. The only other thing that moved out there was the shadow gradually creeping up the wall as the sun went down behind some unknown part of the building – or the rain that dripped from window ledges, and the raindrops that hung below the pipes and then dropped.

Kathy came in.

"Ah, here you are. There's no escape, you know. I've brought you a present."

She presented him with a shiny yellow plastic board.

"It's called a banana board. Guess why!"

She laughed.

"It's so you can get out of bed on your own, or use the commode on your own. I know you hated that hoist. Everyone does."

She pushed the wheelchair next to the bed and slid the arm off. She placed the banana board so it reached from the bed to the chair seat.

"Can you help, Sue?"

"Of course."

"Just put your hand under Mike's stump, so he's got support under his knee."

Mike felt an immediate protest arise, a revulsion that Sue would be touching his bandaged stump, something he had still barely brought himself to do. But the moment was overcome by Kathy's matter-of-fact approach. He had no time to say anything. Sue's hand was there, Kathy had her hands hovering near his armpits in case he overbalanced.

"OK, Mike, up on your hands and slowly move across. Take it steady."

Mike manoeuvred himself to the edge of the board and slowly shuffled sideways along it until he was on the chair. He slumped in there, leaning back into the soft pillows. His face was drenched with sweat.

"No more hoists," said Kathy. "That's a real step forward. And Sue can take you for a walk. Just go up to the main foyer and back, buy a paper or something. Have a cup of tea in the café."

Mike was drained. Somewhere hidden deep down was a sense of achievement, a lessening of humiliation. But suddenly, without warning, he was going public. Sue had taken a neatly folded blanket from a table top and was wrapping it over his lap. She knew hesitation now would mean Mike retreating back into himself. Quickly she wheeled Mike down two long corridors to the café in the foyer. She found an empty table, put Mike's chair next to it and locked the brake on.

"I'll get us two teas," she said.

Mike sat, stunned by his new perspective: he was looking upwards at everybody. If anyone looked at him, they did so with a downwards glance. It seemed to symbolise his new station in life. He quickly noticed one other wheelchair – an old man in pyjamas and fawn dressing gown sat in it, head dozing down on his chest. Automatically, Mike checked – his feet were there, resting on the footplates. Mike found himself almost mesmerised by legs. People were walking or standing or getting up or down. A row of people sat in chairs outside a door marked Oncology. When a number flashed up, one would get up and go inside. They moved so casually, so naturally even if the older ones were slower and more bent over. Mike wondered what endoscopy meant. He had never been in a hospital before and knew nothing of medicine. He watched people patiently queuing at reception. A couple of ambulance men in fluorescent yellow jackets were having mugs of tea.

Sue arrived and sat down with the tea.

"While I was waiting I saw the newspapers. In Beeston yesterday there was a two minute silence to honour the bomb victims. It was in Tempest Street where the police had raided one of the bomber's homes. And they're trying to trace an Egyptian bio-chemistry student who lived near the bomb factory they found."

Mike made no response. He was absorbed in watching people especially the few patients who walked slowly past with crutches, perhaps sent to get some exercise. All had two legs. It was a fact.

He waited for the tea to cool and then drank it, heard the chatter of voices but not the sounds of words. Sue realised he had to get used to this in his own time. From looking round eagerly he had slumped back into himself. Then his eyes closed. She wheeled him back

Not long after, the consultant came in on his rounds.

"Could I have a word, Sue?"

They moved away from Mike's bed.

"He's doing fine," the consultant said quietly. "In fact, he's making remarkable progress. No complications at all. But that's physically. I'm not sure mentally how he's doing. What do you think?"

"This will be very hard for him to come to terms with. I know he could be much worse, much more depressed. He's got a thing about physical deformity."

"We do have a clinical psychologist here, experienced with this kind of situation. Might that help?"

"Mike would run a mile from any psychologist or psychiatrist. In fact, if he believed we thought he needed one that would make him even worse. He'd feel doomed, I'm sure."

"OK, that's fine. I agree with you, you know him far better than I. There is a well know pattern all amputees go through. It's a kind of grieving process – first there's denial, a refusal to accept the new situation; then there's anger, and I think we're seeing some of that. It's better out than in. Then, hopefully, Mike will move on to acceptance and reconstruction – as he puts his body to work again, and renews his life. But it all takes time and individuals work through those phases in their own way."

"I think Mike will be OK. He can be a very determined individual. He'll work round to it, I'm sure."

"We've also got what we call Befrienders – these are people who've been through a very similar experience and could talk to Mike, having come out the other side."

"They might be useful later," said Sue. "I think he has to get somewhere himself first. And presumably he'll meet other amputees as the rehab progresses."

"Yes, and the physios are experienced enough to get him to meet someone with a positive attitude over their coffee breaks. That kind of chat always helps. Mike will see someone ahead of him in the process. He'll see it can be done."

The consultant left to complete his round.

Mike woke later but kept his eyes closed so Sue wouldn't know. He'd felt isolated in the café, seated in his wheelchair. It epitomised his future, a future set apart, a future dependant. He thought of his father. They both knew he was terminally ill with cancer of the kidneys. His Canadian wife had told them he had only months to live. They had been considering flying over once the school holidays had started.

"I want you to phone my father," said Mike.

Sue was surprised but pleased. It was the first sign that Mike was thinking outside himself and taking an initiative. She smiled.

"Just tell him I was involved in the incident, that I'm in hospital but that I'm alright. Don't tell him about my...I don't want him to worry."

"It will be his wife who answers," said Sue. "He's very ill. I'll do it this evening from the flat. They're seven hours behind us."

"Thanks," said Mike. "I suppose I should do it myself but I don't feel up to it and she might want to ask lots of questions."

Buoyed up by Mike's request, Sue wanted to talk to him about her plans for the future, about how they would move to another place and have modifications made to doorways etc, so that Mike could move about in his wheelchair. But she held back, she had to rein herself in, not go too fast. She knew that some time not far ahead he would be able to move to a hospital in Bradfield. Then she would really have him back. On home territory they would begin their new future. She knew she was good at coaxing and cajoling and jollying along, her optimism and hope was contagious and fortifying.

His body had coped with the trauma of amputation, now the challenge was to his mind. She had to be careful to proceed at his speed not her own.

Then Mike said: "Sue, I think you should go back home."

She stared at him. He had been looking directly into her eyes as he said it, in his old way.

"Home? What help would I be there? I want to be here with you. Why should I go home?"

She felt as if the wind had been taken out of her sails. She'd been thinking of them as a team; now he wanted to regain his separateness. He was so locked up in himself, so unaware.

"You're booked on to that school trip," he persisted quietly. "The Highland Hobble. You were really keen on it, backpacking into the wilderness with those naughty kids you've got a soft spot for."

"I've forgotten all about it. It's irrelevant now." Her voice could not conceal her hurt.

"No, it's not. It's fantastic you've been here with me, Sue. But it's exhausting for you – and tedious too, I bet: all this waiting around.

You need a break. It'll do you good – fresh air, exercise, helping kids, midges."

Mike looked at her. How could he tell her that her optimism sometimes got him down, that he found the disparity between them depressing? That sometimes he just wanted to be left alone and not carried forward in her slipstream? Her optimism implied expectations of him that he was fearful he could not live up to.

"I don't need a break. I'm fine. And stop telling me how I'm feeling." Her hurt had turned to anger. "Perhaps the truth is you need a break from me. Perhaps I'm getting on your nerves, is that it?"

She flung the question at him.

Mike cringed at the accusations. Did she not understand? Somehow while she sat with him he could not relax into his weariness. He still had pain, his exercises were tiring , he sometimes even needed an oxygen mask. He still had huge fears for the future. He even felt he was obliged to entertain her, keep her occupied, felt guilty when he awoke from a doze. She was right: he needed space to acknowledge these feelings and deal with them.

She pushed her chair back and stood at the window, looking out. This bloody separateness of his. Only in bed with her and in his running did he ever surrender himself. Did he have any inkling of her anguish for him? He was so self-centred!

She turned to him.

"If you're honest, it's you who needs the space, isn't it? Every man is an island, as you keep misquoting." She laughed bitterly. "You need to be on your own," she said. "Except, of course, from all these good people here."

Does he really not believe I understand how lonely his struggle will be, even with me, she thought? She saw him retreating to the old self he had described, never allowing himself to get close to people. Well, perhaps he should try it and see where it got him.

"OK," Mike said. "Maybe you're right. Is that so bad? Hasn't it all got a bit claustrophobic?"

"Is that what you call it? I call it being close. I call it being supportive."

With the light from the window behind her, he saw only the outline of her face.

"You can have your bloody space," she snapped. "Yes, I will go. Maybe when I get back you will have sorted yourself out. I need to go and get organised."

She strode out without kissing him or glancing backwards. What a selfish bastard he was! He was right: she needed a bloody break as well as him.

Mike stared at the empty doorway, the room suddenly quiet. He hadn't meant to hurt her but he couldn't deny feeling a sense of relief. If he failed to cope over the next few days, if he gave in, he would not have to take Sue's feelings into account. He knew he could so easily relapse into failure and he did not want her to witness it. He breathed more easily.

11.

Gym

St Paul's Hospital, London

The day after Sue left, Mike was wheeled briskly along the corridor by a female porter in flat silent shoes. He felt the slight resistance of his chair's rubber tyres as they turned corners into new corridors. They manoeuvred through swinging doors.

"Careful. Keep your hands off the arm rests or it could be painful."

When she had brought the chair to him in his ward she had begun to fold down the left hand metal foot rest. Watching from his bed he had noticed her suddenly pause, realise her mistake and without looking up at him fold it back into position. He had pivoted onto the banana board and slid across it on to the chair. This was now a familiar routine to him but there was no easing of the indignity he felt for being like a big kid on a slide. He felt the twitching uncontrolled movements of his thigh and knee as they half-remembered their past functions. Kathy had insisted he wear shorts and a T-shirt. He understood with a wry smile her unspoken aim to make him feel more normal, more of an individual than a patient in a hospital smock. Seated in his chair and strapped in, he now felt like a big child in a high chair. All he lacked was a bib.

Now in the corridor the feeling of humiliation continued, he was in a push chair. He still avoided looking at his white-bandaged stumps but he noticed the looks of people in the corridors passing him. In fact, as they approached he locked onto their eyes, waiting for their reaction, soon recognising the pattern: their eyes would first be drawn by a deadly fascination to his stumps sticking over the edge of his chair seat, then a quick glance to his face and, even faster, looking away. He hated their pity, sensed their distaste.

A pair of doors swung open and he got his first sight of the rehabilitation gym. Upbeat rhythmic pop music was echoing around the high room, like a school gym with wall bars all around. He was wheeled across the floor to the far side where there was a table with a pile of folders and plastic trays, and a series of clip boards with biros attached by clean white string. His chair was lined up next to the table, the brakes put on.

"Mike Cooper," said the porter. An unfamiliar physio smiled at him.

"Your first visit, isn't it?"

"Yes."

"I'll be with you in a minute."

He looked around. Was he now part, forever, of this collection of the wounded and derelict? As the music pounded away with its insistent upbeat tempo, these figures forced their limbs and muscles through repetitions on pieces of equipment positioned around the hall. Weights were lifted, pulleys pulled, cross-trainers pounded, bicycles pedalled. There were padded beds, wooden standing frames with sheepskin straps, parallel bars, powered rowing machines. A group of older people walked in a circle, bending knees, changing direction.

Mike looked at them. How had they all arrived at this place? Had they been in car accidents? Had it been their own fault, full of alcohol or drugs? Or were they soldiers, mutilated in their chosen profession? And the old, women as well as men, had they fallen, their broken limb infected with gangrene? Or was it just the insidious creep of old age, the wearing out of joints, the last lap? How many were like himself: random victims who had an extra struggle to fight – the need to make sense of what had happened. A man was on his back on a bed having his flaccid legs manipulated, two others were strapped into standing frames. Two overweight middle-aged men and a woman were passing a rubber ball laboriously between them – for balance and co-ordination presumably.

He looked more closely at their faces: he saw determination and sweat, he saw the sag of weariness or despondency, a dull dogged or resigned face, those who pushed themselves and those who just went through the motions. For the first time he saw close up artificial limbs – weird contraptions of black carbon and beige plastic, with leather strappings and buckles, red Velcro. Why were they so much more horrific than a crutch? One young man had an artificial arm attached below the elbow. His metal fingers were opening and closing as they tried to grasp a stick held by a physio. He saw the young man's concentration, then his head lower in defeat. The physio put her arm around his shoulder, spoke to him. He tried again. Across the room an old man stood stationary on a treadmill, hands on the rests, body slumped forward, looking dazed. He wore long white shorts, grey socks in worn trainers. His legs were scrawny, pale, hairless, knees seemingly swollen. Another physio went over to him, made some remark that made him laugh. He started walking again. Young or old, the keen or the dispirited – the physios seemed to give each the same care and attention. *Sue would make a good nurse,* thought Mike: *developing camaraderie, joining people in a mutually supportive warmth.*

"At this rate," said the physio at the table, "we'll have a strong team for the paraplegic Olympics in 2012."

Mike grunted.

"See that chap over there." She pointed to a huge barrel-chested man in a white singlet sitting in a wheel chair with his back to them. "Go and have a chat with him. He's an interesting man, Jim. He's already training for wheelchair basketball."

Presumably the physio had meant to inspire him. Mike just felt overwhelmed.

"Right, let's get you started," said Kathy, suddenly appearing from

125

an office. "We need to do more work on balance. Wheel yourself over to this bed."

She placed a banana board in position and Mike levered himself up on his hands, swivelled round, and edged his way along the board and on to the cushioned firm plinth bed.

"Sit up straight," she said. "It's party time."

Kathy gave him a fluffy purple bat and brought a red balloon. She batted it to him. He had to reach and bat it back. Deliberately she made him stretch further. A physio stood on either side of his bed in case he overbalanced. As he stretched his arm and bent his torso he felt the muscles working. Only once did he overbalance, and the physio's arms immediately held him and righted him. He was angry with himself. He put in even more effort, fore-handing and back-handing the balloon as hard as he could with his ridiculous bat. He was sweating now.

"OK, that's a great start, Mike. We need to work on strengthening your arms. They'll have more work to do than you're used to. You'll need more upper body strength, stronger back muscles. Into your chair. I want you over there at the lat bar."

Mike slid across the banana board into his chair. He positioned himself under the bar. The physio adjusted the tension and weights.

"I want you to pull that down ten times to start with."

Mike reached up and gripped the bar. He pulled down. After five pulls he felt his muscles working. He was given a brief rest after the ten.

"Right, another ten, in your own time. I've put a little more weight on. Then that will be enough for the day."

It was hard but Mike found himself automatically refusing to be beaten. After the last pull he was exhausted.

"That's a very positive first session," said Kathy. "Congratulations. See you back here tomorrow."

Wheeling himself back along the corridors, accompanied by a porter, Mike felt good. He understood from his running that exercise released endorphins which produced a feel good factor. He was elated. But back on his bed, the exhaustion returned and with it a soreness. He seemed to be aching in every muscle of his body. The elation had been temporary. He recalled the others in the gym, the hard journeys they were all on. He wanted Sue back to bolster him, but he had sent her away. He gave in, cast down by the size of the struggle ahead of him. He asked for and was given painkillers, then drifted off to sleep.

Five days later, after lunch, Mike asked to be wheeled out into the hot sunshine next to a bench that overlooked a small rose garden. It was his birthday. Time for celebration! On his bedside table were cards from the hospital staff. One card had come in the post with Sue's familiar handwriting. Unopened, her white envelope was slotted into the book on his lap. Huge oak trees shaded the place and a slight breeze rustled the leaves. Beyond the rose garden was a stretch of lawn and a motorised lawn mower was moving steadily along it, leaving strips of different shades of green. Mike could smell the new mown grass. He could hear the steady drone of traffic on the other side of the hospital wall, could see the red tops of London buses passing, saw faces turned to look dispassionately into the hospital grounds as the bus stopped at a traffic light or a zebra crossing. The bus started off again and the faces disappeared. Another appeared. The busy noisy world was continuing to go about its business, lawful or unlawful. He relished the air on his face, warm and benign. He thought of Sue but it was in a strange, detached way. He hoped it wasn't raining too much for her.

He thought then of his father lying in his hospital bed, far away on the Pacific coast, neatly tucked in, awaiting his death, medicated into a painless solitude. Was he accepting or fighting it? Fighting it, if he knew anything about his father. Was he even faintly aware it was his son's birthday? Mike opened his eyes and watched an old man in pyjamas and dressing gown move slowly along the path beside the hospital wall, pushing a zimmer frame. The man paused frequently to rest, restore his strength. So much was about being alone, the essential problems of life had to be dealt with alone: the struggle of the mind to cope and come to terms. His father's wife would sit with him and maybe read to him; Sue could hold his own hand and chat and laugh and plan. But that was outside on the surface, in the air waves, a feeling like the warmth of the sun. It comforted but didn't really affect cells in his brain. The old man moved forward again, persisting, shuffled steadily across Mike's vision and out of sight round a corner.

He took Sue's birthday card out of his book but the sound of laughter made Mike turn his head to the left. A group of half a dozen men and women appeared from round the corner where the old man had gone. They were jogging, in shorts and singlets, a nice easy pace. He could hear the crunch of their trainers on the gravel of the path. Faintly he heard their voices and another laugh. He recognised one of his nurses. She gave him a brief wave. He saw the steady rhythm of their legs, their slender bodies upright, bent arms swinging, knees high, strides easy. The group ran in pairs. Mike's eyes followed them as they ran along the path and then swung out through the hospital gates and disappeared. Then the path was empty and silent again.

It had taken them less than thirty seconds to pass across his sight, coming round one corner and disappearing round another. He found himself still staring at the gates. He felt his mouth open and closed it, felt that he had held his breath, that his hands clutched each other tightly, that his shoulders were tense. It was the unexpectedness, the shock – not just of the runners appearing but of the sensations he felt in his own body, the sense even of his own legs moving along with theirs.

He shuddered. It was grotesque. He was not one of them any more: their fluid movement into and out of the shadows and sunlight under the trees. He was marooned captive in his chair. He forced himself to look at his truncated legs, sticking out from the seat of the chair, useless appendages, unnatural, disgusting to any normal person. And the warm sun that shone on him shone on them too, treated him the same. It seemed not a blessing but a taunt.

There were a few other patients now, sitting on benches, sticks and crutches placed beside them. This was his community now, the community of cripples. This was his new home. He had to break with his previous life, avoid all comparisons with it. He had to re-invent himself, live by a completely different set of standards. Sue, children, running the mountains, even his career – all had to be jettisoned. He had to start again. He would never run, but he could learn to walk again. In his new limited world, away from the able-bodied and their hopes, he would re-create his own self-respect. That Islamic lunatic bastard would not defeat him. This was his birthday wish to himself.

The more he had to sacrifice to achieve this, the more would be his grim satisfaction. But it would be a labour of solitude. He knew this now with a final clarity. He had to do it alone. What he had brought to his running he had now to bring to his walking: a solitary perseverance which he had to come to love just as he had loved the pains of his mountain endurance.

He would not move back to a hospital in the north, he would remain in London for his rehabilitation. He could not be near Sue because he had to split from her. If he was near her, the temptation would be to rely on her and that would make him weak. That part of it was selfish, he knew. But deeper in his mind he was utterly convinced he could not mar and limit her life by being with her in his mutated state. He could not bear to think of his scarred stumps, those abrupt ugly sawn-off ends touching her beautiful body, his grotesque twitchings.

He jerked himself away from the horror of their making love. It was so obvious it could not happen. But how could he tell her? How to convince her? How could he hurt her?

He inserted his thumb under the flap of the envelope and slit it open. The card was a water colour of a terrace of dark stone houses on a steep hill backing onto fields with drystone walls, with a brown moorland in the background partly lit in a gleam of sunshine. *Carefully chosen*, he thought: *Yorkshire, home.*

Too late for that, an impossible dream.

He opened the card and read: *I love you, my dear dear man – exasperating and foolish (and wrong) as you sometimes are. See you soon, midge-bitten and weather-beaten.* He counted nine kisses. No, it could not be. Already he was closing himself down, shutting himself off. He replaced the card in its envelope and stared dispassionately at the red and yellow roses.

12.

Rose-garden

26th July

St Paul's Hospital, London

On the day Sue was returning from Scotland it was raining, warm soft summer rain drifting down on a windless afternoon. Mike had asked permission to wheel himself into the summerhouse that stood at the corner of the rose garden. The folding doors had been opened wide so that he could remain dry inside but still feel the air and have an uninterrupted view of the pond and fountain just in front. In a few minutes Sue would be here. He had texted her to say he was in the rose garden. *Very romantic,* she had replied. She was in a taxi on her way from Kings Cross, held up in traffic. Mike sat tense and upright in his chair, fingers unconsciously gripping the arms, knuckles white. He wore a sweater and shorts, a thin waterproof jacket thrown over his lap and stumps. Now the moment had come he was scared – frightened of how much he would be wounding her, frightened that he would waver in his determination, frightened of how much he still loved her. He silently repeated to himself, *I must do this because it is best for her. It is because I love her.* She would be totally unprepared for what he had to say. She would come with her smile and her cheerfulness. Somehow he had to keep her high spirits at a distance, refuse to be drawn in. He must not doubt himself.

He saw her come around the corner and into the garden. Her hood was up and she had a rucksack slung over her shoulder. She waved and he saw the flash of teeth as she smiled. Briskly she walked around the perimeter of the rose beds, that slightly limping walk he was so familiar with. She seemed to race towards him and yet time in his mind was paralysed. He felt a great hot surge of love for her. He could not do this to her. He needed her, loved just being with her.

And then she was with him, stepping inside the summerhouse, her warm rain-moist lips kissing him on the lips, raindrops from her hood falling onto his face.

"Hey, you're looking so well," she said, her fingers stroking his face. "Sunburnt even. They let you sit out in the rain as well as the sun. Brilliant. Scotland was great. I'm so glad I went. Thank you. I know I'm late but look what I've brought you, birthday boy."

He watched her, immediately busy, undoing the straps of her rucksack, her fingers whose touch he still felt on his cheeks so deft. He could not do this to her.

She lifted out a dark green, gold embossed presentation box.

"Forty year old Bowmore single malt – your favourite. You deserve it."

She grinned mischievously.

"And I've brought a couple of little plastic glasses." She looked around conspiratorially. "It'll do you good. We'll have a little celebration."

She started to unscrew the bottle top.

"You were right about making me go, what an experience. Unforgettable. I must tell you about one of the kids, Kirsty. What a life she leads, and so brave!"

How could he start?

"Please, Sue, not now. Thanks very much but I'll have to check I'm allowed to drink it."

"Oh, come on, it will be OK."

But she saw his face was drawn and tight. He hadn't smiled, hadn't responded to her kiss.

"Well, if not now, it won't be long. And I've got another bottle for when you get home. And I've brought you something else. There's a couple of books and your laptop."

She placed them on the wooden floor, next to his wheelchair.

"And …"

She rooted round in her rucksack, in a side pocket, and brought out a small box.

"What is it?"

"Your real birthday present – a new iPod. I've put on it all your favourite stuff: some Dylan and other bits and pieces – and of course the Mahler. You can put your ear phones in and listen to your heart's content without disturbing anyone."

She leaned forward and kissed him, her full lips so warm and soft. She opened her eyes and Mike saw them bright with enthusiasm. She was so full of the joy of being with him again. She had thought about him, planned this meeting because she wanted it to be special. It was Sue all over, making an occasion, a little celebration. This was so hard. Her high spirits, her energy and optimism brimmed over.

"Sue, I have to tell you something."

She finished pouring out the whiskey. She looked up and saw his face, twisted away from her.

"What's the matter? Everything's going all right, isn't it? You look fighting fit, you're getting better. I can see it."

Carried along in her own hopes, she had no suspicions. He forced himself to look at her. Her eyes were concentrated directly on his eyes, searching for a meaning, aware now of something portentous.

"It's not to do with the hospital. It's really difficult. I don't know how to say it."

Sue leaned forward, took his hand in hers and stroked it with her fingers. The warmth and gentleness of her.

"You can tell me, whatever it is. Go on. Try me."

He took his hand away and closed his eyes. In the silence that waited to be filled with his words he heard the soft falling water of the fountain, the drip of rain drops from the summerhouse eaves, the dull roar of London traffic beyond the walls.

"I don't want to move up to a northern hospital. I want to finish my treatment here, all my rehabilitation."

"What!" Sue was stunned. Her words tumbled out. "Why's that? Is that what the consultant recommends? Is it because they have more specialised staff down here? What have they said?"

"No, it's not because of any of that."

He drew a deep trembling breath.

"Well, why then?"

"Because…"

"Yes?"

"Because…This is really hard, Sue. I love you so much."

Sue looked hard at him, wanted to hug him, wanted to stroke his face. But she felt his coldness, felt the barrier he had constructed between them.

"And I love you, you silly man."

From somewhere came to her a sense of desperation, a realisation that this was a key moment.

"I had a chance to do some thinking in Scotland, when I couldn't sleep and the tent was slapping like a wild thing in the storm. The noise was incredible. Mike – it's all going to be fine. You and me. This is going to be the making of us. We're going to be the best team."

"No. Sue, please. Listen to me. We…we have to separate."

He looked away from her. Through the rain he saw an ambulance drive in through the gates, blue lights flashing, heard birdsong. This was unreal, he could not believe he had managed to say it. Sue was dumbstruck. Everything in her head had been about their future. During her journey down from Scotland and then from Bradfield she had been looking forward to seeing Mike again.

"What! You're crazy! No, that's ridiculous."

This was when he had to carry on, drive it through, not turn back.

"I've thought it through. I've had more time than you. Lying in bed, sitting out here in my chair, what else have I been doing but thinking about you?"

She had to rescue this. How could she convince him? He must still be in shock, his mind not able to function properly. She had to be calm.

133

"So how have you thought your way through to this conclusion? You're so wrong. I'm not going to let you."

"You have to understand it's for the best. I'm doing it for the best, for both of us."

She stared at him.

"Well, certainly not for me."

"Yes, certainly for you." A certainty filled him, a sense of unselfishness. "You're young and lovely and full of life and plans, and I love you for being those things. That hasn't changed, and it won't change. But I can't bear you to be saddled with a cripple for the rest of your life."

"But…"

"No, let me finish. You deserve better than someone like this. I'll come to be a millstone round your neck. I'll hold you back. You're a good person, I know that more than anyone. But you'll come to resent me – the extra work I'll be, the drudgery of looking after me, having to turn down opportunities because I can't do things with you."

Sue saw he was far away from her, wrapped up in his own conviction, trapped.

"Mike…"

"No, please. I've started now. Let me try to finish. It's hard enough. I know you'll try not to complain. I know you'll always see the best of things. You're like that, always so positive. And I won't be like that. I'll be frustrated and angry. You know what I'm like. And gradually I'll eat up all that love and high spirits you have. I'll bring you down."

She loved him. It was all she was aware of. She wanted to enfold him, coax him out from behind this artificial barrier he had constructed for himself.

"Oh, my poor Mike, you have been in such misery."

"No, it's not that. There's a selfish side, too. Splitting up would be best for me, too. I know that now."

"Why on earth do you think that?"

"Because I can never be what I want to be with you."

"But you are what I want you to be. You are. You haven't changed. You're still Mike."

"No, I'm not. You're kidding yourself about that." Now he had to push on, resist her, resist his need to let her hold him and make him laugh again. "You want to be so supportive now and that blinds you. I know for absolute certain I can never be what I want to be with you. I'm soiled goods. I'm like a bird with a broken wing that, no matter how you care, cannot be mended. They pinion birds, don't they, to stop them flying? That's what the bomber's done to me. If I was a dog or a horse I'd be put down. So every day with you – and it would not be your fault – I would be reminded of what I'm not, what I can't do that I would love to do, love to do with you. I've thought and thought about this and I can't get away from it. It is how it would be. I couldn't bear it. It would destroy me and so it would destroy you too."

She knew she had lost him. He had made his mind up. When that happened he would not change it. Her heart thumped and her stomach lurched. He had never spoken before at such length about his feelings, never articulated himself like this. How he must have forced himself to get to this point. But she could not give in, could not let him make this huge mistake.

"Mike. It need not be like that. You know that."

He heard her voice, her soft integrity. But he heard something he hadn't heard before: a timidity, a sadness, a pleading. And he hated himself.

"I don't know that." He said it harshly, bitterly. "I know me better than you know me. I know how pathetic I can be. How weak I can be. I see some very brave people in my ward, people worse off than me, people completely paralysed from the neck down, who've been in horrendous car accidents. I knew about paraplegics, I'm one now. But I didn't know about tetraplegics. And somehow they fight it, they make jokes. They have hope, for God's sake. In my good moments I think I have hope too. But I can't patch the old life together, Sue. I have to start again. I have to build myself up – literally from the arse up."

He laughed. Sue heard a weird contortion of sound, a cry.

"And it's not just to do with my legs. That will be hard enough but I think I can do that. That's maybe the easiest part because it's measurable, and it's to do with muscle and exercise and perseverance and I think I'm good at that. It's like when I started running, building up the endurance and the strength. No, it's putting my mind together again, adjusting, coming to terms, finding a new manageable way through."

"But you can do all that with me."

"No, I can't, Sue. I can only do it on my own. With no one watching, no one helping. No one seeing me cry like a baby, rage like lunatic. No one – least of all you – being disappointed in me. And doing it on my own, if I succeed, will make me stronger. And if I fail, well, there's only me involved."

He stopped, his voice breaking. She could see his hands trembling, his face gaunt and taut and turned away from her.

Now Sue was filled with a bitter anger. Her voice rose.

"And me, Mike? Have you thought about me? All my plans were with you, having children with you, being a family. That's what I want. That's what I told you when you were in and out of your coma. That's what I still believe."

Mike was tired now, with a deep weariness. His voice was flat.

"I know this will hurt you, Sue."

"Hurt! You and your bloody precious solitude, doing things on your own, your ice-cold will. You don't want me. You don't want anybody."

Now he must become the world-weary consoler.

"But it will pass, Sue. Time heals and all that. And you're young enough to start again, build up another relationship. You won't think so now but that's how it will be. You'll move on in your way, like I will in mine."

"You're a sad man, Mike."

She looked at him in his wheelchair, wanted to look at him in the eyes but his face was turned away. She hated him now, hated him for his delusion of self-sufficiency, hated him for disposing of her so quickly. Mike turned his head slightly and she saw how haggard he was.

"And what about when you're strong again? Will there still be no room for me?"

Mike heard in her a desperate hope and had to stamp on it.

"Perhaps I won't be strong again. That's the likeliest outcome. Most people aren't heroes. And you can't wait for what might not happen."

Now she felt a childish petulance, as if Mike was giving her a parental sermon.

"You can't stop me," she snapped.

"No, I can't. But that would be worse for me, to know that you were waiting."

Now he wanted her to go, to leave him here alone with the rain softly falling, in the faint scent of roses in the damp air, to leave him here in his broken peace, in his broken pieces. He heard her voice as if from a great distance, powerless, pointless.

"I thought it might help, be something to look forward to, aim at."

Sue sensed her own pathetic yearning, despised herself for it. Mike heard it and hated it, hated it because he had corrupted her from what she was, from what he loved about her. He turned to look at her, his eyes blazing. His voice was hard and bitter.

"Sue, I haven't yet learned to look at myself, at these bloody stumps, these bloody useless fucking stumps, fag-ends of legs. I hate them, I hate it all. I have to be in this community of cripples. This is where I belong until I can walk. I am not normal, not proper any more. And then when I graduate, pass out from this training place, hobble out with my crutches and my chair and my plastic fucking legs – then I have to disappear to some place, some wild desolate place where I might find some peace. Away from eyes that can't look away from me, are appalled by me, away from pity, away from this world where people can blow themselves up and kill children and praise God at the same time."

Sue quailed before his onslaught.

"Mike!"

"I want no part of it. Please understand."

His anger was gone. Sue saw his real loneliness, his eyes moist with tears. She saw his pain. This was the Mike who had called to her and whom she had answered.

"Sue. I have to do it, it's the only way. I'm sorry. I'll hurt no less than you. I love you. I love you and hate me and that's why I must do it this way."

Her heart went out to him. He was right. She saw it now, clear and horrifying.

"There's nothing I can say, is there? Nothing that would change your mind?"

"No. Please, Sue, help me by letting me do this. Try not to hate me."

She took his hand again and enfolded it in hers. He did not resist.

"Hate you! I think you're so wrong and I'm very angry. But love doesn't just stop like that."

She felt his fingers tighten on hers. Felt the bond still between them.

"Not for me, either," Mike said softly. "That's why it hurts so much."

She would let him go, let him make his way in his own way. There was no alternative. She had to accept it. But she would wait for him. There would be a time when he would be ready to come back to her. She knew that. But she must not say it. She would keep it secret, hibernate her love – their love – in her heart until it was time.

"I know what I do hate," she said quietly. "I don't think I've ever hated before. It's so pointless and so self-destructive. But I hate that man who blew you up, and I hate that belief that made him think it was the right thing to do."

"I know, that's something else I have to try and sort out in my head."

"I won't stop loving you, Mike. It's been the best part of my life, and the best part of me."

He held her hands tightly.

"We won't see each other again," he said. He had to say it. He was so near to giving in.

"I can't believe that," she said, her resolution hidden deep already.

"Please, you must."

Sue stared at his face. She was photographing it: his eyes, the colours of his hair, the shape of his mouth, his skin, the lines at the corners of his eyes and mouth. She stood up. She leaned forward and kissed him on his forehead, let her lips lie there. Every sense of his being centred there, on the feel of her lips.

"I will think of you every day," he said. "I cannot stop it. You will be in a secret warm part of my head. But I will not communicate with you again."

He leaned forward and kissed her on the lips. She closed her eyes to record the touch of him. Mike swivelled his chair around so that she could not see his face. She knew he was compelling himself to do this and she knew also it would be a relief for him.

"I will write to you," she said. "E-mail you."

Immediately she wished she hadn't said it. Mike said nothing. He could not speak, his throat was choked. Then she moved away, picked up her rucksack and slung it over her shoulder. She stepped outside the summerhouse into the still-falling rain.

He watched her turn and walk away, slowly but with that same slight lilt that was so touching. Would she turn and look back at him? And if so, would he stretch out his arms to her and would she run back? He could do it, reverse it all. He wanted to, he would. He watched her. At the far corner of the rose garden Sue paused. She turned and waved but before he could wave back she was gone.

He slumped back in his chair, closed his eyes, stretched his head back and gave a cry of anger and frustration and love and fear. Alone on the hills he had felt free; alone here he was terrified.

"No," he moaned. "No, I cannot do it."

Now he was truly alone. He opened his eyes. Goldfish glinted and twisted, circling endlessly in the rain-dimpled pond. Rain drops glistened on yellow flowers. The plastic tumblers of whisky stood on the window sill, golden with the light behind them.

Part 3:

One Valley

August – November 2005

13.

Demonstration

6th August

Maccleston

It was ten o'clock on a Saturday morning when Barry pulled into the car park on the industrial estate. They'd been able to follow small groups of mostly young men who'd all had been ambling in the same direction – like a small crowd unexcitedly assembling for an end-of-season, dead-rubber, mid-table League Two football match. Barry let the engine of his Ford Focus idle as he and Lee checked the scene. The car park serviced a huge warehouse, an oblong building with windowless walls of dark green polymer cladding. The wall that faced the car park had four numbered doors large enough for lorries to reverse into. The yellow steel roller blinds on the doors were all closed down to ground level.

"Bloody hell! Look at that lot. They're expecting trouble."

On the opposite side to the warehouse the car park ended at a grassed bank about twenty feet high. Along the top of it stood a line of policemen in yellow high visibility jackets and visored helmets, some carrying curved transparent riot shields. Behind them was a line of parked white police vans with more police strolling about.

"We'll park at the back," said Barry. "As far away from trouble as we can. I don't want the car damaged."

Barry took care of his vehicles, had them souped up, added throaty-roaring, stainless steel twin exhausts, blue halogen lights, wide wheels and flared arches, an aerodynamic spoiler – all this so the car performed above its basic specification. Or appeared to – it was mostly about appearances, thought Lee. In that respect it was a bit like Barry himself, an extension of him. But there were never any speakers, no sound system. Barry liked silence. Barry brooded, turned things over in his mind, came to conclusions. He'd been like that even as a kid: full of rapid physical action, a ruthless tackling terrier on the football pitch, an enforcer they called it nowadays. But he was also a quiet thinker, someone who wanted to work things out before he pronounced an opinion. He was a calculator. Many of the lads at school had found him slightly sinister, a controlled presence that could erupt into targeted vicious action. But he'd been a good mate. If he liked you he stood by you.

Barry pulled into his chosen parking space, turned off the ignition and opened the window.

"This looks a shambles," he said.

Spread across the car park were groups of men, standing or wandering about. Lee could see only two women. The men all wore jeans, some with faces concealed within hoods. Many were talking into mobiles. Some sat on barriers around the car park, smoking, or leaned on lamp posts, hands in pockets.

"Well, they're waiting for something to happen," said Lee. "And the police won't mind the overtime and a bit of licensed baton swinging when the time comes."

They heard a loudspeaker announcement, spotted the car with a loudspeaker on its roof in the middle of the car park. But the amplification was so bad they couldn't decipher what was said. No one seemed to take any notice, no one moved position.

"So this is the English Patriotic League in all its patriotic glory," said Barry.

Two men wandered past them, one wrapped in a Union Jack, the other in a flag of St George. Both had bull terriers on leads.

"It's all waiting to kick off," said one, his voice excited.

"Yeah, it's going to kick off big time," said his companion.

Barry grunted.

They heard the beating of rotor blades getting louder. Lee looked up to the grey sky, peered forward through the windscreen and saw a small white helicopter circle over head, bank, circle again, then hover.

"Christ! It's getting like bloody Iraq," muttered Barry.

"Iraq!" exclaimed Lee.

It was just a car park on a mild grey day, some men with shaved heads who thought themselves hard, a couple of overweight birds with blonde ponytails, a couple of flags; both sides casually getting ready for a game to start, no urgency. Barry had no idea.

"I wouldn't trust any of this lot with a 50p loan, let alone my life," continued Lee. "They're just a bunch of football hooligans. Casuals United, did you say they called themselves?"

A man in shirt sleeves carefully leaned a placard against a barrier, turned away from the slight breeze, dipped his head and lit up a fag.

GOD BLESS OUR TROOPS.

"Wonder when he last went to church," said Barry.

It had been Barry's idea to come. He'd suggested they suss out the EPL in action, "Judge their quality," he'd said. The occasion was a parade of the 5th Yorkshire Fusiliers in their home town of Maccleston, home from a tour of Iraq. From the internet he'd discovered the EPL planned a presence here, a counter-demonstration against the Muslim protestors the EPL had somehow discovered were going to turn up. With mobile phones and the internet it was easy to organise gatherings but almost as easy to hear about them. Barry had thought Lee would have wanted to come just to support his fellow soldiers, or ex-fellows. But Lee had surprised him by not being enthusiastic.

"That part of my life is all over, Barry," he'd told him. "Since the court martial I've not kept up with any of my army mates. They've texted me but I've never replied."

Barry knew not to probe. Lee would say only what he wanted to say and he obviously did not want to say any more now. So Barry had shifted tack: what could ordinary citizens do to combat Muslim terrorism? What were other citizens already doing to defend their country? He'd talked about Combat 18 and the National Front, about the BNP and other newer organisations that were spontaneously springing up because people were not happy with the politicians and lawyers, with political correctness, with soft-soaping the Muslim community. There was a group called SIE – Stop Islamification of Europe. There was British Citizens Against Muslim Extremists.

They arose out of a frustration he understood, said Barry. Nobody spoke for ordinary people any more, certainly not the mainstream politicians. In the meantime the country was changing for the worse.

"Brought to its knees," Barry had said. "Humiliated. We're a laughing stock."

So they'd agreed to come here to see how effective and impressive the English Patriotic League were. Was this a group Lee could align himself with? Would Lee perhaps see them as patriots he could support?

Lee was looking at the bull terriers. One was black and muzzled, the other white with a black, metal-studded collar. Its pink tongue lolled out between white teeth. A muzzle made a dog more threatening, not less.

"Does it look like your cup of tea then, Barry?" asked Lee as they both looked out of the car windows.

Barry snorted.

"They had some good ideas on the blog. And getting some muscle in to go with the ideas is good. But this lot! There's no organisation. They're just hangers on, looking for something to do. They're not like you and me, Lee. They'd run a mile if there was any real danger. Look at that lot, all dressed up."

Four burly young men passed by, shouting and laughing loudly. They were dressed all in black, their T-shirts announcing MIG, Men in Gear.

"It's the local football firm," said Barry. "Today's just another excuse to play at acting. Like when we were kids – playing at soldiers or cowboys and Indians. They're still at it."

"Yeah, but look over there," said Lee. "That looks a bit more serious."

At the side of the car park furthest away from the police a small crowd was gathering around a group of six men, faces hidden by black balaclavas sewn into masks. Over their beer bellies were black T-shirts badged with the St George flag. Two of the men held up a flag, a white crescent moon and star on a green background.

"That's the Pakistan flag," said Lee.

A third man was trying to light a corner of it with a cigarette lighter. He was not succeeding.

Barry laughed. "Typical!"

Two more of the balaclava'd men held up placards:

SAY NO

TO SHARIAH LAW

A sixth man walked over to a nearby car, opened the boot and lifted out a small green petrol can. Lee saw that police were watching through binoculars. The sixth man rejoined the group and doused the flag with petrol. He addressed the small assembly of watchers:

"Islamist extremists have been unchallenged in our country for more than ten years. They recruit on our streets and in our colleges, and the government does nothing. It is up to us to challenge them if no-one else will. It is up to us to fight for our country."

He took out his mobile phone to photograph the event, and gave a signal. The man with the lighter flicked it gingerly at a corner of the flag. It caught alight and was hastily dropped to the ground, the three men scuttling away. There was a smattering of clapping and ragged cheering. On the tarmac it burned away with bright flames which quickly died down. It smouldered there giving off grey smoke. The watchers turned away and wandered off.

"Not even filmed properly, no newspaper reporters. Bloody amateurs. Hopeless. A joke," said Barry.

He looked at his watch.

"Almost time for the parade. I've had enough of this. Let's see what the opposition's like. I'm not leaving the car here. We'll find a spot in town.

147

They found a parking place and went to stand on the main shopping street. Both sides of the street were lined with people and it had been closed off to traffic. They heard the band before they saw it: drum beats and trumpets. All heads turned towards the bottom of the street to see the band turn the corner: black busbies, grey long coats, glistening brass of the instruments. As the music became louder with the band's approach Lee felt a lump rise in his throat. Beneath the music he heard the march of boots. He'd had no contact with the Fusiliers even though they too for a time had been stationed in Basra. Now the crowd was clapping, old women and children were waving union jacks. Lee saw a few old men in berets, medals pinned to their chests, stand to attention and salute. A middle-aged woman with a shopping bag in her left hand held up a placard in her right:

THANK YOU FOR YOUR COURAGE

Then to Lee's left, ahead of the troops, the entrance to a shopping arcade was suddenly filled with men dressed in black. Lee saw they were Asians, a few hooded, most with beards, all with black skull caps, in Asian dress or black leather jackets. They were yelling and one voice was amplified. Lee saw a man with a megaphone, saw placards raised and waved:

YORKSHIRE SOLDIERS
GO TO HELL

BRITISH GOVERNMENT IS
TERRORIST GOVERNMENT

FREEDOM OF EXPRESSION
GO TO HELL

A line of police in yellow high visibility jackets ran across the road and stood in front of the protestors. The police did not appear to try to move them away. Lee heard booing from the crowd in that area. He turned back to watch the band as it passed, the drum major pounding his great drum. Then came the soldiers, marching five abreast in their desert camouflage kit, about 200 of them, their black SA80 rifles on their shoulders, purple berets worn aslant, chins up, faces proud. The last soldiers carried their regimental standards. The clapping grew louder, the crowd cheered. Still looking straight ahead, they marched passed the protestors. Lee saw another placard held up:

BUTCHERS

OF

BASRA

Behind that there was larger placard: a collection of colour photographs of children, bandaged and bloodied, sitting on makeshift beds, or lying in the street.

Lee surged with anger. He clenched his fists. It flashed back to him as if it was yesterday – Camp Sandbox outside Basra.

"Kebab the fucking raghead, Lee," Jimmy had yelled, knotting cords to fasten the Iraqi's wrists and ankles so that he was slung between the forks of the dirty yellow fork-lift truck, the whites around the man's black eyes wide with terror, his voice whimpering low pleading sounds. Lee had extended the silver mast ram to its full height, five metres from ground level, watched the oily black chains ratchet round as the forks whined past his eye-line and above his head, the Iraqi's body immobile, suspended in the air. At the full extension he had pushed the tilt lever so the Iraqi hung downwards, his weight chafing his rope-tied ankles and wrists. Lee released the handbrake, pushed the short gear stick and swivelled the truck round. They were in the huge old stone-built warehouse used as the camp store. It was crammed with gear, baking hot under the corrugated iron roof, the air thick with dust and insects. Going as fast as he could Lee raced the truck along the narrow passageways between the piled high boxes and pallets of supplies, the neoprame tyres screeching round tight corners, the Iraqi's body helplessly flung around, bouncing on the prongs. The place reeked of scorched rubber, the high whine of the electric truck engine amplified in the confined spaces. Then the smell of the man's shit.

Lee remembered shouting, thumping the truck's metal frame with his fist, laughing wildly – his mind bursting again with adrenalin-pumping frenzy of last night's raid on the militia stronghold and the rescue mission. Again he was flinging his Snatch Landrover round street corners of Basra in the blackness, tyres howling, racing across junctions. Jimmy next to him was screaming: "Contact left! Contact left!" and firing his rifle through his open door, his body arched awkwardly in his seat, his back wedged up against the dashboard. There was the crackle and flash of gunfire, flames from burning buildings, Mac screaming in the back that he was wounded, shot in the artery below his shoulder, his fist clamped fast to it to stem the blood flow, Lee desperate to get his mate back to the base medics.

Remembering it, he feels no shame or regret. He was acting under orders – not explicit orders, of course. But all the men knew the officers wanted the detainees 'conditioned.' All parts of the same world: Camp Sandbox, his court martial, prison, the London bombings, here. All real.

"Bastards! fucking bastards!" he muttered, as he now looked at the protestors.

"Easy," said Barry. But this was the reaction he had hoped for.

"They kill their own," said Lee. "Those kids, those women, are killed by their own. Suicide bombers set off bombs in markets, outside the mosques of each other's bloody sects. They don't give a shit for their own people. A dozen men from this regiment have died trying to help those fucking people."

Barry gripped Lee's shoulder.

"Easy, mate."

Now the soldiers had passed, some of the crowd turned its attention to the Muslim protestors. Lee could barely contain his anger, and he knew he was not the only one. He now saw behind the Muslim men a small group of women standing round a shop doorway wearing head to toe black burkas and niqabs. One held a digital camera and was looking at the LD screen as she pointed it. The bearded man with the microphone was now shouting:

"Our anger has been rising, this parade is the final insult to us."

Another, his head covered in a black and white checked scarf, only his eyes visible, raised another placard:

MUSLIMS RISE
AGAINST
BRITISH REPRESSION

An old man in a tweed trilby stood in front of them, shaking his finger at them, his voice quivering with emotion as he shouted: "How dare you say that! It's disgraceful!"

A woman with a child in a pushchair shouted: "You're disgusting! You upset people!"

Barry smiled. "Upset people!" he repeated. "We're so bloody civilised. Those fuckers tried it again, didn't they, just two weeks after the first bombings that you were involved in, in London. The same trick – rucksacks loaded with explosives. They'd have ripped kids like that in half. Luckily they ballsed it up – only the detonator caps exploded and no-one was hurt. They're merciless."

"Look at those," said Lee. "Unbelievable!"

Two more placards appeared:

SHARIAH
THE TRUE SOLUTION –
FREEDOM
GO TO HELL

ISLAM WILL
DOMINATE THE WORLD –
FREEDOM GO TO HELL

Two grey bearded Sikhs in their turbans turned away in disgust, spitting on the pavement. A white-haired woman with two heavy shopping bags remonstrated angrily to the police who were forming a protective line in front of the protestors, now having to push away some of the crowd.

Lee felt his anger replaced by a great respect for these people, an affinity with them – ordinary people, old and young, shoppers and workers and young mothers, people who felt insulted, invaded, dispossessed. They were decent folk, bewildered by a point of view they could not understand but did not like and were powerless to do anything about. They saw proud brave soldiers mocked and despised, soldiers who were protecting their lives and freedom. Not long ago he had been one of them himself. Yet all they did was point fingers, shout their hurt and wave their Union Jacks. They were so peaceful. He watched an old woman in a headscarf lean on her walking stick and wave her flag. Once it had been so simple: she knew what her Union Jack meant, like his mother knew. Now it was too complicated. Lee knew that he wanted his country back, for himself, for these good people. He wanted to do something for them, something that would make them know they were not alone, that they had support, that something was happening to change things. It would be a duty to serve them again, to protect them.

Barry said to him quietly: "We want these Muslims off the streets of our towns, off the streets of Britain. This is the Maccleston Taliban we're looking at. Look at the police defending them. No one these days dare offend the Islamic community, we treat them with kid gloves. It's like treading on eggshells."

Two younger women cupped their hands around their mouths and chanted: "Scum! Scum!"

Others began to clap in rhythm to their chant adding: "Go! Go!"

Lee just heard the church bells ringing noon as booing started. He saw faces looking down from first floor windows. Then another chant arose:

"We pay your benefits! We pay your benefits!"

Then from behind them and further away, they both heard a new chant:

"En-ger-land! En-ger-land! En-ger-land!"

They turned to see a gang of men marching up the street, some with bare chests and beer bellies, fists thrust into the sky, some wrapped in Union Jacks and flags of St George. They recognised them from the car park.

"The English Patriotic League at last," said Barry. "I wondered when they'd arrive."

The crowd fell back on to the pavement to let them through. From the opposite direction more police hurried in to reinforce their defensive line. Two Alsatian police dogs were barking, straining at the leash. Two police horses clattered in. The EPL men lined up in front of the Muslim group. They started a new chant:

"Muslims out, out, out! Islam out, out, out!"

They made loud jeering whistles. Lee was amazed to see the Muslims stand firm. They were not intimidated. He even felt a grudging admiration for their courage. He had to call it that – though the police were in front of them. A new placard was raised:

ANGLIAN SOLDIERS

ARE

WAR CRIMINALS

"This is our country!" shouted the EPL, eyeballing the Muslims.

Five of the EPL suddenly peeled away and ran 100 yards up the street. They stopped in front of a Tandoori Restaurant and hurled stones through the glass frontage. The glass shattered, women screamed. The stone throwers ran off, yelling. Before the crowd could take in what had happened one of the EPL men shouted:

"Over there!"

He pointed to the two old Sikhs standing in a shop doorway, wearing their purple turbans. Immediately three of the men ran over to them and punched them in the face. The Sikhs tried to protect their faces but the punches rained in. Enraged at the attack, Lee started forward but Barry grabbed his arm and held him back.

"Easy, Lee, easy. We need to keep out of this."

"But…"

Barry was just watching, his face calm as if observing a plan unfold. Lee freed his arm from Barry's hand. He watched, sickened as the Sikhs fell to the ground. Boots went in and then the EPL men raced away, chased by the mounted police who wheeled their horses round and clattered after them. Now the police took out their batons and faced the EPL. Lee saw the grim faces of the policemen, saw the wild eyes and bawling mouths and clenched fists of the EPL men. The police took two strides forward in a line. And then the EPL turned and ran back down the street. The police stayed where they were. The whole incident had taken less than five minutes. The Sikhs were being helped up by a man and two women. The shopkeeper had carried out two chairs for them. The crowd just looked shocked, not believing what had just happened. The police now turned around and began to direct the protestors back into the arcade. The burka'd women had disappeared.

"I don't want to be part of that," said Lee. "That's as bad as those bloody Muslims."

"Yes," said Barry. "Just thugs. Beating up ordinary people, innocent bystanders. It doesn't accomplish anything. It's too easy."

"They're so fucking ignorant they think Sikhs are Muslims. Just beating up those guys. Because they looked Asian."

"It's not the way," said Barry.

"No," said Lee. "But what is?"

"We'll find one. We have to," said Barry.

From: Sue [sue08whitehall@blueyonder.co.uk]
Sent: 7 August 2005 0930
To: Mike
Subject: Thee and me

You seem so far away – London and its bombings seem in a different world. I could so easily have been a victim myself – in that second set of attempted bombings that, thank God, didn't work. The world has gone mad.

I have managed to restrain myself over the two weeks since you said, bitterly – but sadly, too, I thought – that you would never communicate with me again. But you didn't say I shouldn't communicate with you. Will you read my emails or have you already closed me down? I don't know. So, in sending this, am I dropping a pebble into a bottomless well? I fear there will be no splash, no response and I will never know the pebble's destination. But I will do it. Why?

I sit on the well's stone edge, my back warmed by the sun of our time together. Though there is no answering splash, I still hear the echoes of that time, sparkling clear. I wish to recall it, re-live it: a time of great happiness, a sense for me as well as you of coming home (as you used to tell me). If you ever see this message I do not know whether you will glance at it with complete indifference – or with a remnant of warmth in some locked away part of your mind. If the first, no harm is done to you; if the second, then I hope you can still take a smidgeon of pleasure in it. When I remember you, waiting at a bus stop or pausing in the middle of ironing or washing up, I find a smile crossing my face. So I feel the deep need to initiate this contact, not just to let whatever it was, **is,** slide down into nothingness.

Sue

xx

14.

First steps

10th August

St Paul's Hospital

Mike had had a restless night. His mind swirled with images of Sue: shreds of his last talk with her as clear and shocking as two weeks ago when he had sent her away, her face transfixed by his callousness; echoes of her voice calling for him in a dark tunnel as if the second wave of attempted bombings had succeeded. His stumps were more sore than usual because they had chafed against the mattress as he moved. But at about five o'clock, as morning light filled the ward into which he had been moved and other patients began to cough, he fell into a deep sleep. He stirred lazily again as the morning shift of nurses came on with different louder voices and the breakfast trolley came round with jollying offers of tea or coffee.

Then he did jolt fully awake, eyes wide open, anxiously checking to see how close the trolley lady was. He recognised a familiar but long-lost feeling in his groin. He had a hard-on! Quickly he looked down to check if a tent shape was visible. It was, and all too obvious on his shortened neatly tucked sheet. God! Quickly he put his left hand inside the sheets, held his penis and pushed it down between his clenched thighs.

"Rise and shine!" said Maggie the trolley lady in her broad Brummie accent. "Tea, me duck?"

"Yes, as usual, Maggie, thanks. Strong and no sugar."

"I know. You don't have to remind me."

He stretched out with his right arm and swung the over-bed table into place. But not before Maggie had noticed his left arm under the sheets and given him a quizzical look. She poured the steaming tea from the big metal teapot, added the milk, turned and put the mug on the table. She bent close and whispered to him:

"I would say *On socks, off cocks* but you don't have socks any more. You are getting better, aren't you?" She grinned.

"Don't give these nurses ideas. They don't need much encouragement."

With a wink she was off on her rounds. Mike felt himself blushing. He could still feel himself hot and hard between his thighs. Good old Maggie – a spade's a spade. He was amazed. While he was in the ICU he'd checked all his tackle was there – appalled at the possibility of even more horrors to cope with, and been mightily relieved. But he hadn't thought of sex at all. But this, this came as a shock. He used to wake with an erection quite often. His 'morning glory' Sue had called it. She vowed during the warm summer nights to stay awake and watch it rise 'on auto' and then slide herself over it to see if he would wake up. But she never had, to his disappointment. She was too sound a sleeper. What a way to greet the day it would have been!

He took a drink of the hot tea. He heard someone pissing into the plastic bottle behind the curtains opposite. He felt his prick shrinking, like a tortoise retracting its head into its shell. Sue had laughed when he said he had no jurisdiction over his penis.

"Juris what?" she'd asked.

"No, really, it's independent of me."

And here it was, proving it again. The tenacity of the bloody creature, its single-mindedness, hoisting its flag in the middle of a war zone, oblivious of the wreckage around it. It was a late birthday present for him. Twenty nine and now only a fully operational middle leg.

157

But for what purpose? It mocked him. He shifted the table aside a little and looked down at the now level sheet. A rose between two thorns. A bail and two stumps. What a hideous incongruity! What woman could find that ugliness attractive? Even if love was blind – and Sue's love was blind. Thinking of his bleak celibate future, he had somehow ignored that he would still be tethered to lust. He had assumed his sexual desire would have abated, cut short with his amputations in some kind of sympathetic natural symmetry. Now he had unwelcome proof that he was still potent. Would this gross pointlessness be another torture to endure? The power of the prick; it made wise men fools. The one-eyed trouser serpent! He had worked hard to be free of being washed and bathed, sweated to avoid the humiliation of the hoist that lifted him onto the bedpan, would struggle with crutches to walk again. Now he had another fight: to be independent of his prick. It might be the hardest fight of all – to avoid the seedy sleaze of wanking for the next half century.

He'd had no inclination to do any exercises over the weekend: there was no physio presence and he was expected to take responsibility himself for maintaining his progress. He'd been depressed in the days after his dismissal of Sue, self-hating. It had been hard to make an effort, easy to go through the motions. Kathy had been great, coaxing, cajoling, sometimes bullying. Because of her he had continued to make some progress. He was again feeling sluggish after his breakfast when Kathy breezed in.

"Big day, today, Mike. You're ready to try out your new legs. "

"What!" Mike exclaimed. This was a reality he hadn't bargained for, hadn't thought about or prepared himself for.

"I know," said Kathy. "A surprise! I knew you'd brood about it all weekend if I'd told you on Friday. You think too much. The doctor says your wounds have healed. It's time get on the move. They're not the legs you'll eventually have. Those will be individually fitted and made for you. These legs today are more like training aids."

She was bustling about with what looked to Mike like blue plastic bags.

"They're different from each other because you've still got one knee."

Before he could get used to the idea she was folding his sheets back.

"OK, into your chair."

Once he was settled in his wheelchair she rolled down his stump shrinkers, like pink elasticated stockings, from his stumps. She peeled back the dressing, checked the wound and then taped the dressing back on.

"Yes, they're fine. Your body must be in good shape, there's been no trouble with healing."

"Not the description that comes to mind," said Mike.

"Your stumps have shrunk back to their normal size, which is why we can get on."

She placed a cotton tubifast stocking carefully over the stump and folded it round.

Mike was watching her closely, grateful that the activity had taken him out of his self-absorption. He still avoided looking at the naked flesh of his stumps, the lurid red pattern of the surgical cuts, the muscle flap folded over and held with stainless steel staples. At least he was now alright with them when they were bandaged or covered. Kath slid the blue cuff of the femurette over the stump and pulled the long tapering blue bag up his thigh to his groin.

"Comfortable?"

"Fine."

She attached a foot pump and slowly began to inflate the bag.

"You'll feel the pressure increase," said Kath. "You must tell me if it begins to feel sore. If we get up to forty millimetres of mercury then the pressure is strong enough. If that's too much for you, that's OK, we'll do it again tomorrow."

She was watching his face as she spoke, looking for signs of strain. Mike watched the bag inflate like a thick party balloon or a lilo.

"This is like a shock absorber for the metal frame. How's that? Any soreness?"

"No, it's fine."

Kath went through the same process of inflating the blue bag on Mike's other leg.

"Now it's time to attach the frame."

Mike had been half expecting to see a plastic leg. What Kath produced was an oval metal frame with two metal shanks connected by circular metal hoops, and black leather straps and shining buckles hanging down. It was ugly and brutally functional. At the bottom of the PPM-aid was a piece of scuffed black rubber, shaped like a rocker. At the bottom of the femurette was a plastic foot in a worn carpet slipper. Kathy strapped on the socket of the frame, tightened the nuts with an allen key.

"From IKEA then," said Mike.

Kathy slipped a long strap from each leg over the opposite shoulder.

"You're just under 6 feet tall aren't you?"

"I was."

"I'm afraid the tallest we can get you now is about 5 foot 9. We have to lower your centre of gravity to make it easier for you to balance and walk."

She said it in a professionally competent, matter-of-fact manner – as if to deliberately sideline any psychological effects as irrelevant, not wanting to encourage any introspection. *How well she knows me,* thought Mike.

Kath buckled the straps firmly and stepped back. Mike looked at the contraptions that stuck out in front of him, like the forks of a fork lift truck.

"OK," said Kath. "Off we go to rehab. You can wheel yourself now. But be careful round corners. You don't want to knock your legs. Perhaps we should put a red flag on."

As he trundled himself along the corridor he felt like a freak – legs like fucking drumsticks. Yes, he had done right by Sue, expelling her from all this, setting her free.

When they arrived at the rehabilitation gym Mike wheeled himself straight over to the parallel bars. He manoeuvred his wheelchair to the end of the bars, directly between them, and put on the brake. Kathy was behind him and there were physios at each side.

"This is the hard part," said Kathy. "You need to haul yourself up."

She demonstrated. Mike watched then grasped the bars,

concentrated his strength into his wrists, made sure he was evenly balanced, checked that his legs were straight.

"Here goes!"

He pulled himself up. For the first time for weeks he was not sitting or lying. He felt muscles working in his back and shoulders and arms. A physio was chocking each foot so his legs didn't slide forwards.

"It's like pole-vaulting," said Kathy. "If the pole doesn't chock into the hole, the jumper's had it."

Then he was standing, he was upright. He was trembling and sweating. He stood for a moment. He dared not turn his head to look at the physios, but he knew his head was at the same height as theirs.

"Well done, Mike! That's the hardest thing you've had to do so far."

He grinned, elated. Kathy came to stand in front of him. He was looking straight at her, eye to eye. He was standing again for the first time.

"But I can't feel the floor," he said.

He felt he was floating, was slightly dizzy. He swayed and the physios quickly grasped his arms and steadied him.

"Sit down for a rest. Then you must do the hula," said Kathy. "You have to get accustomed to moving your thighs again, getting your quads functioning again. Move your hips in a circle, transfer your weight from one foot to the other."

She gave a demonstration. He looked down at the rubber rocker and the old slipper at the end of his legs. He still could not feel the floor. He circled his hips, tentatively at first, nervously put his weight on each foot.

"Good," said Kathy. "Now we'll try the next bit: moving your leg. Just move one leg forward by hitching your hip. Use your trunk muscles to lift the pelvis. Swing forwards, then back again and then rest."

She gave a demonstration. Mike copied her. The few small movements were amazingly tiring. He had to really concentrate. Kathy made him do five repetitions.

"OK, now we go for the big one: an actual step. Stand on your left leg and move your right leg forwards. Take your weight on your hands."

Mike realised he felt the same excitement and nervousness as at the start of a fell race, somehow tensed and relaxed at the same time. He knew this was a key moment. He looked at Kathy, compressed his lips with determination, gritted his teeth.

"You can do it. Remember, put your weight on your hands on the bars, not on your left leg. And don't worry, we're all here to hold you if necessary," said Kathy.

Mike looked at the white-tuniced physios on each side of him, felt them poised to grasp his arms and shoulders should he stumble, but felt their confidence in him, too. He looked to the front along the length of the shining wooden bars. He gripped them hard and leaned forward. He hitched and swivelled his right hip, felt the muscles working in his thigh. His right leg moved forward. He rested for a moment. He felt a surge of confidence.

"OK the left leg now."

Still concentrating, he put his weight on his hands again and hitched his left hip. His left leg moved forward.

"Congratulations! You've taken your first two steps."

Mike felt triumphant. He felt a warming surge of gratitude to these three women physios. He rested and looked around the room. Each person was intent on his and her own activity; no one was watching him. The only witnesses of his first steps were the physios. He wanted Sue to look at him with pride in her eyes. He wanted to celebrate with her, feel her hug him – and her absence hit him like a punch in the gut, almost took his breath away. He lurched and felt the strong grip of the physios on each arm steady him. And now with grim determination he hitch-hipped along the bars, not pausing between steps, until he reached the end. He stood there trembling and sweating.

"That's fantastic! Now rest for a moment and we'll see if you can negotiate a three point turn."

Mike's brain swirled with fatigue, with elation, with despair. He closed his eyes and felt Sue's close embrace, her hug and kiss of hope and optimism. Kathy saw his shoulders give a great shrug and shake before he began his turning operation. It was more like seven points than three points but he did it and faced back along the bars towards his wheelchair.

"I think you should watch yourself in the mirror. You'll get a better idea of your movements," said Kathy.

Mike remembered the first time he had seen himself in the mirror as he had been wheeled through the swing doors of the gym, holding his banana board. It had been a shock to see himself in his wheelchair as others saw him, confirming his status as an amputee. He had looked ill, pale and gaunt, slumped in the chair. It had been profoundly distressing. Now, though, he knew he would get himself back to the other end of the parallel bars.

"Yes," he said, "please."

Kathy wheeled the portable mirror and put it into position at the far end of the bars. Mike started on the long walk back, already getting into a halting rhythm of hip hitching. He concentrated solely on his movements. Half way back he paused for a rest.

"It's like walking on air. I can't feel the ground. I wouldn't know whether it was carpet or wood, concrete or grass. The only sensation I can feel is a vibration in my thighs."

The satisfaction of the physical effort easily outweighed his fatigue. Even as soon as this, on his first excursion, he saw that he could relish this effort as he had relished the effort of running. He saw a way ahead. He set off to complete his walk. When he finally turned and lowered himself back into his chair he was exhausted. There was a round of applause and cheers, shouts of congratulations from the other patients who, this time, had obviously seen what was happening. The physios joined in with their congratulatory clapping and smiles. He knew it was a team effort – theirs and his combined. How much they had become part of him. He wanted them to be proud of him, just as a child he wanted his father's praise and approval. He wished again that Sue had been there to see him and to wheel him back to his room and talk with him about what he had accomplished. She would have photographed him with her mobile phone, capturing this key moment. She would have renewed him. But he had to put her away, he had cast the die. He had to renew himself.

"Can you get yourself back, Mike?"

He nodded.

"Thank you all very much," he said.

"I should think," said Kathy, "at this rate we'll have you on the high zimmer in three days and in a week on elbow crutches and two weeks after that you could be ready to go home. We'll organise for the prosthetist to come and cast your stumps for your own individually tailored legs."

Mike could hardly take in the momentum of progress they envisaged or the extent of the challenge.

"You will walk out of here."

"I know," he said. He knew with certainty.

Mike felt a renewed respect for his body, a wonder at how it could heal itself and adapt. He felt humble as he spun his chair around and thrust the wheels forward with his hands. They had expectations of him. He knew it would be hard work but he also knew he could do it. He thought of Lee. Without his help in the underground he wouldn't be here. He wondered where he was and what he was doing. Sometime he would try to find him. But for now there were other problems to solve. Kathy's timetable meant he had to find somewhere to live. He had to contact his father's wife in Canada.

From: Sue [sue08whitehall@blueyonder.co.uk]
Sent: 11 August 2005 2236
To: Mike
Subject: Thee and me

Yesterday, driving home on the bypass I see a brown-and-white horse (too big to be a pony) cantering up a steep sloping field. I notice to its right a black horse standing still and facing it. The brown-and-white horse slows to a walk and approaches the stationery black horse. Then I notice that though they are in the same field, they are separated by a single strand of an electric fence. They both approach the fence. The brown-and-white horse stretches its neck over the electric fence and they nuzzle, rub noses. They are still doing it as I drive beyond them to the roundabout and out of sight.

I don't look for them but I see them – images of us.

Sue

xx

15.

Arrest

11th August

Bradfield

Amjad's mother paused in her washing-up and leaned against the kitchen sink. She closed her eyes against the early morning August sunshine. It was 6.30 am. and as usual she'd been unable to sleep. It was five weeks since her son had died. Sometimes his memory was so vivid it seemed it had happened only yesterday. At other times it seemed so impossible that it must have happened in a parallel world.

She turned to look at his photograph on the shelf, his among all the other family photographs: her parents in Pakistan before they came here to England, her daughters in their school uniforms. She looked closely at Amjad's face, smiling and open, honest eyes, his hair well-cut, tie neatly knotted. Her parents had been so proud of his success at school, of his going to college. Their decision to leave Mirpur and all their family and culture had seemed vindicated by Amjad. This was why they had come: to create a better life for their children and grandchildren. She had been grateful they were dead. Amjad had nullified their sacrifice and their struggle. They had been deeply religious and would have been devastated by Amjad's killing of innocent people and the offence he had given to Allah. They would never have understood.

She thought of her daughters still upstairs in bed. Thank goodness it was the school holidays. They had had a hard time of it in the last two weeks of term, not really understanding what was going on but telling her of questions from their friends, of strange looks from their teachers. They had told her of the special school assembly about Islam meaning Peace. All they really understood was that Amjad was dead. And she had no body to bury. That image she shut down fast, the image of the wrecked underground carriage. How could they celebrate his life or mourn his death?

Her daughters and her routine chores were where she lived her life now. Today she was taking them to Leeds on the train to buy school things for the new term. It was far too early but it was something to occupy all their minds. They were still excited by train journeys. She would give the girls another hour, time to tidy the living room before they messed it up again. She lost herself in the repeated routines.

At night she and her husband lay in bed together, not touching, each knowing the other was pretending to be asleep, separated by their grief and anger and bewilderment. Amjad had split them as they had never been split before. This morning he had gone to the taxi rank on early shift.

Nowadays they both barely acknowledged the words of their neighbours. He stayed in his taxi, did his calls, did not chat with the others as they waited by the town hall square. He saw their looks and pretended to read the paper. She went to the shop only when absolutely necessary and hurried back, eyes to the ground, knowing and avoiding the looks of people around her. What both had found impossible were the congratulations that had been shouted at them, the honour of being a martyr's parents. They had come only from a few, all of them men. Hussein, Amjad's uncle, had not been one of them – and they had been pleasantly surprised at that. Hussein had looked at her husband with the same bewilderment and embarrassment as most of their neighbours. It seemed to them he had simply not known what to say. She had not encouraged Amjad to spend time with his uncle because he was too traditional in his

167

beliefs, especially so far as women were concerned. But how could she know what Amjad did when he was away from home? And then the attempted bombings of July 21st just two weeks after Amjad and the others had killed fifty two and injured 700 innocent people. How could people be so ruthless, so arrogant in their faith? It had been incomprehensible, evil.

His father had dismissed the local imam when he had come to visit. He had not attended mosque since that fateful 7th July. They were both lost and drifting. Nothing from outside could console them, no one could give them an explanation. They had only each other yet they were cut off from each other.

Mechanically she began to wipe round her husband's coffee mug in the lukewarm water. Then in the corner of her eye she caught a movement in the street. It took her a moment to understand what she was seeing. To her left, on the opposite side, a group of men in black were advancing along the street, hugging the house walls and the doors that opened directly onto the pavement. Another group was approaching from the right. Both groups were crouching as they moved. They were holding guns – the short-barrelled rifles she had seen on the TV news. Both lines of men stopped, their backs leaning against the stone fronts of the houses. The lines were about 100 yards apart. They were dressed completely in black: black helmets over black balaclavas which concealed their faces, bulky black jackets, black combat trousers tucked into black paraboots, black gloves that held their rifles, pistols in black holsters on their hips.

Then she saw one of them step forward into the road. He raised one arm above his head, his gloved hand clenched into a fist. Suddenly he pumped his arm down twice. Groups of men from the front of each line broke into a run, their boots thudding on the flagged pavement. Some turned into the snickets that ran at ground level through to the backs of the terraced houses. Others ran to crouch behind parked cars. One crouched just in front of her window, peering round a van, his rifle aimed – she realised with a shock that made her lurch backwards – at Hussein's house. She looked at the other men. Their rifles were all pointing at Hussein's front door. For a moment everything was silent and motionless.

Then from the left line two men rushed forward. They were carrying a short black metal cylinder. She watched mesmerised as they ran to Hussein's door and, holding the cylinder between them, smashed it into the door. Twice they smashed it, the crashes bursting into the sunlit silent street. Then the door crumpled open. Immediately they stood aside and another squad, already rushing in from the right, dashed straight into the house, their rifles at their hips. She heard them yelling "Police!"

Simultaneously two police cars raced up from both ends of the street and screeched to a halt outside Hussein's door. More police jumped out. Two blue police vans with blacked-out windows drew up. The back doors of one of them opened and four more armed police climbed out. Amjad's mother hadn't moved, her hand covering her mouth in shock.

Almost immediately Hussein was pushed out of the door, his arms behind his back, each gripped above the elbow by a policeman. He was wearing pyjamas with a jacket over them. They marched him to the van. She saw the rifles swivel to target him. Another policeman opened the van doors, Hussein was bent over by his escort and was bundled in. She saw the glint of handcuffs. Two escorting policemen got in the back. One of the police cars switched on its blue lights and accelerated away down the street, followed by the van.

Then Hussein's wife appeared at the doorway, dressed in her black burka. She too was being pushed forward, this time by two police women who held her arms. She was trying to shake them off. She was pushed into the other police car and driven off. Where were the children? What was happening to them. Then out of the second blue van emerged a team of people dressed in white boiler suits with hoods, and wearing white overshoes. They carried little cases. They went into the house. Two more policemen dressed in yellow visibility jackets were unspooling yellow and black tape across the front of the house and out into the road in front of it, cordoning it off. She could read; YELLOW POLICE LINE DO NOT CROSS.

She saw all along the street, faces peering round curtains. Another policeman walked down the street with a megaphone. As he did so, she saw the curtains twitch closed again in the upstairs windows. She stepped back out of the light. Through the open kitchen window she heard his message: "Stay away from your windows for safety."

She watched as a man in a white boiler suit carried out a computer, another carried out a plastic box full of files.

Why was he being arrested? What had Hussein done? If her own son had been capable of blowing himself up and murdering innocent people, how could she possibly know what went on in any other person's mind?

Coming to her senses, she eventually phoned her husband. He came home immediately, having to leave his car two streets away and being interrogated by the police before he could come in. They let the girls sleep late. They would be disappointed that their shopping trip to Leeds was cancelled. They ignored the almost constant ringing of their mobiles until, in exasperation, they turned them off. Amjad's father had said hardly a word, muttering only: "The world is crazy and sick. We are all sick." He stared dully at the television and drank coffee.

That evening they watched the television news. There were shots of their street and the two policemen stationed outside the door of Hussein's house. A police spokesman explained:

"Today we have arrested five men – in Birmingham, Leeds and Bradfield in West Yorkshire – in connection with the attempted bombings in London on July 21st. A suspect package has been found in one house in Birmingham and local people have been evacuated. Investigation is still continuing. Residents living near to the homes where arrests were made will see a high profile police presence during the day and will be able to discuss issues with local officers."

A reporter interviewed a man outside the corner shop by the boxes of fruit. Neither Amjad's mother or father recognised him but he claimed to be a close friend of Hussein's. He said:

"He and his family have lived here for many years. He is a quiet man who works long hours. He is a decent law-abiding family man. His family are quiet and down-to-earth."

Amjad's mother looked across at her husband but he did not acknowledge her glance and his face did not change.

From: Sue [sue08whitehall@blueyonder.co.uk]
Sent: 15 August 2005 2236
To: Mike
Subject: Thee and me

Summer is finishing too early, with all its richness, fulfilment and complacency. Soon the world will turn to autumn with all its ambivalence. And I re-affirm that as part of this extraordinary complexity of life I will not take the common sense road. I will not 'move on', as they say and as you say, but relish this richness so long awaited, given but now taken away. All I ask, my invisible non-hearing man, is that passively or even disinterestedly you will let me be in my strange passion. Hurrah for the whorls and knots and pied wonders of life. (I was reading GM Hopkins today for next year's A level class!).

I went with Lisa for the day to Filey. We walked on the Brigg and I imagined the Roman soldiers stationed there, looking out over the cold North Sea. How alien it must all have been – they were from Dalmatia, so it said on the information board.

How much I would have liked to help with your walking, watching you make progress.

Sue

xx

16.

Evidence

20th August

St Paul's Hospital

Each day in the rehabilitation gym Mike met other amputees. Their cheery greetings lifted him, there was a camaraderie. Where before he had seen them as a medieval parade of cripples, stumbling and lurching along in a grotesque circus side show with the bearded lady and the two-headed baby, Mike now began to see them as brave and defiant. There was Linda who had lost an arm, Steve who had lost both legs, Marco who had lost both legs and an arm. There was an unwritten agreement that no one asked what had happened, how they'd got here. All that mattered was that they were in similar situations, facing the same struggles. In all of them he saw a determination and a sense of purpose that swept him along. As he progressed from the parallel bars to walking with the high zimmer frame, his weight resting on the frame's armrest, as he tried his first steps with his elbow crutches, walking out of the gym and into the corridor, he found himself frequently exchanging brief words with Chris as they passed each other, both gradually extending the range of their walking routes.

Chris was now an out-patient. His wife Jenny drove him in for each physio appointment and often stayed. Chris was a burly man, his red short-sleeved soccer shirt emphasizing both arms tattoed with dragons, and big strong shoulders. He always wore red shorts to the physio sessions. He'd had one leg amputated, above the knee. One morning Jenny had invited Mike over to join them for their coffee break in the small kitchen off the gym.

"That was brilliant," said Chris. "You're waltzing around now!"

"Not waltzing exactly. It's bloody hard work, isn't it?"

Jenny brought over the three coffees and sat down.

"Kevin Stump's got used to it, hasn't he, Chris?"

"Kevin?" asked Mike.

"Yes, Kevin Stump," said Chris laughing. He patted his stump. "He's an actor, my best friend. He loves football."

Nodding towards Chris's red shirt and shorts, Mike said: "A Liverpool fan?"

"Yes, and Kevin here is the corner and free-kick specialist. I'm his coach. He calls me Jose."

Mike looked bewildered.

"Chris sits at home on the couch," said Jenny, "doing his exercises for strengthening his thigh muscles. He raises his stump to aim a kick, doing a running commentary on the match. Liverpool always win, of course. Have you got a team?"

"No. I've never followed a team. I'm not a footballer. I used to be a runner, over the fells."

There was a silence. Mike was staring into the mug of coffee in his hands.

"It's all about small steps," said Chris, wanting to break the silence. "Setting yourself challenges. I've always been competitive so perhaps it was easier for me. I watched the other guys who were ahead of me when I first came in here, watched their exercise patterns. I thought *I can go faster than that. Get there quicker.* And I did. The first time I could get up from the settee at home without help. I remember ringing my Mum and telling her, I was so chuffed."

Mike nodded, rather glumly.

"And when I did my first walk along the bars or with crutches, I was on the phone to everybody I knew."

"He was a pain," laughed Jenny. "But of course they all backed him up, told him he was doing great. He needed that."

Mike wanted to explain that he too was competitive, but with himself, pushing himself to do personal bests like with his running. And yes, he felt elation when he stood up for the first time, took his first steps. But afterwards, when the adrenalin had gone, he felt terrified at the enormity of the task ahead, the long long road. He wanted to ask if Chris had felt like that.

"You had downs, though, didn't you, Chris?" said Jenny.

"Course I did. Tell me someone who doesn't. Everybody has downs, nothing to do with not having legs. I've had weepies. Just little things, daft things really. I was sitting waiting for a blood test. I hadn't got my artificial leg then. Someone brushed past, very close to me. I flinched and leaned out of their way. They'd gone through the space where my leg would have been. It kind of brought it all out. It was brutal. Do you remember?"

"Yes," said Jenny, taking his hand in hers.

"Another thing: you've not got to stall," said Chris. "You've got to keep your momentum – increase the distance you can walk, improve your walking style, your gait, anything to work on. Keep on going. I'm lucky, I'm determined, always have been."

He looked at Mike.

"You are, too, Mike. I can tell. I'm right, aren't I?"

Mike looked up at him, sniffed and nodded with a reluctant grin.

"Suppose so."

"You've got to be selfish, too," said Chris. "Single minded, have tunnel vision. When I started here there was a young guy, just like you with both legs off. He was brilliant, always joking, bantering. Nothing got him down. He was an inspiration. I watched him, spent time with him, trying to catch his spirit. You've got to do that. But there was also an old bloke, about 82 he was, frail, always just standing about in his pyjamas. The physios were doing their best but he'd given up. I was sorry for him but I knew I had to keep away from him. I daren't catch his defeatism. I was ruthless, in a way."

"Come on, it's time," said Jenny. "We've got to go to the DIY store on the way home."

"No rest for the wicked," said Chris. "See you next time."

Jenny was a good-looking woman: slim, dark hair in a long pony tail down almost to her waist, lovely big black eyes and a ready smile, a warm human being. The way she looked at Chris – caring, loving but no nonsense. He just knew they were a team. But he had to shut his mind off from that. He was glad it was time for more balancing on the red medicine ball, toning the core muscles. He turned to it with a new enthusiasm.

That afternoon back in the ward, a nurse brought Mike a zipped polythene bag, labelled *Evidence* in large black letters.

"A policeman brought it in this morning," said the nurse. "I need you to sign for it."

Mike signed the paper on the clipboard and the nurse went away on her rounds.

He picked it up and looked inside. *I suppose the underground train was a crime scene,* he thought. There wasn't much. He looked at the remains of his trainers. They were now scorched black and charred, barely recognisable. The memory of Lee making him talk, keeping him alive. Lodged in the corner of the bag was his watch, still intact and going. He held it through the polythene. The second digits pulsed on – 15,16 17… He flicked to the stop watch read-out: 2.36.21. It must have been the time of his last run around Ingleborough the day before he came down to London. He felt the muscles of his face loosen, his face begin to slacken and collapse. He felt warm tears welling up on the rims of his lower eyelids. He felt the tears warm on his cheeks, tasted their salt. He had to stop this. He took deep breaths until he was back in control.

The old life was over, Chris had said. *You had to embrace the new.* Mike put the bag on his locker top. The trainers could go. The watch he would wipe clean and keep. He could not yet discard it. He would keep it like the ludicrous relics of burned martyrs: a fingerbone, a tooth from a skull.

It was six weeks and two days after his operation when Mike sat in his wheelchair in the small treatment room next to the gym. Full of anticipation, he was awaiting the prosthetist, due at 9.30 am.. He was simultaneously elated and scared: he thought back over the big moments of his rehabilitation – standing up, taking his first steps, the first walk with crutches along the corridor to the reception area café, the first chat there with a stranger, someone waiting for visiting time, just a chat about the weather, something so normal. This was another step: his stumps were being cast so that he could have his own made-to-measure legs. These were the ones he would go to his new home with; they were tangible solid symbols – no, not symbols, tools – of his new life. With them, his new journey would begin.

"Good morning, Mike."

The voice was cheerful and businesslike, the prosthetist a young man, about his own age, thought Mike. Athletic looking, probably a rugby player, a threequarter. Kath had come in, too, and the doctor.

He shook hands

"I'm Dan. Good to meet you. Big day for you, eh?"

"It certainly is. I can't decide whether it's been a long time or whether time has shot by since the operation."

The doctor did a last check to see that the stump was not swollen and that the wounds had healed. The team had already discussed and agreed on Mike's mental as well as physical health.

"Absolutely fine. Your body's healthy, Mike."

Kath had told Mike the procedure but he was still fascinated as he watched. Dan spread some kitchen roll paper on the floor and placed a plastic washing up bowl of warm water on them. It seemed homely, almost amateurish. Dan wrapped Mike's left stump in cling film, then rolled on a stocking. In special blue pencil he marked the pressure points: the kneecap, the front of his remaining shin which would need space in the socket.

"The anatomical landmarks, we call them," said Dan, shading and cross-hatching. It reminded Mike of a Wainwright drawing of a Lakeland walk.

Then Dan took the bandage impregnated with plaster and dunked it in the bowl of water. He squeezed the surplus water out and wrapped the bandage round the stump. Mike felt the heat from his stump as the plaster set round it. It took only five minutes for the plaster to harden. Dan shuffled it off, unslotted it, trimmed off the excess with scissors so that it was a smooth socket shape. He repeated the process with the other leg.

"That's it," he said. "Done."

"I thought it would be more complicated," said Mike.

"Not so difficult. I'll be back in a fortnight."

"Yes, now I want a shapely pair of calves – just the right shape of sinewy muscle, please. And what about some hair?"

"I'll do my best," laughed Dan as he left.

Kathy thought it was the first light-hearted remark she'd heard Mike make – a good sign.

"You'll have noticed already that your stump shrinks during a day."

"I know, even during a morning's physio."

"That's because as the socket compresses, the oedema – the swelling – goes down. In fact, it will be eighteen months before your stump finds its final shape as the muscle bulk changes. So the socket on your long leg, the locking one, will be padded with a thick cotton terylene sock, and your other one you'll need a gel sock."

Mike realised the process of choosing his legs and making the necessary decisions meant that he was already living within a new normality – working within a framework that only a month ago would have been unknown to him. Sometimes he felt at ease about this. Sometimes it seemed he should rage more, even if the rage was pointless. He would watch Chris strap on his leg, tie the khaki-coloured Velcro strap around his waist as if it was just a normal belt on a pair of trousers. Adaptation was the key, he knew. He was a creature catapulted into alien territory, dispossessed like crofters cleared from an inland glen and told to learn to make a new living on a rocky coast – from tending cattle to burning kelp. Against the odds, most survived. Humans learned and adapted.

The next step was to be measured for a wheelchair.

"As if you're getting a new suit," Kathy had said.

They measured the width of his hips, the length and width of his back, his height and weight.

She explained: "Because you no longer have your legs, your centre of gravity has changed. So we have to set the wheels back about three inches, and we fit on anti-tip bars so you can't fall backwards. It's self-propelling; you'll have to push it along yourself – like in the London Marathon. Maybe you should give that a thought."

There was a thought indeed. He'd watched the wheelchair athletes, full of admiration for them but with pity, too. He couldn't stand the pity, people cheering him on because they felt sorry for him.

Next day, at coffee with Chris and Jenny, Mike unusually initiated the conversation:

"Are you thinking of taking up any sport, Chris?"

"I've been thinking about the triple jump! No seriously, I have thought about it. Archery and shot putting would be possible but I like team sports, used to like a bit of contact too. So it's going to be basketball. I fancy charging round in a wheelchair – doing wheelies."

"I think it's a great idea," said Jenny. "What about you, Mike?"

"Too early to think about that. I can hardly walk."

"OK. But you're a fit young guy," said Chris. "Keep strong. Life isn't over, it's just changed. Embrace it. Think of what you can do, not what you can't. Sorry, I'm beginning to talk in slogans, like one of those motivational speakers."

"I'm always thinking of things he can do," laughed Jenny.

"Yes, she chivvies me along, bullies me. In spring she had me sitting on the couch, putting vegetable seeds into seed trays, hundreds of them. Most places she goes, she drags me along – supermarket, shopping. No excuses. But it's good. Life's good. Couldn't do it without Jenny. That's for sure."

Chris reached across, took her hand and kissed it. Jenny smiled.

"He's a new man," she said. "I'll get us more coffees."

She got up and went over to fill the kettle and rinse out the mugs.

Chris leaned over the table closer to Mike, speaking more quietly.

"While she's over there, a bit of man talk. Not quite a new man, actually. You've probably had what they call phantom pain."

"Yes, I certainly have. Terrifying, it disorientates me."

"Yes, I know, but the point is: one of the drugs they give you to deal with it is pregabalin. When you've been taking it for a few weeks it affects the brain's interpretation of nerve messages. One of the side effects is, you know, it inhibits erection, reduces your libido. I realised that I hadn't been thinking about sex – and for me that was really odd. Now Jenny and me, we're close. Jenny helped, she was great. But I've decided to cut down on the pregabalin, even if it means having to cope with the phantom pain. So, think on. I don't know if you've got a girlfriend."

He looked questioningly but Mike didn't want to get into that and luckily Jenny came back with the coffee refills.

"Have you told Mike about the amputee forums on the internet?" she asked.

Chris winked at Mike as Jenny drew her chair up.

"No. I spend a lot of time with them, on my laptop. People join it looking for information. They're often quite frightened. They want help. So I can tell them about my experiences, about leading a normal life and being positive. It helps them but it also helps me. I feel good because I'm able to give them something they value."

There is an alternative world out there, thought Mike, a world he had known nothing about – but real and authentic, just as real as the one he'd come from.

"It shouldn't be called phantom pain," said Mike. "It's real pain, there's nothing phantom about it. It's excruciating. I'd heard of it but didn't realise you had to take painkillers for it."

"Yes, it's the limb part that's phantom," said Chris.

"I still don't quite understand it," said Mike. "It's a weird form of out-of-body experience."

"It's because the nerve endings have been chopped, but they're still there in your stump. They can still be triggered. The part of your brain that communicates with your leg is still there. For me, it's usually as if someone has poured scalding hot water on my ankle. It's so sudden. It's agony."

"Yes, I get that. But sometimes it's like cramp."

"Or itching, drives me mad. Or sometimes like having an unbearable heavy weight hanging round my leg."

"But the whole thing is a bit spooky," said Mike. "When I walk, I can't feel the ground. There's no feedback. It's like having a deadleg. Ho ho!"

All three groaned at the pun.

"It will get a bit better. I can sense at the back of my stump when my artificial heel touches the ground and then, as I move through the step, I can feel at the front of my stump when my toe touches the ground."

"Sorry to interrupt," said Jenny. "But we have to go. We're having a party!"

"That's what it's about: the sun on your face, the smell of steak grilling on the barbecue, sipping a cool beer, a good woman, your mates. Remember what Kathy always says: *Everybody's achievement is their own achievement.* See you next time."

Mike watched them go. They were a team well-tuned to each other. Chris was a fortunate man.

Mike's physio session was over. He needed time on his own. He wheeled himself down to the rose garden. It was the first time he'd been there since Sue had left. He would never forget the utter dejection in her face. He recalled her last words, her final desperate hope: she would email him. He had hated himself. The porter had wheeled him back through the rain. Once in his ward he had immediately set up a new email account on his laptop. The old one was redundant. He would never use it again. It was a confirmation of his decision, of his callousness. It had been an act of self-harm, a punishment, a burning of boats. He had hurt her. He had to hurt himself more, inflict on himself a painful renunciation. Seeing himself as an emotional outcast was his only way of surviving. He knew he would not cope with hearing from her.

He wondered now if his brain – or the chemicals in it that composed his emotions – had required an emotional amputation to deal with the physical amputation. It might also have been a healing, a cauterization – a protective sealing in, as when a tree withdraws its nutrition from a leaf, to hoard the remaining life force over the cold winter. He was healing, he knew, without a doubt. Chris and Jenny were inspiring.

How had Sue spent the long summer holiday? Had she sought solace with someone? The sudden stab of jealousy almost made him double over with pain. He dare not let his mind go down that way. He must control himself, distract himself. Sue had her own life now. He had made the choice: he must survive without her.

From: Sue [sue08whitehall@blueyonder.co.uk]
Sent: 21 August 2005 2015
To: Mike
Subject: Thee and me

This weekend I bought the most expensive object I have ever bought: a wood carving entitled Departures. It stands about three feet high and is on a small table next to me. It is carved out of a sycamore stump, a beautiful pale wood, oiled and waxed to gleaming. The carving is of two figures, a man and a woman (of course!). The man stands upright, gaunt, his arms stretched above his head, his head thrown back and anguished. Behind him, her body arced in line with his, stands the woman, her face composed, her hair neat and formal. One of her arms cradles the man's head, one of his cradles the woman's head. The prominent grain of the wood acts like ligament or muscle in both their bodies. Both of their shapes emerge out of the natural wood at their feet. The whole is a wonderful sinuous stretching and seeking and comforting as well as a simultaneous separateness.

How could I resist? "These fragments I have shored against my ruin."

I have been touching the carving, running my fingers over the carved thighs and stretched ligaments. I thought of faith. People are said to have faith when they believe in something in the face of total lack of evidence. People have faith in a good God even when confronted with suffering, earthquakes, abused children. It seems that the need is greater than all contrary appearances. Me, too – faced with silence and possibly total disinterest or even aversion now, somewhere along that spectrum. Yet I believe in my feelings: they are valid in that they arise from something, some phenomena, come contact and connection that is indisputable.

It is as if I have taken a black and white photograph and the film lies in the dish in the darkroom. I am not permitted to develop it, let alone print it. Yet I know the photo is there and it is this knowledge that counts.

This is a soliloquy in a darkened auditorium to an audience of one, maximum. And I cannot see, as I peer into the dark, if even that one is there.

This is my dilemma: in my better moments I want you to be happy in the way that is necessary for you even if that means being separate from me; but I also want to remain curled up in a warm corner of your mind. The two are incompatible so there can be no resolution.

Is this soliloquy pointless? Is it damaging me? No, it is vital to me. It confirms the best part of me, an integrity. The cruel irony is that you have locked off your feelings for me out of love for me. I maintain mine out of love for you.

I need this feeling of tenderness for you in order to survive. It sustains not undermines me. It gives me a sense of myself that I approve of.

So I write into a dark and empty space and just hope – for what? For a sudden recollection that you may have, that comes into your mind disobediently. Back to faith! I want this rich experience, this weird form of happiness. Is it a form of courtly love?

Is this soliloquy or self-indulgent ramble?

Sue xx

17.

Dog-track

24th August

Bradfield, St Paul's Hospital, Belle Vue Stadium

In the small kitchen of his ground-floor flat, Barry was leaning on the kitchen sink, smoking his first cigarette of the day. He was looking out of the window, waiting for the paper boy. He stretched his arms, scroggled his fingers in his ears and scratched his balls. He padded across the kitchen in his bare feet and blue boxer shorts, filled the kettle, rinsed out a mug, put a teabag in it and two spoons of sugar. He came back to the window. The paper boy was always later in school holidays. The bin lorry was coming down the road, bin-men in boots and shorts and singlets were jogging from house to house. Two women were waiting at the bus stop, one in the supermarket uniform. The paper boy crossed from the other side of the road on his bike, vaulted off, carelessly leaned his bike against the wall and sauntered up the path. He stopped to open the newspaper, probably page 3. Barry rapped on the window. The boy looked up: expressionless, no embarrassment or guilt. Barry was half-expecting a finger. The boy, in his baseball cap, roughly folded the paper over. He stuck it into the letter box. Barry went through to get it. He pulled it out. It was slightly torn.

Back in the kitchen he brewed his tea, stirred in the sugar and opened the paper.

"TERROR SUSPECT FREED!"

He read the story.

Police yesterday released five men arrested in connection with the failed bombings in London on July 21st. The men had been arrested in Batley and Bradfield in West Yorkshire and Selly Oak in Birmingham.

A police spokesman said: "In the twenty eight days allowed by law we have not been able to find sufficient evidence to allow a warrant for further evidence to be gathered or charges to be pursued. We could not be confident of a conviction should a prosecution come to court. Bail is not allowed under terror legislation and so the men have been released."

It is believed the men were suspected of carrying out reconnaissance missions for the would-be bombers and conspiring to cause explosions. CCTV had identified them as visiting the London Eye, the Natural History Museum and several tube stations.

Detention of suspects without charge or trial, as at Belmarsh prison, has been declared illegal by the House of Lords and in breach of Human Rights. Tony Blair had tried to extend the time police could detain a suspect for questioning from fourteen to ninety days. He was, however, defeated in Parliament and an amendment of twenty eight days had been passed. Police believe this is insufficient given the complexity of electronic evidence.

Although freed from prison, the Home Secretary has decided that the five men will be placed under control orders. The orders are used for people believed to pose a threat to national security but who cannot be brought to trial because this could reveal intelligence sources or because evidence has been collected by bugging the suspects and such evidence is inadmissible.

Under a control order the suspect must live at one address, is subject to curfew so that he must remain in the house for sixteen hours a day, can have only restricted visitors, has his passport withdrawn, is electronically tagged, cannot access the internet or use mobile phones, can attend only one mosque and must report daily to the police.

The men's solicitor added: "This is virtual house arrest. Is this what living in a democracy means? One of my clients has developed an anxiety disorder already."

Barry snorted and threw the paper down on the table. *Anxiety disorder!* Six weeks before and they'd killed fifty two and wounded 700. And then they tried it again a fortnight later. *Anxiety disorder!* It was a fucking sick joke. The police should have all the time they needed to sort those bastards out. ninety days if necessary. Blair was right on that one. Fucking Human Rights lawyers. What about the human rights of those poor bastards on the tubes and the bus!

He sipped his tea, hot and strong as he liked it. He looked at the photograph of the freed men. They looked so fucking superior, self-satisfied, as if they were in charge, calling the shots.

The trouble was they were not scared. They had such brass neck. We were scared but they weren't. Someone had to do something about it. Someone had to do something that would make them afraid, make them have second thoughts. He was that someone, once he'd got Lee on board. He couldn't do it alone. He could trust Lee and Lee had been a soldier, he'd been trained to do the things Barry couldn't do.

Barry drove into the stadium car park, already half full, just before 7 pm. This evening he had to persuade Lee to join him. Up the stairs they went and into the restaurant that faced out through vast windows onto the racetrack. The restaurant was stepped in four tiers, each tier lined with tables with white table cloths, gleaming cutlery and wine glasses. They were shown to their table on the top tier.

"This is a bit classy," said Lee.

"Only the best for you."

Immediately they were seated and a waitress came up, middle-aged,white-shirted, black-trousered.

"I'm Donna," she said. "I'll be looking after your food for you. Tim over there will sort your drinks." She pointed to a man with a face round as a football, great jowls and beard and a belly that overhung and completely concealed his belt. "And Georgina there will take your bets and bring your winnings. Do you want it on tab?"

"Yes, that's fine. Thanks, love," said Barry.

They looked around. Conversation was already loud.

"This is a first for me," said Lee.

"Never been dog-racing before?"

"No. Never been a gambler. Mug's game. My granddad used to say he'd never seen a rich-looking man go into a bookie's. How about you?"

"I go to the big race meetings occasionally," said Barry. "Ascot, the Derby. I like to see the toffs being toffs. The women all glammed up, the blokes in their tails and top 'ats, all braying and flinging their money around. Confirms all my prejudices. Just a reminder of who my enemies are."

"Not like this then. These just seem like ordinary folk, here for a night out and a bit of a flutter."

There were tables with three or four men, a few hen parties, a few family groups, women in too tight dresses or too short skirts, tottering down the steps on high heels, too much cheap glamour.

"Yeah. That's why I like this, too. And the excitement of a bit of a bet."

"Don't get me wrong," said Lee, his eye catching a girl who should have known better than to put her fat thighs into a short skirt. "I usually put a tenner on the National. I used to have to go down the bookies for my Mum. She wouldn't go in. Thought there was something not respectful about it but she wanted a flutter. I used to do the pools, too."

"Me, too. They've kind of gone out of fashion, haven't they? It was a real ritual as a kid, every Saturday night listening to Final Score on the tele, checking the coupon."

"Same for me when I stayed at me Grandad's. He still listened to Sports Report on the radio like he always had done – they still play the same music, you know. He'd send me out for the Green and we'd read the match reports."

Barry was fiddling with his knives and forks.

"Good times, Lee. The old days. Christ, we sound like a couple of old men."

They ordered drinks from Tim. Already a gleam of sweat on his fleshy face – Worthington's for Lee, a bottle of Becks for Barry. Georgina, a black girl in a short red uniform with an identity badge, left them a pad of betting slips on the corner of their table. Lee picked up the menu.

"Carrot and coriander soup or tomato and mozzarella salad. Pretty up market. I'll bet my old Mum wouldn't have known what coriander and mozzarella were."

"Upward mobility, Lee, that's what it is."

They ordered Lamb Navarin cooked in white wine and herbs, and BBQ chicken melt with Monterey Jack cheese. They dispensed with the new potatoes and had chunky chips instead with battered onion rings.

"Hey, they're out," said Lee.

Six greyhounds with numbered jackets were paraded along the sanded track in front of them. The commentator started but the sound system was as bad as a railway station and they couldn't hear what he said.

"Too late to bet on this race," said Barry, "but there's twelve more."

Then the 'rabbit' shot past on its rail and the greyhounds hurled themselves out of their traps and skidded round the bends. There was some cheering and shouting as the dogs came round the final bend. In less than thirty seconds the 470 metre race was over.

"I'm getting into this," said Lee. "Let's have a look at the race card."

"The next one's a hurdles," said Barry.

They watched the four sets of hurdles being put out, like flattened shaving brushes.

"I'm going for Nagrag Jim. It's had a couple of firsts and it's a good stayer, so it says here," said Lee, trying to decipher all the tight-packed information on the race card.

"I always go for trap one or a brindled dog," said Barry. "I'll have Rough Pickings. What's the odds?"

Lee looked up at the bank of four monitor screens over head. One was replaying the first race, another showed the results, one was headed Trio pool which Lee did not understand, the last showed the odds.

They put their slip and a tenner on the corner of the table. Georgina took them and returned with their receipts.

"Every table's full," said Lee. "Popular place."

Waiters were hurrying with trays of food, pints and bottles of beer and tall glasses of coke, thumping up and down the stairs and along the tiers. In their red shirts with buttoned down collars, the betting slip girls passed efficiently along the tables.

"They were good," said Lee, looking thoughtfully at the head on his pint.

"What were?"

"Good, the old days. We had good times when we were kids. We didn't do Leisure Centres and Adventure Playgrounds. Remember, we just took our bikes out into the fields and woods."

Donna set their soup bowls in front of them, two warm rolls and butter on a side plate.

"Ta, love," said Barry.

Then the second set of dogs was paraded, the loud commentary stopped any more conversation, the dogs raced out and the soup was forgotten. Barry watched with a smile as Lee stood and shouted, pumping his fists.

"What a fucking race," Lee exclaimed. "Overtaken on the fucking line, mine was overtaken on the fucking line."

"And mine was barged out on the corner."

Lee sat down. Barry screwed up the betting slip. They chose two more for the next race and filled in a new slip.

"Do you remember that weekend we went camping down that valley?" asked Barry. "There was a ruined mill there. What was it called? Out in the wilds somewhere."

"I took Ben there a couple of weeks ago, I told you. My Grandad used to take me. He loved fishing. That's how I knew about going camping there. Crimhope Dale it's called."

"That's it. Do you remember the toads?" asked Barry, looking across at Lee, his thin lips forming a half smile.

This was going well, he thought. Getting Lee in the mood, pressing the right buttons of childhood friendship, nostalgia. It was like chatting up a woman or playing a fish on a line, angling down on the canal.

"Course I remember them. I was petrified. It was your idea to put the tent up in the ruins of the weaving shed at the mill. It was blowing a gale and we wanted some shelter."

"It was your fault. You wanted to shine the torch out."

"Jesus. We could see them all, hundreds of 'em," said Lee. "All shiny and bloated, their great eyes shining. All looking at us, their throats all inflated and beating. That croaking everywhere."

Barry laughed.

"I've never seen you move so fast. Getting the tent pegs out and carrying the tent out in a bundle, all our stuff inside, pitching it on the open ground outside. Bloody hilarious."

"I still never slept a wink," said Lee. "Scared of nightmares about the toads crawling all over my face."

Lee took a long draught of his lager. He remembered Barry throwing boulders at the toads, aiming them, throwing them viciously, flattening them, exploding them. Laughing. He'd been shocked. There was no need.

Lee turned away and looked out at the track. It was getting dark, great thick black clouds piling up over the stadium. Just above the roofs of the council houses on the other side of the track there was a streak of lighter cement-coloured sky. The brilliant lime-coloured floodlights were on, brightening the sand, the red ashes of the speedway track and the muddy green of the central oval. In the middle of the oval was a large hoarding advertising *Early Bird Discount for a Christmas Package*. Christ! It was only August.

Donna brought their main courses, with separate bowls of vegetables and chips.

"I read about that terrorist being freed this morning," said Lee. "Did you see it?"

Barry paused from piling the chunky chips onto his plate.

"Course I did. Really got me going. It seems we're just bloody helpless, waiting like sitting ducks for the next suicide attack. Those Law Lords don't live in the real world."

Lee was tucking into his BBQ chicken.

"You can't fight people who are willing to blow up their own bodies and innocent people with softy liberal stuff," continued Barry. " It means they've just got a free hand. Appeasement doesn't work. I

189

thought we'd learned that from bloody Hitler."

Lee was helping himself to more onion rings as he said, "But that English Patriotic League demo we were at was pretty useless – football chants and a few lads wrapped in union jacks and beating up innocent bystanders just cos of the colour of their skin."

"Couldn't agree more, mate," said Barry. "Puerile. And I'll tell you something else. I was at a BNP meeting last week. I've been a few times, seeing if they've got the answer."

"And have they?"

"Bloody useless if you ask me. Some of the top ones are just politicians on the make – working towards a cushy number in the Brussels parliament with a fat salary and huge expenses. And the local councillors they've managed to get elected are a bunch of losers, doing nothing except making fools of themselves, shouting and bawling in council meetings. The rest are thugs and loudmouths. You couldn't trust any of them. Crude racists. Almost as bad as Combat 18 and the National Front. Fascists. Violence for the sake of it. A few punch ups and kickings." He stabbed his knife into his Chicken Monterey. "That's not patriotism. It's just so undignified."

"Undignified!" Lee frowned. "That's an odd way of putting it."

"I mean it's not worthy, somehow."

"Not worthy of what?"

Barry was staring out of the huge windows at the floodlit track.

"It's not good enough," he said. " It doesn't do justice to the cause. It doesn't do justice to you, for Christ's sake, Lee."

Now for the bait, thought Barry.

"Me?" said Lee, his fork loaded with chicken and poised halfway to his mouth.

Barry put down his knife and fork and looked directly at Lee, his face serious with what he hoped looked like hero-worship.

"Yeah, you. You've been a British soldier fighting for Britain. Then you got kicked out for obeying orders they couldn't admit to. But you risked your life out in fucking Iraq. Then you saved that guy in the underground explosions. So waving a few flags and having a few punch ups is pathetic. Then there's the Law Lords pratting on about Human Rights, paid for by you and me through legal aid. We're just mugs and I'm fucking sick of it. We're a laughing stock so far as those Muslims are concerned."

Lee heard the passion in Barry's voice.

"You're right," he said quietly. "And a lot of people would agree with you. They want something done."

Was this the time to hook him, to strike?

"They want to see some action," continued Barry. "They want to see there's someone fighting back, someone with a bit of British bulldog spirit, someone prepared to stand up to them."

Lee could see the wound-up tension in Barry's body, saw his fists clenched, knuckles white.

"You must have some ideas, Barry. You've thought about it, you're steamed up enough."

Barry let himself relax. He paused. Now to reel him in.

"Yeah, I have an idea, but I can't do it on my own. And I need someone I can trust."

Without hesitation, Lee said: "You can trust me, we're mates, we go back a long way."

"Yeah, you and me could do something, Lee. Just the two of us, a two man team, relying on each other. No-one else to complicate things. Two Englishmen, straight and true." Barry laughed, his hand on his heart. "They need a taste of their own medicine. Bring them down a peg or two, realise they're not getting it all their own way."

Lee saw Barry's eyes glaze over, far away from the bustle and excited chatter of this place.

Barry was thinking of the beheadings – of Edwin Dyer, of Ken Bigley in his orange jump-suit – and of the shooting of aid worker Margaret Hassan, begging not to die like Ken Bigley. He was thinking of Omar Bakri Mohammad glorifying the 'magnificent 19' of September 11th in New York. He was thinking of the Panorama programme a few nights ago on The Muslim Council of Britain. What a charade – mealy-mouthed apologists for book-burning and holocaust deniers and imams who preached that all non-Muslims were monkeys and pigs, refusing to condemn suicide bombers in Palestine. He was on a mission.

Lee took another drink from his second pint.

"So what's your idea?" he asked.

"Something daring, something that will grab the headlines. We'll create a mystery that will get the public's attention. Something that will shock."

"Yes, but what?" asked Lee.

"I don't know yet. We have to wait, wait until an opportunity arises and then seize it. We have to be prepared. I'll recognise the moment. You'll have to trust me for that. Do you trust me, Lee?"

"Of course I do."

He'd said it straightaway. Perhaps it was the beer, the nostalgia, the companionship, the excitement of the races. Afterwards, for a fleeting almost unacknowledged moment, he felt a nip of misgiving. To hell with it!

"Just tell me what we're going to do."

"I will. But we'll do it together."

He stretched out his hand across the table, his eyes bright with zeal.

"Shake on it, mate."

They shook hands. He was in the keep-net.

"Let's go down trackside," said Barry, "before our lemon meringue pie."

They laughed.

"There's more atmosphere down there."

A tractor was smoothing down the sand track. It was spitting with rain and a few umbrellas were going up. A young child in a push chair watched her sister, all in pink, and brother skipping about on the concrete area. Their mother sat on the concrete step eating a paper cone of chips. There certainly is more atmosphere, thought Lee. Virtually everyone was smoking, there was a smell of burgers and chips. Gangs of young lads, mostly in their twenties, stood around, plastic pint glass in one hand, pie in the other. Shaven-headed, in white t-shirts, overweight, they shouted odds and dogs' names to each other and waved race cards.

"There's a lot that's not pretty," said Barry, gazing round.

Two women stood by the blue wooden track rail, their half empty pint glasses perched on top of it. Both held fags in one hand while eating sausage rolls with the other.

"Hard faces," said Lee. "Rough as prop forwards. Christ, look at those shoulders. They're square."

Their hair was scraped tight back from their faces, hair artificially black and blonde. One had a tattoo on the nape of her neck.

"No sophistication," said Barry. "Except for the ankle chain." He laughed. "Poor sods."

Was he really doing it for them, for 'the people'? Barry knew, if he was honest, he was doing it for himself.

Then the rain came in a sudden flurry and they hurried back into the restaurant. Now there was a richer comradeship between them, a bond, as they placed bets, ate their lemon meringue, collected a few winnings, drank more beer and cheered and shouted with the rest. They ended the evening £30 up and Barry drove them home, religiously obeying every speed restriction in case he got stopped.

He was fired up by his evening's work – he'd got Lee on board. But he knew he had to wait for the right moment. When it came, he was prepared. He'd show them. He'd fucking show everybody.

From: Sue [sue08whitehall@blueyonder.co.uk]
Sent: 26 August 2005 1904
To: Mike
Subject: Thee and me

Yesterday evening I went with my friend Hannah from school and her two young sons for a walk across the fields. Swallows were gathering on the telegraph wires by the lane.

"Look at the moon," I said to little Dan. It was an early-rising, pale gibbous moon in the still clear pale blue sky.

"Why is the moon broken?" asked Dan.

Sue

xx

18.

Telescope

12th September

Crimhope Dale, Pennines

Mike had been at Upper Heights Barn for two weeks and the change from London had been total. He was in a different world now. How incongruous it had been, poring over OS maps in his over-heated hospital room with the constant sound of traffic outside, tracing the brown contour lines, following the routes of his runs, recalling the landmarks. He had been more detached than he had feared. He knew what he was looking for: he wanted to return north, to live in a wild place, isolated but within reasonable driving distance of the hospital for the continued physio he would need. He didn't want it to be pretty, either. His old asceticism didn't want a stream running through a village green, or white painted fences and roses round the door. He must live in a new place, not connected with his previous life of running nor a place he had walked with Sue.

Mike had found this place, far up Crimhope Dale. Local occupational therapists, a physio and social workers had gone out to inspect it and declared it suitable. Jim the farmer had agreed to rent for a year before first refusal on purchase. The support team had come to an agreement with him about the necessary refurbishment:

lower wheelchair-height kitchen surfaces, stair-rails on both sides of the stairs, grab-rails and a lifting frame for the toilet and bath. The cottage already had a ramp to the front and back doors and widened doorways, put in when Jim's mother needed a wheelchair. Jim had been co-operative in every way, wanting to help, even perhaps proud to help one of the victims of the terrorist attack.

Mike knew the cottage was perfect for him: towards the head of an isolated valley, down a track with high banks, leading from a country lane, a single property surrounded by fields. It felt like an island and that was just right. Ever since he had thought about things Mike had believed that each man was an island, essentially alone. This place reflected that view, reinforced it. Islands are separate and individual, bounded. Islands can be secretive places where private hopes and fears and imagination can bloom, a place of possibilities but also of limitations. This was the right place to confront himself, continue the task of re-creating himself.

Mike had phoned his father in Canada about the cottage but he had been too ill to talk. His Canadian wife, Anita, had been so supportive. She had organised the necessary paperwork for the transfer of funds. All along the line people had been helpful. They'd welcomed him, warmed to him and Mike had felt an instinctive reciprocal response.

It was a perfect early September morning. There had been a thin streamer of mist along the valley floor but the sun had quickly burned this off. Mike had opened his conservatory door and the sun was streaming in, already warm. The dark green footprints of his early morning walk were slowly fading in the dew of the lawn. A cow in the adjacent field moo-ed so loudly it startled him, it seemed to be in the garden. He still wasn't used to it.

He was in the kitchen chopping onions and frying off the mince, preparing a chilli for this evening's meal. In his orderly way he had lined up on the surface in front of him the tins of sweet corn and kidney beans, a pile of chopped mushrooms, the Hot Chilli Pepper seasoning and the bottle of Lea and Perrins. He had invited Ali's family – Ali, his wife and two children and, of course, their telescope.

Ali was the volunteer NHS driver who had driven him to his

physiotherapy sessions at the city hospital. He was a Muslim. It had been a shock the first time Mike had opened the door to him. Now he was ashamed of that reaction. They'd even talked about it together on the last forty five minute trip to the hospital and Ali had laughed. But he'd also understood Mike's reaction. Mike liked him. Ali worked with his brother in an accountancy firm they had set up but he took half a day a week off work using his people carrier to take patients to hospital for treatment.

"I'm grateful to the NHS," he had explained. "Our first child, Yasmin, was born prematurely. She only survived because of her time in the incubator. The care they gave her, and the kindness shown to us, were amazing. I wanted to give something back. And I like meeting people. Like I've met you."

He'd laughed.

"I saw your face when you first opened the door to me," he'd continued. "You were scared. When you told me what had happened to you, I understood that. But nearly everyone I call on is wary of me to begin with, until they realise I am just an ordinary bloke. I suppose that's another reason I continue with this: to show there are other kinds of Muslims, that we are not all bombers."

Ali talked easily to him. Britain had been good to him, he had said. It was his home, he had been born here. Britain had given him opportunities and he'd been fortunate enough to have been able to accept them. He had a good job and a nice house, a family. His kids were in a good school which he and his wife had chosen because most children there had English as their first language. His wife worked, too, as Grocery Manager in Morrisons. He had been horrified at the London bombings. He and his wife had cried as they watched the news reports on television: the injuries, the deaths. They had also realised that life for Muslims in Britain would never be the same again. They would all be tarred with the same brush: the enemy within. The only way forward was to carry on, carry on with his volunteer work driving and hope that people would see him as an individual and not label him as an Islamist terrorist.

On their last trip they'd talked about how Mike filled his time, living out in the country on his own. Ali had talked enthusiastically about how he'd been into astronomy, how his wife had bought him a telescope for Christmas one year. But then their children had been born and he had quickly discovered that night was needed for sleeping not watching stars. The telescope was in his loft somewhere. Astronomy was something you could do on your own. He could lend Mike his telescope. He could try it out, see if he was interested. Mike had been interested. As Ali turned the NHS community ambulance into the cottage yard Mike had suddenly invited them all for a meal. Ali, with a broad grin, had immediately agreed, saying he would bring the telescope and set it up. His own kids would be fascinated, they'd never seen it.

Mike had watched the vehicle drive away up the lane, amazed at his own initiative. Spontaneity and invitations to social occasions were just not how he worked. Now here he was, his face wet with tears from the chopped onions.

Ruth came bustling into the kitchen to squeeze out a damp cloth and get some fresh water. She looked at his face.

"You want to turn the tap on when yer choppin' onions," she said. "You won't cry then. It works with me."

"Bit late, I suppose," said Mike.

"Me Mum used to light a candle or chew a match," continued Ruth, running the tap and swilling out the bucket. She squeezed in some Stardrops.

"How was your weekend?" asked Mike.

"We 'ad a lovely time. The caravan site was nice. It didn't rain and we went into York."

She wrung the damp cloth dry and returned to the living room.

Ruth and her husband Dick were two other people that Mike realised he was warming to. Ruth cleaned for him one morning a week and Dick did occasional hours in the garden to keep it under control. Dick had big plans for the spring and had already planted dozens of daffodil bulbs. Mike knew the extra cash came in handy for them. They'd both worked here before Mike came, looking after Jim's parents. Jim was the farmer a mile down the valley. When Jim's parents had retired and passed on the farm to him, they had come to live here. Jim's father had died a year later of a heart attack, herding sheep into a pen at dipping time, unable to stop working. His mother had lived on alone but had died six months ago. Mike knew the old people's deaths had given him an opportunity.

Mike heard the hoovering stop in the living room. Through the half-open door he watched Ruth spool up the cable. He knew if he ever needed any extra help Ruth and the people he had come to know so recently could be relied on. But he was determined not to ask for help. This was his journey; he had chosen it. Chris had shown him the way. He would follow – but on his own.

Ruth came in, taking off her pinnie.

"What you need is a good woman – and not an old 'un like me," she said, putting the hoover under the stairs. She didn't see Mike's face tighten up at her words.

"Look after yersel'," she said. "And don't forget the salt in there. I see ye've not lined it up with the rest of the stuff. Dick 'll be in tomorrow. I think he's bringing some compost to freshen up yer soil, he said. I'll be back next week. 'Ope ye 'ave a good evenin'."

"See you," said Mike.

He emptied the rest of the ingredients into the large pan and turned the gas down to simmer. He hoped he hadn't made it too hot for the kids. He'd give it an hour now, turn it off and then heat it up for another hour just before the meal. Chilli, like curry and casseroles, always seemed to taste better the second time around. It was a good job it did as he usually made enough food at one go to last three days.

Next up was his exercises. He hadn't missed a day yet and didn't intend to. He had a chart, a spreadsheet he'd produced on his PC, on which were listed his exercises with spaces to fill in with the time he'd spent on each or the number of repetitions he'd done. There wasn't an empty space yet and already he could feel the benefits in his muscle strength and suppleness. It gave him a good feeling that he could apply the same determination to his walking that he once applied to his fell-running. He'd come a long way to accepting his stumps, too. It had been easier on his own. He no longer saw them as horrific and ugly. He had sat in his wheelchair or on the couch in his shorts quite happily, even when Ruth was cleaning around him. There were still scars and always would be but they were neat. The surgeons had done a good job. Strapping his prosthetic legs on every day had made him familiar with him. Now that he was walking ever more efficiently he saw how serviceable the stumps were. They had a job and did it well. His muscles were toning up and sitting in the garden in the sun had tanned them. He'd found himself automatically hitching his shorts up so that more of his thighs would be browned.

He levered himself down to sit on the floor with his back leaning against the couch. This was an exercise to develop his upper body strength and triceps. He stretched his hands back to the seat of the couch, paused then pushed himself up, held the weight of his upper body there, then bent his elbows to let himself down. He had to do this twenty times. It was hard and he had to concentrate. Resting after this session, as his heart slowed down and the cottage was silent around him, his thoughts flickered back to Sue. In spite of himself he imagined Sue's voice here, singing some snatch of a tune repetitively, or just the rattle of pan lids from the kitchen or her footsteps crossing the bedroom floor above. With her presence, there would be a busy-ness in the house. He saw clearly how empty his cottage was, how minimalist. He liked it that way, it suited him now. All his belongings were at Sue's, or he supposed they were. He had had to start again. All he'd had were his laptop and his memory stick. Clothes, chairs, a kitchen table, bed, hard drive, printer, discs – he'd bought the absolute minimum. This stringency suited him. But as the evenings became cooler and grey days made the cottage rooms gloomy, he realised how unwelcoming the place was. He saw it was an odd sort of home – in fact, wasn't a home. The flowers Ruth had brought, in her own vase, and placed on the small coffee table looked incongruously colourful and graceful, their faint scent defying the bleakness. Were they lilies? He noticed the scatter of yellow pollen on the table top. The walls were white and bare. He saw too easily how Sue could soon turn this room into a real home with warmth and cosiness. She had a gift for it – colours and textures, softnesses, lamplight, creating homely spaces. He shrugged away his thoughts. He had to keep control.

On his last visit to the hospital, over coffee, one of the other patients had mentioned the amputee forums on the internet. Mike remembered that Chris had spoken about them, back in London. With the chilli done and his exercises completed, he decided to log on and explore the sites. He was amazed. They were a revelation. A whole community existed out there of people who shared his problems and had many more. Questions were asked and fellow amputees answered with their advice and experiences.

Mike scrolled down. There were men and women preparing for amputation who were scared stiff: 'Give yourself room to feel the emotions you're feeling, let them out. They need to be processed. You are not alone.' Someone asked how you dealt with people staring at you: 'I stare back at them, look them in the eye and smile at them. Do they pity me or think I'm courageous? People find it difficult, don't know how to react. They might want to know how it happened or if it was painful.' A man replied saying it wasn't other people's perceptions he had a problem with, 'It's my perception of myself.' He asked if other amputees had problems with 'body image, feeling ugly.' Mike recognised this one. 'I don't feel whole any more,' the man continued. Mike leaned back in his chair. Perhaps there was a role for him here, perhaps he could help. He wasn't through his own problems yet, but that was an advantage. Helping each other, that was how it worked. He smiled to himself. Perhaps you could live on an island and still communicate, share.

The site had sections on amputee funny stories, amputee achievements, amputee inspirational moments. There was even a section that dealt with decorating your prosthetic leg – with tattoos, peace signs, laminates, air brush paintings. Mike followed a reference to a charity site that had been set up to develop and deliver prosthetic limbs to African countries. There were photographs of young children and adults who had lost limbs to land mines left in the ground after civil wars. It was horrendous. The site explained that limbs out there were in short supply, were badly designed and cheaply made because of lack of money and surgeons and equipment. £60 or £100 would buy a good quality limb or pay for reconstructive surgery in some remote location: 'giving people back their lives.' It swept over him that he was so lucky, so fortunate. The pictures made him feel he should never complain again. Here, too, was something he could do. He remembered Chris talking about sport. Was it wheelchair basketball he was keen on? He should do the same, get into paraplegic sport but in a sponsored way, raise some money for those kids out there. Do for them what had been done for him – getting a life back. Wheelchair marathon racing was a possibility – perhaps he should try that. The other project he'd set himself was to find Lee but he had no idea how to start because he couldn't remember his surname.

He wheeled himself into the conservatory, across to the open doorway and looked across the valley. Cows moved in the field, he could hear their munching. There was the lone cottage opposite which Ruth had told him was a holiday cottage but untenanted at the moment. No other sign of life. He felt the sun on him, closed his eyes and leaned his head back. It was odd, this feeling: life expanding beyond the bounds he had set himself, beyond what he was familiar with.

He liked chatting to Ruth and Dick and Jim, Ali and his new physios. That was a new feeling. Perhaps it was because he lived alone. He was really looking forward to tonight, meeting Ali's wife and children, except for being a bit nervous about the food. But security lay on his island. He had never been a sociable man and was suspicious of this unaccustomed sense of fellowship. As well as a freshness, he sensed in himself a new vulnerability that he was scared of. He had constructed a shell around himself: to deal with his stumps, to harden his heart against Sue, to devote himself to learning to walk. If the shell cracked and broke to leave him exposed, if he let other people in, what needs might be released or renewed? The thought made him shiver even as he felt the sun on his face.

With the second exercise session of the day completed in mid afternoon, Mike put the pan of chilli on at 4.30, brought it to boil and then lowered the gas to simmer. He laid the kitchen table with five places, measured out the rice and filled a pan with water. They would eat at 6.00. A dinner party! Who'd have thought it! He knew he wasn't good at small talk but Ali was naturally chatty and you could usually rely on a woman to keep the conversation going. Would their young daughters be politely quiet, he wondered, or full of questions? Get them going on school, he thought, the new term must be about to start. A sudden image of Sue flashed across his mind – her neatly tabulated folders on the shelves, a pile of exercise books, her school bag. Like the kids, she would have been down to WH Smith's to renew her pens and Tippex and post-it notes, yet more ring files. Again he resolutely put away the image and stirred the chilli.

Promptly at 5.45 the Ali family arrived. Mike welcomed them. Ali introduced his wife Shakira, a petite woman, smartly dressed in a black trouser suit, with gold hooped ear-rings and bright lipstick.

"I've heard a lot about you," she said, shaking Mike's hand.

"That always worries me," said Mike.

Shakira laughed gaily. She held the hands of her two daughters, standing each side of her.

"Our girls," she said proudly. "Zara and Yasmin."

They wore jeans, trainers with red and yellow laces and t-shirts. Zara, the youngest, had a T-shirt lettered The Little Mermaid. The mermaid had a bright green tail, long Hollywood-style red hair and, surrounded by bubbles, was admiring a yellow flower underwater. Mike shook her hand. Then he shook hands with Yasmin whose t-shirt showed Pocahontas, glossy back hair streaming into a golden sunset.

"Glad you could come," he said. "Your Dad told me you like chilli. I hope he was right."

"Oh, yes," they said.

"Well, come in, then."

Ali went round to the boot of his car and lifted out his telescope.

"Yasmin, can you take the tripod, please?"

Yasmin gave a low groan but went round to him.

"I'll set it up in the garden while you're sorting out the tea, if that's alright," said Ali. "Then we'll be all set for when it goes dark. Good job it's a clear sky, but it means it could be chilly."

"Go ahead," said Mike.

Over tea the girls talked about the new teachers they'd be having when term started next Monday. There was Mrs Steadman who had long grey hair, was funny and had the room with the blue door.

"I'll be in year two," said Zara.

"But I'll be in year four, because I'm older," said Yasmin.

There hadn't been a quiet moment over tea and all three adults had done the washing and drying up together in spite of Mike's protests. The girls were almost as excited as Mike about the telescope.

They hadn't seen it before.

"Daddy said some naughty words when he banged his head on the trapdoor into the roof, going to get it," giggled Yasmin.

It was quite cool when they went out into the garden but the sky was clear and the moon was rising over the moorline.

"As you can see," said Ali, "it's a new moon so we won't see much there but the advantage is that with less moonlight we can see the stars better. In another couple of weeks it will be the harvest moon – which is always bigger and brighter than usual because of its low arc."

He adjusted and focused the telescope. Mike was as excited as the girls when he took his first look at the moon – amazed at the pattern of craters and ridges, all of them mapped and named.

"Fantastic to know that there are human footprints up there," he said.

Ali pointed out Venus, low to the west, the brightest light in the sky, and Jupiter close to it.

"Stars twinkle, planets are steady," he explained.

Over to the west Ali pointed out the constellation of Ophiucus, the serpent holder. They saw the stars of Cassiopeia but the highlight of the evening was seeing the last of the Perseids, a meteor shower which looked like cosmic fireworks. Mike was fascinated.

When they had all driven away Mike allowed himself to feel the evening had been successful – and he was hooked on stargazing. For the first time in his life he had hosted a dinner party – of sorts! Yes, he had enjoyed the evening, the company. Sue would have been astonished and pleased, seeing him venture out of his shell. He realised it wasn't just a shell he had created since the explosion: he had always lived within a shell, at a distance from people. He wondered why but couldn't be bothered pursuing the thought. Childhood, he supposed. Everything depended on childhood, so they said.

He would have liked Sue to have been there – not as a support, nor as a supporter in his rehabilitation. He just wanted her companionship, her sense of ease in herself that somehow relaxed other people, made them feel comfortable. What on earth had she seen in him? That need for her that burned up in him, that made his heart ache: it was just like phantom limb pain. She wasn't there but she was there. Cutting her off had been essential but how he wished to share things with her again – the heavens, for instance, tracing the movement of the constellations across the sky, beginning to understand the life and death of stars.

That night, in a confusion of thoughts and unable to sleep, Mike deliberately created a scene in his imagination. Sue is sitting next to him on his bed, talking. They are sipping champagne which she has brought. She smiles, her eyes mischievous. She is so full of high spirits, so joyous, so vital.

"You are beautiful," he says.

"And you are pleased to see me," she replies, placing her hand on his groin.

"All I want is to hold you, be held by you," he says.

"Liar," she laughs.

They lie back on the bed. She holds his penis tight in her hand, their mouths lock into a deep kiss, his finger enters her and strokes her. She comes, with a groan. Their mouths part. He sees her lips swollen, her eyes heavy with sensuality.

"You always know what to do," she would say, "you always have that effect on me."

She still holds his penis, still stiff. She begins to move her hand up and down it, still looking into his eyes.

"No, don't," he says." I don't want to come. I don't want this to end. I have come home."

He snuggles his head on her lap.

Mike opens his eyes. Why must he torture himself like this? Because it is all he has of her. Mike is fully awake now. He feels his penis: it is erect. The room is dark. His panic is back. In his imagination she is always present. His self-sufficiency, his lone journey depended on her being there in the background, a presence to be relied on in emergency or desperate straits. Memories of her, feelings for her come to the surface. He cannot keep them submerged. He looks at the clock. It is 2.34 am.. Somehow he must go to her, see her, hold her. He cannot be without her. He aches for her.

Slowly he returns to this time and place, this silence. This is how things must be. This is how he decided it. He cannot break what peace she may have begun to create for herself. He cannot presume.

205

Sent: 13 September 2005 2218

To: Mike

Subject: Thee and me

Did my usual pre-term shop – bought a big bag capable of holding a class set of exercise books. Oh joy!

I have decided that I have reached a kind of wisdom in one area of my life: I can love without being loved back.

Love! What is it? Wanting to spend time with someone, admiring and respecting that someone, share experience, have fun and discussions, enjoy the other's independence, laugh at the same things, plan together, pile up a joint history, help someone, support them, enjoy them as themselves, ride the irritations, enjoy a sensuous joyous carnality, be shameless, talk about feelings. We had most of that, Mike, didn't we?

You are open and honest but there is a part of you I do not know, cannot touch. Nor do I want to – I do not want your soul. I like trekking into an unknown place. Your separateness has left me here and you down there but I loved your separateness, and still do. I somehow find a safety in its strength. Oddly, it is like a haven when I feel my life is too busy. I sometimes wonder if my social life is a cover-up for something, a fill-in. I know you think I am confident and pragmatic and optimistic. I am those things but maybe they are limitations that shield me from more demanding complexities. You invite me into those. And sometimes I know you want to escape from them. You do that inside me, and I love it. It is exhilarating. So you see we have a reciprocity. Ah! Well!

Sue

Xx

19.

Target

Bradfield, Crimhope Dale.

Around ten o'clock on Saturday morning Sue had completed her Sainsbury's shopping and parked her loaded trolley at the entrance to the in-store café. She bought herself a latte and picked up the *Guardian*.

At about the same time Mike, at the bottom of his garden, waved to his neighbouring farmer on his tractor as he passed along the lane. With the help of his crutches, he walked up to the cottage, poured a re-fill of coffee and picked up the *Independent* that the farmer had put in his letterbox. It was an arrangement they had, the farmer and his wife wanting to be helpful. Mike went into the conservatory. The sun was warm and he opened a window to let in some air.

On the same morning Barry got down to the kitchen just in time to hear Radio 5's sports news summary just after ten o'clock. Still bleary-eyed, he checked the kettle had water in it, switched it on and put a spoonful of Kenco instant coffee into a mug. He picked up the *Mirror*.

All three read the same news which made the front page in all their newspapers:

TOP TERROR SUSPECT IS FREED OVER SECRETS FEAR.

That article continued:

The Home Secretary has released a terror suspect from virtual house arrest to avoid disclosing secret evidence.

The man, known only as HS, has been subject to a controversial control order since being freed after the maximum twenty eight days' detention for questioning about his links with the attempted 21st July bombings in London. He is believed to be an uncle of one of the 7/7 London bombers. He has never been charged and the evidence for the allegations has never been heard in a public court.

The control order was revoked last week and the suspect's electronic tag removed, setting him free in spite of the government's claim that he remains a threat.

The Law Lords had already ruled that the suspect had been denied a fair hearing prior to detention because he had not been told sufficient details of the case against him. No reason was given in the Home Secretary's letter to the suspect's solicitor. But he was faced with either releasing the man or disclosing secret intelligence-based evidence such as telephone taps, audio bugs, tip-offs from informants or information from other intelligence agencies around the world. This could have jeopardised intelligence sources or methods.

HS' solicitor said: The orders are incompatible with Article 5 of the European Convention on Human Rights. The right to a fair hearing is fundamental. He has always insisted he has done nothing wrong. It has been terrible for his family since the first day of his arrest, that he is considered a terrorist. His mother is a heart patient and she has had to go to hospital a couple of times because of all this, the custody and the uncertainty.

Sue put her paper down and gave a deep sigh. It was almost exactly ten weeks since the bombing that had altered Mike's life so cruelly. He would be severely confined for ever. She was confident he would learn to walk again but he would never run. For most of those ten weeks she felt that she too had been in a kind of solitary confinement. Mike had kept his word about never communicating with her. She knew that in his view he wasn't just protecting himself, he was protecting her. But she kept the faith: that some time soon, as he adjusted and learned to cope, allowed himself to feel again, he would turn back to her. She understood his need to cut himself off, to channel all his strength into recovery, to prove he was still independent. It was hard, though, not to feel diminished, relegated: like so many women before her, her role was to wait. She was looking forward to the afternoon: a walk with Jade along the canal to the old mill and its attractive tearoom. She finished her coffee and folded up the newspaper, hoping the day wouldn't cloud over.

Mike finished the article and stretched back in his chair. The uncle of his bomber. No one had yet been charged with conspiring with the bombers to plan the explosions or to help make the bombs. It seemed that one of the bombers – not his – had been under MI5 surveillance but this had been discontinued. There had been known visits to training camps in Pakistan but no action had been taken. He felt no bitterness. Humans make wrong decisions, resources are limited, the whole world-wide jihadist movement so complex and fluid. He seemed remote from it now. The past was the past; all his mental and physical effort had to be on the future. He wasn't interested in revenge, not even in justice for himself. The main thing was that the killing of innocent people should not be allowed to happen again. And to prevent it he thought the courts and the government and MI5 should have all the powers they needed. It was out of his hands. He turned to the sports pages, to the football stories of the day.

Barry finished the story in a helpless rage. The world was mad. Especially Law Lords! The government had no final powers, the Law Lords had the final say. Democracy! But, thanks to them, HS did again, free to stroll the streets without even an ASBO.

Barry calmed down and then smiled. The timing was perfect. The powers that be had given him his chance. He enjoyed the irony. Now the fight back could begin. He picked up his mobile phone, scrolled through the names, and tapped in Lee's number.

"Hello."

"Hi, it's Barry here."

"Early for you, Barry."

"Soon enough. I think we have lift off. We have our man. Can't say more on the phone. The Bobbin-makers at 12.30, OK?"

"I'll be there."

*

At the Bobbin-makers' Barry got the pints in and went to sit at a corner table.

"Here's to us!" said Barry, clinked glasses and took a deep drink.

"That's better," he said and wiped his mouth with the back of his hand. He took the *Mirror* out of his pocket, unfolded it, spread it out on the table.

"That's our man," he said, pointing at one of the photographs on the front page.

"I remember that," said Lee, "it was about a month ago, wasn't it? We talked about them. What's happened?"

"What's happened is: they've been bloody freed. They're free to walk the streets like you and me. The Home Secretary has let them out. And this is where we step in. This is where you and me start the fight back, Lee, show the fuckers they may be able to run rings round the Law Lords and the fucking Human Rights brigade but not round us."

Lee had never seen him so alive. His eyes were glittering. He couldn't sit still. Barry jabbed his finger at the photo.

"That one – he's the uncle of that bomber who did your tube train. That's the one we'll get."

"What do you mean, get?"

Barry looked Lee in the eye.

"Are you with me?"

Lee looked steadily back at him.

"Aye, I'm with you, mate."

Barry clapped him on the shoulders.

"Now, this is the plan," said Barry.

Barry did not give details, just the broad strategy and the reasons behind it. Lee listened intently. He had a part to play, he could change things, swing the balance, get back in the action.

When Barry left early – "Phone calls to make, mate!" – Lee

ordered another pint. This was a new start. His mind went back to that northern barracks just over a year ago, to the court martial that had changed his life.

"Corporal Lee Norton, number 73188650 of the 10th Black Watch, you have pleaded guilty to the charges of disgraceful conduct of a cruel kind, behaving in a way which was nothing less than a calculated and premeditated act of cruelty."

Then the dramatic pause as he stood to attention, arms stiff by his side, head tilted upwards, cap firmly on. He would show no reaction, give the bastards no satisfaction.

"You will be dishonourably discharged from the army and will then serve eighteen months in prison."

He had saluted. As he turned to march out he noticed his lawyer shaking hands with the prosecuting counsel. They were smiling at each other, another fee earned. It was as if they had finished a game of tennis and were shaking hands over an invisible net cord. Well played, sir!

What had happened then was done only to an identikit of him. They had dealt with only the husk of him, the uniform. All that ritualized humiliation hadn't touched the real him: the obligatory medical at the garrison detention centre to check he was fit enough to be held in custody, the sample of his DNA, being de-kitted and his ID card taken away at the Military Correction Training Centre in Colchester. Finally he was driven, now no longer a soldier, in a private security prison van to Wormwood Scrubs in London. He was now just a common criminal. But inside, he had been whole. He had kept faith, been honest. And he had come to terms with it, understood it.

He knew he'd been made a scapegoat, been the fall guy. But in the long early sleepless nights in his cell he'd begun to see things a different way. The officers had had to sanction the conditioning because they needed information from the detainees that would protect the troops – from ambush, road side bombs, sniping. They couldn't publicly admit this for obvious reasons. It was a war situation out there, kill or be killed. But at home, here in Britain, where people's lives were not on the line there was leisure time for principles and discussions. They hadn't seen the mutilated bodies of his mates that put them into wheelchairs, their brains so damaged they were barely more than vegetables. So the officers had been right. He was a fall guy, but he had been a protector, a shield for his mates. He'd been right, they'd been right.

And so his anger had been re-focused on to the cause of the conditioning: the Muslim militia who fought behind shields of women and children, who kidnapped and beheaded; the Muslim suicide bombers who killed the innocent and their own kind. They were the ones who were responsible for the conditioning.

He finished his pint. The London bombers had been the English equivalent, Mike and others the innocent victims. Now perhaps, with Barry, he could fight back and make his mark.

From: Sue [sue08whitehall@blueyonder.co.uk]
Sent: 17 September 2005 1300
To: Mike
Subject: Thee and me

I got so angry with you last night as I lay in bed – our bed. Angry at your stubborn refusal, your male obtuseness, retreating behind a bizarre macho mask. I will stop the nonsense of these messages, be sensible, move on. I'll get drunk with Lisa, pull a bloke at a Leeds nightclub. God stop me hating you! No more of this!

xx

20.

Learning

18th September

Upper Heights Barn, Crimhope Dale

There was a knock at the door, at one thirty pm., dead on time. Mike got up, picked up his crutches and walked to the door.

"Afternoon, Mike," said Ali. "How are you today? Ready for the physio?"

"Good. Really looking forward to this meeting. I think he'll tell me I'm ahead of schedule. That'll be good."

"Well, you've worked hard. Very conscientious."

"Thank you."

Ali looked around at the open landscape.

"I love this trip out into the country, especially on a sunny day like today. You live in a beautiful place."

"I know. I'm lucky. I feel like I live on an island, tucked away in secret down this lane."

Ali helped Mike get into the car. It was still a manoeuvre he had to concentrate on, conscious of each separate movement, retaining balance, swivelling into the seat, pulling his legs round.

"I need some education today," said Mike as the car set off up the lane.

"From me?" laughed Ali.

"Yes. You're the only person I know who might have the answers. Have you seen the news today, about those suspect bombers being released?"

"Yes, I have."

"Perhaps it's because I'm feeling better, making good progress with my walking. But for the first time I'm beginning to think about the man who bombed my train. Not about how I feel, but how he felt, why he did it."

Ali slowed down to swing round a corner. The lane was narrow with passing places.

"I know some of the theories," said Ali, "but I still can't comprehend how someone can actually go through with it."

"So what are the theories?"

Ali turned his head to look at him.

"Eyes on the road, please, Ali."

"Sorry. Don't you want to get past all that?"

"Yes," replied Mike. "But this is part of how I can do it: if I can understand it better, rather than it being a mystery. I think it's easier to accept if there's a reason rather than just being the result of a random meaningless accident."

"Even if you don't agree with the reason?"

"Yes, I think so. I'm not sure. I'll find out, I suppose."

Ali sighed. He slowed down for a blind summit and then began to descend the hill.

"It's to do with identity in the first place. Do you see yourself as English?"

"Actually, no," said Mike. "First of all I'm a Yorkshireman. You know, *born and bred, God's own country.* Then I like to see myself as a European, I like this European Union thing. Then British: that's what I always write on forms that want your nationality. I never put English."

"So I'm more English than you," laughed Ali. "I firmly see myself as English. But maybe that's because I had to make a more conscious decision about it. You can float between them, you're at ease in any of those identities. My colour, my religion, my family history – they

215

forced me to make decisions about how to live my life. All of us British Muslims – women as well as men – have to make to make this choice. Who do I support when England play Pakistan at cricket? It's a good question, not a daft question."

"But I'm the same," said Mike. "I missed out one bit of my identity. My Dad was part Welsh, I'm a quarter Welsh. So in rugby matches I always support Wales."

"But Wales is part of Britain, isn't it? So it's not the same."

"Being a Celt isn't the same as being Anglo-Saxon, I can assure you," Mike protested.

They were entering the town now, semi-detached houses and parked cars lining both sides of the road. Cars were filtering in from side streets, darting into the smallest gaps to join the continuous line of traffic.

"Yes, but that's all history and a bit of a luxury, if I may say so," said Ali. "My choices are about now, how we live now in our street, in our town. They're real decisions. And when *you* walk down the street people can't see anything that tells them you're Welsh – or Irish, or Scots, or Polish or Ukrainian or Australian. But they know I'm different even if I'm wearing a suit and tie or T-shirt and jeans. They see my skin."

The bus in front of them had stopped at a bus stop. They couldn't overtake because of traffic coming the other way.

"But what's all this to do with the bombers?" asked Mike.

"Are they British or are they Pakistani? They're neither. They're lost between both identities. So that gap is filled by being a Muslim. They know what that means. Islam tells them how to live, gives them rules. And it means they are part of a worldwide community: what we call the ummah, the global Muslim community. Being a Muslim is what gives them an identity, not being English or even Pakistani. Identity is not about race or nationality, about tribes, any more."

"But that's just like someone being a Christian. It doesn't turn them into killers."

"But it did, didn't it? It used to," said Ali.

"How do you mean?"

"Christians were Crusaders, weren't they? Then they slaughtered the Aztecs and the Incas in the name of the Church. They tortured each other with the Inquisition. The Jews were the same, with the Zealots and the Zionists."

"I suppose so."

Nearer the centre of town the semi-detached houses had been replaced with stone terraced cottages, their front doors opening directly onto the pavement. They slowly passed a row of shops: a butcher's, a greengrocer's with a display of flowers narrowing the pavement, a post office, a fish and chip shop, an Indian take-away. Ali stopped to let an Asian woman wheel her push chair across the zebra crossing, holding a small boy with one hand.

"But it's more than being a Muslim," continued Ali. "For these young male Muslims see their brothers oppressed in Iraq and Palestine, attacked in Afghanistan. And who is doing the oppressing? The West. And who is the West? The USA and Britain. They are the enemy from whom they want to protect and save their brothers. The West is unjust and he wants to fight injustice. It is a noble cause."

"So my bomber mutilated me in the noble cause of justice."

"Yes, of course."

"So I am a victim of justice."

"And of injustice, of course."

There was no by-pass to the town so the main streets were clogged with lorries on their way through. Slowly they worked their way round a roundabout, past pedestrian crossing lights and road junction lights, the yellow diagonalled areas at T-junctions.

"Your bomber was a freedom fighter, not a terrorist. Just like the IRA, like the Mau-Mau. He is – was – a Jihadist."

"Explain, please."

"For these men Jihad is more important than prayer or fasting or even hajj – the pilgrimage to Mecca. It is the best voluntary act a man can perform. Jihad is an individual obligation, an offensive weapon against oppression. Jihadists see themselves as the only true Muslims, all the others are heretics. And all non-Muslims are infidels. So the world is simplified down into Jihadists and everyone else: infidels, heretics, kafirs. Us and them."

"So being a Jihadist is their prime identity?"

"That's right," nodded Ali. "It has filled the gap, it has answered the questions, given them a purpose. And young men need a purpose. It has also given them an enemy."

"Who tells them all this?"

"Osama bin Laden, Al-Qa'eda. They issued a fatwa: 'To kill the Americans and their allies – civilians and military – is an individual duty incumbent upon every Muslim.' Abu Hamza at the Finsbury Park Mosque. He actually wrote: 'If you truly loved God, you'd hate even the shadow of an unbeliever. Those who believe in democracy are kafir, infidels.'"

"Jesus!" muttered Mike.

"Look at that," said Ali, pointing.

They were halted in a line of traffic. On the opposite side of the road was a partially built mosque with a high wooden fence round it. It was all grey breeze blocks with empty spaces for the pointed windows. Over it was the red steel framework for the dome. Ali was pointing at a large poster stuck on the fence. They both recognised the picture of the mangled red London bus that had been bombed. Under the picture were the words: 'Maybe it's time to start listening to the BNP.' Scrawled alongside on the fence in large red letters was: 'Islam out of Britain.'

The traffic edged forward.

"It's not easy," said Ali.

"I suppose if you feel helpless, you do turn to violence," said Mike.

"Of course. It's always true. If talking gets nowhere, if peaceful voices are silenced, violence is the only way. And for the Jihadists scattered over the world a violent act is the most dramatic and visible proof of their community, their collective identity."

"It certainly worked with the Twin Towers," said Mike.

"Yes, to destroy the financial capital of the west, of the mighty USA. And then your bombings: to bring to a halt the great city of London. That was real shock and awe. Real symbolic statements of Jihadist power."

This was one of the Asian parts of town. There were several people walking along the road but not one was white, noted Mike.

Two young women pushed prams, both swathed in black niqabs.

"The suicide terrorist," said Ali, "is the poor man's smart bomb."

They passed a park with an imposing stone arched gateway. The houses now were larger, with driveways that curved into gardens. Ali turned into the hospital grounds and pulled up outside the out-patients' entrance.

He turned to Mike.

"Your bomber was called Amjad Khan, wasn't he?"

"Yes."

"Well, Amjad did what he did out of love."

"Love!"

"Yes. Love of his brothers and sisters, love of jihad, love of fighting a cosmic war on behalf of his God."

"Love!" scoffed Mike. "That's perverted. And what does the Holy Qu'ran say about all this?"

"Oh, it's perfectly clear. 'Do not kill yourself. If someone does so, God shall cast him into Hell. Whoever kills himself with an iron weapon will forever be carrying that weapon in his hand and stabbing his abdomen with it in the fire of Hell, wherein he will abide eternally.'

"So how do the Jihadists explain that?"

"They don't. They put it in a larger context. They divide the world into two, as I said. There is no neutrality in the war they are waging. If you are not with them, you are against them. If you are not on their side you are apostates and deserve to die."

"Quite an education, this trip," said Mike, looking at his watch.

"I'll tell you something my wife Shakira told me the other day. I didn't know it. She is a modern woman, as you know. Those women in their niqabs reminded me of it. Shakira says there is the Qu'ran and then there is the interpretation of the Qu'ran – always been done by men, the Ulama, the scholars. Men interpret the Qu'ran to suit their own ends, as they do everything else, says Shakira. How should men behave towards women? It is very controversial."

"You can say that again," interrupted Mike.

"There is a verse in the Qu'ran about men's obligation to women. Shakira tells me that one translation says: 'Men are the support of women.' But exactly the same verse has another translation: 'Men are in charge of women.' Men choose which interpretation they want."

"It's the same with the Bible," said Mike. "Fascinating! But I must go."

"Do you understand better?" asked Ali.

"A lot to think about, but, yes, I think so. Thank you. And thanks for driving me in. I'm sure for the return journey I'll have thought of some more questions."

"No, that's enough for today. Let's talk about the new football season, or I'll tell you about my wonderful children's latest wonderful achievements."

Mike began to manoeuvre himself round in the seat. Ali came round and opened the door for him.

"A little story for you, before you go in," said Ali. "At college one morning I was chatting with someone over a coffee. He was on my course. He was white, he was English, he'd been friendly. I said to him: 'I was born in this country, I speak its language. What else must I do to become English? Can I ever become English?' And do you know his reply?"

He paused. Mike looked up to him, his hands grasping his crutches.

"He looked straight at me and he said," continued Ali, "he said: 'There is no such thing as becoming English. You either are or you are not.'

Mike saw a hurt in Ali's eyes. Then his smile was back.

"Come on, in you go. I'll see you later. Football, remember. We'll talk football."

"See you, Ali. Thanks again."

Ali watched Mike walk across to the entrance. He had improved. His steps were more natural, he wasn't so tense. Mike wasn't concentrating on his steps. He was lost in thought about love: the kind of love that had lost him his legs, the kind of love that had lost him Sue.

From: Sue [sue08whitehall@blueyonder.co.uk]
Sent: 18 September 2005 1900
To: Mike
Subject: Thee and me

Sorry about that last message. I was so down. I didn't even get drunk. I didn't pull a bloke or even try to – too grotesque to contemplate. Sometimes I wish you were reading my messages, sometimes I'm thankful you don't. If you do, you must think me so pathetic. You probably don't think anything – indifferent. Or maybe you have had to learn to hate me, to put me away.

You kissed me on the lips and then said: "I will not communicate with you any more." Was it cruelty or kindness? Was it a survival technique or were you as cold as you seemed?

I don't want to send this, don't want you to see me so abject, so self-pitying. But I am compelled to send signals your way.

I think I know for definite now that you don't read this stuff.

"Humankind cannot bear too much reality." But something in me won't allow me to avoid it, displace it.

Sue

xx

21.

Kidnap

Bradfield, Crimhope Dale.

Barry came up with the ambulance plan. He and Lee drove over to where Hussein had been arrested at 23 Jackdaw Road, just opposite where Amjad Khan the bomber had lived, in the Asian area of town. They strolled past.

"It's just like my street," said Lee. "What my street's turned into, a takeover. We're the only white people here."

"That's how it is," said Barry. "It all looks peaceful and ordinary but who knows what's going on behind those windows? Watching jihadist videos. Arranging forced marriages, planning honour killings, getting the tribal witch in to cut off the clitoris of young girls."

"Christ, Barry, steady on." Lee laughed. "They're probably just watching tele and getting the curry on."

"Don't you believe it, mate, it's a parallel bloody world in there. And fuck all like ours."

Number 23 was just an ordinary terrace house like the rest, its door opening straight onto the street. Lee watched two young kids playing on their bikes, a couple of old men talking, a woman with a plastic shopping bag in each hand walking home. All brown-skinned, all peaceful.

"Your first job," said Barry, "is to do some surveillance on him. We've got to know the pattern of his movements."

"I've got to give him some time to establish his routine. He's been under house arrest. He'll be getting used to being free. We'll give him a month. He may even get a job and we'll have to work round that."

During that month Barry organised the renting of twin lock ups on a disused industrial site down a cobbled road in town, near the railway bridge. Barry had studied decommissioned ambulances for sale on the internet to identify which vehicles were used. Then he and Lee had driven to a car auction mart on the edge of Manchester. Barry had selected a white Renault Master panel van as being right for conversion, Lee had checked the mechanics. They'd paid cash again and driven it back to the lock up. From Emergency Vehicle Solutions Barry had sourced a second-hand roof light bar with halogen rotator and a siren; and a yellow and green check reflective marking kit with which to battenburg the van. From a separate source he'd also acquired large adhesive letters AMBULANCE. They had replaced the number plates and prepared new ones for Barry's own car. Lee worked on the van's engine and brakes to make sure everything was in perfect working order.

It was down to Lee to find a base. They agreed the criteria: it must be isolated but within driving distance of a town; it must be available for renting for two months. On the internet he found many holiday cottages available now the summer had ended but most were in villages or hamlets. When he saw the one in Crimhope Dale he knew that must be it: it was a sign! A good omen! It was the cottage he'd seen across the valley that day with Ben. There was a one and a half mile gravel track to it, not tarmaced, with a cattle grid and gate at the start. It had indeed been gentrified: mock carriage lamps outside the door, an old stone trough planted with red geraniums and a millstone on the flagged patio. Apart from the ruined mill below, threequarters hidden in the trees, the only other building was a similar cottage on the other side, the one with the For Sale sign he'd passed with Ben. It was far enough away, with no connecting track, a steep walk down and up the valley. They couldn't get better than this and only a forty five minute drive from town. Inside, it was well-furnished for a family, all mod cons, microwave, dishwasher, a vacuum cleaner in a cupboard, rules on the wall about not smoking. Linen and towels were included, and fuel costs. There was even a full log basket next to the wood-burning stove.

But what excited Barry most when Lee phoned him was the keeping cellar. When he heard about it, Barry smiled – a smile Lee could not see – excited by the possibilities. In the old days this was where they stored the bottles and jars of preserved damsons and blackcurrants, jams and chutneys, elderflower wine. The entrance to the cellar was through a low doorway and down three steps from the kitchen. It was barrel-vaulted, had stained stone benches and shelves. But what was unique about it was that from a little opening five feet up in the wall trickled some water. There was a constant flow which ran down the wall, now stained coppery brown over the years from the acid, to the floor where it spread out like a thin film and then drained away in a corner. So the place was kept cool and damp.

Lee negotiated a bit of discount because he was renting it for two months and paid cash.

While this was going on Barry disappeared down to London to organise "some other stuff", as he put it. Lee put to use some of his training in the army to keep surveillance on Hussein Salim.

He was careful but he enjoyed it. At last he was doing something with a purpose. He watched the nervous Hussein walk down the street, turn the corner into Magpie Street and then immediately return to catch a follower by surprise. He saw him stand in front of shop windows, knowing he was looking at reflections in the glass. Hussein walked to the mosque but never alone, to the community centre twice a week, to the shops. He was obviously living on benefits, thought Lee, making use of that 'anxiety disorder' to wangle more out of the state, out of us.

But Hussein did seem to relax after about three weeks, stopped checking he was being followed. The quietest time of day, decided Lee, was between lunchtime and just before school came out. It was then, between 2 and 2.30, that Hussein established a habit of ambling down to the corner grocery store and returning with a bulging plastic bag. He wore beige loose-fitting Asian pyjama-type clothes, bare feet in sandals, and a black waistcoat decorated with bits of silver thread. He always had a black walking stick – must be more of a defensive weapon than a walking aid, because he showed no sign of a limp. He had begun to henna his beard and usually wore a white cotton kufi skull cap.

All this he reported to Barry in The Bobbinmakers.

"Time to go, then," said Barry. "D-day, H-hour approaches. The sooner the better now, he might change his routine, even get a job and then we'd have to start all over again."

Lee explained there was a bend in the road between Hussein's house and the busier area around the shop and post office. The stretch of quieter road was about 200 yards long with a short terrace of houses set back from the road with small gardens and high hedges. It was there that they would take him. Thursday would be the day, November 4th.

"The day after tomorrow, just before Bonfire Night," said Barry. He stared into his half full pint glass of beer, his face set. "It will be the start of the fight back. Just the start. Other people will copy us. They'll start to feel the fear. I'll enjoy that. It will be a good feeling."

"But what are we going to do with him when we've got him? You've never really explained."

"That's not the point, Lee. It's what we decide to show the world we might do to him. Have the power to do to him if we wanted."

Barry took another drink.

"Trust me, Lee. I know what I'm doing. I'm not going to overstretch the mark. The thing is we'll be able to watch others carry on from us. We'll know we started it. We'll be able to watch it grow, the movement. It will be our cause. We'll be the unknown patriots, the unsung heroes. There'll be no vanity in it, no celebration, no fame. Just the two of us, back in our homes, watching it on the news, knowing we were the first, the pioneers. Seeing the shift in point of view, seeing the lines hardening."

Lee nodded. "It's the way to do it. I like it. The backroom boys."

"The keeping cellar boys," said Barry, grinned and finished his pint.

Thirty six hours later, at 1 pm., Barry and Lee drove to the twin lock up in Barry's car. They were wearing dark green paramedic squad suits that Barry had acquired on one of his trips, complete with epaulettes and the NHS crest. They wore identity cards from lanyards round their necks. They backed the car inside, closed the doors and fitted false number plates. In the adjoining lock up they both gave approving looks at the 'ambulance' in its battenburg check uniform.

"Looks the real deal," said Lee. He was impressed by the detailed planning, Barry had worked like a professional.

Barry threw his hold all into the back. They shook hands firmly. Barry held Lee's shoulders and looked him in the eyes.

"It will work," said Barry. "Like a dream. I can feel it in my juices. Go for it, Lee my lad. A cakewalk compared with Basra."

Lee gave him a playful jab to the jaw and climbed up into the ambulance driver's seat. Barry opened the lock up doors and swung them back. Lee drove out. Barry closed and padlocked the doors and climbed into the passenger seat. He checked his watch.

"Let's roll."

Traffic would be thick and it would take thirty minutes to cross the city. They'd given themselves plenty of time. They could dawdle if they were early. They didn't talk. Barry was picturing his part in the scene, going through the movements, rehearsing the bit of patter in his head. It was like practising a set-piece move on the football pitch. Lee was concentrating on his driving. A careless insignificant accident now could wreck the whole venture or being pulled over for breaking the speed limit. He too went through his role: it was vital to get the right acceleration, to turn on the blues and twos at the right time – not too soon, not too late, and then to pull up just in front of Hussein. Then it was up to Barry. If Hussein wasn't there or if he was with someone they would abort and Lee would just drive the ambulance through the street and out of it. Thank God it wasn't raining, thought Lee, that could have complicated matters.

Lee stopped at the pre-arranged spot, kept the engine running while Barry got out and walked to the corner where he could see Hussein's house. Lee watched, heart beating fast. This was really it.

He was there less than a minute, consulting a clipboard, before he walked briskly back and climbed in.

"Put your foot down," he snapped.

Lee pulled out and switched on the lights and siren. He was startled by the volume of noise. It wasn't like Iraq where the noise of revving engines, gunfire and helicopters enveloped you. Here the siren shattered the peace and quiet. This was the part he hadn't been able to practise. Keep cool, he told himself. He turned into Jackdaw Road, saw cars pull over to give him room, smiled. He saw Hussein walking steadily forward, in exactly the right place. He saw Hussein stop, leaning on his walking stick, turning round as he heard the wailing siren. Lee drove the ambulance just past him and screeched to a halt. In his green uniform, Barry leapt out of the near side door, slammed it shut behind him and ran up to Hussein. With one hand gripping the steering wheel and the other resting on the gear lever, engine ticking over, Lee saw Hussein start back a little.

"Don't be alarmed, sir. We need your help, please." Barry spoke respectfully but urgently. "We have a young Asian boy in the back of the ambulance. He crashed his bike and cracked his skull on the pavement. He's not talking English. He's crying, he's in a lot of pain. He's frightened and he needs someone who understands him. Can you help us, please, sir?"

Lee saw Hussein's eyes flicked up to the chequered ambulance, its lights still flashing.

"But I may not speak his language," stammered Hussein.

"Please, sir, quickly, we have to get him to hospital. Try, sir. At least try."

Hussein looked up and down the street. Lee saw that a few passers-by were watching them. *Come on, Barry, get him in before there's a crowd.* He saw Hussein's uncertainty, peering forward at the ambulance man's uniform, the identity badge.

Not waiting for a reply, Barry cupped his elbow.

"Thank you, sir," said Barry, turning and steering him. They walked quickly to the back of the ambulance out of Lee's sight. He heard Barry open the door and step up. Then he felt the heavy thump of Hussein's body landing on the ambulance floor, the door slam shut.

"Go," screamed Barry.

Lee already had the gear in. He let out the clutch and accelerated away, siren screeching again. In the back Barry straddled Hussein, pushing his face into the dirt and dust of the floor. He wrenched his arms were roughly behind him, thrust his knee into his back, wrapped rope round his wrists, jerked it tight and then rolled him over onto his back. Hussein was shouting but his voice disappeared into the noise of the siren. Barry forced a tight rough cloth into his mouth and tied it behind his head.

"OK," shouted Barry. Lee turned off the light bar and the siren. In the sudden silence Hussein tried to yell but just gagged and was almost sick. Barry slipped a canvas bag over his head and tied it loosely under his chin. He roped up Hussein's feet tightly so the coarseness burned into his bare ankles.

Barry sat back exhausted on the floor of the van. He was sweating with the effort and the tension. He climbed over the seat and sat back in the passenger seat.

"Sweet as a nut, Lee, sweet as a fucking nut."

"Yeah," bawled Lee, thumping the steering wheel with his clenched fist.

"That was the hard part," said Barry, beginning to breathe more easily. "Now we've just to let the rest of the plan roll smoothly out."

Half an hour later, Lee drove the ambulance into the cobbled lane between the boarded up premises of what once had been small family-owned workshops. He turned into the compound, past the piles of bricks that once had been a warehouse and down to the lock-ups beneath the railway embankment. Barry leapt out to un-padlock the doors. Lee drove the van in and Barry closed the doors. Lee turned off the engine. Now there really was silence. Lee sat there in the sudden gloom, felt his heart beating hard and fast, listened to it slow down. He could hear Hussein in the back, banging his heels on the floor. He turned to look at him.

"Hey, you bombing bastard! Shut it! We're just taking you on holiday."

Grunts came from Hussein's gagged mouth hidden in the black bag. Lee watched him twist his bound body, struggling hopelessly.

Then Barry opened the back door of the van and stepped in, lowering the two steps.

"Keep fucking still, will you, or you will get hurt."

But Hussein kept jerking about and grunting. Barry kicked him in the stomach.

"OK, Lee, we need to do this together."

Lee clambered over the bench seat. Out of the hold-all Barry took a black body bag and unzipped it down its length. The noise of the unzipping made Hussein writhe even more.

"You take his shoulders and I'll take his feet," said Barry. "And slap his face hard if he makes it difficult for us."

Hussein seemed to give in, went limp. They lifted him up and lay him in the body bag. Barry zipped it up to the neck. The bag crackled and rustled like tin foil as Hussein strained against the ropes. Then they lugged him across the ambulance floor to the steps. Barry stepped down. Lee, bent double, followed him, careful not to bash Hussein's head on the metal steps. They carried Hussein across the concrete floor to Barry's car in the adjoining lock-up. Barry had already opened the boot. Carefully they placed Hussein into the boot. Barry took the black canvas bag off Hussein's face. His eyes were wild and terrified.

"Not nice is it? Now you're learning, getting the first taste."

He slammed the boot shut.

"Now for the ambulance."

It took them only twenty minutes to strip off the checkered battenburg tape and the adhesive lettering, to disconnect and take off the light bar. They worked in silent concentration, efficiently and effectively, not getting in each other's way. They bundled it all into the back seat of Barry's car which was full of other gear that Barry had already brought and covered it with a piece of old green plastic sheeting. They restored the original number plates to the van.

There was muffled thumping from the boot. Barry opened it.

"Keep fucking quiet," he said.

Hussein's eyes stared up at him. He smashed his fist into Hussein's nose.

"I meant keep fucking quiet."

He closed the boot. Lee drove out. Barry padlocked the doors and got into the car.

"OK, now for the country retreat."

They whooped and holla'd as they drove out of town, laughing loudly. Barry started them off singing Land of Hope and Glory but they didn't know the words. Forty five minutes later they were rattling over the cattlegrid.

"Hold your bollocks!" shouted Barry, turning round towards the back of the car and laughing.

He got out to open the gate half way along the track, waited for Lee to drive through, then closed it again. In a few minutes they swung round onto the gravelled parking place at the back of Valley View cottage. Barry and Lee got out of the car. It was four o'clock in this early November afternoon and the light was fading fast. The sky was grey but there was no wind. The silence was complete. They looked around: not a thing moved. The front of the cottage faced over the valley but at the back lay broad empty moors and then a couple of intake fields, once farmed but now patched with reeds and bracken, sloped down to the lane and parking place. There were muffled thumps from the car boot.

"Better get him out," said Lee, "before he suffocates."

"He's no bloody use to us dead," agreed Barry.

They lifted the body bag out of the boot, Hussein's face covered in dried blood from when Barry had punched him in the nose. They laid him on the gravel and unzipped the bag. Barry untied the rope that bound his feet. They helped Hussein to stand, his sandalled feet on the gravel chippings. He stared around. They led him across the gravel, unlocked the door and stepped inside, pushing Hussein in between them. The cottage was cool and damp behind its thick walls.

"Smells like a church," said Lee.

"Turn the fucking central heating on," said Barry.

Lee went up to the bathroom where the boiler and controls were. Barry led Hussein into the kitchen at the front of the house. On the table was a tray with three cups and saucers, a teapot, a small container of teabags, coffee and sugar sachets. There was a wooden bowlful of apples and bananas and oranges. A vase of flowers stood in the middle with a card leaning on it. Barry picked it up.

"*We hope you enjoy our cottage and have a wonderful stay,*" read Barry. He put it back.

"How kind, eh, Mr Salim."

They stood looking out of the window down the garden.

"Lovely view, lovely place for a holiday," said Barry. "I'm not sure how long we're going to stay. Depends a bit on how you behave, Mr Salim."

Hussein stood unmoving, head bowed. Lee came back.

"OK, should warm up soon, I've switched the heating on."

He stood in front of Hussein.

"I'm going to remove the gag," said Lee, "but if you make a single sound I'll put it back on and with it on you won't be able to eat or drink. Understand?"

Hussein nodded and Lee undid the gag. Hussein coughed, almost retched, breathed deeply but said nothing.

"OK," said Lee.

"I want to show you something," said Barry.

With his hands still bound behind his back, Hussein was led round the dining table and across the kitchen. Lee opened the low door into the keeping cellar and Barry pushed Hussein down the steps. He switched on the light.

"Cold and wet, isn't it?" said Barry. "That stone slab won't be comfortable to sleep on, especially with no clothes. And with the light out it's pitch black."

Hussein opened his mouth to speak, his eyes scared. Lee grabbed his arm.

"Remember what I said," and put his finger to his lips.

"Now we could keep you in here. It depends if you co-operate. You've done as you've been told so far. That's good."

Back in the kitchen Lee let down the window blind and Barry made Hussein sit on the floor next to the radiator. He chained him to the pipe that led into it.

"You're very fortunate," said Barry, "that we're understanding people. Some of your lot captured two of our guys called Terry Waite and Brian Keenan and chained them up like this for more than two years, but in a cellar. You wouldn't want that, would you?"

231

Hussein stared at him. Barry bent and brought his face close to Hussein's, noses almost touching. He suddenly screamed: "I said you wouldn't want that would you?"

Hussein flinched and jerked his head back, knocking it against the wall. He shook his head violently.

"Good, just so we understand each other. Now here's three sleeping pills for you."

Hussein began to object and shake his head. Barry clenched his fist and held it under Hussein's nose. Hussein quietened. Lee watched impassively.

"Give him a glass of water," said Barry.

Lee held the glass to Hussein's lips. He drank the pills down.

"Now let's have tea," said Barry. "I'm starving."

Hussein sat and watched them make soup, toast and beans and drink tea. Neither of them offered Hussein anything.

They watched the six o'clock news but there was nothing about their kidnap. Hussein's head drooped and he was soon asleep. Barry and Lee dozed, drank beers and watched TV through the evening. Just before midnight Barry checked the padlocked chain on Hussein's feet and fastened his gag back on. They turned off the cottage lights, locked up and drove off down the track. They went to the lock-ups and transferred the lights and siren and other kit back in to the van. Lee drove the white van out followed by Barry driving his own car. They went to an old quarry out on the edge of the moors, once used for building a reservoir. There they drenched the ambulance-van in petrol and torched it. They stood for a moment, watching as flames flared into the sky.

"Reminds me of Basra," said Lee.

"An early bonfire," said Barry. "Like that one down there."

He pointed to the edge of the town where a fire burned. There were occasional rockets soaring into the sky, exploding into fans of stars which dropped and disappeared. They heard bangers going off like gunfire. They drove off fast, stopping only once when the van's full petrol tank exploded and shot a ball of fire into the sky

From: Sue [sue08whitehall@blueyonder.co.uk]
Sent: 3 November 2005 1900
To: Mike
Subject: Thee and me

I couldn't keep it up, staying away from you, in absentia. Not writing to you has been more draining than writing. I can't tell myself I haven't tried.

This need to communicate with you persists, despite knowing you may read none of it and may be entirely unaware of my messages. So here I am again.

This morning I was up before six and sitting outside in the garden with a mug of tea. It was absolutely still, not a breath of wind. There was complete silence except for one early car and a blackbird. I love this time. The world is empty and unmoving, most folk still in bed. And I have this other secret world with you in my head that no one knows about, probably not even you.

Last weekend I went up to Watersinks, near where I know you used to run. A stream issues from the tarn and flows windingly across a bog and then into a field. Its bed is bouldery there. I sat and watched it flow until it just disappeared underground, beneath its bed of dry pebbles where it once flowed aeons ago continuing down into what is known now as Dry Valley. The stream now emerges a mile further and about 500 feet lower at the foot of the great limestone cliff of Malham Cove.

Looking for parallels and metaphors, allegories to try and understand the flow of life, it is a place at which I had to pause. Not that it explains anything, just expresses something I felt an affinity for.

I wandered down Dry Valley to the limestone pavement that overlooks the great cliff. I look across at the vertical white cliffs of limestone. It is inconceivable that it and the rocks on which I stand

and which spread beneath the thin soil are made of fish bones, of the calcium of unimaginable numbers of creatures dying over unimaginable periods of time. I could not grasp it.

Just as I cannot grasp that I will not see you or touch you again. Ever.

Another mystery: why, out here in the wilds, can I see your face as clearly defined as in a photograph and hear your voice as clearly as if you are on the phone?

All this may mean very little to you now as you are involved in other great struggles. But to me it matters. It is part of my authenticity. I want to still live it even if there is no reality to it outside of my mind and imagination. I am not deceiving myself. I know it for what it is and what it is not. That old adage: the curlew still calls in the hills even if no one hears it.

I hope you are fitting the pieces of your new life together. I know you will because that is the person you are. Why would I hope for anything else? I wish you could tell me you are, entrust me with that. The entrusting would be more salve than wound, because it would be a contact, an acknowledgement that I still exist for you.

Should I cringe that I think that way? And if so, so what?

I am only trying to describe my feelings, work them out to properly experience them.

If my desire for you died, part of me would be killed off. I want to retain it even if consummation is forever impossible. Back to courtly love. How ridiculous it was! Aint life grand and rich and weird and funny?

Teaching is going well. We have a new teacher in the department, a red-head full of great ideas. Her enthusiasm is catching. She has that oh-so-valuable knack of getting on with naughty boys. We share a class and she's really got me going again.

Sue

xx

22.

Kiss

Upper Heights Barn

Mike stood at the window of the conservatory and looked up the valley to where heavy grey clouds were lumbering over the moor top. He loved the way he could watch the weather move in. In about fifteen minutes he would see curtains of rain up there and then shortly afterwards raindrops would rattle on the roof, as if on a canvas tent, and the birch tree branches would sway and toss in the wind. As the clouds rolled down, the other side of the valley would be completely obscured and his isolation would seem complete.

The rain and greyness did not depress him. Observing the weather, sheltered in his house, hearing the bleat of lambs in the fields, he considered his progress. He lived in a beautiful place, he could walk again. He was independent but enjoyed his chats with Ruth and Dick and Ali, his journeys to the city hospital and his sessions with the physios, the busy-ness of everyday living. He felt able to connect with people in a way which was new to him. His days were busy with his exercise regime, his amputee forums and the beginnings of a plan for running an ICT business.

As he looked out through the rain-distorted windows he knew he had found a contentment. He was satisfied with himself. He was well on the way to creating a second self, starting again. He had learned to accept his altered body and even take pride in what it could now achieve. He felt complete again. But that was when his thoughts swung to Sue, as inevitably as a compass needle swung to the north. Usually he put them aside, distracting himself with a chore or doing an extra exercise. But it was not so easy now.

Always there was the temptation of the mobile phone. He looked at it now, sitting on the coffee table. It would be so easy to ring her. The arguments were familiar: it was not fair to her, he had sent her off to lead another life; she would reject his call and he did not want to hear that finality. He was scared, too, that his new-found strengths, born of his determination to be independent, might dissipate. He lived protected within a kind of shell. If it cracked, he wasn't certain what might happen.

No, he could not contact her but nor must he deny his feelings. Maybe it was part of his new self, but he realised he had to grieve properly for what he had lost. He had to re-live those times, accept that they had happened, even take joy in them. That way, as with his stumps, he could move on and not be tethered.

He closed his eyes. Winter, a rainy night, in the car, that first kiss. He remembered everything.

He was driving, going to the pub again for a drink when, without turning his face towards her, Mike said: "Sue, I want to kiss you, properly."

She stopped what she was saying. He didn't know what she had been talking about. He dare not look at her. His fingers gripped the steering wheel, the windscreen wipers beat out their rhythm.

"Where can we go?" he asked.

The heater blower was full on. The traffic lights changed to red at a zebra crossing. He slowed to a halt. A couple, arms round each other's waists, hunched together under an umbrella, hurried across without acknowledgement. Mike waited for the lights to change, looking straight forward, concentrating on the rain falling across the street lights, glistening on the pavements. Waiting for a reply, heart thumping, scared. How had he dared to say that? And yet he was an adult wasn't he? In the darkness of the car he felt a blush rise into his cheeks, felt hot. They were on their way to their fourth evening together in the pub.

"I know a place," she said.

She had accepted, was taking him somewhere. He turned briefly to her, saw the streetlamp light her fair hair, a half-smile on her face, her hands resting in her lap. The lights changed. He drove on, wondering where she would take him, impatient now but with a different nervousness. They were passing houses, set back from the road with big gardens and tall black trees, the occasional porch light shining on a driveway.

She gave him a few directions. He tried to detect what she was feeling in the tone of her voice but there was nothing to help him: it was normal, quiet, controlled. They were coming to the edge of the town and he recognised the golf course.

"Take the next left up the lane," she said.

He did so. The lane was a track, rutted and stony, with dark masses of hedges and bushes on both sides.

"There's a lay-by thing in a couple of hundred yards," Sue said.

"You've obviously been before," said Mike with a flash of jealousy he knew was pathetic, and suddenly tentative. She laughed.

"It's a well-known place for local folk," she replied, apparently oblivious of his anxiety. "There's no way out at the other end but if you go ahead you can reverse at a field gate and come back."

"So you've been here recently then?"

"Don't be silly, this was years ago but I suppose things haven't changed."

He passed the lay-by and reversed as instructed, returned and parked the car, brushing up against the long grass by the hedge. He put on the handbrake and turned off the lights. There was total darkness, rain pattering on the car roof. They sat unmoving. Slowly he turned to her and saw the profile of her face turn to him. He stretched across to put his hand gently on her cheek to guide her face to him. So gently their lips touched, the softness of her lips startling to him. So slowly her hand stroked the back of his neck. So unhurriedly he gently kissed her eyes and brow, exploring her face in the dark with his fingertips and lips. He was absorbed wholly in their touching. There was a chasteness about it. Perhaps she too was taken aback by this as she responded with the same tenderness and lightness of touch.

They moved apart but holding hands, staring forwards through the blank windscreen. Life was simplified into this moment – all the day's mundane events were gone, all the chatter, all the apprehension he had felt. There was only this relaxation into the sensation of touch.

"Mike," said Sue, drawing out the length of the vowel in her soft voice, "are you sure about this?"

He sighed and turned to her.

"Of course," he replied, "and there's a story to tell. But not now. It makes sense to me. Why? Do you want to go back home?"

For answer, she drew him to her and now their kissing was no longer tentative and hesitant but suddenly passionate. They spoke not at all, kissed sometimes with eyes open in the meagre light, stroked each other, laughed in the amazement of discovering their ease with each other. Much later she said:

"I must go. A full day's teaching tomorrow."

"I know. Me too. What now?" he asked.

There was a sudden surging thump in his gut – the possibilities, the image racing in of their bodies together on a narrow single bed in his room, the despair of being rejected.

"I want to see you again," he said.

"I'd like that. Do you not know that?"

He held her fingers in the silence, stroked them.

"Did you feel something special, that first time we met, at that talk I gave? Tell me the truth."

He tried to keep his voice neutral. He had to conceal the urgency with which he wanted her to affirm it – that there was something instinctive, some animal connection and recognition which they shared before words or even touch had intervened. It had to be different from anything either of them had experienced before. It had to be unique.

"You're a strange man," she said. "Don't be so afraid."

He wanted to ask her again for a direct answer but before he could she leaned over towards him and kissed him. Her hands were cupped around the back of his neck, drawing his head gently towards her. Her tongue caressed his lips and then slipped into his mouth, stroking the edges of his teeth and then entering deeper until it seemed to him his whole being was lost and absorbed into her. He shivered with the delicate power of her touch. Inside the warmth of her unbuttoned coat he stroked her breast, felt her nipples harden under the soft material of her shirt, felt her push her breast towards him into the palm of his hand. Then she pulled away and when he opened his eyes he saw her looking at him. He saw the shine of her eyes, her smile.

"Do you have your answer?"

It should have been enough for him: the warmth, the softness, the acceptance the giving, the desire. But some need remained, some question scratching obsessively, trapped at the back of his consciousness.

"What more do you need to know?" she asked. "I'm wet for you," she said quietly. And she placed her hand on his trousers, where his erection strained, and held him.

"As wet as you are hard."

He shuddered when she touched him, and groaned as he involuntarily pushed his penis into her grip. He was shocked at what she had said, amazed, excited.

"And I've never said that to anyone before. I promise you. Never remotely felt as natural with anyone."

The rain rattled harder on the roof of the car. The windows were steamed up. Mike still made no reply. He turned the car heater back on, the sound of rain dulled by the blow of the heater and the ticking of the engine.

"And now I'm scared," said Sue.

"Of what?" Mike managed to ask.

"That you think I'm crude, that I've disgusted you."

"No, not that. It was me who asked the question, wanted an answer."

"And don't you see that because I felt the same as you it made me bold, that I wouldn't prevaricate or be coy. This was different. I'd say it as it was because it was a shining new experience for me and you wanted me to be honest."

She paused again but he did not reply.

She said: "You're hard and I'm wet. We want to make love, don't we?"

It was as simple as that. It seemed as if his mind cleared, the complications and anxieties fading like a passing squall.

"Yes," he said. He laughed and flung his arms around her and covered her face and hair in a shower of kisses. "Yes, yes, yes!"

"But not tonight," she said. "It's very late and we must go – to our separate beds."

And she laughed, too.

He let her go, and they both settled back into their seats. Mike turned on the ignition, switched on the lights, stretched round to try and peer through the back window.

He was suffused with the taste and scent and touches of her, accepted and desired by her, thrilled at her frankness. He had not been mistaken: this was new to both of them. It wasn't just her words.

He put the gear into reverse and slowly backed up to give himself room to turn out of the lay-by into the lane. He could see nothing through the steamed up back window, the reversing light made no difference. Then they were off, her hand resting on his thigh with that straightforwardness which surprised and delighted him, of which he was no longer afraid.

Mike opened his eyes. He saw Sue so clearly. What a woman she was: so honest, so different. He wanted her here with him, sharing this place, watching the crows beat into the wind, hearing the rain, being warm together. It could not be. He had made his choice. She was living a new life, just as he was. He looked at the phone. He leaned forward but could not reach it. Then he shook himself like a dog after a swim. He needed a hard exercise session.

From: Sue [sue08whitehall@blueyonder.co.uk]
Sent: 4 November 2005 2230
To: Mike
Subject: Thee and me

Autumn is almost gone – season of mellow fruitfulness. Hardly for me! But I refuse to be melancholy. The yellow and red leaves have been beautiful and bright. The trees are sealing themselves off only so they can have new growth in the spring. Autumn conceals a promise. I must remind myself of that.

Sue

xx

23.

Terrorist

5th November

Valley View Cottage

Hussein had spent the night on the bottom bunk in the children's bedroom, with one hand and one foot manacled to the bunk frame. He had said nothing, asked nothing except to go to the lavatory before he was chained up. He had slept little. His nose where he had been punched was aching and tender to touch; when he had dozed, his hand or foot jerking against the manacle had woken him. What were they going to do to him? Why had they selected him? He did not know where he was and, wherever it was, no one else knew he was here. His wife and children would be scared – his kidnap would have been seen and stories would already be circulating. The police would be interviewing them again, maybe even taking his wife to the police station. What frightened him most was his isolation: he had no companions, no lawyers. That man who had punched him, had asked him for help in the street, was vicious. The night had been long, and so silent. There had been no street noises, no shouts, no traffic, nothing. He had prayed long and silently, readying himself to accept the will of Allah.

In the morning Lee freed him from the bunk, re-tied his hands behind his back and led him barefoot to the kitchen. Lee raised the window blind and the early sun sparkled on the taps and stainless steel kettle, angled a sheen across the wooden table. There, chained to the table leg but with his hands free, he breakfasted on cornflakes, tea, toast and jam. He hadn't eaten for nearly a day and he would need his strength. He must also try to appear unafraid. He whispered a request for extra toast and Lee gave it to him. Barry came down in his boxer shorts and T-shirt, a cigarette already in his mouth, and set about making some filter coffee, the coffee-maker starting to bubble.

"Sleep well, Mr Salim?" Barry asked.

Hussein nodded.

"It's going to be another nice day," he commented, looking out of the window as if the three of them were on a weekend break. He stretched and cracked his knuckles, farted.

"Oh, pardon me!"

Lee washed the breakfast dishes, dried and put them away, wiped over the worktop.

"He'd make a good wife, wouldn't he?" Barry asked Hussein.

Hussein did not respond. He did not like the man's pale blue eyes, his fair hair, the stubble already on his face. His mouth was mean. The smell of coffee filled the kitchen.

"We should have brought some bird food to fill up the feeders. Poor little things. Winter's coming on. We should give them a bit of help," said Barry, frowning with exaggerated concern.

He stubbed his cigarette out on his saucer.

"But it's time to start the business of the day," he continued. "We need to take your photograph, Mr Salim."

Hussein looked startled.

"No need to worry. We're not going to hurt you, unless, of course, you try to resist. Just a photograph in the garden. I want you to hold this card."

Barry bent down and from his holdall took an A4 piece of white card with *TERRORIST* printed on it.

Hussein shook his head vigorously.

"You can speak if you wish," said Barry.

Hussein croaked and cleared his throat.

"I am not a terrorist," he said.

"We'll get into that later," said Barry. "But for now, are you willing to hold this card while I take your photograph? Or shall I simply kick your shins with my boots and then kick you in the balls until you agree? Understand?"

Hussein looked across the table at Lee who was watching him. Lee's face was expressionless. Hussein looked back at Barry.

"Yes, sir."

"Good, let's keep it simple."

"Better clean him up," said Lee.

Hussein's face was still caked with the blood from when Barry had punched him as he lay in the boot of the car. From a drawer Lee took a tea towel, decorated with Yorkshire landmarks: Kilnsey Crag and The Cow and Calf Rocks at Ilkley. He dampened it and began to dab Hussein's face, cleaning his narrow aquiline nose, the deep lines to the corners of his mouth, his bony cheeks. What if Jimmy and Mac and Alan could see him now! Mac, shot in the shoulder and screaming in the jeep as blood poured out of his artery! Jimmy spitting at the man tied to the fork-lift truck!

There was a stale spicy smell about Hussein. His red-veined black eyes looked up at him and then closed. Lee noticed the deep purple of his eyelids. He had to put more pressure on where the blood had caked onto his beard, a greying beard but partially dyed with henna. But his hair was still that glossy black, thick and oiled. Hussein opened his eyes. Their eyes met, their faces so close to each other. For an instant Lee recognised the terrified face of the detainee at Camp Sandbox.

Barry watched Lee without making any comment. Then he retied Hussein's hands with bright red rope, so that it would be more visible in the photograph, and took him into the garden. The grass was still wet with dew. Barry surveyed the shrubs and finally stood him in front of the glossy green leaves of an anonymous rhododendron bush.

"It could be anywhere," he explained. "Now, hold the card so that we can see your hands are tied. And smile so that your family will know you are being well looked after. You see, your photo will go into the papers. It may even be on TV. That's what we really want."

As he lifted his camera and composed the picture in the LCD screen, he added softly: "You could even be a martyr."

Hussein controlled himself, made no response. He forced himself to give a half smile. So the photo was taken. Back inside the cottage, Barry plugged the digital camera into his laptop, slotted in one of the blank discs that he had bought in London with the camera and downloaded the picture. He checked the quality.

"See, Mr Salim, you look good."

But from his position, chained by Lee once more to the radiator and sitting on the floor, Hussein could not see and made no attempt to do so. Barry made a second copy and then typed out a statement which he read out:

The lawyers, the government and the European parliament have let the British people down.

Dangerous men considered to be a threat to this country have been freed, not because they are innocent, but because the lawyers insist that they can only be brought to court if our intelligence services and techniques are disclosed. This is obviously ridiculous. The public would be even more in danger.

This man, Hussein Salim, is one such man.

We have captured and imprisoned him to show that the British people have had enough of this namby-pamby treatment of those who would kill and maim us. This is the start of the fight back. Mr Salim is just the first.

"That will do for a start," he said. "We'll build on it next time."

He printed out two copies, folded them, and placed a copy and a disc in each of two envelopes which he addressed to the BBC and the *Daily Mail* at their London headquarters.

"And now I'm off to Liverpool to post them. That should put them on a false scent."

Lee had watched approvingly. He was impressed at how Barry had thought things out.

"You look after Mr Salim, Lee," said Barry as he left. "And treat him well. We're not in Camp Sandbox now."

That remark was like a punch in the gut, but the door had closed before Lee could react. He heard the tyres on the gravel and then the sound of the engine died away.

He went out into the garden. The sun had come out but there was that autumn sharpness in the air. He kicked the brown leaves that already lay across parts of the grass. He was angry. Just like Barry to make that last cutting farewell remark. He couldn't resist a put-down. From the stone wall at the bottom of the garden he looked back at the cottage, the gable end bathed in sunshine. Hussein would be slumped on the floor. Barry called the shots and he was good at it. Barry had the big plan in his head but he hadn't told him how it would develop. Lee didn't like his growing feeling that he was just a bloody caretaker. Lee brooded as he looked up to the ridge of moors, a narrow line of cloud just above them. Sandbox had been completely different. That was a war. He'd seen the men he'd conditioned trying to kill him and his mates, beating up their prisoners, abusing that woman soldier. He was suddenly hungry again and went inside.

Hussein looked up from the floor and asked: "Can I say something to you?"

"OK," said Lee, putting the kettle on.

"I am really not a terrorist."

Lee spooned some instant coffee into a mug.

"Well, of course you will say that."

He poured the boiling water into his mug.

"I was in London that day just to see my sister and to see some of the sights. I swear it, on the Holy Qu'ran."

"I don't believe you."

From the fridge Lee took the bottle of milk and poured some into his coffee. He turned round and looked down at Hussein.

"I know who you are. You're the uncle of the man who bombed my train in London. I rescued a man. I saw what your nephew did, how he murdered and mutilated innocent people. I was there. I heard the screaming."

Hussein was silent for a while.

"Yes," said Hussein. "He was my nephew. Amjad, my brother's son. But I was ashamed. It was terrible. I had nothing to do with that."

"But you are a strict Muslim. I read about you. I saw your wife.

You make her wear the niqab, cover her whole body up."

Hussein sighed.

"You are right. I follow the Qu'ran strictly. Mohammed, peace be upon him, says a woman must be covered, must be modest. And I do not force my wife. She wants to be covered, she tells me it makes her feel safe. And yes I go to the mosque to pray, I do not gamble or drink alcohol or borrow or lend money. But I do not have anything to do with violence. The Qu'ran says killing one person is like killing all mankind and that saving a single life is like saving all mankind."

"You could have kidded me," said Lee.

"Do you not believe me?" asked Hussein.

"No," said Lee. "I fucking don't. And I don't want to hear any more."

He took his mug of coffee into the garden. He'd read about hostages: they tried to make a relationship with their captors so they wouldn't harm them. He wouldn't fall for that. All that crap about the Qu'ran, it was just like the Bible. Anybody could read anything into it, find what they wanted to find. Even if it was the word of God, it was men who interpreted it for their own ends. Armies were always told God was on their side.

Later that evening, hunched in his parka and with a can of beer, Lee watched rockets arc up into the sky above the village way down the valley, spraying brilliant coloured stars. He wondered if Ben was at a bonfire and if Nicki still made treacle toffee. He wondered if somewhere Mike was also watching fireworks.

The next day Barry switched on the television just before six o'clock. The three of them were in the living room. Barry had shifted the furniture so Hussein, on the floor attached to the radiator, had a clear view of the TV. Lee was eating an apple and could see Barry, making a roll-up, was tense and expectant. He lit his fag, took a couple of deep draws and sat on the edge of the sofa.

"Come on, you bastards, let's see what you're made of," he said.

"And now for the six o'clock news," said the voice-over, "with Natasha Kaplinsky."

"She really turns me on," said Lee. "I could end up stalking her."

Barry's photograph of Hussein was the lead story. He leapt to his feet.

"Yes!" he shouted, punching the air. "We did it!"

He turned to Lee, as if seeking his congratulations. Lee just smiled and nodded. Barry sat down again to listen. The photograph was on screen.

"See, Mr Salim, we've made you a star!"

Hussein did not respond.

Police and politicians who were interviewed strongly disapproved with grave comments about this lawless vigilante action. But several of the public interviewed on the street said that too soft a line was being taken with terrorist suspects, people were fed up with the way they seemed to get away with everything. The lawyers and human rights people had brought this on themselves. One of the men, middle aged and wearing a suit and tie, even went so far as to call the kidnappers a sort of "people's heroes."

Barry loved that.

"You see," said Barry. "It's starting, we've got to stir up the dissatisfaction, give it a focus. It's the only way the government will even start to listen."

Barry suddenly got up and stood over Hussein, straddling Hussein's legs.

"Oh, we've got plans for you, Mr Salim. Next time you'll have a much bigger role. More action."

From: Sue [sue08whitehall@blueyonder.co.uk]
Sent: 5 November 2005 2239
To: Mike
Subject: Thee and me

I think of you far more than convention or common sense should allow. Do I have any pride or dignity left? They are qualities I dismiss as irrelevant – unless you despise me for their lack.

All I want is contact: the simple uncontentious things, as of friendship and mutual interest. That's rubbish! Sometimes my whole being yearns for you, it seems so virtuous and right.

Is it pointless? No more than the pointlessness of all things in an individual life in the context of all of time and space. So there is a congruity. I want to talk to you about these things. How I wished we had earlier.

You enriched me, enlivened me. You were scared you would restrict me, hold me back. From what? I just miss you so much. You think you freed me but you have confined me. How do I make you understand that? If only I could touch you, you would see.

After I write to you, even after this mass of contradictions and doubts, I feel on a high, as if released, as if I have met you. Even – dafter still – if I know you don't read this.

Your things are here – clothes still in their drawers, neatly folded, washed and ironed. Your books and your few discs – I will not allow myself to listen to your music, it would be too powerful for me, especially on these long dark evenings.

As usual on Bonfire Night I stay in. You know how scared I am, even now, that a stray firework thrown by some unthinking lout can ruin someone's whole life.

Sue

xx

24.

Single Bed

Upper Heights Barn

The clouds had cleared in late afternoon, the temperature had dropped and now Mike stood in the garden just before midnight. Well wrapped up though he was he could almost feel the frost forming around him. High overhead he had located the four bright stars of the Great Square. He looked north to find the five stars of Cassiopeia making their bright W shape, and east of them the small cluster of the Pleiades. He was looking for the Andromeda galaxy. His astronomy was becoming a bit of an obsession and partly, he realised, because it passed the night hours. He focused in on the galaxy which looked like a bright oval embedded in the centre of a long swathe of light. The nucleus shone brightly and the dimmer streaks of light surrounding it seemed to go on and on extending far beyond his field of view.

For an hour or so Mike panned the sky before his shivering overcame his sense of wonder. He packed up his telescope and went inside. He made himself a cup of hot chocolate and sat looking out. Knowing now where to look, he could see Andromeda with his naked eye. He had learned it was 2.5 million light years away, the furthest object the human eye can see. He could predict what would now happen, the pattern was familiar: he would muse on the incomprehensibility of it all, the distances, the time span but then some image, some memory of Sue would emerge through the darkness. And he would not fight it, he would accept it. He still rationalised it as part of a grieving process but increasingly he loved re-living the memories just for the sake of it. That he had loved so strongly made him feel warm, even on the frostiest of nights after his viewing of the stars. He took another drink of the hot chocolate, closed his eyes and let the memory fill his mind: the first time they made love.

They had arranged to meet in the evening at an up-market French restaurant but half-way round his run he had phoned her on his mobile.

"Sue, I have to see you, this afternoon. I know we're out tonight but I must see you before then."

"Are you running?" she had asked. "You seem out of breath a bit."

"Yes, I'm up at the tarn and I feel so happy. Completely happy. It's beautiful up here. I must come round. I have to."

He was surprised by his confidence and decisiveness. Sue laughed.

"You really are out of breath," she said. "Let's see." Mike heard the mischief in her voice. "I've got some marking scheduled while I listen to the Saturday play. But I think I could fit you in. You could come and help me."

"I love you," said Mike. "See you, around two."

Elated, he had turned and begun to run down, loping with long strides as the ground levelled off. Did she know what he really meant?

Back at home he had showered with extra care, felt pleased by the lithe body he examined in the mirror. He'd never done that before. He ate no lunch, wanted to feel spare and hungry.

Heart thumping strongly, he walked across the park at the end of Sue's row of terraced cottages, past the neatly tilled flowerbeds and old women sitting enjoying the brief spell of winter sun, shopping bags at their feet. But now the momentous occasion was imminent, he realised how nervous he was about his own sexual proficiency. Sue would be only the fourth woman he had slept with and he was twenty seven years old – not exactly the experience of a young Lothario. What if it didn't work? If they weren't compatible? Were his expectations ludicrously unreal? What if she overwhelmed him?

He knocked on the door of the mid-terrace house, not able to prevent himself from surreptitiously checking that no one was watching him – as if he was doing something illegal or wrong, something daring. Sue opened the door almost immediately and he quickly stepped inside. In the hall they kissed briefly, diffidently. He felt a tension in Sue as he held her.

"To my boudoir," she laughed but he sensed a new shyness in her voice. Sue led him up the stairs. He followed her, knowing she would be conscious of him watching her legs, the sway of her thighs, wondering whether she was as excited as well as nervous, like he was.

She pushed open the door and he saw her room was small with a single bed pushed into the corner. He saw the pile of exercise books on the dressing table, the two red bars of the electric fire, two small watercolour prints of wild flowers on the bare walls, the small bedside table with its lamp, the plain bedspread. He felt the cosy warmth of the room. He closed the door behind him and immediately Sue came to him and held him. He felt her body relax into his, her hips pressed against him. They kissed. Sue stopped and leaned back a little and looked at him directly into his eyes. Her eyes were soft and grey with that mischievous sparkle he had come to love. She smiled at him. He opened his mouth to speak but she put her finger to his lips. She went over to the window and closed the curtains. They did not really dim the afternoon sunlight but only diffused it so that the room glowed.

She turned from the window and Mike felt a pang of disappointment as he registered the unseductive practicality of the clothes she was wearing: the plain straight skirt, the plain pastel cream blouse. But this brief feeling passed as quickly as it came as they put their arms around each other and kissed, her lips so soft. Without speaking they undressed, in turn taking a garment off each other in an almost ceremonial rhythm, unbuttoning and unbelting with deliberate unhurriedness. They stood together naked, he felt her nipples against his chest, his penis hard against her pubic hair. And then she took his hand and led him to the bed.

"Not much room," she said.

"Enough," he said.

They lay together, arms around each other beneath the cotton sheets and winter duvet. At last naked and in bed, they leisurely explored and traced each other's bodies: the slender firmness of her thighs, the softness of her neat breasts. Her loveliness enthralled him, humbled yet liberated him. For the first time he kissed her stomach, his tongue gently grazing around her navel. Never before had he felt so natural and at ease with a woman, never had he felt such a balance of response. He pushed her over so her back was towards him, their legs bent together in parallel, his arms around her, his hands holding her breasts.

"It's like there are strings," she said, "connecting my nipples to my cunt."

That word! Like a stone thrown into a still pool, it broke his absorption into her. That harsh savage word that he hated. She turned back towards him, his hands now stilled on her body.

"I want to be me," she said. "At last, I can be me."

She kissed him.

"I feel so good with you. I feel I can talk with you. Don't be offended. Cunt can be a tender word, too – the way we use it, not a swear word."

Mike leaned on his elbow and looked at her.

"You really are special," he said.

He stroked her lips with his fingers and she took them into her mouth and sucked them hard while he groaned and sucked her nipple.

"You see what I mean by the strings," she said,

And she placed his fingers between her legs, guiding them into her, into her warmth and wetness.

Then he crouched over her and looked at his fingers inside her, and looked up at her face to see her smiling that smile at him. He took his fingers out and kissed them and put them to her lips. Then he lay over her.

"Put me in you," he said.

She held his penis, spread her legs wider and guided him into her: that first moment inside her, surrounded by her heat, the marvellousness of it. They moved together, easily and then more urgently. He felt her moving with him, together, their moans of pleasure merging.

"Not yet," she said. "Not yet."

He opened his eyes to watch her face, saw a mixture of relaxation and concentration, eyes closed, arms flung back, her whole body open to him.

"Yes, now," she said.

And he thrust in that final unhaltable rhythm and as he cried out she cried out too. Her arms held him tight.

"Stay in," she said. "I want you to stay in me."

They lay together in the narrow bed, Mike on top of her. Their heartbeats calmed. They laughed when he said there was nothing left to stay in her. He rolled off her and she took his penis in her hand, looked at it, and said:

"Little mollusc. Never fear, your time will come again."

"I love your cunt," he said.

Sue laughed softly.

"You see, it's OK."

They lay together, quiet, at ease, peaceful. They dozed and woke to make love again: the late afternoon sunlight on the plain furniture, pale shadows, no music, the faint hum of traffic on the street outside, the dull thump of doors closing in rooms below. The world continued around them in all its ordinariness.

Later, Mike watched Sue's face as she slept, tenderly stroked her forehead and cheeks, her skin smooth as pearl, with the backs of his fingers. Her lips, slightly open, were so full and sensuous. He owed so much to her. He had always believed he had a great potential of love within him, slowly gathering and accumulating within him like an underground lake. But it had been dammed up. Now Sue had released it and it was flowing out of the dark cave into clear bright sunlight. She was, just by being herself, cleaning away the rubble of distrust which blocked him from getting close to anyone, always feeling at one remove from someone. The awful daring of a moment's surrender. She had accepted him.

"I have come home," he whispered to her and kissed her lightly on her belly. He loved to lie there, feeling her pulse beating, the occasional gurgling of her stomach, his hand resting on her inner thigh. She stirred and snuggled closer, still asleep.

Now in the different world of the chilled conservatory with his eyes still closed he repeated the words aloud to himself: "I have come home."

He would phone her now. This was ridiculous, it was becoming a perversity, this refusal to contact her. Perhaps she was waiting for him to do so. Back in the rose garden at the hospital she had said she would wait for him. *Love just doesn't stop,* she had said. He could never forget those words. He looked at his watch. It was 1.30 in the morning. She would be asleep. Her phone would ring on the bedside table and she would stir. Were her arms round someone else? Had she found some other comfort? His heart quailed at the thought. If it was so, it was his just dessert. Did he want to know? Did he want the certainty one way or the other? He dare not. He would not ring.

From: Sue [sue08whitehall@blueyonder.co.uk]
Sent: 8 November 2005 0710
To: Mike
Subject: Thee and me

Autumn is passing, but for her it is already winter. She scrabbles up the tunnel and peeks out of her burrow. She twitches her nose, pink and delicate. It is still freezing cold and there is no food at all. She has no choice: back down to hide in her warm burrow where she will hibernate, living off the fat and nourishment she has stored in herself. She will slow her metabolism. Spring may never come. That's the deal. Her head bobs down out of sight. A blackbird on the surface with its intense hearing may just feel the vibrations of her heart pulsing, steady but of necessity so slight.

I imagine you walking now. I'm sure you will have come through. When you set your mind to it, you can do anything. As I know too well. All strength to your crutch elbows.

Sue

xx

25.

Jigsaw

9th November

Valley View Cottage

Barry was apoplectic when he picked up a newspaper on a trip into town. It had the same effect on most of the British public, according to subsequent phone ins and texts to various radio programmes. An alleged terrorist had escaped deportation to Pakistan. He had been seized eight months ago in Birmingham as part of an MI5 operation which had foiled a plot to blow up various high profile targets in the Midlands. He had never been charged because secret service evidence was not admissible in a criminal court. But he had been detained while the Home Office sought to deport him on national security grounds amid fears he would try again to commit atrocities.

Barry read the report to Lee when he returned from the supply trip:

The alleged terrorist successfully argued he was entitled to stay under Section 3 of the European Convention of Human Rights which is enshrined in British law. It states: "No-one shall be subjected to torture or to inhuman or degrading treatment or punishment."

Mr Justice Wain, sitting as Chair of the Special Immigration Appeal Commission with two other judges, said: "It is conducive to the public good that he should be deported. He is an Al-Qaeda operative and remains a serious threat. But in Pakistan there is a long and well-documented history of disappearance, illegal detention and the torture and ill-treatment of those detained, usually to produce information, a confession or compliance."

"It's a sick joke," said Barry. "An insult. So even though he wants to kill us, he mustn't be exposed to possible ill-treatment back home. Unbelievable."

He threw the paper down.

"So, terror suspects can't be detained in Belmarsh and yet can't be deported to their own countries because they might be ill-treated or tortured. On the other hand they can stay here in England, free to mix up fertiliser bombs, free to travel to Pakistan to training camps and come back full of Al-Qaʾeda propaganda. But they must be protected from being hurt themselves by their own countrymen! Crazy!"

His eyes were blazing with anger and frustration.

"It's obvious – terrorists' rights are more important than ordinary citizen's security," continued Barry. "It's exactly what we're up against. Anyway, it makes it the perfect time for message number two. We'll ratchet it up a bit."

Barry printed out two copies of his next statement and deliberately chose Birmingham as the place to post them this time. He hadn't shown it to Lee. When he had driven off, Lee sat and watched curtains of rain swing under the low clouds and across the valley. He could not see the other side. He was bored; he could not leave the house. Barry was not even consulting him now about the next step. He didn't have any input. Barry obviously didn't think his brain was up to it. He was just the driver and bottle washer. They weren't a team, Lee just had to do what he was told.

He heard movements from the room above, where Hussein was again chained to the bunks. What if he was telling the truth? What if he was innocent – as innocent as he himself and Mike had been in the underground? He could not forgot the passivity he had seen in Hussein's eyes as he washed him, the way he just shuffled barefoot from one chained up place to another, sat on the floor, usually resting his head on his knees, drawn up to his chest, never protesting, never saying anything to Barry except when he compelled him. A pawn in the game, Barry's game. They were both fucking pawns in Barry's game.

He followed a single rain drop as it zig-zagged unevenly down the window. A bird was on the empty bird table. Lee suddenly got up and went upstairs. Silently he unlocked Hussein's chain and helped him down the stairs. He pulled out a chair at the table.

"Sit there," he said. Hussein sat down, facing the window and garden. Lee re-attached the chain to the table leg.

"I'm going to untie your hands again," he said, "so you can eat."

He watched Hussein steadily chewing his way through a large bowl of cornflakes, the packet open on the table, the gaudy red comb of the rooster crowing a welcome to the sun while golden cornflakes bounced out of the pouring milk.

"Thank you," said Hussein.

Lee did not re-tie his hands. He saw Hussein massaging his wrists, flexing his fingers.

"Crap day," said Lee, nodding towards the window.

Hussein said nothing. Lee went into the living room and opened a cupboard that was filled with board games for visitors.

"For rainy Yorkshire days like this," muttered Lee to himself.

He sorted through boxes of Scrabble, Monopoly, Snakes and Ladders, two packs of cards, dominoes. Finally he pulled out a jigsaw: 500 pieces, a picture of Buckingham Palace. That should fill some time, he thought. He took the jigsaw into the kitchen and poured the pieces out on the table.

"First thing," said Lee, "is to get all the pieces the right way up. Second thing is to get all the straight edge pieces together, third thing is to get all the sky pieces together. That's how I always did it as a kid."

Hussein looked at him, confused.

"Come on," said Lee, "you must know about jigsaws. You've got kids, haven't you?"

"Yes," said Hussein. He was amused now, relieved, almost smiled.

Together they sorted the pieces as Lee had explained.

"You know who lives there, don't you?" asked Lee.

"Of course. The Queen."

"I've never been there," said Lee, "to Buckingham Palace."

"I have," said Hussein. "That one trip I made to London, to see my sister, the one I told you about – I stood and watched the guards change. They probably thought I was planning to blow it up."

He picked out two corner pieces.

"Where else did you go?" asked Lee.

"We walked along the Thames, saw the Houses of Parliament across the river, the London Eye, the Tower, St Paul's. It is a beautiful city."

"Weird, isn't it?" said Lee. "You've seen all those places and I haven't. And I'm English."

Hussein decided to stay silent.

"I've only been in London once as well. I was leaving, that day on the underground."

Hussein kept silent, concentrating on finding the edge pieces to connect with his corners. His brown fingers flicked the pieces round the right way. Occasionally Lee's white fingers brushed Hussein's.

"Right, we're away," said Lee, extending the corner by three pieces. It showed part of the crowd waving small union jacks. Hussein immediately added a couple more pieces.

Without looking up, Hussein asked; "Were you injured, on that train?"

"No, I was lucky."

"I told you," said Hussein, holding a jigsaw piece in his hand and turning it round, "I was shocked. It was a terrible thing to do, like in New York. That was terrible too. And then I read it was Amjad, my nephew. He disgraced my family – even more my brother and his wife. They will never recover. They lost their son – that is bad enough, when your child dies before you. It is not the natural way. But that he should die this way. It is unbearable. What can they say to Amjad's sisters?"

Lee slotted in part of the crowd along the bottom edge of the picture.

"But wasn't he a martyr? I thought that meant he brought honour to a Muslim family."

"No. Only to those crazy people. No honour."

He paused to discard a piece, searched for another.

"Do you have a son?" asked Hussein.

"Yes."

He pointed through the rain-streaked window, down the garden and into the valley.

"He's five, at school. A few weeks ago I was down there with him. Fishing in the stream. We had a camp fire. My grandfather used to bring me when I was a kid. You see that chimney, there used to be a mill down there. They made worsted."

Hussein looked down towards the old chimney, the roofless building next to it, trees growing inside it.

"It's why my parents came to this country," he said. "To work in the textile mills. They knew about making cloth when they lived in India. They came here very soon after the British left India. That is strange, isn't it? We are glad the British leave our country, we have our country back to rule ourselves. But then all of us Muslims have to leave India to go to our own new country, Pakistan, that has just been created. My parents told me terrible stories of Muslims and Hindus slaughtering each other. Millions had to move from their homes. My parents were on one of the trains to Pakistan. At a tiny station in the country the train was attacked by a mob. It was set on fire. My great grand-parents and two of my father's sisters were killed. My parents somehow got to Pakistan. But they thought there would be still more violence. So they decided to move again and they came here, so they could bring up a family in more peace."

He took a deep breath.

"And now there is all this. This is not true Islam."

For a time they were silent, extending the jigsaw edges round three sides, the top of blue sky still not connected up.

"Do you have children?" asked Lee.

"Yes, of course. I have two daughters."

Hussein looked up.

"When you said you had never been to Buckingham Palace you said you were English. Well, I am English, too. I have my passport. I have lived here for fifty years. I was born here. This country is my home. I have never lived in Pakistan."

Lee pushed his chair back and got up. He stood at the window looking at the rain still coming down, the grass soaked and gleaming with rain drops. He turned round and looked at Hussein's head bent over the jigsaw, the glossy black hair, the wide sleeves of his gown brushing over the pieces, the long dark fingers nudging them about. Who the fuck was this man? He was his captive, a stranger, a foreigner though he was born here.

Lee himself was beginning to worry about what Barry planned to do next. Though chained to a table, like a dog chained to a kennel, there was a dignity about this man. He must watch himself, he was letting Hussein talk too much. He left him doing the jigsaw and went into the living room and turned on the TV. It was Countdown. He changed channels: the Jeremy Kyle Show. He turned it off.

Barry returned late that afternoon, very pleased with himself. Ignoring Hussein, he saw the unfinished jigsaw, said nothing, pored over it for a few minutes, slotted in a couple of pieces.

The following day – arranged as before on sofa, chair and floor – the three watched the lunchtime news bulletin. The news reader read out Barry's latest text, again it was the lead item.

Our prisoner will be freed only when Shoab Nasir is deported to Pakistan and the three other detainees released with our prisoner are re-arrested. If this is not done within the next forty eight hours, we will begin to give our prisoner some of the treatment meted out to captives of Al-Qaeda. Expect to see a video.

Lee looked questioningly at Barry. Where had this idea come from? He wasn't just the bloody babysitter, he should have been consulted. Barry turned to Hussein.

"I told you," said Barry. "I'll turn you into a star. Your wife and kids will see you."

He turned back to the TV. The report continued with an update on the police search. The police now knew from witnesses in Bradfield that an ambulance had been used for the kidnap, they had learned of the burnt-out white van but were not yet convinced the two events were connected. Barry and Lee watched smiling and fascinated at the shots of police helicopters roaring over the city streets, of armed police searching derelict buildings, of door-to-door police interviews. Brief interviews with members of the public showed anger and disbelief at the court's decision not to deport Shoab Nasir, opinions that were dismissed by a spokesperson for Civil Liberties: "It's no victory even if the young man has won. He has been stigmatised for life and put at risk or even further risk in their own country on the basis of the shocking phenomenon of secret evidence. It's no way to conduct justice. If people have committed a crime, put them on trial."

"Bollocks!" said Lee. "Justice! I think we're way past justice with suicide bombers."

"Of course," said Barry, "they won't do what the public wants. That would be really democratic. They won't do what we ask. They won't deport him. They will say they never give in to blackmail or threats. That's always the line."

"So what happens now?" asked Lee.

"We make the video."

"What video? I don't know anything about a video."

"You'll see, you'll be impressed," said Barry.

Lee just stared at him, always so bloody secretive. Barry went over to Hussein who was sitting on the floor.

"We need your co-operation," he said. "Otherwise we have to force you and you wouldn't like that."

Barry bent to unchain Hussein from the radiator and untied his hands.

Hussein looked bewildered.

"We're going to make a short film. In the cellar. Remember, we showed you?" said Barry.

Hussein nodded. Lee saw a new fear in his eyes as he looked towards the low cellar doorway. Barry picked up his holdall from the corner of the room, turned the armchair around so it was facing Hussein. He sat down and opened the holdall on the floor in front of him.

"Here, put this on, Mr Salim," instructed Barry, and he threw Hussein an orange silk robe.

"What will you do to me? This is like the suits they wear in Guantanamo."

"Yes," said Barry.

Lee was stunned by the sudden appearance of the orange robe. He knew about orange jump-suits – stories of how some renegade American soldiers had mistreated Iraqi captives. An image of the forklift truck in Camp Sandbox flashed into his mind. What was Barry going to do next?

Barry watched Hussein putting on the orange robe. He took a 50p piece out of his pocket and relaxed back into the armchair. *That old party trick,* thought Lee. Barry placed the 50p between the first and second fingers of his right hand, deftly moved his fingers up and down so the 50p was transferred across his fingers and back again.

"Yes, it is like what your mates forced Ken Bigley to wear. You remember Ken Bigley?"

"Ken Bigley?"

Barry flipped the 50p across the fingers of his right hand and back again, flicked it high into the air – Hussein and Lee couldn't stop themselves from watching it – and caught it in the fist of his left hand.

"Yes," he said, "the innocent man from Liverpool. Al-Qaeda cut off his head, on video, and then showed the world."

Hussein fell to his knees. "Oh no, sir." He held his hands in supplication.

"No, please. I am an innocent man."

Lee turned away from the man's cringeing submissiveness. He stared at Barry in disbelief. Barry somersaulted the 50p backwards and forwards across the back of his left hand fingers.

"So was Ken Bigley. It didn't make any difference to your mates in Iraq."

He flipped the 50p up high, the silver coin glittering as it turned, and caught it in his right fist and thumped his fist down hard on the arm of the chair.

"Put it on, I said."

Lee and Barry watched as Hussein slipped his arms into the robe which was like a loose dressing gown – Hussein who only a few hours ago had been fitting jigsaw pieces and telling him about his daughters and his parents.

"Now tie the belt."

Barry nodded, satisfied. He bent forward and out of his holdall took a knife, more like a dagger.

"Please, sir, no, no, sir. Please, I beg you."

Hussein crawled across the floor and held on to Lee's feet, moaning. Lee shook him off. He was disgusted with Hussein but repelled by Barry's brutish indifference.

"For Christ's sake, Barry!"

Barry examined the shining blade, stroked the edge of it with his thumb.

"It is the will of Allah," said Barry. "That's what you should be thinking, isn't it?"

Hussein had curled himself up into a foetus shape on the floor, his hands around his head.

"But not today," said Barry quietly, eyes half watching the race horses parading at Sandown on the TV.

Hussein had not heard him. He continued to rock himself and moan. Lee watched him. All his dignity had vanished. Barry stood up and put his foot on Hussein's shoulder and shoved him over so he was lying on his back, staring up at them both.

"Today," said Barry, "we are just acting."

He drew the knife across his throat and laughed. He looked across at Lee with a smile, seeking his complicity. Lee stared back at him. This was getting very dirty. Barry hadn't told him anything about this.

"But afterwards," he continued, "well, that depends on whether anyone takes notice of us and does as we ask. Now, into the cellar with him, Lee, and sit him on the bench."

Lee didn't move, his mouth tight with resentment and anger.

"It's OK, Lee. I'll explain afterwards. Please. And here's your balaclava. And I need you to sit next to him."

Hussein struggled to his feet. Lee waited a moment longer in disapproval, then held out his hand for the balaclava and led Hussein into the cellar, his bare tied feet shuffling through the thin covering of cold water. He sat him down on the stone bench. It was chilled in there and Hussein shivered. Barry had fixed the brightest bulb he could get in the light fitting and Hussein shaded his eyes. On the wall behind the stone bench Barry had fixed a large flag of St George, its white background emphasised by the dirty grey stone wall. The folds of Hussein's orange silk robe shone and flashed in the light. Lee sat down next to Hussein. Carefully, Barry placed his camera on a small table he had carried in. He adjusted it so that it framed Hussein and Lee and a space on the other side of Hussein where he would sit. He connected the remote control lead into the camera and turned the dial to the movie icon.

He gave Hussein a piece of paper.

"When I tell you, you must read this out. You will read it slowly so people can hear it clearly and you will read it as if you mean it. You have to persuade people so they do what we say, so that you can be freed. If you fail…"

Barry tapped the knife that he had slid into his belt. The paper was shaking in his hand as Hussein read through it.

"I cannot do it, sir," he muttered.

"You will do it," yelled Barry, and he whipped the knife out of his belt. "Don't think I won't use this. I would enjoy it."

He lifted Hussein's chin with the flat of the knife blade.

"As you read, you will feel the point of this knife sharp on your skin. It is a sort of encouragement. When I say the word, you will begin. Understand?"

Hussein nodded.

"But the film must begin with you blindfolded. When I take it off, you will begin to read, immediately. Read to the camera."

Hussein was about to protest but he thought better of it.

Barry tied a dirty white handkerchief over Hussein's eyes.

"Looks good, eh, Lee?"

Lee nodded grudgingly. "It's like a bloody film."

"That's exactly what it is. Now we put on our balaclavas and we are ready to roll."

They pulled their black balaclavas over their faces.

"You take his blindfold off when I give the word," said Barry.

Barry sat in his place, pricked the skin of Hussein's neck with the knife, pressed the button on the remote cord. He waited ten seconds.

"OK."

Lee pulled off the blindfold. Hussein stared at the camera. Barry nudged him. Hussein held the paper and read, his voice shaking:

"I am a simple man who just wants to live a simple life with my family. The patience of these people is wearing very very thin and they are very serious people."

His voice failed, he felt the point of the knife. He cleared his throat.

"Please, please give them what they request – deport that terrorist to Pakistan and re-imprison the three terrorists who were freed with me from their control orders. You must broadcast this tape and then you have seventy two hours. If you do this, I will not be hurt. Thank you."

He looked into the camera, he was trembling. Barry let the camera run for another twenty seconds then clicked off the remote button.

"You did very well, Mr Salim. Let's hope they listen to you. If they don't, the next film will be less pleasant for you. We will have to show them that we really are hurting you. Give him some coffee, Lee, while I sort this."

Lee helped Hussein to the kitchen table and then made three instant coffees. Barry was pushing it too far. It wasn't right. He hadn't signed up for this sort of stuff. Barry took the camera, plugged it into his laptop, slid in a disc and transferred the film. As before, he made two copies. This time he would post them in Manchester.

Lee took his coffee to his room and lay on the bed. Barry was changing, he didn't like how he dealt with Hussein. He hadn't liked the knife and Hussein's humiliation. Barry was just imitating the worst of Al-Qaeda. This was worse than those thugs at the demonstration. Maybe, after all, Hussein was just a decent man caught up accidentally in all this, a victim, like Mike. All that talk about his family. It made Lee think of his own mother. Thank God she was dead. It was terrible to think that, but she would be appalled at what he was involved in here. He could not repay her for what she done for him by behaving like this. She had devoted herself to him; what he was doing now dishonoured her.

He remembered on one of his leaves he'd taken her to Bolton

Abbey and they'd had afternoon tea in the Cavendish Pavilion and walked a little along the river, his mother now so slow and careful, having reluctantly accepted her need for a stick. He'd asked a young mum with her child in a push chair to photograph them on the wooden bridge. He could see her face now, smiling for the camera, still the traces of humour in her mouth, her grey hair done specially for the outing, her eyes watery behind the lenses of her glasses. She had led a brave life. He wondered if some of his own courage came from her, rather than from the father he had never known. It always came, this merciless stab of guilt, when he thought of his mother who had brought him up alone, working as a checkout clerk in the co-op, taking in other people's ironing, cleaning big houses for a few hours a week. It had been hard for her, a lonely life he realised long after.

Three weeks after the passing-out parade, at his new garrison near Preston, he had received a phone call and was summoned to his Captain's office to be told that his mother had been involved in a hit-and-run incident. She'd been walking back along the main road from the corner shop when a car had swerved up onto the pavement, hit her a glancing blow which propelled her into a stonewall and fractured her skull. By the time he arrived at the hospital she was dead of a huge haemorrhage in the brain. By her bedside someone had placed a small posy of real flowers and a copy of psalm 23. He had picked it up, read *Yea though I walk through the valley of death, I will fear no evil.* He vaguely recalled the words from school assemblies and put the card back down. He was shocked when he lifted the sheet that covered his mother's head, to see the green and purple bruising disfiguring her face. This was a different kind of death – random, ugly, alone, trivial.

Back at the home he had shared with her, he had wandered through the rooms. Just so many small and meaningless objects, a life gathered up into so little: a couple of glass vases, an embroidery of a rose she had made from a kit, some cheaply-framed prints of flowers, an old Black Magic box full of cheap jewelry in her dressing table drawer. She had brought him up alone. She had been a good mother. He was never hungry, always had clean uniform and sports kit for school. She took a job as a dinner lady so he was never a latch-key kid. She helped him with his homework, especially the arithmetic she was good at. She stung his grazed knees with iodine, bought him a bike, took him for a week's holiday every year to a caravan in Filey. Thinking back now, he understood she expressed her love in a practical, down-to-earth way. She seldom hugged him except when he was hurt. Never, so far as he could remember, had she told him she loved him. But she did, would have done anything for him, would have died for him. But who would remember her, and for what?

Now downstairs was a man he had made himself responsible for, Hussein. It was turning out in ways he had never imagined. Barry was clever and persuasive but Lee wouldn't go along with him. He didn't believe all that fairy stuff about his mum watching him from heaven, but he owed her. He owed her to act decently in her memory.

From: Sue [sue08whitehall@blueyonder.co.uk]
Sent: 9 November 2005 0721
To: Mike
Subject: Thee and me

If only I could dislike you or be bitter. It would be easier. But I can't and so it isn't.

Feeling low and sorry for myself tonight. A dreary time stretches ahead. I can't bear to think of Christmas and New Year without you.

Sue

xx

26.

Piano

10th November

Upper Heights Barn

Mike could not sleep. Wind bludgeoned the house, rain lashed the windows. His grieving plan wasn't working. His detailed recreation of scenes with Sue were not cathartic. They left him with only a temporary peace. Increasingly they brought a longing to be with her. This evening he had gone further than ever before. He had picked up his phone and dialled her number. But before it could even ring he had closed his phone. He must not do it.

Lying in bed, he was not able to shut out – even relished – the memory of their last evening and night together, before he had left for London and his leadership course.

He had been stretched out on the couch, flipping through a copy of Fellrunner. He listened to the soft tapping of the keys as Sue worked at her computer on the table in the corner. He looked at her bent back, her arms bare in her short-sleeved shirt, her computer surrounded by open books and papers. Her fingers were fast as she typed. Occasionally she straightened her back and stretched her arms upward, rotated her head slowly to soothe stiffness in her neck. Mike loved to see her so absorbed, intent, committed.

"Will you have time to play the piano?" asked Mike.

Sue half-turned to him and smiled.

"I think so," she nodded. "Not much more to do. Just got to download some pictures for this poetry lesson. My famous bad lads are on a writing roll and I want to keep them going."

"You love that lot, don't you? Always a soft spot for the scallywags."

Sue laughed and went back to her keyboard.

"I'll make you some coffee to help you through," said Mike.

"What do you want me to play?"

"Oh, I don't know. You choose."

Mike made the coffees and went back to his magazine. Sue typed away for another twenty minutes or so and the printer whirred into its complicated digestive system. Then he watched her systematically pack her school bag, always neat and properly fastened, the pictures safe in a transparent pocket file. She put the bag and her laptop in the hall ready for the morning. She was almost compulsively organised, timed things to the minute. He had always loved her neatness, her punctilious smartness, her control. Those long fingers that sorted and filed so carefully had other skills, equally efficient. That loss of control.

Sue bent over and kissed him on the forehead.

"How about that arrangement of Mahler?" she asked. "No doubt you're fretting about tomorrow, so prepare to relax."

Mike watched her playing. This was a piece of music they often made love to. Mike closed his eyes as the sounds filled the room. They drew him into them and wrapped around him. Her touch on the keys was so soft. The notes were infinitely slow and delicate, drawn out with sadness. Yet he heard in them aspiration as well as resignation. They swelled to a richness which was on the edge of breaking – delicate and as full of potential life as a bird's egg, he thought. Then that final slow swaying rhythm that ended in a quiet surge of hope.

She enriched him. He looked at their shelves of books. She had told him that her childhood home on the council estate had contained no books. Her father, a train guard, usually brought home a newspaper he had found on the carriage seats and that was the only reading matter her home contained. But her parents had somehow found the money for her to have piano lessons from a friend of her uncle's, and they had encouraged her in her ambitions to be a teacher. Mike admired her for the determination she had shown to better herself, the strength to be different from her council estate friends, to aspire. Now that aspiration was directed to her students: she was determined to open doors for them that she had opened for herself. What opened those doors was passing exams and that was dependent on high quality teaching. She was so self-contained. Her fingers flitted across the keys, her shoulders swayed slightly and the room resonated with sound of the final notes.

Slowly he opened his eyes.

"Come here, sweetheart," he said. He sat up on the couch.

She sat beside him and he turned to lie with his head on her lap. He felt the steady beat of her heart, felt the heat from her body, heard the quaint chemical tricklings in her flat belly. It was his favourite position. He felt absorbed into her, all the busyness of his mind stilled. He breathed deeply and sighed.

"Thank you," he said quietly.

"I love playing that piece."

"No, I mean thank you for all of this."

Sue had stroked his hair.

He groaned and turned over in bed. Even now, months later, he could feel the touch of her fingers. This was torment, he could not carry on like this. He resolved that tomorrow or the next day he would ring at a time when she should be at home. He had to know how she would respond.

From: Sue [sue08whitehall@blueyonder.co.uk]
Sent: 10 November 2005 2239
To: Mike
Subject: Thee and me

These are the longest days: going to school in the dark, coming home in the dark, home to a place full of your absence. At school I can lose myself in my work – the classroom doesn't allow time for self-pity, the kids one way or another draw me out of myself. Marking fills my evenings but I can find myself looking at the same page of some kid's essay for ten minutes, not taking anything in, lost in a daze, not even thinking. The kids are already talking about Christmas. I cannot bear the thought of it. It's quite simple: I just miss you. Sorry to be so gloomy and introspective. But writing this, even this, is a form of contact with you – even if you don't read it.

Sue

xx

27.

Argument

Valley View Cottage

Only stills of the video were shown on television the following night but Barry was not disappointed. The editing and commentary emphasised the brutality and the threat to the hostage, as he was now being described.

"You did well, Mr Salim," congratulated Barry, looking round at him on the floor and clapping his hand in mock applause.

The police search was being intensified, further arrests of suspect Islamist conspirators were being made but they were getting nowhere with the kidnap. The video stills had produced a distinct change in the public mood and this was expressed in other interviews in the report, in later radio phone-ins and in blogs on YouTube. The sense of justifiable revenge, the applause for tit-for-tat action – these were now being replaced by a sympathy for the hostage, with a distaste for the humiliation he was suffering, with a growing condemnation of the further threats of violence against him. This vigilante stuff wasn't the way. Without the rule of law, however much you may disagree with it, there was anarchy where the bullies won.

Mike, a book about astronomy on his knees, looked up and watched the item with increasing disgust.

Miles away Sue also reacted with horror. It was the general public's reaction, too: a ghoulish fascination for the next instalment together with disapproval. The police were desperate for any lead but none was forthcoming. Politicians were afraid of a Muslim backlash and criticism for lack of progress in the investigation. Watching the television together with Barry, with Hussein watching from the floor behind him, Lee recognised some of his own feelings in those expressed in the street interviews. But Barry sneered at this new public opinion.

"They've just edited in the bits they want. They're just kow-towing to the Muslims again. That's not what people really think. And even if some do, I don't give a shit. They've just been brainwashed. They don't think for themselves. Fucking sheep. I'll show them what justice is."

Lee knew Barry wasn't saying these things to him. He might as well not have been there. Barry was telling himself. Lee saw him tightening up, shutting himself up. He was going it alone, locked into his own motives.

The following day about noon, Lee returned with further supplies and dumped the supermarket bags on the kitchen table. Barry was sitting on a chair he had pulled into the cellar doorway, playing with his knife, looking at Hussein who was in the cellar, kneeling, naked this time, on the stone floor. The bright cellar light was focused directly on his face.

"What the fuck is going on?"

"Watch this, Lee," said Barry.

He leaned forward towards Hussein.

"Get up," he said.

He watched Hussein struggle to lever himself up, hands tied again behind his back, his feet chained together in shackles.

"Where did you get those from?" asked Lee.

"I just got them."

Hussein was shivering in the cold damp place, his bare feet in the film of cold water that constantly flowed across the floor.

"What the fuck is this about, Barry?" asked Lee.

"He won't confess. He won't write or read a confession that he was involved with his nephew on the day you were bombed, that he was helping plan other atrocities against us. I'm just jogging his memory. It's for the next video."

He turned to Hussein.

"Now, bend your knees until you're crouching. Lower, lower, I said. No, not squatting. Higher. Good, that's it."

Hussein was half-squatting so that his thighs were almost at right angles to his knees.

"Now, hold your arms out straight in front of you and hold them there."

Hussein held his arms out. Lee saw the strain on his face, turned and saw in Barry's face a cold-blooded pleasure.

"Come on, Barry, this is way over the top. We don't need this crap."

"Look familiar, Lee? Just like you used to do, wasn't it? Out in Basra?"

His voice was calm and matter-of-fact as he sat on the pine kitchen chair with its cushion neatly tied on to the spindles. Lee saw his back bent as he leaned forward towards Hussein, saw him take a drink from his mug of coffee. How relaxed he was, how in control, how comfortable.

"You don't know the first fucking thing about it," Lee said in a low intense voice. "You know fuck all. You weren't there. Don't ever again say that what you are doing was like me. Ever. See?"

Barry turned slowly round to look up at him from where he was seated. He was smiling. He bent to put his mug on the floor and stood up. He turned back to Hussein and walked over to him. Hussein was still crouched, his whole body trembling with cold and strain. Barry unzipped his fly and pissed into Hussein's face. Hussein collapsed onto the floor. Barry re-zipped his fly and turned to face Lee.

"He's just shit," he said. "Terrorist shit."

"For Christ's sake, Barry, what's got into you? That's not fucking on."

"Why are you bothered?"

"I'll tell you why," said Lee.

Barry heard a new menace in Lee's tone but he walked casually up the cellar steps into the kitchen, placed his half-empty mug and his knife on the table and leaned back in the chair. Lee threw a towel onto the stone shelf in the cellar, then Hussein's clothes that lay on the kitchen floor. He shut the cellar door. He stood on the opposite side of the table to where Barry sat.

"This is not what I signed up for, Barry. This wasn't the deal."

"You're not getting soft, are you, Lee? I thought we agreed that was the problem with all that lot out there, letting the Islamists ride over us, take the piss out of us. All I'm doing is giving them a taste of their own medicine, and a very slight taste. He has to confess, Mr Salim, for our next video. I haven't even hurt him."

"It's torture," said Lee, "that's what it is."

"Nothing compared to what they did to Ken Bigley and the others."

He paused, weighed things up, then continued: "Nothing compared with what you did in Camp Sandbox. I read about it. Why so sensitive about it?"

Lee strode one step forward and gripped the edge of the table, his knuckles white. He leaned forward towards Barry's face, Barry sprawling in his chair. Lee stared into Barry's eyes.

"Don't push me, Barry. I reckon I can still take you if I have to."

Barry smiled and picked up his knife, began to clean his nails with it.

"Maybe, maybe not."

Lee looked at the knife in Barry's hand, shook his head in disbelief.

"Would that be on the video too?"

Barry put the knife back on the table, pushed it across to Lee.

"My fault," said Barry. "Sorry, I got carried away."

"It's not as simple as that," said Lee. "You haven't seen your best mate's face burned away, you haven't heard his scream, you haven't heard him begging you to kill him, to put him out of his agony. You haven't walked among body parts in Basra market place after a suicide bomb, seen a little girl screaming with her arms blown off, the same age as my Ben. You weren't even in the underground. I've seen what I'm fighting against, smelled it and heard it, tasted it on my tongue. You've just seen pictures in the papers while you ate your breakfast, seen it on the tele while you sat in your easy chair and picked your bloody nose."

He moved from the table to the window. He was breathing heavily, fists clenched.

"I was angry in Iraq, I was fired up. The Arabs I dealt with were mujuhadeen, so-called soldiers who hid behind women and children and taunted us to kill them. They were trying to kill me." He pointed to the keeping cellar door. "This here is just so cold-blooded. He's helpless."

He paused. "And I believe he is innocent."

There was a long silence, Barry at the table, Lee gazing out of the window. Finally Barry said: "OK, Lee, have it your way. Do we just let him go?"

Lee thought, watched the wind in the trees, had a sudden memory of Mike in the underground.

"No," he said. "It's still right to fight back, to show them they haven't got it all their own way. Just not like this. We send one more video to show he's still alive, that we still have him, to make them look over their shoulder, feel nervous."

"Then what?" asked Barry.

"I don't know," said Lee.

"Sort him out then," said Barry. "I'm going up for a kip."

He picked up his knife and went upstairs. Lee heard the lavatory flush, the bedroom door close. When Lee opened the cellar door he saw Hussein sitting on the stone shelf, shivering, his clothes laid over his knees drawn up to his chin. He went across and untied him.

"Come on," he said. "I'm trusting you."

In the bathroom, while Hussein showered behind the curtain, Lee sat on the toilet seat. He despised Barry now. He was a cold-blooded sadist. Hussein dried his long dark spare body and put his clothes back on. Downstairs, Lee gave him hot soup and toast.

"I have to do this," he said as he took him upstairs and re-chained him to the bunk. "I have to think."

"I am grateful to you, sir," said Hussein.

Downstairs again, on his own, Lee wandered out into the garden.

It had stopped raining but the clouds were still low and grey. He scuffed his way through the leaves on the grass. He thought about the men upstairs: Hussein's acceptance of his captivity, his dignity changing to humiliation. He had his faith but he was not a bomber or a conspirator.

As for Barry, Lee saw that the situation was allowing his cruel streak to flourish. He'd always had a cruel streak, as a kid been cruel with words, razor sharp. Lee remembered when he'd asked Barry to burn his hand with a cigarette. He knew Barry would have done it had he not chickened out himself. But Lee also remembered when Barry had rescued him. One night on a side street where the street lamps weren't working four big lads had surrounded Lee, pushed him up against the wall and demanded all the cash he had. Two of them had knives. He'd been terrified. Then Barry had come round the corner, seen what was happening, and immediately rushed at them, screaming like a maniac. They'd fled. You never knew which side of Barry was operating. Now Lee saw that when Barry was in the cellar with Hussein he was no longer concerned with Hussein's possible part in any conspiracy. He had passed beyond that into the sheer joy of power. He got a kick out of inflicting pain and humiliation for its own sake. His cruelty was authorised not by a quest for justice but by retribution. What Barry was doing was plain wrong. So he was in the wrong too.

Lee leaned over the stone wall at the bottom of the garden. There were a few sheep on the lower slopes of the field that led down to the wooded valley. The mill chimney stood clear above the trees. He had started to teach Ben how to fish down there, how to make a camp fire. What was he teaching Ben by being here? If Ben found out when he was older, what would he think of his father? He could explain about what had happened in the army but there was no justification for how this was turning out. No way could he defend this to Ben. He could clearly see in Ben's trusting eyes first the bewilderment then the disappointment and then the disgust. Nikki too, she would be appalled – and he realised he still valued her approval. His mother would turn in her grave, and his grandfather. All these people believed in him, even Nikki. They had seen good in him and, in doing that, had fostered that goodness.

He turned back and looked up at the bedroom windows of the cottage where Barry and Hussein lay, with just the width of a stone wall between them. No more. He had to get out of this. But he couldn't abandon Hussein. He would be as guilty as Barry for what befell Hussein.

From: Sue [sue08whitehall@blueyonder.co.uk]
Sent: 11 November 2005 1946
To: Mike
Subject: Thee and me

When I am alone I gorge on you: in the bath, in the garden, in the pale sunlight dead heading the flowers, at a bus-stop on the street, in the book room. You are my mind's default position. You make me happy/sad, the memories of you.

But it is creeping up on me, the awareness that to imagine you is becoming more risky, more ambivalent, more difficult. But it makes no difference. I still believe in you.

I hope you read this, but I become more convinced you don't. I still have to express myself to you, try to explain.

It is now four calendar months since the bombing. You will be walking now, I know you will. I know your strength of purpose. It is the same strength that shuts me out and leaves me here away from you.

Sue

xx

28.

Decisions

11th November

Crimhope Dale

It was going dark before Barry came down downstairs again. He opened the fridge door and rooted round.

"There's not even any fucking cheese left." He opened the freezer door. "And not a single ready meal."

He slammed the door shut and stomped across the kitchen. "I can't survive on bloody teabags," he said, putting on the kettle. "And we're almost out of milk."

Lee watched him. He was reading Barry's *Mirror*. Barry had that coiled up tension in his body, that grimness set on his face when he was frustrated, padding round like a caged tiger. So, no comments on their argument, then.

"I'm not the bloody housekeeper, Barry," said Lee quietly.

Barry turned and registered his tone of voice. Lee saw Barry slip on another face like a latex mask.

"Sorry, mate. I shouldn't have slept. Sleeping in the day doesn't suit me. Never did. Not your fault. Want a cup of tea?"

"OK."

Barry brought over the two mugs of tea and sat down at the

table. He sipped the hot tea and watched Lee reading the paper. He had decided on what he had to do. He'd thought it through up there on the bed. He could see no alternative. Lee had disappointed him; most people did in the end. He'd thought Lee would be different after what he'd been through. Typically English – he didn't have that killer instinct, couldn't go for the jugular. It used to be different: we hadn't built an Empire being soft, hadn't forged the industrial revolution by being namby-pamby. Men had forced things through by sheer strength of will and vision: individuals who'd gone it alone, dared to think and do what others couldn't even imagine. But now the nation shilly-shallied, dithered, had lost direction. It was collapsing into mediocrity – like that rabble down trackside at the dog stadium, like those people interviewed on the street for the TV news. Limited. No sense of purpose, drifting, drinking, eating crap food. He knew he was a cut above them, a throw back to the explorers and inventors. He knew where he was going.

"I'll go and get some supplies this time," Barry said. "We need to stock up. And get some beer in. We're out of that, too."

"No, I'll go, if it's alright with you," said Lee who had done his own decision-making. "I need to get out, a change of air. I feel I've been locked up here. Wander the wide spaces of the supermarket."

Barry laughed.

"Sure? I don't mind going."

"Yeah, sure. I'll get a bottle of whisky, too. Might even have a quiet pint in a pub."

"Why not? Good idea."

You had to seize the moment, thought Barry. Opportunities always came, you just had to be prepared. Like with the kidnap. Like now, when Lee was away. He would have a couple of hours.

Lee drove away in Barry's car, Barry watching the beams of the headlights cross the ceiling, welcoming being alone with Hussein.

*

Mike did not notice the headlights moving across the valley. A wind had blown away most of the clouds and the sky was clearing. He was preparing Ali's telescope to concentrate on Mars. But first he focused on the moon. It was still a revelation to him, the craters and plains, all named. He focused in on the Mare Serenitatis, one of the most regular of the lunar 'seas' with its single small bright crater, Bessel. There too were the great walled formations of Aristoteles and Eudoxus. He wanted to open Sue's eyes to the beauty, give her entry to this new world. Once again, he wondered what she was doing. He was more anxious about it now, felt a lurch in his stomach when he imagined another man chatting her up in a pub. He shut that away. He had decided: tomorrow he was going to phone her. He focused in on the waxing gibbous moon. Clouds were re-forming near it. Would Mars be hidden?

*

Barry carefully positioned his camera, composing the kitchen table and the chair on which Mr Salim would sit. He widened the field of vision so that his own body, standing over Mr Salim, would be in the picture. He checked his watch, plenty of time.

*

Lee strolled up the almost empty aisles with his trolley. There had been an offer on a carton of Worthingtons. He'd added a bottle of Bells at £2 off. The supermarket seemed a melancholy place at nine o'clock in the evening. The other shoppers were also on their own, almost as if they were finding a way of filling the time, seeking some vague human contact as an alternative to sitting at home watching TV on their own. Shelves were already being filled for next morning. He put in a loaf of bread, cheese, selected a boxed Indian meal for two. Funny, both he and Barry liked Indian. When he returned with the supplies it had to look normal, nothing to make Barry suspicious. Barry was sharp, his quick eyes flicking everywhere. He would spot immediately if anything was up. Lee knew what he had to do, and he had to do it this evening before Barry pushed his 'encouragement' further. He'd think through the details over his pint.

Mike swung the telescope to the north west sector of the moon. Already he could identify the deep prominent crater of Eratosthenes between the mountain ranges of the Carpathians and Apennines which bordered the Mare Imbrium. He looked for the ghost crater of Stadius, its surface pitted with craterlets. He loved crater hopping.

*

Barry brought Mr Salim downstairs into the kitchen. All the lights were on: the main light, the spotlights over the sink area, the concealed lighting over the surfaces.

"Your mate's not here any more, is he?"

Hussein was silent. He looked at the small silver camera set up on the cupboard top.

"I said, your mate's not here any more, is he?"

Hussein looked at Barry. Barry saw his eyes were so fucking calm. He'd soon change that.

"No," said Hussein.

"Just you and me now, to play our little games."

Barry threw him the orange robe.

"Put that on."

Hussein began to put his arms through the sleeves.

"No," said Barry. "Take your ordinary clothes off first."

Hussein paused a moment and then did as he was told. He took off his shalwar kameez.

"I said everything."

Hussein paused again briefly, before bending to take off his underpants.

"Good boy," mocked Barry.

Unhurriedly, Hussein put on the orange silk robe.

"Now sit on that chair."

Hussein did so, muttering to himself: "Inshallah."

Barry tied Hussein's feet to the front legs of the chair, his arms behind his back to the spindles. He went round and looked at the LCD screen on the back of the camera.

"Perfect," he said.

He walked back and stood next to Hussein.

"Now, don't be alarmed. This is just for your next appearance on the tele."

Barry pulled his black balaclava over his head and gently placed an empty yellow cement bag over Hussein's head. He felt Hussein start and strain against the ropes. He adjusted the sack so the symbol Blue Circle faced the camera.

"Neatness is all. I cleaned it as well as I could," said Barry. "But I should keep your eyes closed in case there's any cement dust left. It will sting you. See how I look after you? Now I won't be a moment. I just have to set the camera running."

He heard Hussein muttering words he could not understand. He flicked the dial to movie mode and stood by Hussein again. He held his shoulder. Hussein's body was perfectly still, no trembling. Barry felt a moment's admiration for him. Then he took his pistol out of his pocket and jammed it against Hussein's temple. He felt Hussein jerk his head away. His mutterings were louder now, a chant, low and rhythmic from within the sack. He felt Hussein relax again, even leaning his head slightly into the pistol nozzle. Barry clicked off the safety catch, the sound clear and metallic in the silent kitchen. Hussein's head did not flinch. His prayers – for Barry realised they were prayers – were no longer mutterings. He was speaking them aloud now, muffled though they were in the cement bag, with an expectancy, almost an exaltation.

∗

Lee sat with his pint, staring at its white head. He had to free Hussein. Barry was going to kill him, it was inevitable. But what about Barry? He could take out his mobile now and call the police. They would go together to the cottage. The police would be armed. It would be over. Hussein might even be still alive. He and Barry would go to gaol for a long time. He might get a lesser sentence because he had called in

287

the police but it would still be a long time. They would both be vilified in the media, he would be lumped together with Barry, equally guilty of what had happened in the cottage. Ben would know about it. He would be taunted at school, perhaps bullied. He would hate his father. Shit! It was impossible. Barry was cruel, worse than he had ever imagined. But he had been a life-long mate. Even in this situation, did you grass in a mate? Was there another way? And even if Barry was wrong in how he was doing it, was he wrong in what he was doing – taking direct action, making a stand?

*

Mike groaned in frustration. Clouds had covered the moon and were spreading across the sky. He had wanted so much to see the red-orange planet of Mars with its polar hoods and maybe a dust-storm. Amazing to understand that tonight Mars, Earth and the Sun were all lined up in opposition. Frustrated, with his eye still on the telescope sight he swivelled the telescope from the clouds frayed with moonlight, traversing time and space, arcing it across the sky to darker clouds that hid the seven sisters of the Pleiades, past a single star that shone millions of light years away in a cloud gap, sliding smoothly down thousands of space miles across the constellation of Taurus and then of Orion and finally the Plough, down across another bright streak of cloud-free sky, down to the blacker straight line of Blackstone Edge, down across the dense darkness of the moor, down to the first intake fields. He could see the stone walls, blacker patterns across the dark fields, and then the roof of a cottage, the chimney stack, down past the shadowed shapes of upstairs windows, down to one lighted window. Mike stopped. What was that? Curious but knowing he shouldn't spy, he turned the declination knob and refocused on the window. He adjusted the finer focus wheel. Total clarity. He saw a man standing, wearing a balaclava, he was pointing a pistol against a man's head, covered in a brown bag. This man was seated at a table. He wore a bright orange robe. That shining orange robe. Immediately he saw the image he had watched on the TV screen. It was the same.

Barry lowered the pistol. There was an indentation in the cement bag where it had been tight against Hussein's skull. Hussein's chanting voice didn't change. Barry lifted off the bag. There was grey cement dust on Hussein's hair, on his cheekbones and beard. Hussein stopped his chanting but kept his eyes closed.

"You see. I said we were only playing games. But you didn't believe me."

*

Yes, there was a way, thought Lee. Using a piece of army training Barry hadn't made use of. If it worked out Hussein would be freed, Barry would have a choice and a chance to escape. What happened to him, Lee, would depend on Hussein – Hussein the devout Muslim. Bizarre how life worked out. But there was no alternative.

He finished his pint. The rest of his life would depend on what happened in the next couple of hours. If it went wrong would Ben understand? As he got older would he understand his father had tried to right a wrong, to retain some kind of honour?

*

As the balaclava'd man lifted off the bag, Mike could see the hooded man's face. He recognised him. He was the man on the TV news, he was the man whose photograph he had seen in the newspapers. He remembered him: he was the uncle of the man who had bombed his underground train. What was name? Salim something. The balaclav'd man went out of shot as he walked across the lighted kitchen window.

*

Barry played back the video clip on the LCD screen to check it had worked properly. It had. Tomorrow, when his work was completed here at the cottage, he would post the discs as he had before. It would be his last gift for this benighted country. They could fucking sort themselves out now. But of course, they wouldn't, they didn't have the balls. He was off to the sun. He had a mate in Tenerife who had a betting shop and a bit of a low level protection racket. He'd do some work for him. He'd get by. There was just one more scene to add to the video.

He untied Hussein from the chair.

"This is where it gets serious, Mr Salim," said Barry. "You still haven't confessed to being involved with the London bombings. And I need that confession to wrap the video, to complete the narrative. You know that word, wrap?"

Hussein, still sitting, said nothing.

"Well, you soon will."

He untied him from the chair. Hussein's feet were still chained together. Barry shuffled him across the kitchen to the cellar door, as if he was on a chain gang, the chain scraping across the wooden floorboards.

*

In the pub car park Lee switched on the ignition. He sat for a moment, watching a couple of smokers by the pub entrance. He felt better. His mind was clear. It was the only way. And it all came down to Hussein. How Barry would like that! He put the car in gear.

*

Mike kept looking through the telescope but there was nothing to see. The two men had gone. He was stunned. He sat back. What was he to do? What could he do? The answer was obvious: contact the police.

But was he remembering the TV news accurately? There had been an Asian man in an orange robe, a hostage. He had virtually been pleading for his life, reading that note. Had he really seen the same man in the window? He realised he was not used to differentiating Asian faces. Was that man related to his bomber? Was it the same man sitting there with a bag over his head? Could all this be happening here, here in this half-hidden valley in the hills? That sort of stuff was city stuff. Everything that had happened with terrorist suspects had happened in cities – the arrests, the searches.

He looked into the telescope again. It was a kitchen: a table, chairs, units on the wall, a fridge freezer, a calendar. He couldn't have imagined it. But it was so shocking, so incongruous. The scene had lasted for less than a minute.

And yet a man had been threatened with a gun to his head. What was happening to him now? If his memory was right, contacting the police might prevent a tragedy. If he was wrong he might look a fool but for all the right reasons. He wheeled his chair across to the phone.

*

Hussein halted at the top of the three steps down to the cellar. The bright light was on and he saw a plank had been placed on the stone shelf, one end raised on another piece of stone. On the floor was a green watering can without its rose, full to the brim. Barry pushed him down the steps and shut the door behind him.

"Come on, we've only got about half an hour but that should be enough," said Barry.

He took off Hussein's orange robe and made him lie naked on the plank, his head at the lower end of the slope. His feet, already chained, were tied to the top end of the plank. Another rope fastened his thighs to the plank, another over his chest. Barry fastened a belt over Hussein's forehead so that his head was held tight to the plank. Finally he linked the belt and the three ropes to rusting iron rings in the wall. Barry stood back. Hussein was thoroughly trussed. All through, he had not resisted. Barry was disconcerted and a little disappointed. He would have enjoyed the need for a punch or a flash of his knife blade. Hussein lay there, still, eyes closed. Only his lips were moving but he was silent.

"This will not be pleasant for you," said Barry. "It's called waterboarding. It works like this. I will pour water down your nose

291

and throat. You won't be able to breathe. Your heart will pound faster and that will use up even more oxygen. You'll think you are drowning. Maybe you will drown."

Hussein's naked body began to shudder, his penis shrunk to the size of a small acorn. How spare he was, his skin almost purple. Hussein now began his low muttered chant. Barry set up his camera in the doorway, made sure it was composed and focused correctly.

"All you have to do, Mr Salim, is to confess your part in the bombings. Remember? The 7th of July, the 21st of July. Agree to confess and to tell the camera, and I will not be so hard on you. But when people see this little film they will know I'm serious."

Barry took a piece of muslin out of his pocket and spread it gently over Hussein's face. He could see Hussein's lips still moving, nudging the muslin, heard his chant. Then Barry lifted the watering can and poured water over the linen that covered Hussein's face. He kept pouring it, varying the flow slightly, never too strong. The water soaked into the muslin, pushed it onto Hussein's mouth as he opened it to catch a breath. The cloth prevented him from spitting the water out; involuntarily he swallowed it. At the same time his nose filled up with water. He began to choke, his trussed body jerking and straining.

Barry put the watering can down and lifted off the linen cloth. Hussein was gasping for air, then he vomited and almost choked again. The vomit lay on his face and beard and neck. Slowly he calmed.

"Anything to say?" asked Barry.

"I am innocent," croaked Hussein.

Barry made no reply. He put the muslin back on to Hussein's face. This time he would do it for longer, really push him to the edge.

"The edge of Paradise, Mr Salim. Maybe you will see it. Meet and greet your prophet."

Hussein was chanting, the words tumbling thick and fast, losing control. He could not stop his body from straining against the ropes in a futile instinctive attempt to escape. Once again Barry placed the muslin over his face, as gently as if it was some holy veil. Once again he poured the water, as reverently as if it were a libation or a baptism.

Coolly he watched Hussein, his bucking body, managing to turn his head slightly; heard his choking and retching and gasping. He let the water slow to a trickle, put down the can, held the vomit stained muslin by a corner and lifted it off.. Hussein's eyes were wide and staring, bloodshot, terrified. The veins in his neck stood out as if to burst. He took great grasping breaths.

Barry leaned over Hussein, close enough to smell the vomit on Hussein's breath, to feel its heat.

"I'm going to leave for a few minutes," he said, "to decide whether you want some more."

He shut the cellar door behind him. Now to deal with Lee: he would be back shortly.

*

Lee drove out of the town, past the lighted windows of take-aways – Kentucky Fried Chicken, Indian, Balti, Chinese – past the furniture showroom and the shuttered QuickFit, past pubs which had smokers loitering on the pavement. He passed the terraced stone cottages with doors opening directly onto the street, then the long lines of semi-detached houses with their front gardens and hedges. Dipped headlights approached and passed him. Finally, on the edge of town he passed the Waste Re-cycling Centre. The street lamps ended there and the dark countryside began. At the roundabout he turned off and drove towards the narrow valley road. There was no traffic now and he could concentrate on what he had to do. He turned the headlights on to full beam.

It was a long time since his training in unarmed combat but he remembered it clearly. When your life depended on something, it stuck in your mind for ever. He would have one chance, he had to get it right first time. As Barry said, you had to seize the moment. He had to carry the bags of food, the carton of beer into the cottage and put them down in the kitchen, perhaps shout to Barry if he wasn't there, that the beer was in. Be casual and normal, perhaps even a bit distant after their row. Then as he moved about the kitchen, perhaps opening the cans of beer and passing one to Barry, he had to get to

the right side of him. His blow had to be swift and hard and accurate
– just below and slightly in front of the ear. If he got it right, the shock
to the carotid artery and the jugular vein and the vagus nerve would
make Barry unconscious instantly.

He turned onto the unmade gravel track that led to the cottage.
100 yards up it he stopped to open the five-barred gate, drove
through, stopped again, closed the gate. He stood for a moment
gazing up at the cloudy sky, a faint gleam of light from the unseen
moon. He got back into the car. His full-on headlights picked out the
stone walls on both sides of the lane, fallen in places and patched
with fencing. A rabbit ran across, or was it a stoat, fast and black and
low into the undergrowth. He looked up at the moon. A small light
shone on the far side of the valley, must be that other lonely cottage,
must have been sold.

It was time. He depressed the clutch and put the car in gear. On
the rough track, as he negotiated the dips and ridges, the headlight
beams swung across fields and moors, up into the sky.

*

Mike lifted the phone and turned to take one last look across the
valley. Headlights. He saw headlights moving slowly in the direction
of the cottage, their beams swaying across the black. Quickly he put
the phone down and wheeled himself back to his telescope. He
picked up the lights, bright as stars now, and tracked them. They
disappeared as the vehicle pulled in behind the cottage. Then they re-
appeared, stationary now, two parallel white beams slicing the dark
horizontally. The driver must have parked. The lights were
extinguished. Someone else was involved. He remembered the news
item about the kidnapping: there had been two men in balaclavas.
This must be the other one. He focused in on the window again.

*

Barry had watched the headlights approaching, bobbing up and
down on the potholed track, piercing up into the moonless night

294

sky. Standing in the unlit living room at the side of the deep-set windows, hidden by the folded curtains, he watched the car pull in. He'd cursed as he'd stumbled in the dark, kicking over the pile of boxed games that Lee must have taken out of a cupboard. Tomorrow it would all be over. The three of them would watch the news together, very homely except that Lee and Mr Salim would be gagged and bound. They would see the video he had made. Then the final scene in the cellar, the scene that wouldn't be on any video – the end of Mr Salim. But what about Lee? Lee he had brought it on himself, been found lacking in the last resort, not come up to the mark when it really counted. And then the sun in Tenerife for rest and recuperation. R&R – well, he was a soldier, after all.

He watched Lee unload the ASDA bags and the carton of beer. Lee closed the boot of the car, put the carton of beer under his arm and walked up the path as the automatic light came on. Barry heard the front door open and close, saw through the half-closed living room door Lee turning right into the kitchen.

*

Lee dumped the shopping on the kitchen table. He ripped open the carton of beers.

"Beer's in," he shouted.

He opened a can, took a swig and walked to the window.

*

Mike watched the new man move forward with his beer and stand, staring out of the window. It seemed as if he was staring directly across the valley darkness to him, their looks meeting somewhere between the lens of the telescope and the window, the man's eyes looking to him, almost seeming to ask a question.

And Mike knew with absolute certainty who this man was. There was no doubt. It was Lee, the man who had saved his life in the underground tunnel.

Barry moved silently into the small hallway, peered round the kitchen doorway. He saw Lee standing looking out of the window, his back to him. Barry gripped the baseball bat tightly in his right hand and, light on his feet, swiftly crossed the kitchen.

Lee saw the movement reflected in the kitchen window, half turned and then felt a crunching smash to the back of his skull. He crumpled to the floor.

*

Mike watched him fall. He saw the other man bend and disappear below the window sill. Then saw him lugging Lee's body across the lighted window. He could only see Lee's lolling head, his mouth already gagged.

Lee was involved with this? Lee was the other man, the driver? Lee was a hostage taker? Lee must have helped force the man to make his statement, dressed him in the orange Guantanamo style robe. He was the other man in the balaclava sitting in the cellar in front of the flag of St George. It really had all taken place over there, just opposite him.

But what was happening there now? Why had Lee been attacked by his companion? They must have argued. The last statement on the news had talked about further threats and hurt to the hostage. Had Lee disagreed?

Then the Asian man appeared, shuffling, naked, his face caked with some sort of dirt, his mouth gagged, his eyes blindfolded. He was being pushed forward by the other smaller man. The Asian was then roped into a chair, the orange robe thrown over him. Mike watched the smaller man moving around the chair looping the rope before he moved across the window out of sight. He returned to place another chair on the opposite side of the table to the Asian. Mike saw Lee, half stumbling, led to the chair and forced to sit. Then he too was roped.

He looked at the two men tied up. If he contacted the police there would maybe be a siege, maybe the other man would kill Lee and the Asian. His action would have killed the man who had saved his life. If not, they would be arrested. Lee was involved but he was a victim now as well. But he would be found guilty whether or not there were extenuating circumstances. The judge would take a stern view towards kidnapping, towards Lee and the other man taking the law into their own hands, being vigilantes. The judge would want to make an example of them. The politicians would want a heavy sentence to deter a Muslim backlash and copy-cat kidnappings. He, Mike, would be responsible for putting the man who saved his life into a long prison sentence. When Lee pleaded that he had tried to stop the other man from ill-treating the Asian he would not be believed.

He looked down at his legs, his stumps. The old anger, the bitterness returned. What could he do on his own? He was helpless. He had no alternative but to involve the police. Lee would have to take his chance.

Then the light in the kitchen went out. Moments later, a first floor light went on, a bedroom. Ten minutes later that too went out.

In that ten minutes Mike had decided: Lee must be rescued. There was only one person who could help him, one person he could truly trust, one person he had wanted to phone so many times. Not tomorrow, now – this was it. He took a deep breath, picked up the phone and dialled Sue's number.

From: Sue [sue08whitehall@blueyonder.co.uk]
Sent: 11 November 2005 2308
To: Mike
Subject: Thee and me

I can't sleep so my second message of the day.

Almost every day I still log onto our email address and every day the unchanging message: *There are no unread emails in your inbox.*

A daily disappointment but a daily relief: your address has not been closed down. My messages are not returned with *address unknown.* They are in the ether somewhere, floating in cyberspace, compromising evidence of my frailty and – I must believe – my strength.

I still write and my feelings are as strong as ever: evidence of a truth not to be denied, my best effort, real, authentic. My messages have been infantile, puerile, adolescent, self-pitying, pathetic, ridiculous, self-abasing; but all of them honest, unedited by any sense of self-pride or dignity.

Surplus to requirements – for the most loving of reasons, if most misguided.

I am becoming what I never was – introspective. You will remember me as all action, busy. Now I choose to be alone a lot, choose to live with memories and wishes. Perhaps, ironically, you would not love the new me. But hope has not withered yet.

I must live my own kind of truth. I love you not wisely but too well. I do not even know where you are – still in London? Somewhere back up north? Abroad even?

Enough! Will you never relent – you stupid, obstinate man!

Sue

X

29.

Arrivals and departures

11th November

Crimhope Dale

He took a last look through the telescope: the cottage was all in darkness. It seemed that Lee and the Asian would spend the night tied to their chairs while the other man slept upstairs. Mike wheeled himself over to his phone. If she wasn't there or wouldn't help, he had no choice but to contact the police. Lee would have to take the consequences. Doing nothing was not an option.

Mike looked at the phone on its stand. How would she react when he phoned her? Would she even be there? Perhaps, as part of her new life, she had moved home, cleaned the slate to make a new start. He would have done that – had done that – to make it easier for himself to accept the relationship was over.

His heart was thumping hard. He didn't have to look up her phone number – their phone number – it was still clear in his mind. What time was it? Eleven o'clock on a Thursday night. She'd be in bed, tired towards the end of a long week in school, towards the end of a long tough Autumn term. He anticipated her voice. She always ended a phone call with "Bye just now" in that cheery tone that implied she looked forward to the next call. No one else he knew said that. She had told him it was what her grandmother used to say, growing up in the tiny village of Longside near Peterhead. Her voice sounded clear in his memory, and brought with it her face and smile. He had tried not to envisage her in such detail, afraid of the immediacy and how he would cope. Now he found himself afraid again but expectant, caught up in her already. Nothing ventured, nothing gained. How quickly it all surged back. But he had to control it, not get carried away. He tried to calm himself. How could he expect her to leap up and come running after the way he had treated her? Yet he had to try. He needed her help as he had never needed it before.

He picked up the phone and dialled. He felt his heart racing, an ache of anxiety there. He heard the ringing tone. His throat suddenly felt dry. She had to be there, speak to him, help him. He was nervous, ashamed, diffident, hopeful, despairing – all at the same time. The ringing tone continued then clicked off. The answer phone came on.

I'm sorry I'm not able to get to the phone at the moment. Please leave a message after the beep and I'll get back to you.

Mike slumped. Where was she? Staying with someone? Sleeping with someone? A dagger of pain stabbed into him. A great howl filled his head; a howl of protest, of self-hate, of loss. He had thrown away a pearl. He thumped the wheels of his chair in frustration. He had dared to hope. Now his defences had crumpled. And all because she was not there. *I did it for her sake,* he told himself, repeating it again to convince himself. *I removed myself for her sake.* It had been more than four months since he had sent her away from the hospital and banished her from his life. True to his final cutting words he had not communicated with her again. He had set up a new email address which she did not know. He had changed his mobile number for the same reason. She had no idea where he now lived. The break with her had been absolute because it had to be – for both their sakes. Sue had to know she must move on. He had rehearsed the arguments all too often, persuading himself he too had his own solitary journey to travel.

He knew it was only partly true. He had been protecting himself, too, shielding his wounded self from scrutiny. He had been cruel to be kind – but kind to whom? Himself? It had been his basic selfishness; easier for him to remove his feelings than rebuild them, easier to live in an artificially limited way.

He took a deep breath. It had to be the police. And then the phone rang. He panicked, paralysed. The phone continued to ring. He reached out, his fingers hovered, then closed around the receiver. He picked it up.

"Hello," he said.

There was a long pause.

"Is that you, Mike?"

Her voice, the way she said *Mike,* her voice tense and wary.

Emotion welled up in his throat, choking him. He could not speak.

"It is you, isn't it?" she said.

"Yes," he stammered. "I'm so sorry."

Sorry for disturbing her, sorry for his ludicrous hope, sorry for everything, wanting to flee now.

"It's OK. I was in the shower, didn't hear the phone. Then when I came in saw the light flashing that someone had called. Didn't recognise the number. Was curious, as usual."

She was speaking fast, gabbling a bit, a nervous laugh at the end.

"Where are you?" she asked.

Again, he could not get the words out.

"Are you all right?" she asked.

He heard the concern in her voice.

"I've got a big problem. I can't deal with it on my own," he managed to say.

"What sort of problem?"

"I can't explain over the phone. But it's urgent, really urgent."

Sue made no reply. In the silence he heard some electronic interference on the line.

"I need your help, Sue."

There it was, out, spoken: the request, the need – not just for tonight, but for her. But there was no way she could understand the depths from which he dragged the words. He had denied it himself for so long.

"Trust me, Sue, it's vital that you come. And I know it's very late."

Trust him! How crass could he get! Why could she trust him?

"You'll understand when you're here. I have something to do that I can't do on my own. It's life and death for someone. I know that sound melodramatic, but it's true."

He found himself holding his breath, his whole body taut.

"But I'll understand if you don't come."

Another pause.

"You haven't told me where you are," said Sue.

He told her. It took her some time to work out where it was.

"Do I need to bring anything?" she asked.

"No, I don't know, I don't think so."

"OK, I'm on my way, mystery man. Stay by the phone. I'll be about an hour and a half, I think. I'll copy your number into my mobile and ring if I have a problem finding you. But I've got an OS map – one of yours, actually."

Did he sense humour, affection in that last remark?

"Thank you, Sue, thank you so much! Drive carefully."

"Bye just now."

Those familiar words again, the hope in them.

The line went dead. After a moment he replaced the receiver. The tension disappeared. "Yes! Yes! Yes!" he shouted. It was as if a crushing, smothering weight had been lifted from him. She was coming. They would sort this together.

He wheeled himself over to the telescope. The cottage was still in darkness. He had no idea what to do next. He looked at his watch. 11.25 pm. Sue wouldn't be here till about 1 am. He didn't want to be in his wheelchair when she arrived. He wanted to greet her at the door on his crutches, display his walking to her. He looked at his watch again. 11.28 pm. He went back to the living room and the telescope. If anything happened over there, if the downstairs light went on again, he would phone the police. There was no knowing what that thug could do. In the meantime he needed a plan. He wanted to present Sue with a plan, explain her role to her, ask her what she thought about it and see if she had a better idea. She was a good problem solver. He wanted it to be them together, a team.

She would have no idea what she was coming to. She would be astounded. He realised it would be like walking into the middle of a film shoot. How much did she know about the kidnap and the hostage situation? Had she been following it on the news? How much would he have to explain? The key was Lee and she knew about Lee. She would understand how he had to try and save him – not just from that thug over there in the cottage, but from prison.

Still no light across the valley. He sat down in the armchair to think up a plan. OK, so they would drive to the cottage. What then? He couldn't even get past that point, couldn't get past the man with the gun, the man who had smashed Lee over the head. He was dangerous, cruel, violent. He and Sue could not deal with him. He didn't want Sue anywhere near him. He gazed out into the darkness. He'd been ridiculous. He shouldn't have got Sue involved. He should just have phoned the police. This was way out of his league. What state was Lee in? Tied up, gagged, smashed over the head, what would happen in the morning? He slumped, a wave of fatigue and depression washed over him. He wanted to have worked it all out for her. He closed his eyes.

Why had Sue decided to come? Just to help him out in an emergency? How would he know? Had she any feelings left for him? Or had she moved on as he had wanted her to, forced her to? How could he think so obsessively about himself? Lee and the Asian man: he should be thinking about them. God knows the state they were in and what that man might do next.

He was numbed in a reverie of doubt and fear and indecision when he started up. Had he heard a car? He looked at his watch. 12.45 am. Sue should be nearly here. Time had slid by so fast and he had no plan to give her. She hadn't phoned, he had known she wouldn't. She would find her way here, with her quiet competence.

He got up, slipped his arms into his crutches and went through to the back room that overlooked the yard she would drive into. He switched on the lights. Then back to the hall to switch on the outside light. He went outside to the gate, opened it and wedged it with a stone, peering down the valley lane. No sign of a headlight, but the road down the valley bent round a shoulder of moorland out of sight.

He went back to the doorway. As usual there was a wind in the silver birch. He looked up at it, tall and graceful, swaying against the dark sky, the clouds broken with patches of lighter grey, the moon emerging and then being covered. Had this night really begun with his calm perusal of the Sea of Serenity?

Then to his right headlights came round the bend in the lane, cutting through the darkness like searchlights. His heart was thumping again now. He took a deep breath. The lights slowed, dipped, and then turned in through the open gate, the tyres loud on the crunching gravel. She would have seen him standing in the doorway. The car stopped. The lights went off, the engine died. There was a pause and then the car door opened, the interior light went on. He saw her face, her body twist as she got out. She stood up, leaving the car door open, looked at him then walked towards him. He took two steps forward on his crutches, felt his arms trapped in them, wanted them free to embrace her. Sue put her hands lightly on his shoulders, kissed him on the lips, so briefly. He felt his lips tingling. She stood back and looked him up and down, smiled at him.

"Walking already? You're looking good. I'm impressed."

She blinked. Turning away, she said: "I'll just get my bag. Didn't know what to bring."

He watched her bend to take a holdall off the back seat. She closed the car doors and pointed the remote. The locks clicked.

"No need, I suppose, out here. What a place! You certainly find wild places."

They stood there. Mike realised he hadn't said anything.

"Thanks for coming. I didn't know if you would."

A pause.

"It's good to see you, Sue, really good."

"And you, too. Shall we go in?"

"Of course!"

She passed him with her bag slung over her shoulder. He followed. She put her bag down in the small hall. He closed the door, switched off the outside light, turned back to her. The closeness of her, just the two of them, she in her jeans and sweater and short black coat, blonde highlights in her hair, the faint scent of her hair, so new, so familiar.

"You better explain what this is all about," she said. "In here?" She turned into the living room.

"But first, tell me how you are."

She sat on the couch.

"You seem to have made amazing progress."

Mike was relieved to be able to speak.

"As you can see, I'm on my pins. Literally."

She smiled, the same smile as ever, beautiful, lighting him up as it always had.

She said: "You have a problem. Something urgent, you said. What is it?"

A flash of fear that she was putting him off, keeping him at a distance. He pointed to the telescope.

"A telescope! Are you a star-gazer now? You've always had stars in your eyes."

Was there affection in that slightly mocking question?

"There's a cottage over there, on the other side of the valley. And I accidentally saw something terrible there. Lee's there. Remember Lee?"

"Of course. The man who saved your life. You told me. He's there? Does he know you're here?"

"No. It's a long story. Have you been following the story of the hostage?"

"Yes, I have. It's terrible, isn't it?"

She peered through the telescope but there was nothing to see. He told her what he had seen through the lighted kitchen window of the cottage: the orange robe, the gun at the head, recognising who the Asian man was, and then recognising Lee and seeing him beaten.

"But you must ring the police, Mike. The man is armed, only the police can sort this. And fast. You don't know what might happen in there."

So Mike explained about wanting to keep Lee out of prison even though he was obviously a partner in the kidnap plot.

"Lee doesn't want to be part of it any more. I'm sure of it. It's gone further than he thought. They must have had a huge row. That's why he was smashed unconscious and why he's tied up on the chair."

Mike looked at Sue. She had to agree with him, surely.

"I'm not sure, Mike. They could have argued about something else. Money? Payment? No honour among thieves, you know."

"I've just got this feeling."

"Yes, I understand that. Lee saved you. But even if I do agree, what are we going to do about it? From what you've said, neither of us can tackle that madman in there Have you thought up a plan?"

"No, I've tried but I can't see a way through."

He had relied on her practical competence to find a solution but though they racked their brains they found no way forward. They kept checking the cottage through the telescope but nothing changed. They began to go round in circles, returning to the same obstacles with increasing frustration. Gradually their talking ceased. They were drained of ideas. Sue was right – he and Sue were no match for an armed thug. If Lee survived whatever was to come, he would have to take his punishment. Mike, after all, couldn't help him, even with Sue. As the possibilities of action disappeared, as the night slowly passed, as silence fell between them Mike despaired. They'd spoken together as though they had never been separated, as though he had never cast her away. Now he felt them slide apart again, sitting opposite each other in the lamplight, dispirited by indecision. Tiredness came over him again. It was 4.30 am.

"If we can't think of anything you have to call the police, there's no alternative," said Sue. "We can give ourselves another hour. No more. I'll make us some tea. That might revive us."

Mike checked the telescope again. No change. He moved ahead of her into the kitchen.

"I'll show you where the stuff is."

"Your walking is brilliant," she said.

He stopped and lifted his crutches.

"I can stand, but I can't walk without my crutches yet."

"It's still brilliant."

In the kitchen they moved around each other, careful not to touch, saying nothing, synchronised in the mundane task but separate and wary. Sue brewed and poured the tea. They sat at the kitchen table in a gloomy silence, hands cupped round the warmth of the mugs. She was exhausted. She thought of the men over there in the darkened cottage and her responsibility for them. How badly injured were they? What was that thug planning next? This was a situation way out of their league.

Mike broke the silence.

"I didn't know if you'd come," he said. "How you'd feel – a phone call late at night, suddenly, out of nowhere."

"But you know how I feel," she said.

Did he? Should he? What did she mean? He knew how she used to feel. How it was. It couldn't still be the same, after all this, after what he'd said, after he totally cut her off.

"What do you mean?" said Mike. "I know how you feel."

"My emails," said Sue. "Did you read my emails?"

"What emails?"

So he hadn't read them, had not even seen them. She'd come to accept it, even written about it, but she'd always hoped. Surely he hadn't been able to cut her off as thoroughly and immediately as that? Had she been a fool? Should she actually feel relieved that he hadn't read all that lovey-dovey needy stuff. She looked across the table at him. Had she re-invented him, idealised him in spite of herself?

As if elbowed by the force of her sudden coldness, Mike got up and went to the telescope again. No change, all in darkness. It was 4.45 am. now. What time did it get light? Time to give up, ring the police. It was all going wrong, a disaster.

He went back to the kitchen, sat down again.

"Is anything happening over there?" she asked.

"No, still the same. No lights on. I just can't work out what we can do, but I can't just abandon Lee."

He looked up at her as she leaned forward on the table.

"What about those emails?" he said.

"I sent you some," she said softly. "I said I would when I left you at the hospital. I know you said you wouldn't communicate with me but I decided to ignore it. You were ill, still in shock."

"I'm not like I was back there in the hospital, Sue. I feel so much better."

Mike looked at her, her hands round the warm mug. He wanted to pour it all out now, say how he'd hated himself, his ugliness; then how he'd met Chris and Jenny, and slowly learned to walk and see himself in a new way, feel good about himself again; and how he'd thought about her, and how hard it had been to put her out of his thoughts but he had made his bed and must now lie on it. It was only fair. And was she happy – and was she still on her own? Was she?

"Sue, I'm so sorry. I was so wrong."

She stared into her tea.

"All this time," she said, "I've been sending you emails."

"But, Sue, I don't use that email address any more. I set up a new account when I was down in London, at the hospital. I haven't seen anything from you."

Sue stood up and leaned against the kitchen cupboards.

"What did they say?" asked Mike softly.

"I wrote what I was feeling. Daft stuff. I'm quite glad now you didn't read them. At first they were to you. Then they became more of a diary, talking to myself."

She walked into the living room. He followed her. It was still pitch back outside the window.

"Ring the police, Mike. You must do it now, before it's too late."

He heard the flatness in her voice.

Seeing him standing alone with his crutches outside his cottage when she arrived – at that moment she knew that all she had written to him was true. She still loved him. His rejection of her had been self-defence. But part of his healing had opened him up to her again. She had seen it straightaway.

And then this amazing situation together – the excitement fading to helplessness. She had not been able to help him. She looked out across the valley, past the telescope into the darkness.

There was a light in the cottage window.

"Mike!" she called. "There's a light. There's two lights in the cottage."

Mike strode across to the telescope, his crutches creaking with pace and purpose.

Barry had slept well – the untroubled sleep of someone who'd got things sorted, made his decisions, knew what to do. His conscience was satisfied. He had done his best. It wasn't what he'd hoped for. If people were so ignorant they couldn't see he was right, at least he'd made his personal statement, made a stand against his country slipping into chaos. Later they'd come to know he was right. In his room he went through the now familiar process of downloading the video clip from camera to laptop and copying to disc. He had the two scenes he wanted: the gun to the head, the waterboarding.

It was still dark outside. He'd have a quick brew, check again that Lee and Mr Salim were securely tied up. Doubtless Lee would have had some training in escape techniques. He'd give them some water before he gagged them again. He'd leave the TV on for them. Why not? They could test themselves in a quiz show or decide which was the best bargain. He chuckled.

He'd drive in early to Leeds before the rush hour. He'd park the car round the corner from the BBC North Studios, walk round and deliver the disc to reception. He'd pull his hood well down, in and out of the building quickly, just handing the envelope to the receptionist. He'd already put it in an envelope marked. *Urgent, news editor.* Then he'd use the same tactic at the offices of the Yorkshire Post. Say fifteen minutes. He'd be back pretty quickly for a proper breakfast. He'd fry himself some bacon, make himself a couple of sarnies. He smiled to himself again. He liked the idea of Mr Salim spending his last hours in the smell of fried pig. It was the little things that counted, the details. He'd always been a good organiser. He felt pleased with himself: not a bad end in the circumstances. The disc would make the lunchtime news. He could get off in the afternoon.

*

Sue was looking through the telescope when she saw a man enter the kitchen.

"Mike!"

He hurried over and looked through the telescope.

"That's him! He's the thug!"

They took turns to watch the man go to the two men in turn, lift up their chins, say something to them. He took off Lee's gag and let him drink from a water bottle. There was blood dried on the side of Lee's face from the previous night's blow, a huge purple bruise. The man re-fastened the gag. He moved over to the Asian man and did the same. He shifted the chairs so they faced the same way and then went out of sight beyond the window frame.

Mike and Sue saw the kitchen light go out. Its yellow light was replaced by a flickering blueish light.

"He's put the TV on," said Sue.

The man crossed the window again and seemed to wave farewell to the two men. He disappeared. Mike and Sue sat back from the telescope. They saw the glow of a light go on behind the cottage, then watched a car's headlights drive away, bobbing along the valley, stop for half a minute and then drive on again. The light behind the cottage went out.

Mike and Sue sat together, looking out across the dark valley.

"Now's our chance," said Mike. "We have to try it now."

"Please get the police, Mike."

"No. We have to give Lee a chance. I have to, Sue. I wouldn't be alive if it were not for him. This is it!"

His eyes were glittering with a renewed life.

"But I promise I'll call the police immediately if we can't do it."

"But what are we going to do?"

"We'll drive round and break in and take it from there."

"But the man may come back."

"I know. We'll have to take our chance. No time to lose. Let's go."

Mike was up across the room on his crutches. There was no hesitation now. She had no choice. She had to drive. He'd made up his mind and wouldn't change it. Sue grabbed her coat and followed him, the adrenalin already flowing. He was already on his way across the yard.

"Got your door keys?" she shouted.

"Yes."

She slammed the cottage door shut behind her, clicked open the car door locks. Mike opened the passenger seat door, turned to get into position. Sue stood and held his crutches as he lowered himself into the seat and twisted round to face the front.

"Thank you," he said.

She handed his crutches in, closed the door and went round to the driver's seat. She turned the ignition on and looked round at him. He looked at her. She held his hand, squeezed it. He smiled. He leaned towards her and kissed her. Briefly she kissed him back.

"I'm scared!" she said.

"So am I!" he said. "But we have to do it, have to try."

⋆

Lee and Hussein sat roped to their chairs, four feet apart. On the table in front of them was the plastic bottle from which Barry had given them a drink. Up on a shelf next to the recipe books was the portable TV; its flickering light gleamed on the tumbler standing on the table in front of them, still with half an inch of water in it. The green figures on the electric stove showed it was 6.10 am. On the TV screen a man was walking along the base of a cliff, gesticulating and talking about fossils. His enthusiastic voice pounded into Lee's head, still throbbing from last night's crashing blow. His gag was so tight he had to concentrate to stop himself from retching and possible choking himself. He looked at Hussein and saw his face slumped forward, eyes closed. Lee tried to move his hands but Barry had knotted them tightly. He could move his fingers but not his wrists. He grunted as loud as he could. Hussein lifted his face and looked across at him. Lee grunted again and nodded his head, trying to convey some ridiculous sense of re-assurance. Hussein nodded back.

On the screen a man and a woman sat on a sofa, talking. They had newspapers on the table in front of them. Lee flexed his fingers again. When Barry came back that would be the end of them. To save his own skin Barry had no alternative now but to kill both of them, probably in that cellar. How long would it be before their bodies were found? Only the estate agent knew they were there and he wouldn't

311

need to contact them for another seven weeks when the rental contract ended. What a squalid meaningless end to his life. Barry would just shoot them both, leaving their bodies on the cellar floor, the cold water flowing silently, constantly, around and under them. When they were found it would be big news: the mystery of Hussein's disappearance, the videos of his torture replayed, Lee incriminated as much as Barry, the public disgust: Ben's final picture of his father as the disgraced cowardly murderer, then murdered himself – just desserts. Lee groaned, strained against his ropes, slumped. On the TV he heard a woman announcer explaining that a lorry had overturned and shed its load of crated live chickens across the M25 and the tailback was already two miles long.

*

Mike and Sue fastened their seat belts. Sue took a deep breath, switched on the lights, put the car in gear, took off the hand brake. Each felt the same but said nothing: they were side by side and together, a team.

"How do we get there?" she asked.

"A couple of miles back down the valley there's a rough track that cuts across to join the track on the other side that goes up to the cottage."

Bushes and stone walls loomed a deeper black against the night's darkness, seeming to narrow the lane and hem them in. They bumped across the link track, grass growing in the middle, their headlight beams swinging into the sky. Sue turned right onto the cottage track. They drove slowly on, past an open gate into the even thicker darkness. They pulled into the cottage yard and the security light switched itself on.

*

Inside the cottage Lee was conscious only of droning voices on the TV, not listening to the words. His tongue was dry and seemed swollen against the rough cloth of the gag. He was desperately thirsty.

His head was throbbing and pounding. Then he jerked suddenly alert as he heard a car engine. He saw headlights swing across the ceiling and down the walls, then disappear. He knew Hussein had seen them too, his body instinctively straining for freedom from its bonds.

This was it. Not long now. It wasn't fear for himself he felt, it was knowing he was leaving Ben without a father, his final betrayal.

*

Sue ran round to Mike's side and helped him up and out of the car. They hurried across to the door, Mike's crutches peg-legging in the gravel. It was locked, of course.

"It's a yale," said Mike. "We should be able to open it. We need a stone."

Sue quickly found one tumbled down from a stone wall in the garden. She brought it over.

"I'll do it," she said.

"Close your eyes," said Mike.

She lifted the stone and smashed it into the glass panel above the lock. Listening intently in the kitchen, Lee and Hussein heard the smash of glass. Had Barry forgotten the key? That would put him in a really foul mood. Sue knocked away some shards of glass with her elbow, carefully put her hand in and turned the yale lock. The door opened.

Sue looked back – no sign of returning headlights. They had to move fast. God knows what that thug would do if he came back and found them. The one thing Mike couldn't do was run away.

Mike stepped in, his feet crunching on the glass then clicking on the wooden floor. Lee and Hussein heard the sounds, tensed themselves for some foul-mouthed swearing from Barry. Mike heard TV voices and laughter coming from his right and strode into the kitchen, Sue just behind him. She switched on the light. They saw Lee and Hussein sitting upright on the chairs, the TV chattering away on a shelf. Mike crouched down to look Lee in the face.

"You're OK, mate. We're going to get you out of here. Remember me?"

Lee's eyes lit up with recognition.

Mike moved round to the back of the chair and leaned his weight on the elbow supports of his crutches, using the fingers of both hands to loosen the gag. It was tightly knotted, his fingers struggled. Sue went to the Asian man and ungagged him more deftly.

"What's your name?" she asked.

He gasped for air, taking in deep breaths and croaked: "Hussein. Thank you so much. Praise be to Allah."

Finally Mike unfastened Lee's gag and took it out of his mouth.

"Mike! It's Mike! How the fucking hell did you get here?" Lee croaked.

"A long story. Tell you later. We've got to move fast. Do you know when the other guy will be back?"

"Barry? No idea but we don't want to be here when he comes. Christ! Am I glad to see you! Barry's coming back to kill us. I know he's got some plan."

Sue had already found a carving knife in the drawer and was cutting through Hussein's ropes. She freed him and he stood up, swayed a little. She steadied him. He rubbed his wrists and shook his hands to get the blood circulating.

"Thank you," he said again. "I'm OK."

He hobbled unsteadily to the sink and began to clean his face up. The smell of his stale vomit hung in the kitchen. Sue then worked on Lee's ropes.

Mike said to Lee: "I live in the cottage opposite."

He pointed out of the window.

"I saw that bastard hit you last night. And there's fresh blood on your face. Are you OK?"

"Yes, just sore," said Lee.

"Do you think you can make your own way across there?" asked Mike.

"Yes, I'm sure I can," said Lee. "I know this valley. There's a footpath from near here down to the old mill and up the other side. It comes up just along the lane from your cottage."

"Great!" said Mike. "Our car is too small to hide you both. I'm terrified Barry's going to come back as we drive out, and you know he's got a gun. We can put Hussein in the boot but we've nothing to cover you with in the back and it's too risky."

Mike had done some good quick thinking in the car, Sue thought. She cut through the last of the ropes around Lee's ankles. They were chaffed and smeared with blood. Lee leapt up and threw his arms round Mike's shoulders, hugging him.

"And you're walking, my bloody guardian angel!"

He kissed Sue.

"Scuse the gore," he said. "You must be Sue."

"The very one," she said. "Proper introductions later. Let's go. We've got to get out of here."

Sue explained to Hussein what was going to happen with the car. He nodded his agreement. Lee was pacing the kitchen getting his legs going again. They left the kitchen full of synchronised TV laughter again and went out through the front door.

"Oh, just a minute," said Lee and he ran back into the kitchen.

The sun was still below the horizon but its first light was thinning the night to grey; still no sign of headlights. Sue opened the car boot. She snatched out the bag of emergency kit she kept there and two empty cardboard boxes she used for carrying school books and threw them onto the back seat. Hussein was curling his long legs into the boot, resting his head on his arms, as Lee came out of the house and slammed the front door shut.

"Only for a few minutes," said Sue to Hussein, patting his shoulder.

She slammed the boot shut.

"Now," said Mike to Lee. "Get yomping. We'll see you the other side."

Lee jogged a few yards down the lane then clambered over a field gate and hurried down through the grass into the darkness.

"He'll be OK," said Mike.

He and Sue got back in the car.

"If we meet that Barry on the track, leave it to me," said Sue.

This time she grabbed both Mike's hands and kissed him full on the lips. Her eyes were shining.

"I think we might have done it," she said.

315

She drove off, this time with no lights, twisting between the rain-filled potholes as carefully as she could. An overhanging hawthorn branch scratched the side of the car. Mike looked ahead for the approach of any car. They passed through the open gate.

"Back the same way," said Mike. "It'll be bumpy for Hussein, poor sod, but it's the shortest way out."

In five minutes they were turning in to Mike's cottage. While Mike manoeuvred himself out, Sue went quickly round and opened the boot. Hussein lay there looking up at her, exactly as she had left him.

He uncurled himself and Sue helped him lever his long thin body out of the boot. Standing, he stretched his arms high, bent his torso backwards and forwards. He looked around, breathed deeply. It was a grey, overcast November morning, the first glimmerings of light listless and reluctant.

"The most beautiful morning of my life," said Hussein.

The trio stood together and looked over the stone wall across a couple of fields. Then Lee appeared out of the trees, his burly figure toiling up the steep hillside, angling across to the corner of the field. He waved to them. He went out of sight behind a line of hawthorn trees. He re-appeared, jogging along the lane.

"Nothing like a bit of exercise and fresh air to clear the head. No problems then?" said Lee, joining them.

Sue put her arms round both their shoulders.

"Inside out of sight, and time for some tea, I think," she said.

Mike led the way into his cottage. He took them straight in to the living room.

"That's how I found you," said Mike, pointing to the telescope. "Pure chance, luck."

"Fate, maybe," said Hussein.

They were standing around the telescope, looking across at the other cottage, alone on the far side of the valley.

"Valley bloody View, it's called," said Lee. "A quiet break in the Pennine hills, all mod cons, no smoking and a picturesque keeping cellar."

They stood for a few moments, each in their own thoughts.

Then Hussein asked quietly: "What happens now?"

"We call the police now," said Sue. "Now we're all safe."

"Ah," said Lee. "Can we talk about that?"

Mike looked at him.

"How do you mean?" he asked.

"Remember I raced back into the cottage when Hussein was climbing into the boot of your car? Well, I left Barry a note. I scribbled it and left it on the kitchen table."

"What sort of a note?" asked Sue. "A thank you note?"

Lee smiled. "Not exactly. I simply told him to get out of the country today before the police caught up with him."

"Why on earth did you do that?" asked Sue. "He was going to murder you. If we ring the police now, anonymously, they can be ready and waiting for him when he arrives back. Or they can pick him up when he drives off. It's an easy place to cordon off, there's only the one track in and out."

"Why anonymously?" asked Lee. "And they can trace calls anyway, even mobiles. If Barry is arrested I'm sure he'll implicate me. And they'll be over here asking if you've seen anything suspicious happening over there. You're the only house in the area. It won't take them long to put two and two together, even the local police, especially with that telescope."

"But we're not telling the police," said Mike. "We've already discussed that, Sue." He looked at her. "Remember?"

She nodded. He was right. She looked at Lee: his bruised face, his clothes wet with his walk through the rain-soaked bracken and grass. Without him, Mike wouldn't be here.

"And there's another reason," said Lee, "which you'll maybe find hard to understand." He paused a moment. "I've known Barry since we were kids at school. We had some great times. He was my mate. He saved me from a very dangerous situation once."

He gingerly touched the bruised side of his face.

"And despite what he did to Hussein. I can't just grass him in. In my world you just don't do that. I'm sorry."

"We need you to tell us what was happening over there, Lee," continued Mike. "But you saved my life back in the tunnel and I'm

317

not turning you in for whatever part you played in there."

Hussein had listened carefully to this conversation, standing further back from the window, listening to them, fitting together the pieces of their story.

"I would like to pray," he said. "Is there another room?"

"Of course," said Mike. "Could you take him up, Sue – there's an empty bedroom at the front."

Sue led him up the stairs. At the doorway he turned.

"Thank you," said Hussein. "I won't be long, but I need to give thanks to Allah."

Looking at his dark-skinned face – angular, haggard, bearded, inclined slightly to one side and leaning down to her – she suddenly saw in him the head of a medieval Christ she'd seen carved in wood in a Breton church, his wrists crossed over his belly and tied with rope. Christ aux Outragés, it had been titled, the Christ of Abuses and Indignities.

"I understand."

He closed the bedroom door behind him.

Downstairs she went into the kitchen to make some tea. Lee was telling Mike what had happened over in the other cottage. She listened from the doorway while the kettle boiled.

*

Upstairs Hussein took off his sandals. There was no water to cleanse himself, no prayer mat. He needed guidance from his God about what to do. His decision would affect not just Lee and Barry, Mike and Sue but all the people around him – his family, his community, his mosque, his imam.

In an unfamiliar place and with no sunlight he could only guess the direction of Mecca. He stood upright then placed his hands on his knees and lowered himself slowly to a kneeling position. He touched his forehead, his nose and the palms of his hands to the faded green carpet. He bent his toes so the tops of his feet faced towards Mecca.

Subhaana Rabbiyal 'Alaa, he chanted quietly three times.

318

Allahu Akbar!

He rose to the sitting position then prostrated himself again. First, he gave his thanks for his freedom, for the strength Allah had given him to survive, for the bravery of those three below, for the compassion of Lee.

Oh, Allah, who answers prayers and answers those who ask you, I am asking you for your help. I am asking you to lighten my way.

Arms stretched out, back bent, face to the carpet, he prayed. Then his mind was a blank. The room was silent. Eyes closed, he sought a word or a sign, an image, a sense of what to do. He pleaded for a confirmation and a direction. He began to feel a slight ache in his knees, smelt an itchiness from the carpet.

*

Sue took three mugs of tea into the living room. They sat down around the coffee table, clearing Mike's papers to put their mugs down.

"It's down to Hussein, then," she said. "What he wants to do."

"Yes. It is," said Mike. "Do you really think he's innocent, Lee? He's my bomber's uncle, after all."

"How do I really know? But I think so. We spoke quite a bit together. He's obviously religious." He indicated upstairs with his head. " I don't think he's a violent man, or even political. But I could be totally wrong. Those bombers seemed ordinary decent blokes."

"Why shouldn't he involve the police? What's he got to lose?" asked Sue. "I imagine he could make a hell of a lot of money by selling his story to the press."

"Other Muslims would have no doubts," said Mike. "Tell the police, a trial to show all the gory details, put them in prison for a long time. Exemplary punishment – to put others off taking the same kind of vigilante action."

There was silence for a moment. They sipped their hot tea.

"As you said, Sue," said Lee. "It's up to him upstairs."

Mike got up to look through the telescope.

"Nothing happening over there."

319

Upstairs Hussein sat up and straightened his back. He understood: Allah could not decide for him. He had the words of Allah. That should be enough: he had to find his own meaning in them. He looked at the grey sky outside the window. He looked round the bare room: the narrow empty fireplace, two deeper yellow oblongs on the faded wallpaper where pictures had been. There would have been births and deaths in this simple room. He thought of his children and his wife. Soon he would be back with them, their anxieties ended. Then he understood what he had to do. He stood up.

*

Barry had made his calls to the BBC and the *Yorkshire Post*. He'd changed his mind: no need to race back to spend all morning staring at the bloody moors waiting for the one o'clock news. He'd turned into Starbuck's and was drinking a cappuccino. He would buy a couple of paperbacks from Waterstone's. A couple of thrillers, that's what he needed for the plane. He'd take sandwiches back for them. He wasn't that unfeeling. Lee wouldn't complain about a triple BLT. He'd get a spicy chicken sandwich for Mr Salim. He was quite sensitive, really, felt virtuous. But he would fry his bacon, couldn't get over-sensitive. Were you hungry when you knew you were going to die?

He'd booked a flight last night on the internet – internet connection was one of the facilities in the cottage blurb. He'd thought the internet would be irrelevant at the time but it had come in useful. Always use your resources. They'd watch the lunchtime news together, the three of them. It would be edited, of course, but the full disc would be seen by those in authority, in the government, the police. They would know how he'd succeeded. Then he'd take Mr Salim into the cellar and shoot him. When he knew it really was death would he still accept the will of Allah, chant that *Inshallah*?

He'd leave Lee tied up but without a gag. No need to kill Lee.

Then he would drive to Manchester. In the departure lounge he'd ring the estate agent and tell him there was a problem at the cottage. The plane flew at 4.00 pm. Just right. Barry congratulated himself.

He ate the last of his pain aux raisin, with his sticky fingers picked up the last crumbs of flaky pastry. Tomorrow morning he'd be in the sun, by a swimming pool with a long drink and bronzed bikini'd bodies to look at. Lee had been a good mate, a hard man in the army, no doubt, but he was soft inside. He finished his cappuccino, using a teaspoon to scrape the last bits of chocolate covered foam from the inside of the mug.

*

They heard the bedroom door close quietly upstairs. They glanced at each other nervously. They heard the slap of his sandals descending the staircase. The door opened and Hussein entered. From their seats they looked up at his tall figure and waited.

"I have to thank you, Lee." He had paused briefly before using the name, it was the first time he had used it. "Like you saved Mike in the tunnel, you also saved me. That man Barry would have hurt me much more if you had not been there. You helped me. That's why he attacked you. He was going to kill me, and you too for helping me. It was the only thing left for him to do."

He came forward and stood over Lee who was sitting on the sofa. He held out his arms and took Lee's hands in his own.

"I will be for ever grateful to you, and so will my family."

Lee looked up at him.

"When I go back," Hussein continued, "I will tell the police nothing. I will not press charges, I will give no information. They have the discs, and that is all they will have. I will make everyone angry, I know. The police, the government, most of all many of my own people. They will want an eye for an eye. That is in Shariah law, the ulama's law, the scholars' law. But I am alive and free. That is truly the will of Allah. He worked through you, Lee."

Lee looked nonplussed. Hussein smiled.

"I know you are not a believer. You are shocked at the idea. We are

321

taught to call you infidels, kaffir. But in the end we can only help each other, whatever we believe and don't believe. The Qu'ran even says so: *Our God and your God are the same and it is to him we submit.*"

Lee stood up. He put his arms around Hussein and hugged him tightly. Sue watched Hussein's arms lift in instinctive response, hover tentatively at Lee's back, then let his hands touch and then hold Lee's broad back. The sides of their heads touched. Lee stood back.

"Thank you," said Lee. "You're a fine man. I trust you."

"Thank you. In the end, it is perhaps all we can do in this life: learn to trust each other."

Hussein turned to Mike.

"And, Mike," that same almost shy pause again before he used the name, "my nephew Amjad did this to you." He nodded towards Mike's legs, the crutches leaning against the sofa. "He was wrong. What he did is not Islam. I cannot undo that. But perhaps I help a little to right the wrong, to get the balance correct."

"Give us a hand up, Lee," said Mike. "I'm knackered."

Lee helped him to stand up. He shook hands with Hussein, all four hands interlaced, then walked across to where Sue sat in the armchair. He bent forward and kissed her gently on the forehead.

"I love you," he said. "It's only because of you that we're all here. And only you know how much I owe you."

She smiled up at him. "Well, thank you, kind sir! So what do we do now?"

"You phone your school," said Mike, "and tell them you won't be in."

"School!" laughed Sue. "I'd forgotten all about school."

"If you could drive me back to Bradfield, I would be grateful," said Hussein. "Just drop me off round the corner from where I live so I can walk home. I will see my family. Then I will endure the TV crews and the newspaper men. They will soon tire of me. Then tomorrow I will go to the mosque."

"And you, Lee?"

"The same for me: just drop me off in the town. I'm off to see my son, Ben."

"Back to our lives," said Sue, "as if it all never happened."

"Oh, no. It happened," said Mike. "Starting with these creatures." He patted his stumps. "And, I suppose, before that – with God," he added.

"No," said Hussein fiercely. "Not with God, not with the word of God. But with the words of men, men interpreting the words of God for their own ends."

Epilogue

9th July 2009

Mike watched from the window as Sue stood at the edge of the garden border. She was watering the lupins and petunias, spraying them from the yellow hosepipe. Her arms were bare. The heat of the day's sun had at last faded and in the early evening the border was shaded beneath the hedge. Where she had watered, the earth was darker, looked richer. Leaves and petals glistened with water drops. Somewhere a blackbird was singing a late song in the soft air.

Accidental beauty: he had learned to catch it, see the moment. That afternoon, sitting under the cherry tree with his young son, Matthew, a few red cherries fallen on the grass around him, he had pointed to the leaves shaking in the breeze. The sunlight flicked their undersides with silver as they turned. Dark green shadows of other leaves momentarily fell across the bright translucent green of leaves back-lit by the sun. Patterns of light shifted and reformed, never still. Transient. Matthew's fingers had grubbed around the cherries, wanting to eat them.

Now, with Matthew asleep in bed, he watched Sue lean her weight onto her left leg. Her legs were bare and sun-browned, the line of her calf muscle changing as she shifted her weight. Lovely – the shape of her legs, the ankles precise. As she leaned forward to water the back of the border, her blue and white flowered skirt swayed and lifted.

She turned off the nozzle and dropped the hosepipe onto the

grass. She moved to the garden bench and raised her hand to her head to push some stray hairs back into place. He saw her profile now, slender, lithe, her breasts neat in her T-shirt, her movements easy and young. She picked up a trowel and a packet of seeds, crouched down at the border and tore a corner off the packet of seeds. With her trowel she roughened and freshened the damp earth, and sprinkled the seeds at the back of the bed. They had chosen hollyhocks which would flower deep crimson in two years time.

She had her back to him, did not know he was watching. Just like the cherry leaves, she was unconscious of her beauty and her grace: the few inches of her back bared as her T-shirt rode up. How well he knew the shape of her again; the generosity of her loving, the pleasure she took in pleasure, the mischief of her tongue and fingers.

She had come back to him, continued to love him when he had turned her away, had persisted at a deeper level than he could envisage or even understand.

He watched her bare hands spreading a layer of damp soil over the seeds. He liked it that she did not wear gardening gloves, liked the earth on her fingers, the dampness of it clinging to her. She stood and moved a step or two along the border, touching a flower, bending to pull up a weed. She was so self-contained, content in nurturing the plants into growth. She raised her arms to brush the back of her neck, an insect perhaps or a fly. In his fingertips he felt the traces of the down of her fine hair there, on the nape.

Tonight he would lay his head on her belly and confirm again that he had come home, she had come home.

He heard her mobile ring on the garden bench. She skipped across to pick it up. He heard her greeting but could not discern the words. He heard her laughter. She tucked the phone between her shoulder and her neck, her head tilted sideways, talking while she tidied her garden implements away. He was learning from her about being with people.

Tomorrow they would be in London, staying with Chris and Jenny. They would meet up with Lee and Hussein at the memorial in Hyde Park. His father had been right: "It's a good life if you don't weaken."

Sue sat on a rug on the warm grass in Hyde Park, the pushchair parked beside her. She watched them – Mike leading little Matthew by the hand as they walked between the pillars, Mike bending to talk to him. There was a stiffness and a limp in Mike's walk but not many would realise he had two artificial legs.

It had been a good decision, she thought, not to come on Thursday when Prince Charles unveiled the memorial to the 7/7 bombings. They didn't want the photographers and the cameramen, the formalities and speech-making. They had come on the early evening train yesterday and been met at Kings Cross by Chris and Jenny. She soon understood how they had been an inspiration for Mike. She and Mike had asked for some time on their own at the memorial, with eighteen month old Matthew. Later this morning they would all meet up again here. Lee would join them from Bradfield, travelling across London even now with his son, Ben. Hussein was staying with his sister south of the Thames and he would join them too. The weather had been good to them and they would walk through the park and have lunch together. These were the people who had saved Mike's life and helped put it together again.

Matthew was toddling off as fast as he could. She could hear him laughing when he fell over. Mike picked him up. Matthew went to stand by one of the fifty nine stainless steel pillars, leaned against it and stroked the sand-roughened steel. Then Mike lifted him up and put him on his shoulders. Sue watched them wander slowly between the pillars, between the pillars' shadows cast on the gravel. Mike paused at the group of seven pillars, representing those who had died at Paddington. She saw Mike tilt his head to read the inscription halfway up one of the pillars: the exact time, date and location of the individual death were inscribed on it.

There were flowers at the foot of some pillars. A few other people were wandering through, deep in thought. A man suddenly looked up into the sky. She saw him struggling to control the muscles on his face, his mouth working. A young woman bent to read a card on a bunch of flowers. The sun was shining and beyond the sound of the breeze in the trees she could hear the ceaseless noise of traffic.

Mike now had taken Matthew off his shoulders and was crouched by him, holding his hand, reading the blackened steel slab which had the names of all the fifty nine victims carved on it. They were people he had never known. Sue was moved by the whole place, by the tragedies and sufferings it implied. The amazing thing was how people coped and adapted even though their lives would never be the same. She would never forget the months that followed the bombings: the loneliness and very different struggles each of them had had. But out of them had come a deeper appreciation of each other. Some quality constricted in Mike had finally been freed. He was such a wonderful father. He had been liberated. She had never doubted her love for him, for the complexities of him. She knew she was essential to him.

Yes, we have come through, she thought.

"It's a guid life gin ye dinna fooner," as her Granny used to say up in Buchan.

So much of life was random – fortuitous meetings, coincidental events. Life had its own haphazard flow that carried you along. Every moment could contain an explosive secret; could release the love of strangers.

Behind her she heard men's voices raised in animated conversation but in a foreign language. She turned and saw a group of Asian men walking along the path, some in western clothes, some in eastern. One or two glanced towards the memorial but they didn't pause. Perhaps they were talking about the Pakistani cricket victories. But we could never be rid now of suspicion, she thought. That was the real legacy of the bombers.

Then she heard Matthew's voice and turned to see him toddling towards her, laughing and throwing himself at her.

"Yes!" she shouted to him, gathered him up in her arms, raised him above her head and kissed him.

"And here's Daddy," she said.

Acknowledgements

In my research I relied heavily on Reza Aslan's *How to Win a Cosmic War* and *No God but God*, Ed Hussein's *The Islamist*, Melanie Phillip's *Londonistan* and two uplifting books by survivors of the bombing: Rachel North's *Out of the Tunnel* and – in particular – Gill Hicks' *One Unknown*.

Thanks: to my readers along the way – Steve Britten, Pat Dearden, Moira Downie, Bruce Downie, Ian McPhail, Ian Plimmer, Martin Roberts and Diana Roberts. To Elizabeth Garrett in whose Cliff Cottage haven in Muchalls much of the first draft was written.

To the army staff at Catterick Camp, who arranged for me to watch a court martial.

To the present and past staff (especially the physiotherapists) at Airedale Hospital in West Yorkshire, who were so helpful and introduced me to patients, especially Dieter and Julie, who shared with me their experiences of amputation.

To my children and their vital encouragement, who know how much writing means to me, have suffered my melancholy short stories and poems and demanded the ending to this book should be different.

Finally, my partner Jan who endured many readings of many drafts, was my critical friend and gave me the endless support I needed.

Thank you, all.